I0761238

THE HADACOL BOOGIE

Also by James Lee Burke

Don't Forget Me, Little Bessie
Clete
Harbor Lights
Flags on the Bayou
Every Cloak Rolled in Blood
Another Kind of Eden
A Private Cathedral
The New Iberia Blues
Robicheaux
The Jealous Kind
House of the Rising Sun
Wayfaring Stranger
Light of the World
Creole Belle
Feast Day of Fools
The Glass Rainbow
Rain Gods
Swan Peak
The Tin Roof Blowdown
Jesus Out to Sea
Pegasus Descending
Crusader's Cross
In the Moon of Red Ponies
Last Car to Elysian Fields
Jolie Blon's Bounce
White Doves at Morning
Bitterroot
Purple Cane Road
Heartwood
Sunset Limited
Cimarron Rose
Cadillac Jukebox
Burning Angel
Dixie City Jam
In the Electric Mist with Confederate Dead
A Stained White Radiance
A Morning for Flamingos
Black Cherry Blues
Heaven's Prisoners
The Neon Rain
The Lost Get-Back Boogie
The Convict and Other Stories
Two for Texas
Lay Down My Sword and Shield
To the Bright and Shining Sun
Half of Paradise

JAMES LEE
BURKE

THE HADACOL BOOGIE

A DAVE ROBICHEAUX NOVEL

Atlantic Crime
New York

FIRST EDITION

Printed in the United States of America

Text design by Norman E. Tuttle at Alpha Design & Composition.

This book was set in 13-pt. Spectrum MT with Albertina MT
by Alpha Design & Composition of Pittsfield, NH.

First Grove Atlantic hardcover edition: February 2026

Library of Congress Cataloging-in-Publication data is available for this title.

ISBN 978-0-8021-6660-9
eISBN 978-0-8021-6661-6

Atlantic Crime
an imprint of Grove Atlantic
154 West 14th Street
New York, NY 10011

Distributed by Publishers Group West

groveatlantic.com

26 27 28 29 10 9 8 7 6 5 4 3 2 1

To Linda Pai, my sister-in-law, my friend, a great artist and writer herself and my supporter during the good and hard times of life, no matter which.

Your brother-in-law,
James Lee Burke

THE HADACOL BOOGIE

Chapter One

The events in this tale occurred very close to the turn of the century, when some early celebrants were popping rockets and raining sparks on Bayou Teche, although the tree frogs paid them no mind and droned with such volume the night air seemed to have a voice of its own. Who would have thought such complexity would fall upon us?

As usual, the Acadian Saturnalia was a grand and innocent mix of paganism and Christianity, the breeze balmy, smelling of fish roe, more like spring than winter, more like a fecund and pastoral piece of Eden that had drifted loose from the South Seas. But for me, lying on top of my bed in my shotgun house that creaked with loneliness, listening to the long-dead voice of Jimmie Rodgers yodeling in the dark, I wondered about the plantation world in which I was born and the one in which I now lived. Sometimes I felt the year was 1861, although my Acadian family certainly did not descend from the agrarian aristocracy that readers of *Gone with the Wind* would associate with the historical South.

Both my parents were illiterate, although my mother wanted terribly to learn. Education of any kind was a luxury in the world in which she lived. She worked in a laundry for twenty cents an hour, alongside black women who spoke no English at all.

My father's world was certainly more lucrative but more severe in its own fashion. He racked pipe on the monkey board of an offshore drilling rig and thought his drinking and womanizing and carefree ways under the stars would never end, until the drill punched into an early pay-sand and blew oil and gas and half the Gulf of Mexico through the rig, the floor spikes popping like corks, pipe clanging and bouncing in the network of steel stanchions. My father hooked his safety belt on the Geronimo wire and leaped into the darkness just as the wellhead exploded, sending a ball of flame into the heavens and taking my father down to the bottom of the Gulf, the heat boiling the surface, the bodies of the dead bobbing in the waves, their faces burned off, the unlit oil as black and shiny as paint rolling in the waves.

Those were the kinds of images floating through my mind while Jimmie Rodgers sang, maybe because he was tubercular and doomed to an early death. Maybe that was the true South, the best of it strewn across a cornfield at Dunkers Church or littered in front of the cannon on Cemetery Ridge, the worst of it in the cockneys' whip whistling across a black man's back.

When I was growing up, the people in the Victorian and antebellum homes along East Main Street in New Iberia were never hurtful toward me, although my class of people would often be asked to go to the back door. To me, however, they seemed kind. They were not profane, nor harsh nor curt, and were called "genteel." I wasn't sure what the word meant, but it was obviously associated with the way they did things. If a difficult situation came about, such as an argument over money or a disrespectful remark from a person of humble origins, a lawman or landlord or an employer would appear and the situation would be settled.

It took me a while to understand what those gestures indicated. It might not be 1861 to others, but in our world the calendar meant nothing and the mention of a surname could freeze the sweat on a black man's face or leave a white field worker unemployed and not certain his family would eat that night. Serenity along Bayou Teche sometimes was acquired at a heavy price.

From its inception, Louisiana has been a home for pirates, brothels, gambling halls, corrupt politicians, legal and illegal slavery and terrorism. The torch and the whip. The slave insurrection of 1811 in Orleans Parish was the most brutal atrocity in the history of our country. To this day it is hard to believe it happened. I won't even describe it here.

Later on, the White League made General Forrest's Ku Klux Klan look silly when they invaded New Orleans and shot former Confederate General James Longstreet and struck a deal with the Republicans to shut down Reconstruction. Angola Plantation, on the Mississippi River, became one of the first rental prisons in that nation. It was called Angola Prison or Angola Pen or the Farm, but Hell would have been a more accurate title. Even today no one knows how many of Angola's convicts died of disease or gunshots or beatings or starvation or the sweat boxes on Camp A. Their bodies are still in the levee along the river, the bones and teeth broken into chips.

For many years the Farm's electric chair was kept in the Red Hat House. A black convict I knew by the name of Guitar-get-it-and-go Welch wrote a song about it. And here's what he had to say: "How come they electrocute a man twelve o'clock at night? The current much stronger, the peoples turn out all the light."

I don't wish to continue. Evil is evil, and giving it another life, other than to prove it's real, serves no purpose. But I will tell you about one event that for me was worse than the memories I brought back from Indochina. The emblematic nature of the story needs no interpretation; evil requires support and consent and organization. It doesn't create itself.

A hundred-dollar hit man, Johnny Massina, whom I busted in New Orleans, asked me to visit him when he was about to be electrocuted. I didn't want to do it. But he had become an AA member on death row and I couldn't turn my back on a fellow member. When I was about to leave, he stuck his right hand through the bars and slipped it into mine. The rims of his eyes were red, his head already soaped and razor-shaved, the tiny remnants of his hair like flecks of dirt on a rock. I could smell the stink on his body and the bile in his stomach. I thought his grip would break my hand. It didn't. His voice was a whisper, his hand as light as air. "I ain't up for this one, Streak," he said. "I cain't control my sphincter."

Two hours later I watched the executioner go about his procedure. I could not look into Johnny's face. My heart was thudding. I could not imagine the stress on his organs, the dryness in his mouth, the incontinence that was inevitable.

The electrician, as he was formally called, dropped the black cloth over Johnny's head and waited for the warden to look up from his pocket watch. One second after the warden nodded, the electrician pulled the switch and Johnny's body jerked, as though he were trying to run away, the leather straps straining and squeaking against the oak chair, the metal cap on his head clattering as loud as dishware.

A smell bloomed inside the room that seemed familiar, one I didn't expect. It was like the warm, damp clothes my mother ironed at the laundry with the black women. Exactly like it.

Sometimes I still cough when I think about the connection in my mind with my mother and Johnny Massina in his last moments. Was it because they were both pawns of the same system? No, I don't think so. I *know* so. My mother was as disposable as Johnny was. Now as I lay in my bed, a recording of "T for Texas" by Jimmie Rodgers playing over and over on my ancient record player, I wished my mother was there with me. Even though she tried, she never learned to read at an eighth-grade level. If she were alive, I would teach her. Time surely gets away.

Chapter Two

I got up from my bed and walked, sock-footed and in my trousers and strap undershirt, into the kitchen, took a carton of chocolate milk from the icebox and sat at the breakfast table and drank it watching the fireworks exploding above City Park. I also had a carton of eggnog, but I had bought it only on the premise that it was for guests who might drop by, perhaps with a bottle of Jack or brandy.

In all probability, my subconscious was finding another way to get me to the package store. See, alcoholism is a disease that says you don't have a disease. And "disease" is the word for it. The carrier taints everything he touches or breathes on. Family, friends, employers, and even other drunks. My friend Clete Purcel says most alcoholics belong in old-time diving suits with brass helmets. Better said, alcoholism is a form of psychological and moral insanity. The schemes you perpetrate on yourself are the deadliest of them all.

It had rained earlier, but now the rain was only a mist that had been followed by a blanket of cold fog, one that was as white as cotton bolls between the mudbanks and cypress trees along Bayou Teche. I saw some kids in a boat fire up a bottle rocket and send it across the water into my backyard. They sounded young, and I don't think they meant me any harm. But that's what they did. The rocket bounced off a wood post on my little dock, then went right through the flap on an old army tent I had propped up for an armadillo who had lost a foot after laying her pups, which are what baby armadillos are called. In minutes the tent was glowing with an unwelcomed flame and dark smoke.

I slipped on a pair of boat shoes and grabbed a fire extinguisher and headed down the slope. It didn't take much to put out the fire. I went to my toolshed and picked up a tarp and flashlight and replaced the burned army tent, then tried to round up the mother armadillo. The hardest job was to find the pups. They had scattered over the slope and were difficult to see in the fog and tall grass. My kind feelings toward the kids who set fire to the tent were beginning to thin.

"Hey, you guys!" I yelled. "How about obeying the law and not shooting fireworks inside the city limits?"

"Sorry, Mr. Dave," a boy replied. I could see the boat now. There were three or four kids sitting in it. They were all about fifteen or sixteen. Maybe two of them were girls.

"We thought somebody was up to no good on your lawn," the boy said. "We don't have a flashlight. I thought I could light up your yard."

"You lost me, podna," I said.

"There was a man there, suh," the boy said.

"Yes, suh. An ugly guy," one of the girls said.

"Y'all row to the dock," I said.

"We ain't in no trouble, are we?" the same girl said.

"Of course not," I replied. "I appreciate y'all looking out for me."

I heard the oars move in the locks and the wood blades dip into the water. It's funny about Cajun kids in what we call Acadiana. The accent never changes; the simplicity and humility and vulnerability remain the same, generation after generation. When a tragedy finally wends its way into their lives, the destruction is total, like a kitchen match flaring around a rose.

The bow of the boat scraped on the mudflat.

"Okay, tell me about this ugly guy," I said.

They glanced at each other, not sure what they should say.

"I will not give out your names to anyone," I said.

"You cain't make a promise like that, can you?" the boy said. He wore a baseball cap backward. His face was soft and grinning. He was afraid. They all were. Cajun parents can be strict.

"He was a tall man in a black raincoat," the same girl answered. "His hair was black. It hung straight down. It was dirty, like it had sticks in it. For a few minutes the moon came out from behind the clouds. His skin looked like it had knots on it."

That was a pretty good description, the kind that can cause a witness a lot of trouble.

"Mr. Dave?" the boy said.

"Yeah?"

"He was dragging a big plastic garbage bag. I ain't seen what he done wit' it. He was standing by the cattails wit' the bag, then he walked off in the trees and I couldn't see him no more."

"Maybe he doesn't like to pay for his garbage pickup," I said.

The kids didn't laugh. I bounced the flashlight beam on the bank so I could see them more clearly. Their foreheads were furrowed, their arms folded across their chests. They kept looking over their shoulders, like they wanted to row back across the bayou. "What is it, you guys?" I asked.

"He was really scary, Mr. Robicheaux," the boy said. "I'm glad you come out. We gotta go now."

"Give me a minute or two," I replied.

I walked toward the cattails, the flashlight's beam carving through the dark, the eyes of the tree frogs glittering on the cypress limbs. When I got close to the frogs, they scattered over the water like birdshot. A big black plastic bag tied in a knot at the top rested half in the mud and half in the reeds and the water and cattails. With one hand I dragged it onto dry ground. I couldn't say it was heavy, nor could I say it was light. Nor was it lacking solidity. That last part bothered me.

I opened my Swiss Army pocketknife and sliced across the top of the bag, just below the knot, then folded the blade and replaced the knife. I set down my flashlight, then with two hands tore the plastic wide.

My breath went out of my lungs, audibly, as though someone had dropped a steel storm sewer lid on my chest. The woman was young and thin and nude and had olive-colored skin and was in a kneeling position. She was also dead. Her eyes looked straight at mine. They were pale blue, like a Creole might have. Each breast was tattooed with a large rose. Her body had no odor.

"You okay there, Mr. Dave?" asked the boy from the boat.

"Yeah," I replied. "Y'all stay there, please."

"Anything wrong, suh?" he said.

I kept the flashlight's beam on the dead woman, with my back to the kids. I've seen many bodies, overseas and in this country, and in each instance I did not want to see how they died. I always felt I was a voyeur, an intruder who had no right to violate the most private moment in a person's life. Most importantly, I did not want to witness retroactively the suffering that had been imposed on them.

But I was a cop, and cops don't get to make the rules. With my left hand I held the flap I had torn in the bag and with my right hand I lowered the light into the hole, flattening the beam's brilliance on the woman's throat. A thin, bronze-colored wire had sunk deep into the woman's throat. I couldn't be sure, but I thought it was a guitar string.

I heard a rustling sound behind me and quickly clicked off the flashlight and rose to my feet. The three kids had gotten out of the boat and were staring at me. "It ain't garbage in there, no?" the boy said.

"No, it's not," I said.

"It's an animal?" the second girl said.

I couldn't keep the kids straight in my mind, even though they obviously knew me. I thought the boy used to throw my newspaper.

They seemed like visitors from another dimension. I pressed the heel of my hand to my forehead. "I have to take back my word," I said. "Y'all come up to the house. Your folks are probably wondering about y'all."

They followed me up the slope into the kitchen, and I gave each of them a cold drink and a piece of cake, then went into the living room alone and dialed the private dispatcher's number at the Iberia Parish Sheriff's Department, then made a call to Clete Purcel at his motor court farther down the bayou. I wanted to tell Clete everything about the young woman's body before my colleagues got to the crime scene, as odd as that sounds.

"What are your first thoughts?" I said when I finished.

"Sounds like a real perv wants to do you some damage, noble mon," he said.

I guess that was one way to put it.

Clete beat the ambulance and Sheriff Helen Soileau and the coroner and two cruisers and a new homicide plainclothes named Valerie Benoit to the house. I was sorry for the kids, but glad that Helen was there. She took their statements herself, then told them to beat it and keep their mouths shut and don't violate our fireworks laws again. The real issue, of course, was the possible danger to the kids. If they saw the man with shaggy hair drop the body in the cattails and shallows, he probably got a good look at them, too. How would you like a guy like that looking in your kid's window? Sometimes I really hated my job.

If I seemed to have portrayed Helen as rough, it's intentional. She worked her way up as an NOPD meter maid with no help from several NOPD males who were one cut above white trash, plus she was bisexual, which gave them an extra handle to make her life miserable.

Clete not only stayed out of the way, he sat in my stuffed chair with his feet on a stool in the living room and watched Turner

Classic Movies while eating a ham-and-onion sandwich loaded with extra tomato and lettuce and mayonnaise, his porkpie hat crown-down on the TV. Clete was a movie addict, and believed *The Godfather*, *Shane*, *My Darling Clementine*, and *For Whom the Bell Tolls* were the best films ever made. He also believed he had spoken several times to Joan of Arc, the real one. He even visited the town in which she was burned to death and cried openly in front of a group of tourists from Iowa who treated him with great kindness. Clete Purcel led many lives.

He was a recipient of the Navy Cross, the Silver Star, and three Purple Hearts, and would never discuss any of them. His complexity was such that he was never predictable, which on occasion made him an instantaneous threat to the Mob, slumlords, jackrollers, drug dealers, racist cops, pimps, women-beaters, and con men who cheated the elderly, primarily because a collection of shitheads like this never saw their destiny coming, namely, having their heads twisted off and spat in.

Example? In New Orleans Clete threw a visiting greaseball from Miami off a balcony into the swimming pool. Except it was the wrong end of the swimming pool. That was minor though. He dropped a steel wrecking ball through the roof of a porn theater that had just set up across the street from a black Baptist church. The pastor was a friend of his. Those were warm-ups.

After Helen and the investigating team left the property, along with the body of the woman who had rose tattoos on her breasts, I walked into the living room and sat down across from Clete, my energies gone. He was drinking a Diet Dr Pepper. He turned off the television. "Better get some sleep," he said.

"So I can have nightmares?" I replied.

"Did anybody have an idea who the guy was? The tall guy with sticks in his hair?"

"Nope."

"You said there was one girl who could probably sketch him or help a police artist do it?" he said.

I nodded but didn't speak.

"There's no chance she's seen him before?" Clete said.

"Could be, but I don't think so. I think she would tell us. I think this one is going to be a bucket of shit. Are you going to stay here?"

I waited for his answer, breathing through my nose, deliberately letting my eyes go out of focus.

"Yeah, if I can listen to your Jimmie Rodgers record," he replied.

"Sure."

"What do you like about Jimmie Rodgers most?" he asked.

"Jimmie Rodgers died recording on a cot at age thirty-five, knowing every minute his time was up."

"I knew you'd say that," he said.

Clete's neck was as thick as a fireplug, and a scar like a flattened nightcrawler ran through his left eyebrow. The latter was from a gang beef when he was seventeen in the Old Irish Channel. His eyes were green and intelligent and never dulled-over, his hair freshly clipped and combed, still blond, like a kid's. He was also overweight and sometimes split the shirts on his shoulders. The liquids he drank and the fried food he ate were a study in coronary and arterial abuse, but he claimed, seriously, that his liver and kidneys were already petrified and hence none of it was worth worrying about.

I wanted to think of Clete as a happy elephant playing with an umbrella on a high wire, but that was too easy. Clete was a tragedy, and most of his problems were buried in his unconscious. I had probably gone along for the ride. In our days at NOPD we called ourselves the Bobbsey Twins from Homicide. At various times the Mob put a hit on both of us, breaking their own code about killing flatfeet. As an addendum, I think most of the department was pulling for the Mob.

"Why are you looking at me, noble mon?"

"No reason," I said.

He pointed his index finger at me. "You're thinking about the past, Streak, a great guilt you haven't paid for. The girl with the rose tattoos is the warning sign."

"Streak" was a nickname given to me as a child. My hair was black, but there was a white patch in it, caused by malnutrition. "Everybody eventually has to pay his tab," I said.

"Hey, we're the good guys, remember?" Clete said.

"I'm just saying, Clete. You can't reverse time. Dead means dead. I'm not talking about overdue library books."

"Are you talking about mistakes here or Shitsville?" he asked.

I opened my palms to say, *What difference does it make?*

Clete got up and went into the dining room and started up my old Jimmie Rodgers LP. Even in his last days, the Mississippi Yodeler's mournful voice rose to the ceiling like a balloon cut loose from its string:

Now whether I'm right or wrong
I'm gonna be gone before long
And I'll hush this crazy song
And I never will sing
No mo, no mo.

Chapter Three

The next day was Saturday. I was glad. I felt a lassitude I couldn't explain. I felt that my life was catching up with me, as though I had ignored the past and needed somehow to change it. But I didn't feel this just about myself. I believed it of everything around me. In a live oak tree on the bayou were iron spikes and lengths of chain left from the auctions conducted by James Bowie and Jean Lafitte in violation of the 1808 ban on slave importation from the West Indies.

Another instance of our wayward past lay in St. Martinville, ten miles away, the home of the legendary Evangeline. In 1947 a fourteen-year-old black boy was convicted of murdering a white pharmacist. The trial was a mockery. At least one of the executioners was drunk and botched the electrocution. The plea for mercy was turned down by Governor Jimmie Davis, the man who wrote "You Are My Sunshine." The boy's name was Willie Francis. He died the second time the state strapped him on the lap of Gruesome Gertie, the nickname for the Louisiana chair. Few people remember any of this.

As I've said before, I could go on. But the past is the past, huh?

I drove down East Main to Clete's cottage at the Teche Motel. He ran his P.I. business in both New Iberia and in the French Quarter in New Orleans, chasing down bail skips, spying on adulterers, working as a bodyguard for celebrities and witnesses to serious crimes, searching out employees who sold information they stole from their employers, and doing grunt work for lawyers who wore sharkskin suits and looked like they combed their hair with motor oil. About twice a month he swore he was going to set fire to both his offices.

His cottage was at the rear of the motor court's driveway, right by a grove of old live oaks that sloped down to the bayou. He was washing his latest Cadillac convertible, one of many he had owned. This one was orange, the top ragged and gray with mold, a spray of rust on the fenders that was as delicate as lace. He had parked the Caddy so no one could see the other side of it. About two weeks ago five holes appeared in the passenger's door. The pattern looked like buckshot or rounds from a small-caliber pistol. Obviously he had decided not to explain their origins.

He was wearing navy blue boxer trunks, brand-new white tennis shoes, a T-shirt with Ernest Hemingway's face on it, and an immaculate straw cowboy hat. He grinned with a big smile. "Noble mon," he said.

"What the haps, Cletus?" I said.

"No haps," he said. "You look good."

But I didn't feel good, and he knew it. As I was just saying to you, the past seemed stamped every place I looked, in fact right here as I walked to the other side of the Cadillac. "Those holes bother the hell out of me, Clete. Is that supposed to be your flag?"

"It was just a little accident."

"Really?"

"Yeah," he said, squeezing a sponge over his wash bucket. "This black gal in the Ninth Ward was having trouble with her ex, you know, clubbing her in the face with the stock of his twelve gauge in front of their baby, and I talked to him about it and he said he'd give up his twelve gauge, except he was drunk and got dramatic about it and flipped it end-over-end and it butt-fired."

"Who's the guy?" I asked.

"Who cares?" he replied.

I was standing by the passenger door now. I probed three of the holes with my little finger. "So the buckshot fired into the air, but the trajectory was downward? The drunk ex-husband has invented a new kind of gravity."

"You worry too much, big mon," he replied. "If we didn't have these guys to toilet train, we wouldn't have jobs. Face it. It beats selling used cars."

He gazed at the bayou, the current running fast, the sun spangling in the oak limbs, his eyes like empty holes. "You heard anything from the coroner?"

"About the girl? No."

Clete nodded. "You need to get out of this funk, Dave."

"How should I do that?" I said.

"The day we got our badges at NOPD was the day we went to the other side of the moon. We play make-believe with everyone around us. We know how the real world works. Most people don't."

"I think we fool ourselves, too," I replied.

"You've got a broom up your ass, Dave, but I don't think it's about the dead girl."

"You're not hearing me, Clete. You've got either buckshot or bullet holes in your car door, but you're telling me I should bugger off."

"No, I did not."

"Evil is evil," I said.

"I think you should go to a meeting."

"A meeting isn't going to get rid of a guitar string around a young woman's throat," I said. "Don't shine me on, Clete. You know what I'm talking about."

"The hell I do."

"Slaves chained to a tree. A fourteen-year-old black kid condemned to frying twice. Cops who say, 'I feared for my life,' and plant a drop on an unarmed corpse. Fuck."

He pulled the lid of his cowboy hat down on his brow so it shaded his face, and huffed air out of his nose and kept his back to me. It was a golden day, perhaps seventy-five degrees, the oak leaves rustling above our heads.

"I feel like a dry drunk is coming on," I said. "I'm sorry."

"Screw it."

"It doesn't work that way, and you know it," I said.

"Just don't drink. It'll pass."

He was right. But a dry drunk is easier talked about than dealt with. My head was light, as though my old friend the malarial mosquito were laying her eggs in my heart's blood. I began walking back to my pickup truck, off-balance, the sun like a burst of glass in my eyes.

"Come back, Dave," Clete said. "Hey, big mon, hold up! I'll go with you! I apologize. I had my head stuffed up my butt. You know me!"

But I got into my pickup and drove away. In my rearview mirror I saw him pick up the sponge from the wash bucket and fling it at his car.

When I got back home, there was a piece of notebook paper neatly folded in my mailbox. The message was printed in pencil, all of the letters capitalized. It read, YOU CAN CALL ME BOO.

Valerie Benoit, the new homicide plainclothes, pulled into the driveway just as I was reading the note. Her car was a piece of Japanese junk that leaked smoke from the hood. She was only twenty-eight and designated as a woman of color to fill out our departmental Affirmative Action requirements.

Helen Soileau, our sheriff, didn't need the federal government to be a virtuous administrator, but nonetheless she was thankful the Feds backed her up. Valerie Benoit got an unearned break, no doubt about it. But she was industrious and intelligent and humble, and was doing everything she could to be respectful of her colleagues. Yeah, I know, that should have been enough to earn her a little mercy, but power is power, and cops aren't any different from academics or bankers when they're broke: For a two-hundred-dollar raise, they'll rip out your throat.

She got out of her car and walked up to the porch, pausing to look at the flowerbed. She wore tight, stonewashed jeans and a purple jersey (she was known for her athletic intensity at Red's Gym in Lafayette and her marathon competitions). She also had a narrow face and blond streaks in her hair, which had immediately drawn attention from the wisenheimers in the department who named her Goldilocks. I'm talking about some five-star assholes.

"How you doin', Miss Valerie?" I said.

"All right," she said, glancing at the piece of notebook paper in my hand. "You get anything back from the coroner?"

"No."

"Sheriff Soileau said we'll be working together."

"That's good," I said.

Her eyes went again to the notepaper.

"This was in my mailbox," I explained. "It says, 'You can call me Boo.' Know anyone named 'Boo'?"

"No," she said.

"Cranks come to my house with regularity."

"I know you like to work informally with your friend Mr. Purcel. That doesn't bother me."

"Clete is my sidekick from NOPD Homicide," I said. "He's a pro. He won't get in anyone's way. You want some coffee?"

"Yes, that would be great. You surely have a nice place."

I let her walk ahead of me, through the house and into the kitchen. My home was indeed a nice place, what is called a "shotgun" house down South, meaning a boxcar you could shoot through the front door and the lead shot would fly down the corridor and out the back screen without hitting a single board.

She looked at my books and music albums and framed photographs. None of the pictures were from Vietnam. Several were of local musicians. "You collect old 78s?" she said.

"Yes, since I was a kid."

"Like who?"

"Bessie Smith and Robert Johnson. Benny Goodman. Hank Williams and 'Lovesick Blues.'"

I couldn't tell if she recognized the names or not. She stood in the middle of the kitchen. The windows were open and blowing up the slope. She removed a lock of her hair from her forehead. It was gold and perhaps dyed, I couldn't tell.

"I'm sorry to ask you this, Detective Robicheaux, but are you going to handle that piece of notepaper or try to get a print?" she said.

"To tell you the truth, I've given it no thought."

She widened her eyes and looked at the walls and ceiling as though she had never seen the inside of a kitchen, probably because she had just insulted me. "This is such a nice house. And your trees and flowers and the animals in your backyard are lovely. It must bring you great pleasure."

I kept my face empty. I can't say my stomach was churning, but it was close. I cannot stand people who make observations of me or my life.

"Did I say something wrong?" she asked.

"No, ma'am, not at all," I replied, staring through the screen.

"Please don't call me 'ma'am.' "

"I would not dream of it."

The next morning, Sunday, I was weeding my flowerbeds when Valerie Benoit turned into my driveway again. This time she was wearing a dress and a floppy straw hat with a wide lavender band around the crown. I stood up as she walked across the grass, the leaves crunching under her shoes, an attempt at a relaxed smile on her face.

"Good morning," she said. "I owe you an apology."

"Not to me, you don't."

"I didn't know about your losses," she said. "I kept running my mouth about your creating such a nice house. I shouldn't have been making observations about your private life. I'm kind of left-handed about that sort of thing."

"Don't worry about it."

"I didn't know you had the Silver Star and two Purple Hearts."

I shook my head. And I did it as fast as I could. "I don't talk about those things anymore."

"I'll say this only once. You're a piece of work, sir. And you and Sheriff Soileau make me proud to be a member of the department."

"Thank you," I replied, hoping she would shut up.

She looked down the street and rubbed the back of her neck. She was obviously looking at Shadows-on-the-Teche, a home built in 1834, one that made use of more than two hundred slaves, all of whose graves could be anywhere, perhaps fertilizer in my gardens.

"You know about the Shadows?" I said.

"Yes," she said. "But I don't dwell on it. I just talked to the coroner. The woman in the garbage bag didn't die of strangulation. Cause of death was a hotshot. Brown skag, probably from across the Rio Grande."

"Why the guitar string around her throat?" I said.

"Who knows?" she said. "Can I ask you a question?"

"You bet."

"How many of your colleagues are dangerous?" she asked.

"What?"

"Yesterday somebody put a dead nutria in my locker. It was bagged in a Ziploc and full of tiny worms. This morning a windshield wiper was broken off my car."

"Did you tell Helen?"

"Not yet."

"Do it first thing tomorrow."

"I can take care of myself."

I shook my head. "That's a bad attitude. There're a couple of deputies at the jail you don't want to mess with."

"What are their names?" she asked.

"You'll know them when you see them."

"Why don't you tell me now?" she said.

I blew out my breath. "Talk to Helen."

"Yeah, I can do that. I'd better let you get back to work. Thanks for the heads-up."

"Miss Valerie, you're putting me in a bad position with these other guys."

"I understand," she said. "Don't worry. I spent three years in the army."

She had no idea what she was talking about.

"You want some coffee?" I said.

"No, I'd better go. Have a nice day."

She backed her car out into the street, then drove past the Shadows, slowing down, looking sideways at the bamboo wall around it and the second-story verandah and its Caribbean architectural magnificence, or maybe she saw it as the entrance to the necropolis it actually was.

Late in the evening there was a tap on my door, although I had a mechanical bell with a handle the visitor could twist. I looked through the glass pane before I opened the door. I didn't know why. Perhaps I sensed the man standing there didn't want to get germs on his fingers or leave his fingerprints. This is what happens when you spend a lifetime in law enforcement. The door-to-door Girl Scout selling cookies suddenly looks like Lucrezia Borgia.

The man was of medium height and build, his dark hair recently clipped, his cheeks shaved, his face pleasant. He wore starched navy blue strap overalls, a light blue shirt and black tie, steel-toed work shoes, and a black suit coat. A cheap briefcase lay next to his foot. "Did you get my note?" he said.

"What note?"

He was smiling now. "The one that says 'You can call me Boo.' That's me, Boone Hendrix. I do all kinds of repairs. My prices are always on the square."

The vowels in his speech sounded like wooden shoes clunking down a hallway.

"I don't think I have any repair problems right now," I said.

"I noticed a Spanish-moss buildup on your roof. I have my panel truck and aluminum ladder close by. I can have a look-see. You can never be too careful when it comes to dry rot."

"No, my roof is sound and I can pull the moss down with a rake."

"I wouldn't be so sure about that, Detective Robicheaux. A tin roof is a vulnerable roof, particularly if the nails are torn loose, like yours, probably from the last hurricane."

To make his point, he tried to wobble the handrail on my little porch, although it would not budge.

"How did you know my name?" I asked.

"I've seen your photo in the newspaper. You're a famous man."

"No, I'm not. Look, partner, there is nothing wrong with my roof."

"Have you had any backup in your sewage line? I suspect it was put there a century ago. All the lines on this street are like that. I pulled a gob out from your neighbor that was hard to deal with. But I will not go into detail. All my jobs are done with iron-clad privacy."

"Thanks for your offer, sir, but I have some things to do."

He nodded firmly, then reached down and picked up his briefcase, poking the inside of his cheek with his tongue. Then he extended his hand. It was sheathed with callus. His fingers reached almost to my wrist.

"Where are you from, Mr. Hendrix?"

"Nowhere and everywhere. Know why that is?"

"No, I don't," I replied.

"The man who does not claim the world is the one to whom it will be given."

There was a strange light in his eyes. "If I'm in your neighborhood, I'll drop by again, unless you'd rather I not," he continued.

"Do you have a card?" I said.

"No, sir, I keep it simple. If the customer is not satisfied, I take no money or I rip up my work and do it over. Yes, sir. But I seldom need to do the latter."

He waited for me to speak. "That sounds like a good way to do things," I said.

"Yes, sir, it is," he said, saluting with two fingers. Then he walked away with his back as stiff as a broom, the unraked leaves in my yard swirling around his knees.

I closed the door and went into the kitchen and started to fix a sandwich. But Mr. Hendrix bothered me. Was he an autistic savant? If he was, he may have seen the shaggy man who dragged a dead woman on my property. I wished I had asked. Why hadn't I? Was I afraid of him? Now I was really troubled.

The last ember of the sun was buried in a purple rain cloud in the west. I hurried down Main Street to catch Boone Hendrix. It wasn't hard. He was standing on the lawn of Shadows-on-the-Teche, inside the locked gate, his cardboard briefcase hanging from his hand, the massive antebellum brick-and-wood building barely visible in the gloom.

"Hey, partner," I said. "That's private property. It belongs to the National Trust for Historic Preservation. You'll have to come out of there."

He walked toward me. "It belongs to who?"

"It doesn't matter. It's closed."

The live oak trees and Spanish moss had drained all the light in the yard, as though the sun had never shone upon it.

"There's people walking all around here," Mr. Hendrix said.

"What people?"

"Back yonder. A mess of them."

"Last chance, partner."

The streetlamps suddenly lit up, startling me, causing me to turn around.

Then I turned back around. He was six feet closer to me, one hand gripped on a fence pike, his eyes as round as half dollars. He pushed the gate open and stepped out on the sidewalk. The roots of an oak tree had wedged up the concrete, cracking it in half. "Why are you staring at me like that?" he said.

"I wondered if you had seen a man with long black hair, like it has twigs in it. He also had knots and bumps all over his face."

"No," he said, faster than he should have.

"This guy dropped a young woman's body on my property, Mr. Hendrix," I said.

"I don't listen to those kinds of things."

"I see," I said. "If you run into this fella, I'd appreciate your letting me know. Can you do that for me?"

"Don't talk to me like a simpleton, sir," he replied.

"I understand. You said you saw figures on the grounds of Shadows-on-the-Teche?"

"I did not say 'figures.' I said people. Black ones. Look at the sky in the west, Mr. Robicheaux. The stars are dropping over the edges of the earth. It's a warning, sir."

Then he walked rapidly down the street, passing the old Evangeline Theatre and turning onto the drawbridge at Burke Street. Then he was gone altogether, as though he were wrapped in a cloak from an earlier time rather than the ordinary suit coat he had been wearing on my porch.

Chapter Four

The next day was Monday. At 5:30 P.M. Clete Purcel came over to the house in his orange Caddy convertible with the gray canvas top, the one that looked like it was dug up from a graveyard. He had a Bud propped on the dashboard, a folded paper towel under the can. I was sitting on the front steps, reading the newspaper. We had made no progress identifying the dead girl or the man who had dragged her on my property.

Clete cut his engine and picked up his beer and got out. The fact that he was drinking in front of me meant only one thing: Clete really wanted to drink and was about to shift gears into overdrive, namely, boilermakers or worse, a dozen or more glasses of shaved ice and cherries and orange slices and Russian vodka and Collins mix, a combo he called a "guaranteed rocket to Venus" that left him crawling around on his knees.

"Can I sit down?" he said.

"What's the haps?"

"I was gonna tell you about the buckshot in my car door," he said.

"Forget it."

"No, this is how it went down. I was working under my car when this black gal's ex accused me of improper behavior, which was a lie, then he shot my car door and shucked out the shell to give it a second try, so I pulled my ankle gun and aimed along the ground and popped him in the foot, then threw him in his car, which is a shit-mobile, and crammed his shotgun through the windshield and told him the next time he bothered me or my client, namely his ex, I would kick the shotgun up his ass until it was coming out his throat, and then blow his head off."

"Where did all this happen?"

"I told you, in the Ninth Ward."

"At her house?"

"Yeah, that's where she lives. Have you had a hearing check recently?"

"Sounds professional to me," I said. "Just family friends getting together. I'm glad you're setting the standard."

He drank from the can. "Will you stop picking on me?"

"You're going to get yourself killed, Clete. Over nothing."

"The guy's a sadist. Before his last five bit, he did specialty work for the greaseballs. Want me to describe his handiwork?"

"No," I said. "I apologize. Now give it a break."

He looked at his can. He knew he shouldn't have brought it. He tilted it back and swallowed every drop in it, then crushed it.

"What's the gen on the dead girl?" he asked.

"Nothing."

"Whether that guitar string killed her or not, it means something," Clete said. "Maybe a message."

I looked straight ahead. There were shadows on the street under the oaks, the giant limbs swaying in the wind. "Keep going," I said.

"The shaggy guy or whoever killed her knows you're drawn to music?"

"That crossed my mind," I said. "But why now?"

"Maybe he just got out of the system. Recidivists have long memories."

"But why kill somebody else?" I said. "Why not just pop me?"

"He wants you to see the suffering of others and make you feel it's your fault. He knows how you think, Dave. You got a big heart. I'd bet my money on it."

"Maybe," I said.

He brushed at his mouth. "You got some hooch? Anything."

"No," I lied. "What's eating you?"

"I got the heebie-jeebies. The shit-bird I busted up, the torture specialist? I can't get this stuff out of my head. I think he's a serial killer. Maybe including a child. I want to take this guy out. A guy like that doesn't belong on earth."

I pointed my finger at him. "Get those thoughts out of your head."

"Where's Alafair?" he said.

Alafair was my adopted daughter I pulled from a sunken plane flown by a Maryknoll priest who was trying to save the Indians from the death squads in El Salvador. The little girl and I burst to the surface with perhaps ten seconds to spare. Her mother died. So did the priest.

"She's coming home tomorrow," I said.

"Great timing," Clete said.

"Knock it off," I said.

He rubbed the back of his neck. It was red and greasy and pocked and as hard-looking as a fire hydrant. "The fuck," he said to himself.

"Come inside," I said. "I've got a bottle if you want it."

"I buy my own. I'm going to walk on down to Clementine's. Don't let them get behind you."

That was Clete's war call he had brought back from Vietnam. If you were there, you know what it means. It was the last order given by a young lieutenant in a place called My Lai.

Yeah, I was right, Clete got soused that night, so bad a good-hearted uniformed deputy in the department dragged him out of a garden of elephant ears and caladiums and piled him in a hammock suspended between two pecan trees in my backyard. At sunrise I heard a thud, then a shout, followed by a moaning sound, then someone stumbling through my lawn furniture. I pulled back the curtain on my bedroom window. Clete had rolled over in the hammock and landed on his face, and now had fallen down again. By the time I got outside he was taking a whiz on my azaleas. Hunched over in the thin light, he looked like Frankenstein.

"How about showing a little respect?" I said.

He stared at me, bleary-eyed, wobbling, probably not sure where he was. He cut a belch that sent the squirrels skittering through the trees. I would like to say that Clete's drunkenness was funny, but the truth was otherwise. Clete was about to burn his kite. When he laid off the flack juice, he looked thirty years younger, his eyes happy and green as Ireland in the spring. Now he looked like he had been beaten with a bathroom mop.

"You got to stop doing this to yourself, Clete," I said.

He was trying to pull up his zipper. "Doing what?" he said.

"You've got puke on your clothes. You pissed in the pet bowls."

"I wouldn't do that," replied. His voice was adenoidal, like he had been punched in the nose. "I just got to get my gyroscope straightened out. I think maybe somebody doped up my drinks."

"Yeah, it's called Jack Daniel's," I said.

I was ashamed of him, even though I had no right to be. I had degraded myself again and again, much worse than Clete. Actually all drunks are objects of pity and contempt and disgust, no matter what we tell ourselves. It's just a matter of degree. Clete started out a happy drunk and slipped over the edge. I was over the edge long before I got to a saloon, usually armed with my 1911-model army .45, the gargoyles climbing the walls before the first shot glass of Jack hit my stomach. Then I would turn up the volume on "Full-Tilt Boogie" and find a de facto whites-only bar populated with neo-Nazis or bikers looking for a beef, then ask one of them how he would like to be the deadest bucket of pig shit ever poured in the ground.

"I'm sorry, big mon," he said. "I was thinking about the black guy who tortures people and gets away with it. Jesus Christ, how do these guys stay on the street? We don't need DNA. You can smell death on them soon as they walk into a room."

Then he lost it, and pushed the heels of his hands into his eyes and began to weep.

I took his big arm and draped it across my shoulders. It felt as heavy as a pressurized firehose, his armpit soggy and rank.

"Ready?" I said.

"Ready for what?" he replied.

"*Your mother was home when you left, you're right,*" I said.

"*Your father was home when you left, you're right!*"

"Come on, help me out, gunny," I said.

"*Your sister was home when you left, you're right!*" he said.

"*Your brother was home when you left, you're right!*"

"*Sound off, one, two, three, four! Three-four!*"

That's how I got him into the house and into the shower and steamed him until he was red and oozing grease and sweat. Then I picked up his clothes from the bathroom floor and placed everything on the counter and threw the clothes into the washing machine, then went back to the bathroom, the mirrors and walls dripping with moisture. I had paid little attention to the things he carried. The object that stuck out most was a stiletto. It had a long, slim blade and a small brass eye-drop of a button inset in the black handle.

Do you have those moments when you bumble into knowledge you do not wish to acquire, particularly when it involves a friend? Then a little voice tells you not to be afraid, to help your friend, to not be daunted by evil. Then you walk into a spiderweb.

I picked up the stiletto. It was a real gut-ripper. I had not seen Clete carry one before. The heft was perfect, the release button right under the thumb. I pushed it, and the blade leaped from the handle, a blue, oily light winking on the steel. But there was something else on it, too: blood. And it was not old.

Clete had said I had a generous heart. I didn't know if he was right or wrong. My heart was too sick to feel anything. I held up the shank. "What are you doing with this?"

"What are you talking about? That's not mine."

"It was in your pants."

"Somebody planted it there or something."

"Clete, Clete, Clete," I said.

"Don't talk to me like that. That hurts. It really hurts."

Not as much as it hurts me, I thought. But I didn't say it.

Chapter Five

I had to get to work and I didn't have time to put Band-Aids on Clete's life, at least not then. There could have been many scenarios to explain the stiletto. Maybe he stopped a fight and took it off the owner. Maybe someone attacked him. Maybe he won it in a card game. I could not imagine Clete stabbing someone with a knife. For that matter, I never saw Clete hurt anyone who didn't have it coming.

I opened the drawer under the kitchen counter and dropped the stiletto inside, then shut the drawer and started fixing breakfast.

"You're not gonna say anything?" he asked.

"Yeah, stay here until I come back."

"Was there any blood on my clothes?" he said.

"Not that I saw."

"Not that you saw? You put them in the washing machine."

"I hadn't seen the knife with the blood on it."

"That ensures I can't find out what happened," he said.

"Yeah, I'm afraid so."

"My systolic is going through the top of my head, Dave. I'm not up to this."

Who is? I thought. I've had blackouts I never want to probe.

"Don't beat up on yourself, Clete," I said. "The world does enough on its own. So far no one has knocked on the door, and the deputy who brought you to my backyard evidently had no calls on you, right? Plus, you walked to Clementine's. So you were out and about for only two blocks, right?"

"Yeah," he replied, nodding.

"So there you go."

And once again I had slipped into the role of his enabler.

"Uh, there's one thing I didn't mention, Dave," he said. "I got some images crawling around in my head."

"What images?"

"Guys shooting craps. A dark interior with red neon. Four or five dudes with a mean gleam in their eye. The women are on the stroll, but they're not all women. An open-minded joint. A guy was on a small stage with a bottleneck guitar. He was playing Robert Johnson's song about the 'Crossroads.' It's down by a swamp. Or maybe it's hell."

He stared at me, his eyes unblinking, his face poached. In the silence I could hear the beating of my heart and feel a coldness in my hands and a dryness in my mouth, a moment of fear that is like a *klatch* on a night trail in a long-forgotten war.

Clete had called Alafair's arrival the next day bad timing. Obviously I didn't take that very well. Why is that? Your children are your children. Your organs belong to you or they don't. You don't rent a locker at the bus station for your child. It's not complicated. Yeah, I know Alafair is not my flesh and blood. But so what? Your bond is your bond. Over the gunwales with the rest of it. Sometimes I get mad at Clete.

However, no matter how you cut it, I wanted to get a jump ahead regarding the body on the back lawn. I also wanted Clete's latest trouble out of both his life and my life. For whatever reason, Clete could not resist swatting a hornet's nest everywhere he went. The "images" in his head may have been unfamiliar to him but I knew them well. I'll explain. Clete grew up in New Orleans, in the

Irish Channel, among people who spoke with a mouthful of corned beef and cabbage. He might as well have grown up in Boston or Little Italy in New York. Ever hear Louis Prima sing? He sounded like a sewer pipe. The point is, sometimes Clete still doesn't understand blue-collar Cajun culture out in the parishes, particularly down by the Gulf. Forty percent of Louisiana is considered functionally illiterate. People think the Communist Chinese bombed Pearl Harbor, and Idaho is a potato. We thank God for Mississippi.

Clete had stumbled into a marshy settlement on the edge of the Atchafalaya Basin, the biggest swamp in the United States, including the Everglades in Florida or the Okefenokee in Georgia. How he got there, I don't know. He said he was going to walk from my house to Clementine's. I suspected he got drunk and hooked up with the wrong dude or woman and decided he'd take a late fling on the wild side of life, in a place where the pterodactyls still streak the sky.

That's no jive. These were not simply Cajuns; most of them pulled the plug on civilization during the War Between the States. I doubted the people who lived in Jerry Carlucci's Landing gave much cognitive time to the environment in which they lived, or cared about the long formation and destruction of ancient volcanos that had once existed there, or the beasts that thrashed in the sand bogs, or the lightning storms that electrified the heavens without making a sound. For them I suspected the issues were immediate and personal, such as staying off the computer, avoiding the IRS and vaccinations and marriage licenses and car tags, instead staying stoned and shooting whatever birds and four-leg creatures they felt like. In other words, during the French colonial period it could have been a lovely prison.

In more modern times crank hit Louisiana in the 1980s, and Jerry jumped on it. The Landing became a fresh-air sanitarium for people who glowed in the dark or who had to tape their mouths to stop talking because they were blitzed on speed.

I spent considerable time there when I came back from Southeast Asia. I also went there after my wife Annie was murdered in our bed at point-blank range with a shotgun. I was also an irregular visitor when I thought I could drink myself to the other side of Mars and keep my badge at the same time. Even Jerry eighty-sixed me from his saloon. That's like getting kicked off a garbage truck.

Worse, though, from time to time I still had an attraction to the world of Jerry Carlucci. It wasn't all bad down at the Landing, I told myself. It was like Van Gogh's paintings. Or the paintings of his friend, Paul Gauguin. In Carlucci's Landing the sky turned yellow at evening and stretched out over endless miles of marshland and swamps that dipped into the Gulf of Mexico. The thunderheads in the south were purple and swollen with rain and lightning, then the day began to cool and renew your spirits, the links of bays wrinkling like old skin in the wind, the mullet flying through the air, and the funnel of a waterspout twisting like spun glass, the sun bloodred on the horizon. Yes, that's right, it was a postdiluvian world that was free of authority and rules, where the blue-pink emanations on the earth's rim seemed to lead us into eternity.

But I knew it was too good to be true. In fact, these moments frightened me. Why? Arks and animals walking two by two make wonderful tales, but when I find myself justifying a trip to Jerry Carlucci's Landing, I know I'm putting the slide on myself. Way down in my unconscious a screenwriter is typing twenty-four hours a day in order to get me back on the dirty boogie. One day I'm going to meet that screenwriter and stuff him in a septic tank. But that's how he works. Anger is the common denominator of all drunks. We get drunk *at* people, not *with* them.

It's rough being a drunkard. You spend half your time worrying, then the other half of your time feeling guilty about it. As Helen often says, some fun, huh, bwana?

But I had made up my mind and took a drive into the geographical bottom of Louisiana the evening before Alafair was to arrive, certain that my intentions were good. I was a police officer, and in the program, and on the square with my Higher Power, and I wished no harm on anyone. Besides, it was a grand evening, a rainy green cloud on the horizon, pelicans flying in formation low over the water, their bills pouched with fish. What could possibly go wrong in an environment like that?

Jerry Carlucci owned a ramshackle saloon and brothel and café at the bottom of a levee a short distance from the saltwater that was eating away the Louisiana coast. Because of the eroding landscape, no authorities were quite sure where Jerry's property lines were, which gave them an excuse to leave him alone. Jerry had a stare like a slap and an odor like testosterone ironed into his clothes. He was also over six feet and handsome, his hair as black as patent leather, except barbered like a bullfighter, with a pigtail. He wore five-hundred-dollar suits, too, and ofttimes an immaculate shirt with puffed sleeves and a lavender vest and a gold watch and chain and a thin mustache, much like a late nineteenth-century frontier lawman or a gambler or a leader of the Know Nothing Party or an upscale procurer. Jerry was a chameleon.

Except you didn't call Jerry a pimp. At age eighteen he was a door gunner in Shitsville. I shuddered sometimes at the thought of Jerry aiming an M60 out the door of a Huey racing over a rice paddy. His favorite song was "Going Up the Country" by Canned Heat.

I parked my pickup in front of his saloon and walked across a wood footbridge onto a compacted pad of oyster shells and through two rusty screen doors into the bar. It was gloomy inside, a small stage against the back wall, with a keyboard and two or three stringed instruments propped against a purple curtain. It was officially winter, but outside Indian summer glowed on the acres of marsh, and thousands of insects hung in clouds above the water, and the tide was frothy and rocking with organic debris, as though it were about to give birth.

Jerry was standing at the back of the bar, his tall frame backlit by the window, counting the money from the cash register, writing on a notepad, his eyes lifting for just a second when he heard me close the door. "What's happening, Dave?" he said, voice as flat as a board.

I put my arm on the bar, my foot on the rail. I didn't want to answer. I didn't like Jerry, or I didn't like the man he had become, and I didn't like pretending that I did. I didn't sit down, either. "I wondered if you'd seen Clete Purcel recently."

"Nope."

"No sign of him?"

"I've been out of town. I just got back."

I nodded. Some women were drinking at a table on the other side of the stage, a couple of men knocking back shots with them. I wondered if they knew it was watered. One of the men went to the bar and filled a pitcher of beer from the spout. He gave me a look, then went back to his table.

"You got a band playing tonight?" I said.

"No, only weekends," Jerry said. "My bartender is off tonight. Come back tomorrow."

"I'm sure Clete was here," I said. "Maybe he stopped a beef. One that included a switchblade."

"Purcel stopping a beef? That's a laugh."

"You're talking about my friend, Jerry," I said.

"Sorry. The plaster is probably falling from the ceiling of the Sistine Chapel."

"What do you have against Clete?"

"He was born. That's enough. Got a secret for you, Dave. The pair of you should start wearing jockstraps outside your pants. It'll help you with all this macho shit you can't get enough of."

I took a hard-boiled egg from a glass jar and cracked it on the bar. "How much?"

"On the house."

I took one dollar from my wallet and placed it on the bar so it stood stiffly on its edge. Why? I don't know. I wanted to do something he couldn't.

"You got nothing to say?" he asked.

"You're in the life, Jerry. You hurt people who trust you and think you're their friend."

He stopped counting his money and walked slowly toward me, the heel of his hand barely touching the bar. He was wearing pointy, spit-shined Tony Lamas that echoed off the plank floor. "Excuse me?"

"Most of the cocaine and brown tar here'bouts comes right through your backdoor."

He rested his hand on the bar, the balls of his fingers cupped on the surface. He gazed at the green veins under the brownness of his skin. "Go somewhere else, okay?"

"Somebody dropped a body on my lawn," I said. "I think she was probably in the life. She was also attractive. She had roses tattooed on her breasts."

"I don't know anybody like that."

"How can you be so sure?" I asked. "You've given breast examinations to all the women in Southwest Louisiana?"

He shook his head. "You just don't get it, Dave. People feel sorry for you because you've lost three wives. I've got a different take on that. I think they were lucky."

I touched at my right eye, like an eyelash was in it. But I had no trouble with eyelashes. An electric switch had just clicked behind my forehead. It lit up a basement where I seldom went. Unicorns and pink zebras played there, and gargoyles liked to climb the walls.

"Cat got your tongue?" he said. "You look a little sick. Like you swallowed a toadstool."

I could feel a tremble in my right hand, a dryness in my mouth, a bright flicker behind my eyelids, like a guttering candle.

"What about it, Dave? You know what's funny about us? I think you could be me or I could be you."

"Not in a billion years, Jerry."

"How many people have you killed, Dave? Does your badge make you feel good? You like to smoke some dude who can't count past ten? What a laugh."

I pointed a finger at him but I couldn't talk.

"Is that the best you can do?" he said.

I stepped backward. "I'm going to walk away from you, Jerry. I won't be back. That's a promise. Do you hear me?"

But his interest in me had gone. He was staring through the glass in the front door, then he went to the pool table and began dropping pool balls in his coat pockets. Then he ripped open the front door and walked out on the porch. "I told you to get out of here!" he yelled.

On the remnants of the old board road that led to Jerry's saloon were several shacks with sheets of plastic flapping on the windows and crawfish and shrimp nets drying in the yards, and portable toilets probably stolen from a construction site. Boone Hendrix, the wandering handyman who kept secret "the gob" he had extracted from my neighbor's sewer line, was knocking on one of the shack doors. Jerry let fly with the pool balls, firing them one after another. Like me, Jerry had pitched American Legion ball. Jerry's forkball could knock down a Piper Cub. He speared one between Boone Hendrix's shoulder blades. I saw the air go out of Hendrix's lungs, his mouth open, and the pain leap in his face.

"You heard me, you crazy fuck!" Jerry said. "If I see you here again, I'll put you in my crab traps."

I was standing right behind Jerry. "No, you will not, Jerry," I said.

He turned around, his right hand ready to fire another pool ball. "Don't make me hurt you, Dave."

"Put the pool ball away and go back inside, Jerry."

"You don't know this guy. He's a geek, a child molester, and a peeping Tom."

Jerry had gripped the ball so tight his fingers were white.

"That's not my impression of him," I said.

"Because you're a bleeding heart. You worry about the enemies we kill in foreign countries, but you don't give a shit about your own people. This is my property. Neither you or Purcel got any authority on it. Now get the fuck off my land before I lose my temper."

I took my badge holder from my coat pocket and slipped my .45 and the holster from my belt, and put all of them on the porch steps of the saloon. "Go ahead," I said.

He was breathing through his mouth, the pool ball still in his hand. "Go ahead, what?" he said.

"Go ahead and finish what you want to say," I replied.

"I'm done."

"No, you're not. The last time I was here I was drunk. You said some things about my family. You did it before because you're a born killer. In fact, your whole family is. And you want my family to be like yours and live in the same gutter, you motherfucker."

"You mother was a whore," he said. "What can I say? Big deal."

I could hear a whirring sound in my ears now, like an airplane engine starting up or an electric generator I once heard spinning outside a parish prison, back in the days when the electric chair traveled on a flatbed truck from parish to parish.

"Take it back," I said.

"What's to take back? She was poor. Your old man was a drunk. So she got desperate. People get hungry. So your family got screwed. Literally. Boo-hoo."

What he said was ugly, but I almost let him go. Then he said, "If you want an addendum on that, I heard she couldn't get enough. Your old man couldn't get it up."

I hooked him in the mouth, snapping back his head, then spat in his face and clubbed him wherever I could see a vulnerable spot. He went straight down, and I went with him and pinned him with my knees and drove my fists into his face until there was blood on my shirt, but even then I couldn't stop.

My lack of control here was the same as in Shitsville. My enemy was not the NVA and Sir Charles. They were bystanders. For me the issue was a man named Mack, who ruined my family and turned my mother into an addict and finally a prostitute.

It took several people to pull me off Jerry. Through their legs and arms and the sweaty haze in my eyes I could see the handyman Boone Hendrix standing in a yard, staring at me, his face quizzical, as though he had no idea what was going on.

I went into a blackout all the way to New Iberia, then turned into Popeyes out on the four-lane and ate an entire bucket of fried chicken and biscuits dripping in butter. I didn't wake up until five the next morning. All my clothes were still on my body, and Jerry's blood was caked on my shirt. How do you like that for your local sheriff's detective?

Chapter Six

But I showered and put on fresh clothes and was at my office at 0800 hours, anxious to put yesterday behind me and pick up Alafair at the Lafayette airport later that day.

At 10:47 Valerie Benoit tapped on my door, simultaneously peeking inside. "Need to give you a heads-up," she said.

"Come in and have a seat," I said. But I was wary of her. I always am when people deliberately raise an alarm but without any exactitude.

She closed the door behind her. She was wearing khakis and a long-sleeve white shirt with two horses sewed on it, her badge and a holstered nine millimeter on her belt. She combed her hair off her eye with her fingers. The gold streaks in it were hard not to notice. "I've got your man locked down at the jail," she said. "He didn't take it very well."

"Can you tell me who 'my man' is?"

"Jerry Carlucci."

"What about Jerry?"

"He attacked the handyman, Boone Hendrix. I've also got him down for obstruction. You really laid it on him, didn't you?"

I put down the ballpoint and vacation application form I was filling out, and leaned forward. "You arrested Jerry?"

"Of course. Mr. Hendrix called me."

"Hendrix didn't say a word to me at the scene."

"I know him," she said. "He does odd jobs for me."

"Why did you put my name in this?"

"Pardon?"

"He didn't obstruct me. I hit him of my own volition."

"You told Carlucci to desist from throwing pool balls at an impaired man. He kept throwing them. That's obstruction."

"Hendrix didn't say squat to me, Miss Valerie. You shouldn't have done this."

Her face went out of shape. "That's a new one. You're pissed because I saved you from a liability suit or a beef with a couple of those jerks in Internal Affairs, one of whom put a nutria in my locker."

"I have private feelings about Jerry, Miss Valerie. You should have talked to me first."

"What do 'private feelings' have to do with anything? You told him to put down the pool balls and he refused to do it. I feel like I'm in Bongo Bongo Land."

"I wanted an excuse to tear him up, so that's what I did."

"So why did you want to tear him up?" she asked.

"I believe he killed children and women in a rice paddy. I heard it too many times for it to be a lie."

My office was on the second floor of the department; the sun was shining on the bayou and dappling the trees and striking her face. One of her eyes was wet, as bright as a diamond.

"I didn't know about that," she said.

"Maybe he's tormented. But I've yet to see it."

"If you want to cut him loose, you'll have to talk to Mr. Hendrix."

"I don't care what you do with either one of them."

"You're a hard-nosed guy, Detective," she said. "I thought you were a little different than the others."

"Who's the jerk who put the nutria in your locker?"

"Mine to know," she said. "His to watch out."

I puffed a ball of air in my cheek. "My daughter is flying in today. I think she'd like to meet you."

"Thank you," she said. "I've heard about her."

"Miss Valerie?"

"What?"

"Don't underestimate Jerry Carlucci. He's not only a psychopath, he's the stealer of other people's souls. Stay away from him. He has no conscience."

She looked at me for a long time. "I'm looking forward to meeting your daughter. But don't give me any bromides, will you? I can handle any of these fucks, either in the department or out of the department. Mr. Carlucci should be a grease spot."

Then she walked out, leaving the door unclosed.

I picked up Alafair at the Lafayette airport that afternoon. She had graduated Phi Beta Kappa from Reed College in Portland, and now was writing her second novel. It was hard to believe she was the same little Indian girl I pulled from a submerged single-engine plane, or the same little girl who had screaming nightmares about a column of soldiers who walked into her village and massacred hundreds of peasants, burning and machine-gunning them, destroying their homes, killing babies, and raping large numbers of little girls. The officers who condoned the atrocity, which went on for hours, were men we trained at the School of the Americas at Fort Benning.

I saw her coming through the glass doors into the waiting area, smiling, wearing jeans and sandals and a purple shirt with flowers printed on it and a draw-bag on her shoulder. She was beautiful, and I don't say that just because I'm her father. Almost every man who ever sees her turns around for a second look, whether it gets them in trouble with their wives or not.

"Hi, Dave," she said, putting her hand behind my neck and pressing my cheek against hers. "It's so nice to be back home."

I had not told her about the body that was dropped on my lawn, and the dark man with hair like sticks who left it there. "How's your novel going?" I said.

"I still try for seven-hundred-and-fifty words a day. I'm getting pretty good at it. How's Clete doing?"

"Fine," I said, clearing my throat. I felt her eyes on the side of my face.

"Uh, what's going on?" she said.

"Clete got on the grog again. But that's nothing new."

I grabbed her suitcase off the conveyor belt, and we went through the front doors into the parking lot.

"What are you not telling me, Dave?"

"I think Clete got into it with Jerry Carlucci, but I can't prove it. I thought I'd straighten things out, but instead I came down pretty hard on Jerry. We also have a new homicide case open. A black woman's body was found by some kids on the back of our property."

"That's all?" she said. "Nothing else of interest? Genghis Khan marching down East Main?"

"It's not funny, Alf."

"When did all this happen?"

"The past few days," I said.

"Do you know who the black woman is?"

"Nope. She had a rose tattooed on each breast."

A frown came into her face. "That makes me think of *The Rose Tattoo*. You know, Tennessee Williams and Burt Lancaster and Anna Magnani?"

"Yeah, what about it?"

"There was an older black girl I knew in St. Martinville. She wanted to be an actress. She was always talking about *The Rose Tattoo*. Later I heard she got both her boobs tattooed with roses."

I stopped ten feet from my pickup. "You're kidding."

"Would I kid about something like that?"

"What was her name?"

"Benoit," she said. "Clemmy Benoit."

I pinched my temples.

"Did I say the wrong thing?" she asked.

"We've got a new homicide detective in the department. Guess what her last name is? And guess where she's from?"

"And she never mentioned any of this?" Alafair said.

"No."

"Well, I'm glad to know that everything is going along smoothly as always," Alafair said.

"Are you leaving, Alfie?"

That was her pet name. She grew out of it, but I still used it, even if she minded.

"What are we having for supper?" she said. "The plane didn't have anything on board." Then she hit me playfully on the arm. "When did I ever blow Dodge on you, Dave?"

That was Alafair, from the time she was a little girl to the present. She would never let her family down. My skin tingled with pride.

I've been married four times. My first wife was from Martinique and cheated on me with regularity, which could be expected from a wife who had a drunk like me for a husband. How about this? I literally knocked one of her lover's teeth down his throat at a cocktail party. I had to press down his tongue with a spoon to save his life.

Annie was my second wife, a Mennonite girl from Kansas, who never deliberately hurt a living thing in her life, and was murdered while I tried vainly to swim across the bayou to our bait business while the flashes of the killer's shotgun leaped inside our bedroom window. Those memories have never left my dreams.

My third wife was Bootsie Mouton. She grew up on Spanish Lake, where one afternoon at age nineteen with raindrops chain-ringing the lake we lost our virginity inside a boathouse and much later got married and had a wonderful life, until Bootsie contracted Lupus and died a difficult death.

My last wife was Molly, a former nun who never took vows, worked as a missionary in Central America, saw firsthand the neo-colonialism of our times, and was killed by a drunk driver in New Iberia.

In the attic I had saved many pieces of memorabilia from Alafair's childhood. In one way or another it was tied to many people—her stepmothers, her school friends, Batist the black man who ran my bait and boat-rental business, and herself. She was the cutest little kid I ever saw. Whether she ate a lot of food or little food, she was always round—her arms, her legs, her face, her stomach. Her expression was always quizzical, no matter where we went. I used to call her my portable question mark.

I don't know what I would do if I ever lost Alafair. But my profession may one day take me from her. It's easy. Most cops who die on the job never see it coming: Walking into a domestic argument, approaching a car with a running engine and tinted windows, answering a "shots fired" and eating a sniper's bullet. The families never get over it. Why? Because citizens do get over it. Clete calls it *Semper Fi*, son of a bitch.

Look, at one time in our history criminals had some class and a degree of restraint. That is not true today. Since the 1960s, narcotics have become part of our culture. The familial damage is devastating. In terms of chemical-induced insanity, we have no precedent. The increase in robberies, prostitution, homicide and social degradation can only be estimated. Don't be surprised if the contemporary Beaver Cleaver has a synthetic beehive for a brain. The term "recreational" should be kicked up the ass of anyone who sells it.

The next morning I went into Valerie Benoit's office without knocking. She looked up from her desk as though she were about to smile. Then she said, "Something wrong?"

"Yeah, you know a girl from St. Martinville named Clemmy Benoit?"

She held her eyes on mine. "I'm not sure."

"How can you not be sure about someone who has your last name and grew up at the same time in the same town as you did?"

"I lived in other places. Besides, there are a lot of Benoits here'bouts."

"St. Martinville is a small town," I replied.

"Yes, that was one reason I always wanted to leave it. It's also the place where Willie Francis was electrocuted. He was fourteen when he supposedly killed a white man. They burned him not just once but twice. And 'burned' is the right word. How sickening does it get?"

"Yeah, you're right," I said.

The execution of Willie Francis was long ago, but as late as 1964, on the evening Lyndon Johnson signed the Civil Rights Act, not one black person could be seen on the streets of St. Martinville. Why? The sport was called "nigger-knocking" back then.

"You still don't get it, Detective," she said. She was breathing heavily, her hands knotting and unknotting, either from anger or fear. "You're accusing me of hiding information in a homicide investigation. How dare you?"

I kept my eyes flat, my expression neutral. Across Bayou Teche I could see a man selling ice cream in the park. He was sitting on a bicycle that was attached to a cold box. Balloons were tied to the bicycle frame and the box. The vendor was dressed in a white coat and white pants and a white cap like a naval officer would wear. The bill on his hat shadowed his face.

"Hello?" she said. "Have I lost your attention?"

I walked closer to the window. "Take a look. You recognize the ice cream man?"

She got up from her desk and gazed into the park. "No, I don't have my glasses."

"That's Boone Hendrix," I said.

She looked again. "So what?"

"I don't know," I said. "He shows up all over the place. Now he's got you in an entanglement with Jerry Carlucci."

"I think it's the other way around," she said. "You're on some kind of crusade."

"I try not to borrow trouble."

"Yeah, I can see that," she replied. She sat back down at her desk, clicking her ballpoint, her eyes flashing. "Would you please get out of my office?"

"Alafair knew Clemmy Benoit in her teens," I said.

"Fine. Write it up. Put it on the men's room wall."

"They were both in an amateur acting group. Know anything about that?"

She put a stick of gum in her mouth and began chewing, her pulse throbbing in her neck.

"Problem?" I asked.

"Yes, you're still here."

"I wanted to be a helping hand," I replied. "I guess that hasn't worked out."

She got up from her desk again and stared out the window, her arms folded across her chest, her back shaking.

"You okay?" I said.

"I'm sorry," she said. "Somebody sprayed the word 'nigger' on the inside of my locker this morning."

I said I didn't like to borrow trouble. I felt like shooting myself.

Chapter Seven

I crossed the drawbridge and drove into City Park and pulled up beside Boone Hendrix and his cart and the balloons tied to it squeaking in the wind. The temperature had dropped, and the park was empty and the sunlight brittle, red and brown leaves scraping along the asphalt trail that wended through the trees. I could feel myself shiver, even though I wore a jacket.

"How are you doing, Mr. Hendrix?" I said. "Not many kids about, huh?"

He parked his vehicle by the jungle gym. His sideburns were freshly clipped, his eyes empty.

"Did you hear me?" I asked.

"Decide to let me have a go at your roof?" he said. "I'll give you a good price and good workmanship, Detective."

"No, I was just wondering why you're selling ice cream in January."

"Some mothers and their toddlers will be along," he said. "You'd be surprised by how many."

What he said was nonsense. But I went along. "Mr. Hendrix, you seem like a nice man. Do you know much about Jerry Carlucci?"

"I know enough to stay away from him," he said.

"When you file assault charges against a man, you sometimes find yourself with your necktie in the garbage grinder."

"Want a popsicle?"

"Mr. Hendrix, what were you doing down by Jerry Carlucci's Landing?"

"Giving children Christmas presents their families couldn't afford to give them."

"That's a fine thing to do."

"You have children?"

"A daughter," I said.

His eyes clouded as he studied the bayou.

"Did you hear me, sir?" I asked.

"Of course, why would I not hear you?"

I'd had my fill of Mr. Hendrix. "All the best to you," I said. "You're a kind man and a gentleman of the old school, but *hasta luego* or *adios* or something like that. And thank you."

He might as well have been stone-deaf. When I drove away he was still staring at the bayou.

Just after one P.M. Helen came in from a luncheon with the chamber of commerce and blew out her breath and threw a pile of tourist material on my desk. "Take care of this, will you?"

"What am I supposed to do with it?"

"I don't know. Bury it."

"Why not give it to the tourists?" I said.

"Forgive me, I'm just tired. Our little city is changing. I can remember when fifty percent of the people still spoke French. Now subdivisions are covering the cane and every school in town is full of drugs."

I hated to add to Helen's obvious problems with the twenty-first century. "I've got some news," I said. "The body with the rose tattoos has a name. It's Clemmy Benoit. She grew up in St. Martinville. Alafair was in a drama club with her."

"Alafair told you this?"

"Yeah."

"The family didn't know she was missing?" she asked.

"I haven't had time to get on it."

"This makes us look like shit. Is Clemmy related to Valerie Benoit?"

"She said she's not sure."

"My ass," Helen said. "I feel like I'm in a sanitarium rather than the sheriff's department. Get that girl in here."

"You might go a little easy," I said. "Somebody sprayed the word 'nigger' inside her locker."

Helen clenched one hand, her knuckles whitening "Who's behind this?" she asked.

"Most probably Lloyd D'Anjou."

"Where's your baton?"

"In my drawer."

"Give it to me," she said.

"Are you serious?"

"Follow me. I want a witness," she said.

Detective Lloyd D'Anjou was standing at his window, slurping a cold drink from a carton, watching a speedboat on the bayou, when Helen threw open his door without knocking.

"What the fuck?" he said, almost dropping his drink, flicking the crushed ice off the back of his hand.

"Close the door, Dave," Helen said.

"What's going on?" Lloyd said.

Lloyd loved power. He dressed like it, too. But the steroids and shaved head, the bright smell of the deodorant he layered on his armpits, the visceral light in his eyes when he told jokes about a situation in the projects—these were cosmetic. Lloyd was a solid cop. So what if a freebie was sometimes more or less superimposed on him? He considered himself a savior. His unmarked car was often seen at the projects. He threw a wide net.

"*You're* asking what the fuck?" Helen replied. She smashed a ceramic bowl full of paper clips in the center of his blotter.

Lloyd's jaw flexed, but he said nothing. He could do squats with three hundred pounds on his shoulders. He set down a cold-drink carton on the desk and stepped back. "I got no beef with you, Helen."

"You've been harassing a fellow detective," she said, her chest heaving.

"Dog shit," he said.

"You watch your mouth."

"I take back my profane words."

"I know your record, D'Anjou. Your worst nightmare is a black, educated woman who's not afraid of you."

Lloyd D'Anjou was a dangerous and violent man, and I didn't like where she was going. I believed Lloyd had a sickness so detestable to himself he would spend a lifetime purging it by harming or killing others. Tell me you have not seen the same.

"Hey, Lloyd," I said. "You're old-school. Dial it down, podna."

Lloyd massaged a crick from his neck. "Yeah," he said. "We go back. I can see that."

He straightened his tie and lifted his chin.

Helen was breathing like she had run up the stairs, her grip still tight on the baton. The last few minutes had not gone well for her. "You can write me up with the attorney general's office, Lloyd, but I'd better never see you harassing a person in this parish again. You reading me on this?"

"You never saw me the first time," he said. "That's because it didn't happen. But let bygones be bygones."

He peeled open a roll of breath mints and thumbed one between his lips. "Want a mint? I like to suck 'em. They keep your mouth fresh that way. Or you can just crack 'em."

He snapped the mint on his molars.

* * *

I spent the rest of the day trying to run down the family of Clemmy Benoit in St. Martinville. From what I could tell, they belonged to that group of people who thought a mailbox with an address painted on it was a symbol of success. Truman Capote talked about them. They were the New America, a drifting, invisible, drug-addicted, uneducable class who would never see that shining city on the hill. The dusty skies of Oklahoma were not their enemy, either; a hole in the heart was. A mother or a father told them they belonged nowhere, and they believed it.

Her parents had died when she was a child, and she lived in an orphanage, a placement home, a shack in an alley, and with a grown man in an alley. Her only job had been in a drugstore, from which she was fired. Her only pleasure was her drama class, the same one Alafair joined. The last anyone saw of her was on a Greyhound. It was bound for Miami.

Each person I interviewed was obviously uncomfortable. "Why did Miss Clemmy get fired from her job?" I asked. "Did she use drugs?"

These were some of the answers:

"I ain't sure."

"She might have drunk some cough medicine."

"There's was a lot of that going around. I done it myself. I don't t'ink she done it, t'ough."

"I cain't wrap my head around dat, no."

"I t'ink her boyfriend was in Angola. Them kind ain't no good."

I gave it up for the day, and drove home in an unmarked automobile, which was the only kind we used in investigations, particularly in minority neighborhoods. Just as I turned into my driveway and started to get out, a splattered Jeep, one painted with camouflaged patterns, turned in after me and came three inches from my bumper, as though making sure I would not leave the property. Jerry Carlucci got out of his vehicle. He was dressed in a three-piece silver suit with a fleck in it and arrow-lined pockets and a black Stetson hat. His face was swollen and stitched above the lip, and he had an odd-shaped blood clot in one eye.

I got out of my car. "What's the haps, Jerry?"

"Not much," he said. "Toolin' around, enjoying the evening, contemplating some plastic surgery. How about you?"

"I've been trying to find a guy who dropped a dead girl behind my house," I replied. "Say, I'm sorry you had to take a bust on my account, but the lady who jammed you is new and doesn't know how we do things around here."

He wadded a handkerchief over his nose and blew into it. "My lawyer is gonna hang you from your toes, Dave," he said. "I'll have liens on everything you own. You'll be mowing lawns after work."

"What are you doing here, Jerry?"

"Telling you to wise up. If you do, I might bring you in as a business partner."

"Really?" I said.

The streetlamps clicked on all at once, threading light and shadow through the canopy of oaks above East Main. I could smell the coolness and the damp from the storm sewers and the honeysuckle and night-blooming flowers in the yards along the street.

"This place is gonna be like Reno," he said. "A giant neon toilet."

I had to pause on that. "And you'll cut me in? The guy who kicked your ass?"

"You didn't kick my ass," he said. "I let you throw a few punches because I thought you were looking a little old."

"I got it. You're St. Sébastian, hanging upside down on a tree?"

"At least I can pay my bills, which I don't think you're gonna be doing," he replied. "One other thing: There's some out-of-town guys visiting who might drop each of your feet in a bucket of cement and let you watch it dry, then slide you off a boat. Just kidding." He winked an eye.

"I feel like wiping you off the driveway," I said.

"Grow up," he said, and got back in his Jeep.

I went inside the house, trying to hide my hands. Alafair had just fixed supper. "Anything wrong?" she said.

"Not that I know of," I replied. "What's for eats?"

Chapter Eight

Alfie had put deviled eggs and potato salad and ham-and-onion sandwiches on the kitchen table, right next to the back window, where we had a view down the slope to the bayou. "You didn't answer my question," she said.

"Jerry Carlucci was just in our driveway," I replied. "If you see him around, try not to acknowledge him."

She was putting two Dr Peppers on the table now, the way people do when setting a table makes them happy. "What did he do?"

"I got a little angry in front of his saloon and maybe hit him a couple of times."

She paused as though she had stepped inside a camera lens. "Why would he come here?" she asked.

"He said he's suing me and he wanted to let me know."

"But that's not why?"

"No one knows what goes on inside Jerry's head."

"This really bothers me. Why'd you get into a fight with him?"

"He said some things about my parents," I replied.

"He's hooked up with the cartels, Dave."

"We'll nail him one day. Come on, let's eat."

She sat down by her plate, a shadow on her face.

"You don't believe Jerry is going to take a fall?" I said.

"If you say so."

I knew what she was thinking. For Alafair a safe home or a safe nation was a gift. She never understood how the majority of the American electorate seemed to take it for granted.

A flotilla with candles burning in all the boats was drifting down the bayou. I had no idea why. I suspected the boaters were a high school or musical group. The candles were flickering in the wind, forming a collective glow on the current, like ancient light-bearers on a moat below a castle. The sky was deep purple and etched with the last glimmers of an angry sun. Soon it would be dark, and the wind would blow out the candles of the boaters, but they would not give up their cause, whatever it was.

Why are we not like these innocent young people? I asked myself. *Why do we allow men like Jerry Carlucci to spread his narcotics and corrupt our youth and stain our soil and sexually exploit the poor?* But I knew the answer. In any society, a vice flowers in only one way: Permission.

I squeezed the top of Alafair's hand. "This food is wonderful," I said.

But my words bounced off her face. "You and Clete don't listen, Dave. One day or night your luck is going to run out." Her eyes started to brim.

"No, Jerry is too smart to kill a cop," I said.

"He'll launder the hit. Try to stop him from doing that. I hate him."

That was Alafair, always ahead of the batter. I bit into my sandwich, my eyes lowered, my heart sinking. I wanted Alafair's homecoming to be a good one. I wanted her to stay in New Iberia and make us a family again, even though I was probably acting selfishly. I would do anything for that to happen.

"I shouldn't have taken him down," I said. "But I can't undo it. Look, Jerry loves money. He probably has millions. He's not going to sacrifice that for a revenge hit. Give the guy some brains."

"You're not thinking clearly, Dave. The body of Clemmy Benoit was dropped in your backyard for a reason."

"Like what?"

"I think it's me."

"No, that doesn't make sense," I said.

"Listen to me," she said. "When I was in the drama class with Clemmy, Jerry used to drive by in his convertible."

"He was after young girls?"

"No, he always had black dope vendors with him, young guys from New Iberia that sold twenty-dollar bags out on their front yards as soon as the school bell rang."

"Did Clemmy Benoit buy dope from these guys?"

"I don't know," she said. "Just like now, it was everywhere. What bothers me is how she died."

"I don't follow."

"It was an overdose. But somebody took extra time to wrap a guitar string around her throat."

"That's right," I said.

"How does Jerry dress?"

"Mostly Western."

"What kinds of bands does he have at his saloon?" she said.

"Rock and country," I replied. "But who cares what he plays? What's his motivation? Clemmy Benoit was dead and dragged on our property before I punched Jerry Carlucci."

"You already said what the motivation is," she replied.

"You mean money?" I said.

"Or your property," she said.

I put down my sandwich and looked down the slope at the bayou. The boats had floated almost to the Shadows-on-the-Teche and the drawbridge, the candle flames flattening. I was sad to see the flotilla go. Then I saw several black people rise from the back lawn of the Shadows, dressed in rags, their numbers beginning to swell, more and more of them, walking down to the water and through the flooded bamboo, and into the center of the bayou, deeper and deeper, their waists and shoulders and heads finally submerging, their hair shiny with moonlight, just like that.

My heart was booming like a Congo drum.

"What did you see?" she asked.

"I don't know," I said, sitting back down at the table.

"Don't lie," she said.

"People behind the Shadows-on-the-Teche."

"What's odd about that?" she said.

"They were dead."

She stopped eating. Her eyes went away, then came back. "You're serious, aren't you?"

"They had rags for clothes, as thin as cheesecloth. They had dirt all over them. They walked into the water and disappeared under the bridge."

"What happened to the people in the boats?"

"They kept going down the bayou," I said.

She took a flashlight from a kitchen drawer. "Want to go?" she said.

"It's a waste of time."

She paused, then dropped the flashlight back in the drawer and closed it, louder than she needed. "You've been under some stress."

"So has everyone," I replied. "We're about to complete the bloodiest century in human history."

I could hardly look at her face. There was a great sadness in her eyes. "Dave, I want to help you fight the people who want to hurt you. But how can I do that when you hurt yourself?"

"Maybe I imagined it," I said. "Plus, if those were slaves, they're no threat to us. They're our friends."

"That gives me the chills."

I pinched my temples. I was ruining the supper she had made. "Boone Hendrix, the handyman Jerry Carlucci was hitting with pool balls before I stopped him, saw the same black people I did. I was standing there in front of the Shadows and saw nothing, but he did. Ask him."

She looked at me a long time. Then she took a breath and smiled. "Like you say, I guess it doesn't matter, does it?"

"You mean we're on the right side?"

"Maybe that, but something much more important, I think," she said. "The issue is the suffering that occurred in the nineteenth century. Not only the slaves who died but the genocide that continued unto Wounded Knee? How about the slaughter of fifty million buffalo? Those things are not taught in the public schools."

"You know how to say it, Alfie," I said.

"I love you, Dave."

What do you say after that?

The next morning, Saturday, Clete Purcel pulled his orange Cadillac into my driveway, the one with the buckshot holes and the gray top that looked like hundreds of moths had died and rotted on it. He was wearing a sports coat and his porkpie hat, his face beaming. I met him in the driveway. "You look good," I said.

"I found out how I ended up with the stiletto," he replied.

"The one with blood on it?"

"What do you think, the one I open dog-food cans with?"

"So what's the gen?"

"I'll line it out for you. I was plastered out of my mind and I got on my cell and called Erma Poche and she came and got me here on the sidewalk in New Iberia, because she is now living outside Morgan City and is no longer in the Ninth Ward. At least that's what she told me, because I was totally bombed when she picked me up here."

As usual, Clete's descriptions of his excursions into alcoholic insanity were like silverware in a garbage grinder.

"Who is Erma Poche?" I said.

"I told you, the black gal who was getting knocked around by her ex, the guy who does torture hits for the Mob or anyone else and who put the buckshot in my Caddy. Got it?"

"I'm not sure. Maybe I should take notes."

He gave me a look. "According to Erma, who now works in a blues joint close to the Gulf southeast of Morgan City, we went there to pick up her check, because she discovered the other waitresses were supposed to take their rest breaks in a trailer out back. This is a real dump I'm talking about, full of mean motor scooters whose mothers shit them in a bucket, I don't mean oil people, either, I mean guys who've got a shine in their eyes, one that says they'll pop you in a blink and love it."

"Clete, how did you end up with the stiletto?"

"That's what I'm telling, even though it's secondhand information, meaning I was slugging back B-52s. Then her ex showed up because it was payday for her, which was payday for him, plus Erma was gonna quit. Yeah, I'm talking about the torturer, the guy with no parameters, Elton Foot. He put his hand on me or something, I'm not sure. It gave me the creeps. Erma said I hit Foot with the condom machine, and that's when Emma said we should probably go, that this definitely was not working out."

"And leave a great class of people like that behind?" I said.

"Come on, Streak, lighten up."

"How did you end up with the shank?"

"I guess I didn't want to get stabbed in the back and took it with me. Besides, I kind of like stilettoes."

I let it pass. "I'm glad it worked out the way it did, Cletus. But it's time to put yourself on a short leash for a while."

"There's more. Erma told me the daytime bartender knew the dead girl, the one that got dropped in your backyard."

"She was a hooker?"

"No, a singer," he said. "Want to take a ride and have a talk with the bartender?"

"No, I'm going to talk to Helen and tell her."

"Play it the way you want, noble mon. I thought you'd be happy."

"I'm happy you're alive."

The green luminescence in his eyes stayed on mine for a long time, and I knew why. He was hurting inside, deep inside, and the fact he wouldn't admit it hurt him even more. "Talk to you later, big mon."

"Come back, Clete."

He fired up his Caddy and twisted his neck and backed out of the driveway, the rusted-out muffler as loud as a straight-exhaust on a tank, an oily black cloud rising from under the frame.

"Where's Clete going?" Alafair said.

"Back to a dump where he could have been killed," I replied. "Or where he could have killed someone else."

Then I told her everything he had said to me.

"Don't be mad at him, Dave. He thinks the world of you. Clete is a depressive. When it hits him, every one of your words is broken glass."

"Yeah, I know."

"You want me to talk to him?" she asked.

"It couldn't hurt."

Alafair had a degree in psychology, and was good at it, primarily because she never judged and was never harsh. She opened her phone and dialed Clete's number. "Hey," she said. "Where'd you run off to?"

She nodded while she listened. Then she said, "Clete . . . no, no . . . Clete, listen to me . . . Dave told me where you're headed . . . What you're doing is magnificently unwise . . . Are you hearing me . . . No, I will not see you later. I will hunt you down and smack you upside the head."

I believed Alafair was the only person in the universe who could speak to Clete Purcel like that. He talked to her for a long time while she looked into space, breathing through her nose.

"Clete," she said. "You're the only family we have, and we're the only family *you* have. Does it make sense to lose your life putting yourself on the same level as people who have never read a book or a poem or cared about anything outside their viscera?"

There was a long pause, then Alafair said, "I can hardly hear you . . . An electric storm . . . ? Turn around and come back."

We were in the living room. She looked through the window and the sky darkening above the trees, and the veins of lightning leaking in the clouds. "It's your life, Clete," she said. "But listen to your own words. Never do the bad guy's time . . . Oh, you didn't say that . . . ? That's . . . I give up."

She tossed her phone on the couch.

"What are you thinking?" I asked.

"Clete grew up unloved," she replied. "That's hard to fix."

Chapter Nine

It had taken Clete less than an hour to find the bar in the swamp south of Morgan City. The road to it was little more than a line of cracked and sunken asphalt, backdropped by marshland with spots in the grass that resembled quicksand. The saloon where Clete took down Elton Foot was at the end of the road. At one time it was a plantation store, with a peaked tin roof and a gallery where people sat on straw chairs and cracked pecans and drank Jax beer, although black people had to sit on the edge of the gallery.

Behind the saloon was an old trailer up on cinderblocks, orange-red rust leaking from the corners of the windows. On the southern horizon, lightning was striking the water, but without sound, like gold wires in the bottom of the clouds. At the saloon hailstones were bouncing off the roof.

Only two cars were parked at the saloon. Clete parked his Caddy next to them and ran for the gallery, then pounded through the door, slamming it behind him.

"Wow!" he said, wiping his face, not looking yet at the personnel or the customers. "I thought those mothballs were gonna blind me."

The two men at the bar sucked leisurely on their cigarettes and stared at their own smoke as though it contained a mystery. The bartender walked toward Clete on the duckboards. He was big, unshaved and wore a checkered wool shirt with the sleeves rolled, his forearms covered with swirls of black hair. “You look like you’re lost,” he said.

“No, I’m trying to do a good deed,” Clete said. “I think I got into a little argument with a dude named Elton Foot and I think maybe I tore up your place while I was at it,” Clete said. “I’d like to pay for your repairs, if any, and maybe buy a little information as well. You’ve probably guessed I’m a private investigator.”

“Number one, you can put your badge away. Number two, there is no number two. Number three, hit the road, Jack, and don’t come back. Sorry to be harsh.”

“I was told the bartender here knew Clemmy Benoit, a singer from St. Martinville. Is that correct?”

“Give me a break here, Mack.”

“You know Elton Foot?”

The bartender’s eyes climbed up the wall. “What’s your name again?” he said.

“Clete Purcel. Is there another bar around here, one that has a trailer in back?”

The bartender untied his apron and wadded it up and threw it under the bar. “No,” he said.

“Let me start over,” Clete said. “Clemmy Benoit was a young woman singer who overdosed or who was given a hotshot. Then somebody wrapped a guitar string around her neck and put her in a garbage bag. I know this is all pretty disgusting.”

One of the men at the end of the bar left; the other went into the restroom. The sky was full of rain now. Hammering on the tin roof.

“Are you still here?” the bartender said.

“Give me a beer.”

“I’m half owner,” the bartender said. “I just bought into the place. Talk to the cops.”

“You don’t know Elton Foot?”

The bartender gazed at the tops of his hands.

"You want a guy like Foot as a customer, a guy who tortures people? For hire?"

The bartender reached under the bar and lifted up an aluminum baseball bat and laid it on top of the bar. "Hey, I'm a Teamster. Long haul. I've been around. What's it take, pal?"

Through the back window Clete could see the rain whipping across the wetlands and the swamps and the winding bayous, dissolving finally into a colorless, torn sky.

"There's a whole bunch of old machinery out there," Clete said. "It must be sinking by the day. Y'all trying to rebuild the coastline?"

The man who had gone into the restroom returned to his barstool, then picked up his raincoat and left without looking at the bartender or Clete.

"That's two customers you've cost me," the bartender said.

The bartender began walking toward the end of the bar. Clete walked along parallel to him. "Don't do this," Clete said. "I'm begging you."

"You dialed it, buddy."

"Here's fifty bucks for a cup of coffee and an address for Elton Foot."

"You got some kind of obsession?"

"Yeah, I fought for this country. I don't like being thrown out of public places."

They were at the end of the bar now. The bartender started to drape his bat on his right shoulder, then stepped off the duckboards and lost his balance. It was probably an accident, and the bartender was indeed a new owner and didn't have his sea legs. Regardless, all Clete thought about was the bat rising into the air. He picked up a full sugar shaker and thudded it into the bartender's face. The bartender crashed into a stack of boxes that fell on his head.

"Why'd you make me do it, man?" Clete said.

The owner was on his back, his eyes crossed, his nose as bright as a broken tomato. He tried to get up, boxes all over him.

"No, no, no," Clete said, squatting down. "Take my handkerchief. It's clean."

"What's your name?" the bartender said.

"Clete Purcel."

"I should have known," he said.

"Known what?" Clete asked.

"You got a reputation. Not a good one."

"Sorry about that," Clete said.

"Clete went behind the bar and filled a towel full of ice and crouched by the bartender and helped him sit up straight and placed the ice towel in his hand. "Keep it on your nose a few minutes. I'm gonna leave the fifty dollars."

Then he stood up again and started to walk out.

"Hold on," the bartender said.

"What?"

The bartender, or part owner, struggled to his feet. "Get a couple of Coca-Colas out of the cold box. My name is Tommy Driscoll. I put up my life savings to buy a partnership in a swamp. Except I didn't know the state was washing away twenty-five square miles a year. So when I wised up I thought I would make something good out of something bad. The first thing I did was shut down the trailer out there. Then I tried to get Clemmy Benoit off drugs."

"You knew her?"

The light went out of his face, his eyes dulling.

"You all right?" Clete said.

"No," the man named Tommy Driscoll said. "Clemmy went out hard?"

"I don't know."

"A guy who would wrap a guitar string around a young girl's throat wouldn't hurt anybody?"

"You asked me a question," Clete said. "I gave you the best answer I could."

"Yeah, you did," Driscoll said. "You have kids?"

"A daughter. I tried to do good by her. She makes motion pictures."

"That's good," Driscoll said. "A lot of times a guy doesn't know what a gift he has, huh?"

"Yeah, I guess," Clete said, not wanting to relive many events in his life.

Tommy Driscoll had been a carnival man and coal miner and steelworker as well as trucker. He also had a daughter who wandered away from the Res up by the Canadian border and was never seen again.

"Know how many Indian girls get kidnapped every year?" he asked.

"No," Clete said.

"That's because nobody knows," Driscoll said. "Sometimes they get dug up in the spring." His face went empty again. He was eating a hamburger with one hand and drinking a Coke with the other. "Think I'm lying?"

"No, I don't think that," Clete said.

The relationship with Driscoll and Clemmy Benoit was obvious and of a kind that would not help Clete in his investigation. Clemmy Benoit, the girl, or young woman, was probably addicted, strung-out, repeatedly raped, dissolute, in despair, and with the resources of a leaf blowing across a continent. The Great American Plains were full of them.

"You don't have any idea how she got here or where she went?" Clete said.

"No. I liked her though. She had a fine voice."

"Who's your business partner?"

Driscoll wiped some mayonnaise off the corner of his mouth. "A guy a whole lot sharper than me."

"Can you be a little more specific?"

"Jerry Carlucci."

"I see," Clete said, biting into his hamburger, veiling his eyes, wondering how anyone could be taken in by a guy like Jerry Carlucci.

"I paid for all the machinery on the property, too," Driscoll said. "Except it's no good. If they move Atlantic City in here, I get the big score. In the meantime I'm supposed to remove the junk."

Clete nodded, his face blank. "I got the cards of a couple good lawyers."

"I should have busted up Elton Foot. I should've taken better care of Clemmy." He stared at the rain beating against the window. "There are a lot of things I should've done."

Chapter Ten

Monday morning Valerie Benoit was waiting for me in my office. She was sniffling and dabbing at her eyes, and having a hard time looking me straight in the face.

"I hate myself for hiding in your office, but I didn't want anyone to see me," she said.

"What happened?"

"Somebody poured sand in the gas tank of my car and rubbed dog shit all over the seats. I had to take a cab to work."

She had just scrapped her own junker and bought a secondhand Japanese car with new tires and a new paintjob.

"How did the vandal get inside?" I asked.

"Broke the window."

"Is it at your house? I want to send a team."

"Yes, but you're not gonna get any prints."

"How do you know?" I asked.

"Whoever did it had on gloves. You can tell from the shit-smears. I shouldn't have come in here."

"Do you believe anyone other than sheriff's department personnel did this?"

"No," she replied. "They spray-painted the driver's side with their favorite nickname for me—*Goldilocks*."

Her eyes began to mist again. I got a box of Kleenex from my desk drawer. She dried the skin around her eyes, but I had no doubt she was about to lose control again. I also had the feeling she had lost sleep for many nights if not weeks and lived every day under stress, fatigue, and alienation. I wanted to beat the hell out of someone.

She looked up at me. Her face had grown thinner, but it made her prettier, and the streaks of gold in her hair, which I thought might be dyed, now seemed natural. Maybe her ordeal had made her stronger and more beautiful—at least that's what I wanted to believe. I have a confession to make. I love all women. Maybe that's because my mother left me. But I don't care about the origin of the syndrome; all women are beautiful and perfectly made. I think they're more intelligent than men, more loving, more courageous, and certainly more inured to pain; they are also more understanding of males than we are of them, otherwise the human race would no longer exist. If some of my fellow men are mad at me, fuck them.

"You're looking at me a little strangely," Valerie said.

"Me?" I said.

"Yes, *you*."

"I'm over sixty," I said. "I'm allowed to act foolish."

"You're over sixty?"

"What about it?"

"Nothing," she said, and put the Kleenex box on my desk. "Thanks for your time. I needed somebody to talk to."

"Hold on. Did Lloyd D'Anjou give any sign he was going to hurt your automobile?"

"He doesn't work that way. He makes you resent yourself."

"In what way?" I asked.

"He lets his eyes wander where they shouldn't, then sneezes into a handkerchief and bumps into you while he apologizes."

"When is the last time he did something like that?"

"Two days ago. Don't bother with the security cameras. He always stations himself in a blind spot, always humble after he puts his stain on you, then he squeezes your arm to reassure you of his sincerity. I'd like to kill him."

"Wait here."

"No, I'm gonna clock in," she said. "You're a nice man, Detective, but—"

"*Dave*," I said.

"You can't do anything about it, Dave. There's no proof, and truth be known, no one cares."

"Wrong," I said. "I do. Helen does, Clete does, and a lot of the guys do. Stay here."

"Nope, I need to call my insurance man." She got up from the chair. "Don't get yourself involved in my problems, Dave."

She had used the plural, but I made no mention of it. "Stay away from Lloyd D'Anjou," I said. "Got it?"

"No, I don't 'got it.'"

I casually massaged the back of my neck, then stepped into the hallway, closed the door, and locked it from the outside, making sure Valerie could not go anywhere. Then I walked to Helen's office. She wasn't there. Actually I was glad. I headed for Lloyd's office. His door was partially open, but no Lloyd. I went into the men's room.

Did you ever think about the way some men hang out and/or behave in bathrooms? They're exuberant, as though the room is interchangeable with sexual expression; their voices boom at the trough; they fire-hose the bottom of the toilet bowl to demonstrate their manhood; they think their flatulence is entertaining. Their language would get them thrown out of a whorehouse.

Lloyd D'Anjou and three of his buds twisted around when I came through the door, their faces caught in the middle of a joke. I'd rather not repeat the joke. The centerpiece was a word that starts with "C." In the South, it is the most offensive word a man can use.

It's used mostly by white trash, which itself is an extremely bad term, along with "lying son of a bitch."

"Hey, Dave, where you been?" Lloyd said.

"What's the haps, Lloyd?" I said.

"I'm just waiting on my pension, letting the days go by, at peace with the world."

"Why are you so cruel to Valerie Benoit?"

"Whoa," he said.

"You didn't vandalize her car, the one she was so proud of?" I said.

"You better wake up, Robo," he said. "Our jobs are on the line. I'm talking about white jobs. That doesn't mean I hurt her car, but anybody in St. Martin Parish, they'll tell you the troot' about her."

"The *troot'*?"

"She's a liar. She's corrupt. She busts up marriages. She'll hang your equipment on the wall."

"It's funny you say that, Lloyd. That sounds like some of your visits at the projects."

"I just got back from a seminar in Monroe. There's no way I could have done anything to that black bitch. Yeah, I said. She's a bitch and she's black, and she was put ahead of the guys who earned the job she didn't."

"The sheriff's department holds seminars on Sunday?"

"My sister lives in Monroe. I stayed over wit' her."

I looked at myself in the mirror, as though I was no longer interested in the subject, then rinsed my hands.

"You're not gonna say anything?" he asked.

"If you didn't do it, one of these guys did," I said. "How about it, fellas?"

Lloyd and his friends smiled sheepishly, leaning against the lavatories, looking at each other, their arms folded across their chests. In the past one of them was charged with using his baton to sexually violate a black inmate in our prison chapel.

I took a paper towel from the dispenser and wiped my hands. "Y'all got nothing to say?" I asked.

Their lips were curled on their teeth. I knew one day we would get rid of their kind, but it was down the track. I think the problem is in the gene pool. They all have the same grin. They immediately recognize one another and always feel safe among their own kind, without exchanging one word. Check out a Klan gathering. Don't expect them to be rational, either. They laud ignorance.

"Looks like you struck out, Robo," Lloyd said.

"How about it on the nicknames, Lloyd?" I said.

"Sure. You ever get it on with her?"

"Say again?"

"Have you got it on with Goldilocks?"

A smile was breaking on his face. The others were barely able to hold their mirth.

"Come on, Robo," Lloyd said. "You've cut a big swath through Iberia Parish, particularly when you were on the sauce."

"I'm talking about your crybaby, your black—"

Then he said the rest of it, but I will not repeat it.

I hooked him with all my power in the middle of the face. As a young man I was a finalist twice in the Louisiana Golden Gloves and once in the nationals. My right cross was devastating, to the degree I held back on it in an amateur ring. People like Lloyd D'Anjou were a different matter. A red-black cloud would blind both my sight and my conscience. I caught Lloyd in the face at least five times and splattered blood on the wall above the trough. I drove my elbow into someone who attacked from behind, then heard him groan and go down on his knees, both of his hands clamped on his mouth trying to catch his teeth.

I was unrelenting with Lloyd and his minions. I knocked him into a stall and slammed his head against the pipes and tried to stomp his face into jelly. One or two were on the floor. I think I broke his hand. One man was crying. One begged for mercy. Then

I stopped, but I don't know why. I heard a siren screaming in my head. Helen was outside the stall, the door wide open, two or three people on the floor, that floor soaked with piss. Helen's ears were covered by her hands.

"Are you okay?" I said.

"Me, okay? Good God, Dave, what have you done?"

"Done with what?" I asked.

"Have you gone insane?"

I looked around. "Yeah, it could use a tidy-up," I said.

She went to the restroom door and yelled down the corridor, "Mayday! Mayday! Medic on the double! Code red!"

"I'd better go home," I said. "Give me the gen later, would you?"

There was a tragic light in her eyes, one that had nothing to do with death or madness or the violent singularity you might expect in a police station, far more reaching, a vision Helen captured that had no name, a painting that even the sky could not encompass.

I walked past her and down the stairs and out into the driveway, by the grotto of Jesus's mother.

"Oh, Dave," she said.

"What is it, Helen?"

"Something came into my head. But not words."

I tried to shine her on. "Don't worry about it, Helen. You're a good person. It's me that gets into trouble."

"There are no words for it. I've never felt this way."

I do not know what she saw. Obviously it had to do with me. Or something in my eyes or my mind or the deed I had just done in a brick building with a reflecting pond that suggests an earlier time, for good or bad.

"Talk to me, Dave," she said.

But I didn't want to. I hurried down the long, curved driveway under the oak trees, lined with piles of burning leaves, the core of the fires breathing yellow-and-red in the wind, the smoke merging with the sweetness of the world.

* * *

I went home and took a shower and bandaged my hands rather than hang around at the department and get cuffed. Nobody tried to stop me, either. Most of my colleagues did not like Lloyd D'Anjou or his buds. Of course, Helen was disappointed. But the real problem, at least for me, went much deeper. It was Alafair. She had come to New Iberia to spend time with me and to work on her novel. This Monday I had promised to get off early so we could play tennis at Red Lerille's Health & Racquet Club in Lafayette, then go to a fine restaurant. Instead, I had decorated the walls and lavatories and toilets of the Iberia Parish Sheriff's Department with people who weren't worth spitting on.

Alafair came home from the library at 11:47 A.M., a bunch of notebooks in a beach bag hanging over her shoulder. I was scrubbing the kitchen floor, not that it needed it.

"Hi," she said. "You forget to put the pets out?"

I did that sometimes. But it was not intentional. It's one of the first signs of age.

"No, I spilled some coffee."

"What's with your right hand?"

"This?" I said.

"Don't be cute. Please don't do that."

"Something got loose in my head. It's over now."

"You got it on in the department?"

"That pretty well sums it up."

I hated to see the sorrow and defeat in her face, the way family members look when the head of the family comes in drunk. "Why did you do it?"

"It's just my way."

"No, it's just the opposite. That's why it's so awful. What happened?"

I told her everything. When I finished I couldn't look at her.

"Why don't you just burn the house down?"

"I apologize."

"I think you want to get drunk. So why not just do it?"

"Don't drag AA into it," I said.

"Why do you think you and Clete live here? South Louisiana is the drunkest place on earth. It also has the most fatal car accidents and the highest rate of coronary and vascular disorders. Just get it over with."

I took the wash bucket outside and threw the water in the grass, then flung the bucket down the slope and went back in the kitchen.

"Everything you said is true, Alafair. But I don't know what to do about it. Lloyd D'Anjou is a disease. Valerie Benoit has no one to protect her. My mother was turned into a whore because my father let her be taken from her home by a pimp. Right out of our yard. While I watched. So something goes wrong in my head sometimes."

"I didn't know that. I mean about the pimp taking her from the house. Why didn't your father stop him?"

"That was his way of saying 'good riddance.'"

I saw her swallow, her eyes fixed on the animals in the backyard. "Are you under arrest?"

"Not yet. I doubt if I will be."

"There's something I've never told you," she said.

"What?"

"When I was sixteen, Lloyd D'Anjou put his hand on my breast. I still have ugly dreams about it. I never told you because I knew what you would do to him. So he got the justice now he didn't get years ago."

"I wish you had told me, Alfie. Want to play some tennis today?"

Chapter Eleven

I didn't go back to work Tuesday. Instead, I took Alafair to Red's and played racquetball with her, then we showered and dressed and went to a movie and then back home, just as the sun was setting, in the same way it always does in winter, as though the natural world is committing a treasonous act, that the day has shortened itself, that in its bloodredness it has begun to create its own shadows on the Earth's rim, denying what we thought was ours.

"What are you thinking about?" Alafair asked as we turned onto East Main, under the oaks and the Spanish moss, then into our driveway, our yard as dark as the lawn on the Shadows.

"Did you know that at a certain time in your life you regret the things you didn't do rather than the ones you did?" I said.

She was looking straight ahead. I knew she didn't want to enter this kind of conversation. Who does? This is why older people don't waste time on vacuous subjects among themselves: They know a great deal, but they also know they cannot pass the truth on to the young. What did Twain say? Why is youth wasted upon the young?

But Alafair was not an ordinary young woman. "The things you have on your mind don't have anything to do with mortality," she said. "And you're not old. And your mind is always on humanity. How many slaves are buried in the cane fields? Or how many Indians buried across the nation? How about the Baker Massacre in

Montana? If you want to get sick, and I mean really sick, study what was done to the Blackfeet on the Marias River."

"I read you, Alfie."

"Stop calling me that name."

"Okay, Alafair." I cut the engine. I could hear the heat ticking under the hood. "The people with knowledge are the ones who suffer the most and are always the least respected. Intelligence ensures loneliness, and usually to the grave."

"Are you talking about me?" she said.

"No," I lied. "How about some ice cream?"

"I'd like that," she said.

It sounded like a good way to watch the stars drop from the sky and listen to the creatures in the bayou and breathe the fish roe among the lily pads, and try to remember that the Earth abideth forever. Or at least that's what the Bible says. It was certainly a better subject than the massacre on the Marias, a place I had visited many times, although I never told Alafair. I started the engine. Then cut it again.

"What's that?" I said, peering through the windshield and the porte-cochere at the back lawn that sloped into Bayou Teche.

"Where?" Alafair said.

"A man. Down where the body was dropped. It's the guy."

"What guy?"

"The guy who dragged the body there. Stay here and get on the phone, Alfie."

"My butt," she said, her phone in one hand.

I got out from behind the steering wheel and began running toward the water. The last of a red sun had melted in a cloud behind the Shadows, like a scene from *Gone with the Wind*, like Tara, a molten sun behind it, a scene that fills you with yearning but also with guilt and shame, none of which you can explain. The oaks and moss were as motionless as carved stone, the air dead, the grid on the drawbridge rattling whenever an automobile banged onto the steel plates. I tripped over a garden hose, got up and ran again, then heard the feet of a man who seemed to come out of a dream, no, a nightmare, a figure only a medieval necromancer could conceive.

I wondered if indeed that had been the case when I originally saw him. Maybe the shadows had made him look larger than he was; maybe the inflamed knots on his face and the sticks in his hair were an affect from running through the trees and brush with Clemmy Benoit's body in the garbage bag. Maybe all these things were a farce. Or maybe I was going mad.

Why was I thinking this way? Because I was an ex-drunk. That's how it works. You become a souse, a rummy talking to yourself in front of a Salvation Army mission, hoping your *bête-noire* doesn't eat your liver when you finally get a cot. That's why drunks like me don't want to encounter the creatures that dwell in the unconscious. More importantly, you don't want to know how they got there. I'll tell you how they got there. It's a barrel of laughs. For ghouls and reptiles to take over the basement, they have to exist. And someone had to make them. Who might that be? Guess. Yeah, you got it; you turned yourself into a monster. That's a hard one to live with.

I heard a boat on the far side of the bridge, and the clanking of gears and wheels and cables, and almost welcomed the sounds of the industrial world, ensuring that the phantoms that live in the mind are simply that: the imagination at work. Yes, I said, my eyes had tricked me. A cloud of rolling white fog had puffed itself under the bridge, and the red and green lights of a boat were inside the fog. What had I seen? Maybe a gator splashing around in the cattails? Or even a nutria? Many creatures called Bayou Teche home. Surely the bridge-keeper would walk out on the coolness of the steel grid and light his pipe and blow out a white column of tobacco smoke to show us that all was well.

But that was not happening. Instead, he walked back to his little pilot house and closed the door and turned out his light; the boat under the bridge disappeared into the fog, and I saw stars in the trees and smelled an odor that was like offal.

I also saw the man who delivered Clemmy Benoit's body to my lawn. He wore a black rubber jacket with a peaked hood, and boots the size a shrimper might, but they looked to be made of leather and were laced up with cord or straps that a medieval person might wear. A slice of moon was hidden inside the rain clouds, and this time I saw his face in far more detail than I had seen previously.

"This is private property, bub," I said.

I had never seen a face like his. The skin was not simply full of knots. It looked like the flesh from a freshly butchered pig; his eyes were liquid, or perhaps diseased, or thumbed and left with blood clots.

"I bear you no resentment," I said. "I suspect you work for others and perhaps were forced to do things that were not of your choosing."

He stared at me from deep inside his cowl.

"Come on, podna," I said. "I have some food at the house. Or maybe you'd like a soft drink."

He looked over his shoulder at the bayou and City Park and the playground on the other side.

"You want to tell me something?" I said.

He raised his right hand, and turned it up flat, his head recessed in the cowl.

"You're telling me to stop?" I asked.

He shook his head. Then held up three fingers.

"You've got to give me a little help," I said.

He made a deep, snuffing sound in his nose.

"Tell me why the young naked woman had to die?" I said.

He began to shake, his right hand now turning into a fist.

"Ease up on me, podna," I said. "I've done you no harm."

A rumbling sound rose from his throat.

"I'm going to back off, sir." I lifted my hands in the air. "See? I have no weapons and no bad feeling against you."

But my attempt at the role of pacifist did not serve my cause well. He hammered his fist into my chest, knocking the breath from my lungs, twisting and gnarling the knuckles into the sternum, as though he wanted to break as much bone as he could. I choked on my own blood, bent over, and vomited on my shoes. I could hardly straighten my back.

I staggered away from him. "Buddy, you really know how to hurt someone," I said. "In this case, you did it to a man, namely me, who did you no wrong. You're going to straighten up your ways."

He looked back and forth, as though he had been tricked into doing something wrong.

"Yeah, you heard me right," I said. "Get out of here and don't come back again. And if your mother is still living, tell her she made a mess of your upbringing. The short message is you've really pissed me off."

Then I turned my back on him and walked to the house. Alafair had switched on the backlight and was coming toward me. "A cruiser is on the way," she said. "Are you okay?"

"Not really."

"What happened?"

"I don't know. I think I either talked my way out of getting killed or I've lost my mind. Also I think I'm about to puke. Did you ever smell a stink like that?"

On Wednesday morning I still stayed away from the department, although I had not been charged. In fact, I think Helen salted the mineshaft. That means she planted evidence. In this instance it was a throw-down in the men's room urinal where I took down Lloyd and his friends. I know it sounds strange to say a sitting sheriff would frame one of her own personnel, but law enforcement is consistent only in appearance and in all other ways a malleable and subjective culture.

Secondly, I didn't care if I got canned or not, and neither did Helen. We were old-school, which meant we didn't give a shit, pardon the fecal metaphor. My immediate objective was to find the man or creature who left me with huge bruises on my chest, and the best flatfoot badge or no badge to do that was Clete Purcel. Even mobsters who hated Clete's guts admitted he was the best cop they ever dealt with, primarily because he always kept his word. Also, street people borrowed money from him, with no vig, and were happy to give him information.

By the way, the best judges of people in any society are criminals and people of color because they have to survive as a minority. That may offend some people, but it's the truth.

Clete picked me up for breakfast at Victor's Cafeteria on Main Street, and told me all about his newly found friend Tommy Driscoll who had invested his savings with Jerry Carlucci and was determined to find out who killed Clemmy Benoit by way of beating the daylights out of Elton Foot, the sadist button man used by the Mob.

Yes, that's a mouthful. But that's how criminality works. It's a network. They all work with each other; it's an aberration of capitalism, but a very effective one. Professionals call it "in the life." Strong-arm lowlifes are looked upon with scorn. They're treated in the joint just as they are on the street. Remember my friend Johnny Massina, the button man who asked me to witness his execution? I asked him once about some smash-and-bash jewelry robbers in Fort Lauderdale, and he replied, "They got no class. I don't associate wit' them kinds of people."

Johnny claimed to have clipped the cousin of Benny Siegel on a train. That was class.

Clete was talking and eating at the same time, his jaw full, a napkin tucked under his chin, his usual breakfast laid out before him: scrambled eggs and sausage and hash browns and biscuits soaked in butter and coffee with cream and a small bowl of prunes that he claimed would preempt the pounds of grease and fried food he vacuumed up all over the state.

I told him of my encounter with the man who left the imprints of his fists on my chest, which, this morning, felt like I had been hit with pig iron.

Clete stopped eating. "Excuse me, big mon, but your description is giving me boils on my main bowel," he said.

I saw the people at the next table look sideways.

"Sorry," Clete said to them.

They shook their heads to show they weren't offended.

Clete wiped his mouth with his napkin. "The guy's the real deal, I mean some kind of monster or something?"

"No, there is no such thing as monsters," I said.

"But he couldn't talk?"

"Maybe."

"And he was trying to tell you something that has to do with the number three."

"That's what it seemed like."

"What's the name of the Cajun monster who supposedly lives in the swamps?"

"The *loup-garou*," I said. "But he's a werewolf."

"What's the difference? I got chills all over me. You sure you saw everything you think you did?"

"No, I made it up."

"Don't get mad."

"Clete, I feel like hitting you in the head with that bowl of prunes."

"Talk about sensitive," he said.

Then both of us looked into space and were silent. And for this reason: If you're a cop or a police reporter or an emergency medic, there are things you do not want to see or even know about. Once you blunder into a particular kind of scene, you're stuck with a memory you will never rinse from your nocturnal hours. For me that happened when a police photographer showed me photographs taken of a family in Wichita, Kansas. I was a war veteran and thought I had seen horrible things. It took me a half pint of Jack straight-up before I dared go to sleep. There are deeds you wish your fellow human beings were not capable of. The day you discover the truth is the day you become much older.

"It's a geek of some kind," Clete said. "Some guy has got it in for you, and he's sending the geek to unscrew your head and spit in it."

"Yeah, you said that before, and, yeah, I told the guy that."

"What'd he say?"

"He made a bunch of grunting noises."

"You know what I think?" Clete said. He didn't wait for me to answer. "Maybe this has something to do with Alafair. She was in the dead girl's drama class. Plus, Clemmy Benoit is probably related to Valerie Benoit, who just cost you your badge."

"Thanks for breaking it down, Clete. Now I feel a lot better."

"Or maybe there's no rhyme or reason to any of this," he said. "Most of these idiots skipped toilet training and think it's macho to take a dump in their jockeys."

The people at the next table moved themselves and their trays to the front of the building. I got up and put a five-dollar bill on our table. "Talk to you later, Cletus."

"Oh, come on, noble mon, don't do that."

"Got to go," I said. "Everything is okay. Guys like us are transitional people, Clete, the last generation that will remember what's called traditional America. So no matter what happens between us, we'll always know what the real score was like."

"I think that's the most depressing thing I have ever heard anyone say," he replied.

I couldn't argue that. I walked home and put a Jimmie Rodgers record on. The song was "T.B. Blues," recorded in 1931. How could a man carry such pain, yet sing such beautiful music? I suspected the price of the artist's talent has been the same from Homer to the present. But the artist isn't alone. Silent people are often touched people. They're touched by an invisible hand, but they don't talk about it, because the day they share their knowledge of the unseen world is the day it will be taken from them. That's why Clete Purcel is Clete Purcel. He lives in a world of beauty and horror and courage and pity, and welcomes no one to it, lest they lose their minds. And while doing all this, he never lets the sunshine leave his face.

I hated to get into it with Clete. So I walked back to the cafeteria with my baseball and both our gloves, and we went to the park like kids and flung the ball back and forth until our arms were sore and Clete's shirt was ripped down the back.

When I got home, I felt like I had pitched nine innings of nothing but fastballs. Clete retaliated and returned the ball probably faster than seventy miles an hour. My left palm and fingers felt like someone had put it in a waffle iron. Then I saw I had a visitor, and looked at the heavens and said, *Please don't do this to me.*

Chapter Twelve

The wandering handyman who said his name was Boone Hendrix was on my roof, prizing a sheet of tin with a crowbar from the rafters.

"Hey!" I yelled. "What do you think you're doing?"

He was wearing a cork helmet and a freshly pressed denim shirt and cargo pants loop-strung with tools. "You weren't home, Detective, so I went forward with my initiative to beat the rain."

He ripped a piece of rooted plywood free from a beam and flung it down in the yard. "I'll be done in a couple of hours. You neither have to thank or pay me. You took my side when an evil man almost broke my ribs and my spine throwing pool balls at me."

"I took no one's side in the incident with Jerry Carlucci, Mr. Hendrix," I replied, my head tilted back so I could speak to him, an arthritic crick working in my neck. "I'm a police officer. Protecting people is part of my job."

"That has not been my experience, sir. I have seen policemen who are as wicked as the wretches they put in their prisons."

"Mr. Hendrix, I need you to finish the job and let me pay you for your time and materials. That is not a request, sir."

He walked to the roof's peak like he had suction cups on his work boots, his taut body sculpted against a ceramic blue sky. "I am a carpenter, Detective Robicheaux. I do not leave a job undone. Put me in your jail if you have to."

What do you do in a situation like that?

"Okay," I said. "But this is the last time. Right?"

"I will take that under consideration."

His features seemed artificial, as though they were painted on his skin, perhaps like a Puritan whose clarity of thought had never allowed him to frown or leave a wrinkle on his face.

"Is there something you want to ask me, Detective Robicheaux?"

"Yes, why does Jerry Carlucci have such animosity toward you?"

"Because he's a killer of the innocent and hence a killer of children."

"How do you know this?" I asked.

"He has a black aura clinging to his body. It's filled with soot and dried blood. He hates you, too, Detective Robicheaux."

"Call me Dave. Why does he hate me?"

"You saved a child from a plane, while he killed them from planes."

"Come down here," I said. "No, no, don't turn your back on me. Come down and come down now."

"When I'm done," he replied.

My hands were shaking, opening and closing, my throat full of rust. I started up his ladder, but he went over the roof's peak and down the other side. I didn't want to break my neck, so I climbed back down and lifted the ladder and carried it around the corner of the house. Hendrix was standing by the azalea bed.

"How did you get down?" I said.

He had the expression of a snowman, his features molded with charcoal. He was breathing through his mouth, as though he had been running.

"Answer my question," I said.

He took the ladder from my hand and flipped it on his shoulder and began walking toward his truck.

"Don't turn your back on me, Mr. Hendrix."

But that's exactly what he did, walking to his panel truck, one that looked twenty years old. I wanted to pick up a rock and smack him in the back. I started after him, then gave it up. I felt foolish and confused, the way you do when you have said too much or too little. No, I can't say that. I felt I had put my hand through a veil, parted it, and looked at something that was better left alone. You're familiar with Hawthorne's story "Young Goodman Brown," aren't you? Goodman's pride and curiosity lead him into a dark forest that becomes his ruination, and the pain is all the greater when he has to acknowledge that his daring was unnecessary and was born out of pride.

"Aren't you going to finish?" I shouted after him.

But he slipped his ladder into the back of his truck and drove away, as though he didn't know me.

Guess what. After supper that evening, as Alafair and I were washing the dishes, we heard hammering on the roof.

"*What* is going on?" Alafair said.

"I suspect that's our handyman Boone Hendrix. Leave him alone."

"How do you know he's not dangerous?"

"I doubt he's any worse than some of the people in our legislature," I replied.

"I see. He's only torn a hole in our roof without asking?"

"I have to admit it needed repair," I said.

She wiped her hands and went out the kitchen door and looked up at the roof. "Have you eaten anything, Mr. Hendrix?" she called.

I couldn't hear what he replied. They talked for a while. Alafair always took in strays. Of any kind. She came back inside and opened the icebox.

"What are you doing?" I said.

"Fixing him a sandwich."

"He asked for one?"

"No. But I can tell when somebody is hungry."

"I'm proud of you, Alfie," I said.

She shrugged, then said, "It's mutual."

The next day was Thursday. Helen had still not called me back to the office. I had a feeling I was going to skate on the beef in the men's room with Lloyd D'Anjou and his buds, if I just stayed out of things. Helen understood cops. But many cops didn't understand Helen. She believed in justice, but she also understood that justice was blind. Often I saw her eyes go flat and her face turn to concrete. She knew too much, and for that reason she confided in only two or three people. Guess who they were.

I knew what she was thinking though, probably because we had the same kind of childhood, although the devil in my childhood was a pimp named Mack who stole and ruined my mother. Anyway, predatory behavior was a big part of Helen's childhood. So was lying and greed and cruelty and control—all the inflictions that tormented her she is forced to remain silent about. I think that's how Helen got her multiple personalities. They were her escape, and had she not created them, she would have killed herself.

In other words, I wasn't a big player when I took down Lloyd D'Anjou and the others, and neither were they; they were just flatfeet who liked to chat in front of the urinals in the Iberia Parish Sheriff's Department. They were also trash, guys who had the same cranial chemistry as sociopaths. I wouldn't call them evil; I think they were insentient and unable to understand pain in others, either people or animals. The great oddity in them is the amnesia that takes hold of them in the aftermath of their deeds, and consequently never allows them to feel guilt.

Hey, do you want to see the real thing, the backstreet sewer of the entire country, an aggregate of cynicism, greaseballs, prostitution, kids selling dope on every corner, money-laundering, union gangsters, cops on pads, and murder-for-hire?

You ask me where?

Probably every place except Vermont, and that's because no one is interested in stealing maple syrup. Mario Puzo said something about legalized gambling I never forgot. Here's a paraphrase: "What kind of government would instill a vice in its citizenry?"

When you hear about a cop eating his gun, he probably had a reason, and it was ugly. The criminal world is not a romantic place. Clete came to the house that same Thursday, knocked once, walked through the living room into the kitchen, clean-shaved, a soft white dress shirt on, his face the color of a fresh sunburn, his green eyes in manic-overdrive. I put down my coffee cup. "Something happen?" I said.

"My new friend, Tommy Driscoll," he said, his throat catching. "The sheriff in St. Mary Parish sent me a photo over the wire."

"The Driscoll guy who partnered-up with Jerry Carlucci."

"Yeah, and the guy who said he was going after Elton Foot, the piece of shit who maybe killed Clemmy Benoit."

I didn't want to hear the rest of it. "You want to sit down?"

"No, I don't. I printed the photo."

"I don't want to see it, Clete."

It was an eight-by-ten. He held it between his thumb and fingers, as though he didn't know what to do with it. I took it from him and looked at it, then turned it over and placed it facedown on the breakfast table and took a breath. "What did the sheriff say?" I asked.

"The body was in a pile of banana stalks. My number was in his wallet."

"What else did the sheriff say?"

"Nothing. He said if I wanted details, I could meet him in Morgan City."

"Want me to go with you?'

"I'd appreciate it."

"Sit down and let's have some coffee."

"Yeah, I'd like that," he said. He cupped his hand over his mouth. "Jesus Christ, what kind of sick fuckhead could do that?"

"Just as you said, a sick fuckhead. Now clean it out of your mind. Maybe your friend passed out before the worst happened."

"You know better than that," he replied. "And you know who did it, too."

"You're talking about Elton Foot?"

"Who else?"

"Don't put your money on it, Clete. We don't know what we're dealing with. We—"

I didn't get to finish. I couldn't blame him, either.

"We're talking about a chainsaw, here! How do you account for people like that? He got strapped on the potty too long? He had diaper rash?"

"Nobody says that, Clete. Now stop it."

I know, I was too sharp with him. There are times when you can't put your anger anywhere and you hurt your best friend, and I had just done that to poor Clete. This is how I see it. There are different kinds of evil. Some you run from, some you don't. And some you pretend you never saw. Take Manson. Know why his followers stayed swacked out of their mind twenty-four hours a day, probably on acid? My guess is they couldn't stand what they did for him on a daily basis.

"I'm sorry, Cletus," I said. "There's no explanation for a bastard like this."

Alafair walked in from the backyard. "Hi, Clete," she said. "Is everything okay?"

He retrieved the photo from the breakfast table and folded it casually and slipped it into his back pocket. "I just got to borrow your old man a little while," he said, his eyes crinkling. "It's a fine day, isn't it?"

There was nothing to be learned in St. Mary Parish, the parish down the Teche from New Iberia. Tommy Driscoll was an outsider, a northerner, a passing oddity, neither liked or disliked for his origins, looked upon as a visiting Babylonian who speaks in a strange dialect about which the natives have no interest.

Think I'm kidding? Come see us.

But our visit was not funny. The remains of Driscoll were laid out on a steel tray in a small mortuary in the local hospital. The sheriff was a big man, with rolled sleeves and wide shoulders and gray hair on his arms and faded navy tats peeking out of his clothes. His accent was from northern Louisiana or Mississippi. "I hate to be the one to show this, Mr. Purcel," he said. "You know him long?"

"No, sir," Clete said.

"I understand he has family up by the Great Lakes. Near a Res or some shit like that."

"That's right," Clete said. "He told me he had a daughter."

"You know her name?"

"No," Clete said.

"I guess I better start digging then."

"He said she wandered away and was never seen again," Clete said.

The sheriff had the clear-blue eyes of a man who retains nothing unless it's important to his immediate needs. "Y'all got any ideas about who did this?"

"Have you heard the name of a button man in New Orleans named Elton Foot?" Clete said.

"I haven't had the pleasure," the sheriff replied, then waited in silence.

"If I were you, Sheriff, I'd dial up Jerry Carlucci," I said. "It's not his line of work, but he might be connected."

"Why's that?" the sheriff said.

"This stinks of prostitution," Clete said.

"Is that your opinion, too, Detective Robicheaux?"

"Yeah, that's possible," I said. "But Jerry is a businessman. He doesn't like attention. Maybe you can rattle his cage."

"You couldn't rattle that bucket of goat piss with a firehose, boy," the sheriff said.

There it was, the poor-white buried resentment that passes from generation to generation, the contemptuous insult, the condescending sneer. They cannot survive without it. "I didn't quite catch what you said, Sheriff," I said.

"Maybe get yourself a hearing aid."

I stared at the trunk and body parts of what had been a human being. "Thanks for your time, Sheriff. I like your accent. It puts me in mind of all kinds of things. Yes-sir-ree-bob."

We went over the top of the Atchafalaya bridge, then descended onto the four-lane and miles of swamps and serpentine channels spangled with sunshine and chained with rain rings, white-cabin boats bobbing out on the bay. Clete was in the passenger seat. He had been quiet; he didn't like rednecks, but as a rule he didn't let them bother him. He took out two Diet Dr Peppers and a sandwich from the glove box.

"Want half my sandwich?" he said.

"No, thanks."

I shook my head. He bit into the sandwich and went back to gazing at the boats in the bay.

"Worried about something?" I asked.

"We don't know who our enemy is. I think the issue is in the past, like you were saying. I mean all the dog shit we've never dealt with. I think it's got something to do with people in St. Martinville, like Valerie Benoit. I think maybe she's trying to put a leash on you, big mon."

I looked sideways at him, the pickup crossing the yellow stripe. "What was that last part?"

"You heard me," he said. "She's beautiful, lonely, and a victim, then an old-time swinging dick comes along and decides he'll be twenty-five again and swings on the first pitch that comes down the pipe. Know anybody like that?"

"You're talking about me?" I said.

He studied the sky, then at a pelican flying low over the water. "I don't know. What's your opinion?"

"That's incredible," I said. "Particularly coming from you."

"Some army friends of mind dug up some complaints of racial and sexual harassment she filed at Benning and Fort Riley."

"So what?"

"Do you see a pattern?"

"Yeah, there're a lot of sex addicts in the military who should have had a wood post kicked up their asses. Do you doubt Lloyd D'Anjou was on her case?"

"No."

"Then why do you doubt the other instances of harassment?" I said.

"You got me wrong, Dave. I like her. But she has a way about her, like she really wants to get it on, the real deal, not just hauling your ashes. Those gold coins in her hair have a way of wiring me up, also, then my Jolly Roger starts flipping around and I get a little hyper and it's a little embarrassing. What I'm saying is I think she wants to keep a man close to her, but only so close, so she's got you by the joint. In other words, if you get it on with her, you'll probably end up in therapy. Do you copy that, big mon?"

"Have you lost your mind?" I said.

"All right, I'll shut up. But tell me if I'm right or wrong." He stared at me, then pointed his finger. "Yeah, that's exactly what I thought."

We drove for maybe another five minutes in silence. Clete drifted off, then lifted his head with a jerk. "Wow," he said. He rubbed his face. "Where are we?"

I refused to answer.

"Are you pissed off?" he said.

"No," I lied.

"How'd we get in this business?"

"Nobody else would hire us," I said.

"Smart people. Know what we haven't talked about?"

"Money?" I asked.

"You got it, big mon. But whose and where?"

Then he went back to sleep. A waterspout was wobbling across the bay, the funnel like spun glass, the top as big as a thundercloud and dark as cannon smoke.

Chapter Thirteen

Call it vanity if you want, but Clete got to me with his remark about Valerie Benoit strapping a collar on me. After I dropped him off, I drove the ten miles up the Teche to Valerie's gingerbread house not far from the town square in St. Martinville. The sun was red and low in the sky, like a red flame behind the moss in the oak trees along the bayou. She was cooking on a barbecue pit in her backyard, and wore a purple wool jacket with tight, faded jeans, the knees split. I knew what Clete meant when he said she looked like she had gold coins in her hair.

"Hope I'm not bothering you?" I said, stepping out of my pickup.

She shaded her eyes, then smiled. Her stomach showed above her jeans, like a little girl. The bayou smelled cold and dank, and the trees were gray with smoke from a stubble fire. "You might give Helen a call."

"My battery is dead," I replied.

"Use mine. You got your badge back."

"No kidding?" I said.

"You bet. Congratulations. And thank you for all you did for me."

"You owe me nothing."

"That's not the way I see it," she said.

"We've got to get this straight, Miss Valerie. Are you reading me on this? You're a nice lady, but Helen had your back, not me."

"If you say so. Want a hamburger?"

I could hear myself breathing. "Now that I've got my badge back, you and I will be spending a lot of time on the Clemmy Benoit homicide and the death of a man named Tommy Driscoll. He was taken apart with a chainsaw. Clete and I just got back from viewing the remains in Morgan City."

Her spatula and hand froze above the grill, the smoke rising into her face. "What?"

"He was in business with Jerry Carlucci. Clete believes a depraved murder-for-hire guy named Elton Foot might have done the job. Know who Foot is?"

"No."

"You will. What do you know about the Mob in New Orleans?"

"Most of them are dead," she said. "The others smell like hair tonic. The big ones smell like a dirty clothes hamper. I'm not a fan."

"You're a little hard on the Italians, aren't you?" I said.

"Not Italians, the Mob. I worked in one of their restaurants. One used to pinch the inside of my thigh when I was hurrying down the hallway to night school. Yeah, they're really cute."

I folded my arms on my chest and watched the meat constrict on the grill. There are times when you should be silent. This was one of them. But I seldom follow my own advice. "Why are you mad, Miss Valerie?"

"Because you treat me like a ball of shit," she said.

"Me?"

"When I thank you, you take me to task. When I try to describe my experience with the nastiest people I've ever known, you accuse me of being a racist. As soon as you got out of your truck, I congratulated you for getting your badge back. You responded by giving me a lecture. So fuck you."

I nodded. "Fuck me? Anything else?"

"I asked you if you wanted a hamburger. You still haven't answered. So fuck you twice."

Actually most of what she had said was true. I looked up at her house. A cat was sitting on the porch, yawning, then stretching and yawning again.

"You like cats?" I said.

"Yes. But I fear for him. And that's because Lloyd D'Anjou and his friends aren't finished."

I looked down at my feet.

"Tell me that's not true," she said.

"Helen's had it with those guys, Miss Valerie. Have some faith."

She paused, as though arguing with herself. "Okay, I'm gonna drop it on you and you can do whatever you want with it. Come inside, it's getting cold."

"What are you talking about?" I said.

"I'm going to tell you some things other people don't know about. You want to listen or not?"

I was tired and didn't want to hear any more from her, even though I believed she was sincere. She put two meat patties on a plate and closed the barbecue pit. "Coming? It's about Willie Francis, the fourteen-year-old boy my hometown couldn't wait to electrocute."

I followed her into her kitchen. Her cat came with us, his tail straight in the air.

"A few others and I are gonna sue St. Martin Parish and the State of Louisiana for his execution," she said.

"Willie Francis died in 1947."

"He didn't die. He was murdered in 1947," she said. "And the date doesn't matter. There's no time limit on prosecution of a homicide."

"If you haven't noticed, the people who killed him are all dead."

"The individuals are not important. The entity they represent *is*. That means the state and the parish and Angola Prison and the governor's office. It's similar to racial reparations."

"Yeah," I said, nodding, my eyelids fluttering. "Whose idea was this?"

"Mine," she said.

"I see. I'd better run along."

She had just layered two hamburger buns with lettuce and sliced tomatoes and onions. "You're not gonna eat?"

I was afraid she was going to slap a burger across my face. "I'd like one. Thank you. It's kind of you."

"What's the matter with you, Mr. Robicheaux? You don't think that little boy deserves justice? You think a tax bump is more important than his suffering?"

"I have the same feelings you do about Willie Francis, Miss Valerie. I don't like the way you're talking to me."

"Too bad. I'll give you some more to brood on. When we finish, those pitiful pinheads in the state legislature will beg to make a settlement. And I'll tell you something else. They'll put gold bars in our hands."

"They'll get the gold bars from Fort Knox?"

"No," she said. "Courtesy of Jefferson Davis."

I was pretty done with the conversation. Her cat was sitting on the drainboard, its seat flattened to the surface with the same kind of nonchalance my animals had. "You surely have a nice home. You should bring your cat to visit mine. I'll have that hamburger another time."

"Everything I've said here is the truth, Mr. Robicheaux. I know the risk I'm exposing myself to. The suit could possibly bankrupt the state, and the possibilities with President Davis's hidden wealth are enormous."

"I'm sure you're right," I replied.

"You don't believe me?"

"Who am I to judge?" I said.

I went out the back door and walked down the wood steps into the gloaming of the day. I knew I had offended her, but I didn't know what else to do. The things she had said were dreams, perhaps the kind that suppressed people need to survive, but nonetheless dreams. Some might say my attitude was simply one of white superiority, and maybe they would be right. But I did not mean to hurt her.

I got into the pickup truck and pulled the door closed. Then I saw her running down the steps and into the yard, one hand holding a fat ground-beef burger wrapped in foil. I rolled down the window. I could almost feel the heat in her body. She pressed the burger against my chest.

"Eat it. I made it for you. Be the man you are."

Then she grabbed the back of my neck and kissed me hard on the mouth.

"I don't care what you think of me," she said. "Nor do I care about rules. Life's too short, Mr. Robicheaux. I can rip the ass out of an elephant. I don't care what people think of me."

Then she pressed my head to her breasts.

I was a little dizzy for a while as I drove away on the two-lane back to New Iberia, even swaying back and forth across the yellow stripe. Then I was safely in my driveway, the hood ticking with heat, the clouds purple and about to burst. I wondered if the world was mad or if I was, and rather than brood on the question, I decided I would take a pair of scissors and snip away the last twenty minutes of my memory and let it blow away in the wind and never mention it to anyone.

Then lastly I looked at the heavens and said, *God bless all Your children, Sir. You surely created an unusual bunch.*

Chapter Fourteen

It rained all night, flooding East Main and all the yards up to the steps. Then the sun came out, and I went back to work at the department, my shield hanging on my belt, the handshakes, thumbs-up, and winks more visible than I wished. Valerie Benoit was right. Lloyd D'Anjou had a long memory, and so did his buds. Oddly I think D'Anjou caught the drift of my colleagues and at least for the time being had decided to shelter in place.

He opened my office door without knocking and leaned inside. "I got no beef, Robo," he said. "Just keep Goldilocks out of my face. Can you accept that?"

"She goes her own way, Lloyd."

"Yeah, right on your dick."

He closed the door silently.

This is why Clete Purcel says that trying to reconstruct white trash is like trying to mix shit with mashed potatoes.

Anyway I decided to forget Valerie Benoit's bizarre behavior and D'Anjou's depravity and do my job and find out who put the body of Clemmy Benoit in my yard. Right now the investigation had produced virtually nothing. A second homicide, the murder of Tommy Driscoll with a chainsaw, might or might not have a relationship. More problematic, it was out of our jurisdiction.

At the center was Jerry Carlucci, primarily because he had been a festering boil since he came home from Vietnam. The image of an M60 cutting down children and old people from a helicopter would not go away from our community. Cajuns with no knowledge of foreign events literally fled from a grocery or movie line when they found themselves next to him. But Jerry was like Shakespeare's Prince of Darkness, always a gentleman, and avoided violence if he could, which made me wonder why he had rained down pool balls on the handyman Boone Hendrix.

The other figure in the investigation—the more disturbing one because we had actually seen him—was the man whose hair was filled with sticks and his face sown with warts and sores, his shoulders humped with a great weight he seemed to carry.

I did not like to think about these things in my solitude. If you stay in law enforcement, you think less and less in terms of individuals; you begin to see an aggregate that's like a whale plunging among the waves and the depths and its own wounds in a dark sea, rusty harpoons and infection dripping from its sides, its eyes blind, its sperm mixing with the waves' foam, a pod of calves birthed dead upon arrival before they ever saw light.

Oh, I know that's a sickening depiction of the world I live in. But it's there. Those who step willingly inside its circle rarely come out. Ask them. Either the cops or the criminals. Don't believe the shuck that's passed on to the public.

At 2:14 P.M. Valerie knocked on the door with one knuckle and opened it. "Can I come in?" she said.

"Uh, now?" I said. What I really meant was, *Can you come back a year from now?*

I pulled everything I could on Elton Foot," she said. "Want to talk about him?"

I hooked one leg over the arm of my chair and hung my foot over the wastebasket. "I'd love to."

* * *

She had done her homework and then some. Foot's sheet went back thirty-five years, when he set a garbage can afire in the Prytania Theatre in New Orleans' Garden District. He moved on from arson to petty theft, animal cruelty, pushing old people down the stairs in the Iberville Projects, bicycle theft, motorcycle theft, car theft, strong-arm robbery, grave robbery, procuring, assault with a deadly weapon, rape, molestation of a minor, forgery, extortion, blackmail, attempted murder, and depraved indifference (leaving a child in a hot car).

I finished thumbing through the inch-thick stack of material she had clipped on a writing board and set on my desk. "You got all this done today?" I said.

"It wasn't a big deal," she said.

"Got any idea where he is?"

"Right down the bayou in that trailer slum by the Jeanerette drawbridge."

"How do you know?"

"A couple of tips, plus I drove down there."

That was a warning. She had gone out on her own without checking with her partner.

"I thought Foot was pretty well-off for a criminal," I said. "What's he doing in that place?"

"Getting his ashes hauled."

"Are there any warrants on him?"

"Nope."

"Then we can't do anything," I said.

She was sitting in front of my desk. She placed her hand on it. "Foot doesn't need to know that."

"This guy has been con-wise for probably ninety percent of his life, Valerie. Who's the woman he's with?"

"He has two or three. I think he's transporting them to some hook-up situations in New Orleans. Rich guys who want a fling out on the Gulf."

"Did you see any connections with Jerry Carlucci?"

"I don't have to," she replied.

"What do you mean?"

"Carlucci is in everything."

"Really?" I said.

"Why are you holding back, Dave?"

"I like all the work you've done, Valerie. But when you tap into guys like Foot, you can't make a mistake. Look, he accidentally shot up Clete Purcel's Caddy. We might be able to get a warrant on that."

"In Orleans or St. Bernard Parish? That shouldn't take more than the second coming of Christ."

I drummed my fingers on the clipboard. "We do it at night."

"Why?"

"He'll probably be stoned or have his pants down. That's why criminals are criminals. They're stupid."

"You want to check out the toys?"

Another warning. I pulled on my ear. "Didn't catch that," I replied.

What she meant was tear gas, beanbags, stun guns, Tasers, slapjacks, retractable steel batons, flash grenades, and shotguns. These are the kinds of things that supposedly give police officers latitude when dealing with dangerous people (the shotgun's visibility can be extremely effective). Or sometimes a couple of cans of beer and a pack of cigarettes can do the same thing. But I said none of this to Valerie and instead checked out an unmarked vehicle and drove to Popeyes on the four-lane and ordered a bucket of fried chicken and mashed potatoes. The last spark of the sun was gone when we arrived at the drawbridge on the edge of St. Mary Parish, which before the Civil War had a population that was 77 percent enslaved.

Valerie had said nothing about the food I had bought. The bucket was sitting in a bag on the floor.

"Take a piece if you want," I said.

"Is this how you treat who you think are simpleminded people?"

Up ahead was a line of live oaks next to the bayou and three antebellum plantations whose porches were lit with carriage lamps. On the other side of the drawbridge was a trailer park filled with clotheslines, burning trash-barrels, and trailers that leaked rust from all the seams.

"Stonewall Jackson said mystify, mislead, and surprise your enemy," I said.

"Oh, good, that clears it up," she said. "From such a grand person, too. How many slaves did he own?"

"None to my knowledge," I said, and went around a pothole in the road. "You know the worst thing you can ever do as a cop, Miss Valerie?"

"Please. I can't wait."

"To kill somebody when it's not necessary. You live with it the rest of your life. Night after night, unless you're pathological."

I could feel her stare on the side of my face. "You did that?" she said.

"In Vietnam. A sapper was caught in our wire. I thought he had a potato-masher. It was a can of food he probably took from a French plantation." I could hear the tires on the asphalt and nothing else. I glanced at her.

"You okay?" I asked.

"Yeah, sure," she said. "Sometimes I say too much."

"Join the club," I replied.

We banged across the bridge and into the trailer park. She pointed at a trailer that was newer and bigger than any of the others, with a wood porch and shed built on it, and a deep-blue Chrysler and an outboard boat on the patch of grass in front. There were also flowerpots on the porch.

"How do you want to play it?" she said.

"Straight down the pike."

"Meaning what?" she asked.

"We ask them if they want some fried chicken."

I probably sounded like I was taking her over the hurdles. I wasn't. In dealing with a malignant personality, you do the opposite of everything he expects. A benign expression, a reassurance in the voice, even flat indifference, can emotionally disarm a violent adversary. Why? Because he doesn't understand people who have no fear, and that's because every aspect of his own life is predicated on it.

I turned off the headlights and the engine and rolled down the windows of our unmarked car. We were perhaps twenty yards from the trailer Valerie said was Foot's. The first odor I smelled was weed, a lot of it, dense and musky, like a squirrel's nest, maybe with angel dust sprinkled on it. The latter, called PCP, is the equivalent of putting a bullet in your brain.

"Stay here, please," I said. "I want to go around back before we knock on the door."

"What for?"

It was time to be candid, although I didn't want to. "Miss Valerie, you came earlier without telling me. If Foot or his girlfriends made you, we might walk into a shitstorm. Clete Purcel knocked him around a couple of times. I'm sure Foot knows I'm Clete's friend."

I tried not to berate her. Her nostrils were dilating, as though she were about to speak. Then she let out her breath and stared at the light shining from the curtains in Foot's trailer. She cleared her throat. "Copy that," she said.

I winked at her, then got out of the car. All of our unmarked vehicles had the inside lights turned off or removed. I made a loop around Foot's trailer, then came up on the backside of a darkened storage room. I had hung my badge on my belt and put a titanium five-round .38 Special in the pocket of an old bomber jacket. The ground was wet, the weeds sodden, the humidity of the park's security lights glowing like flares. Fortunately I brought a fedora that shadowed my face. I wanted to believe I had neutralized any mistakes Valerie may have made, but my organs knew better. My armpits stunk and my heart was thudding in my ears. I took a deep breath, peered inside the rear window, then took my small flashlight from my trouser pocket, pressed it against the window glass, and clicked it on.

My eyes were stinging, my nose itching, my nostrils running, and stomach churning, a taste like pennies in my mouth. I wiped my eyes on my jacket sleeve but could not believe what I was looking at. But there it was in the flashlight beam—the black hand-guards on the machine, the starter cord on one side of the fuel tank, the oiled chain and the steel teeth of the long, flat, silver blade. It sat on top of a wood toolbox, gleaming, the rest of the items in the room nothing more than junk.

I clicked off the light and stepped back from the trailer as though I could rid my mind of what Tommy Driscoll's last minutes on earth were like. A wave of nausea went through my organs, and I shook all over and felt my eyes water, then I spat between my legs into the weeds and wiped my mouth with my hand and walked unsteadily back to our car.

Before I opened the door, I could see the apprehension in Valerie's face.

"He's got a chainsaw in the back of his trailer," I said. "We're on the edge of screwing up its evidentiary value."

She started to speak, obviously confused.

"We can't discover the chainsaw without a search warrant. Got it? We didn't see it. We didn't talk about it. We are the dumbest, deafest people on earth. Look at me."

"We can't call a judge?"

"No. We're going to slide out of here, call Helen, then go home and go to sleep. Tomorrow is Saturday. We'll find a judge then, or maybe we'll have to wait till Monday. You okay with that?"

"Yeah," she said. "Did I fuck this up?"

"No, you didn't," I replied. "And stop using that language."

"God, you're weird," she replied.

Just as I pulled on the driver's door handle, a man opened the front door of the trailer; he was bare-chested, and his feet bare, too. "Who's out there?" he said.

I had heard about Elton Foot, but had never seen him. He looked part Indian and part black, and wore sweatpants below his navel, his abdomen and chest greasy and plated with muscle and blue tats. His whiskers were silver, as stiff as wire, his hair braided so tight it looked like hard snakes.

He stepped out on the wood porch. I could see some women behind him, like rag dolls on the furniture. "I said who's out there, motherfucker?"

I picked up the sack with the bucket of chicken and mashed potatoes inside, and put my hand on Valerie's arm. "I'm going inside," I said. "Stay out here. That will keep him uncomfortable and off guard. Then get on your phone and try to find Helen or a judge. Don't let Foot see the phone. And keep your face pointed downward. You don't want them to recognize you. Got it?"

"Why all this shit?"

"Shut up, please."

"I think this is a mistake," she said.

I wanted to hit her.

I walked up on the porch, my right arm curled around the Popeyes bucket. "What's the haps, Mr. Foot?" I said. "I'm Dave Robicheaux, Iberia Parish Sheriff's Department. I usually work homicide, but I had some time-off tonight and I wanted to see if I could do a good deed and smooth out a beef between you and my friend Clete Purcel. You follow me?"

"No," he said.

"You know, that accident y'all had when you dropped a shotgun and the gun misfired and punctured a few holes in his Caddy?"

"You don't got to tell me about that cocksucker," Foot said. "He tried to get into my ex's panties. Who's in the car?"

"A rookie. Affirmative Action, know what I mean?" I replied.

He stepped farther out on the porch, indifferent to the cold. "Y'all want to see Affirmative Action at work?" he said. "Come out here." He looked over his shoulder at three women in the small living room of the trailer, seeming as though they were going somewhere. None of them moved or spoke. One was looking at a television set stacked on an icebox; another sat on a lopsided, stuffed chair, one leg over the chair's arm, her mouth open, staring at me, stoned out of her head. The third was wearing a sundress, apparently with little or no undergarments. Her hair was dyed a deep, dark red.

"You got to excuse them," Foot said. "We've been meditating. You're the one called Robo, aren't you? You got a taste for Jack, beer back?"

"You could say that," I replied. "You want some fried chicken?"

He rubbed his chin with his thumb, pushing it hard against his whiskers. "You on a pad?"

"Why would I come to a rathole like this to get on a pad?"

"Oxy sales are booming. Not that I go near it."

"Here's the gen," I said. "Clete Purcel is my friend. He took your shank and beat the shit out of you with a condom machine. I've got your shank in my vehicle and will be happy to give it back to you. But that means you give up your grievance against my friend Clete. I know your rep. I'm not knocking you. I just don't want my friend hurt. You *diggez-vous* on that?"

"You read those lies about torture?" he said, his eyes lighting.

"Yeah, I thumbed through it," I replied. "It's interesting material. You could write a book. Maybe put it on the side of the Goodyear Blimp."

He lifted one arm and smelled himself. "I like that about the Goodyear Blimp. But take the shit out of your mouth and tell us what you want?"

"Somebody dropped an overdosed dead girl in my backyard. She also had a guitar string twisted around her throat. She was also naked. You know why anybody would do that?"

He shook his head. "There's some very low-class people getting into the neighborhoods these days. It's probably something like that."

"Can I come into your trailer or not, Mr. Foot?"

He thought on it. "What the hell," he said.

I closed the door behind me and set the bucket of chicken on a heavy wood table that looked like it was stolen from a public park and sawed in half. The woman with the dark-red hair placed paper plates on the table, then looked at Foot as though asking for permission. Foot lifted his hand, and the three women started eating.

"How about I get you your switchblade?" I said.

"Did I ask you for it?" he replied.

"No."

"That's because it's not mine," he said. "Secondly, I got no knowledge about a fight with Clete Purcel, or hitting somebody with a rubber machine or firing a shotgun at his car. Like I say, he tried to grope my ex; I reported him to my P.O, and that was that, Detective Robo."

"Just call me Dave."

"Whatever," he said. "Want to sit down?"

"No, thanks."

"I think you should," he said. "You look like you worked a hard shift."

"I'm fine."

"Did you pull my jacket at Angola?"

"Yeah. It was the usual grind."

"What's that mean?"

"Bleeding-heart behavioral stuff. You were left in your dirty diapers, you were rejected by your parents, you were sexually abused. The kind of social worker drag you hear about in all orphanages."

His jawbone was flexing, the women now looking guardedly at one another. He worked a crick out of his neck. "All orphanages, huh?"

"Hey, I'm not laughing at you," I said. "What I'm saying is you're an exceptional guy. You didn't let the past drag you down. You're mainline. You've worked for the Mob. The greaseballs don't hire just anybody. I bet you've worked for Jerry Carlucci."

"Jerry ain't no greaseball," he said. "If I was you, I wouldn't be calling him one, either."

"Yeah, but you've worked for him, right?"

"Sit down," he said. "Have some of your own chicken."

"Did you hear me?" I asked.

"Why do you care if I worked for Jerry Carlucci?" he asked.

"He's got bad Karma. He enjoyed Vietnam. He's a baby-killer. Why get his stink on you?"

The woman watching television turned it up louder. The other two women were eating with their hands, not using a paper towel, their eyes dilated with fear, their lips and fingers greasy.

"Why won't you sit at my table?" he said. "I'm starting to take this as an insult."

"I'm in my office all day," I replied. "I like to stretch myself in the evening."

He rubbed the backs of his fingers on his whiskers under his chin. "Know what you didn't see on my jacket? They put me in the microwave."

"They did what?" I said.

"My mother and the guy porking her. They laid me in the microwave and closed the door and turned it on. Because I was crying."

His face looked dead, as though he were beheaded. There was no expression in it at all—no pain, no anger or disgust or sorrow, not even pity for himself.

"That's straight-up?" I said.

"Sit down, Robo. I'll tell you how the world works."

"Forget the world," I said. "Look at me again and tell me if your mother and her partner actually did that."

"Does napalm burn? Am I part nigger? Does your girl in the car give good head? Fuck you, Robicheaux. You got no idea where I've been and what I've seen. You'd wet your pants."

I had known many bad men. But not until that night did I ever see such hatred in the eyes of a human being. However, I didn't have time to meditate on these thoughts or tell him the system that raised him and delivered him to monsters was compiled of assholes.

I saw Valerie pick up a clay pot on the porch and heave it through the front window, crashing glass and packed black dirt and tiny white roots and pottery shards in the midst of the chicken and the mashed potatoes.

"He's got a rig under the table!" she shouted as she came through the doorway. "It's a cut-down! He was gonna blow up your shit, Streak!"

That was the first time she had called me by my nickname.

"Welcome to Popeyes on the bayou, darlin'," Foot said. "Would you like a plate?"

Chapter Fifteen

The next day, Saturday, I told Clete, Helen, and Alafair what happened in the trailer park right across the bayou from a row of plantation homes that represented a culture many secretly wished was still with us. To me, the juxtaposition of the trailer slum with the world of Scarlett O'Hara was a great irony, namely, that the world is more like the past than we think.

I expected the ambulances and firetrucks and sheriff's cruisers from two parishes to acknowledge that I could have been eviscerated by the sawed-off .410 shotgun rigged under the table. But technically, since it was not loaded, no crime had been committed, even though Foot was an ex-felon and forbidden to own or carry a firearm. The woman with the dark-red hair had her name on the trailer and the .410.

Technically the only person who committed a crime that night at the trailer park was Valerie Benoit. I have to say I felt sorry for her. Fortunately none of the cops who caught the 911 said anything about the chainsaw. If we had queered it, we would have destroyed the one piece of evidence that could strap Elton on the injection table.

Valerie and I got back in our unmarked car and drove across the bridge and watched the emergency vehicles leave. It was not a good night. But I didn't care. I had changed my attitude about Valerie. I didn't know if Foot would have blown up my grits had the .410

been loaded, but I think he would have been tempted. Back then, the whole country was drunk with the idea of "stand your ground" craziness and couldn't wait to drop the next-door neighbor.

That same Saturday afternoon, after I had done all the paperwork, I went to Valerie's gingerbread house in St. Martinville. She was giving her cat a bath in a washtub in the kitchen. Her long-sleeve denim shirt was splattered with soapy water. The cat seemed to be having a fine time, whipping its tail in Valerie's face.

"The neighbors are looking out their window," she said.

"So let them look," I said.

She raised her eyes from the cat and looked through the screen. "Why borrow trouble?"

"I'll make it short," I said. "I owe you a big one. I also owe you an apology."

"No, no, none of that."

"I mocked your remark about Jefferson Davis's gold."

She gave a short shrug and smiled.

"You're serious about it?" I said.

"Yeah," she said. "I've seen some of the coins."

"You're kidding?"

"When I get finished with my kitty, I'll show you a couple," she said.

"Supposedly it was buried in Georgia," I said. "Right before he was captured."

"No, he buried it right here. In a graveyard. But the saltwater ate away the root system and took the dirt out to sea."

"Go on."

"I found some things. But that's all I'm saying." She made a motion like she was twisting a key in her mouth.

She had me hooked. Maybe it's built in all of us. We want to believe the earth offers a treasure rather than just a hole where darkness and cold and worms await us. "I'd sure like to see those coins."

"Okay," she said, drying the cat, then her hands.

"One other thing, Miss Valerie?"

"Yes?"

"You're brave."

She tried to shake it off. "That's nice of you."

"No, ma'am, it's not nice. It's the truth."

She looked up in my face, a private thought taking her somewhere else. Then she blinked and seemed to come back into the room. "Follow me," she said.

I walked behind her into her bedroom.

She kept a nice house, like most former military personnel do. Except she had photos on most surfaces, and in them were girlfriends, high school ceremonies, children swimming in the Gulf, a play rehearsal in an old theater in New Orleans. None of the people wore working-class clothes. Most of the photos looked posed. She pulled out a dresser drawer loudly, as though she were angry or trying to distract me. She probed inside a pair of socks and removed two small gold coins. "What do you think of these?"

They were U.S. coins minted in the early nineteenth century. They had no physical connection to the Confederacy, at least none that was demonstrable. I tried to hide my lack of interest. "I don't know much about coins, but I bet these are quite rare," I said.

"You might say that," she replied, her eyes following mine, which were looking at some photos in aluminum frames.

"Alafair is in this picture," I said.

"Oh, yes, she is, isn't she?"

"That's your drama class?"

"Yes," she answered, her voice thinning.

I looked back at another photo. "Look here," I said. "Alafair is not in this one, but you are and so is Clemmy Benoit. That's your same drama class. The one in which you studied *The Rose Tattoo*."

"Well, yes, people came and went. Some didn't stay very long."

"You said you didn't know Clemmy."

"Maybe I did. She was younger. That was a long time ago."

"She was a black girl with blue eyes and tattoos on her breasts, for Chrissakes, Valerie. You can see them in the picture. It's not your common classroom photograph in St. Martinville, Louisiana."

"My life went to shit for a long time. People do what they have to do sometimes."

All the good thoughts and positive feelings I had acquired about Valerie in the last twenty-four hours were draining through my shoes. I hate a lie. I hated a lie then, and I hate a lie now. A lie never heals; it destroys your faith in your fellow man; it can be forgiven but not forgotten; it festers and makes you resent yourself. Is there any sin more harmful?

I didn't want to hear any more of what Valerie had to say. I wanted to flee her bedroom, or put facedown the photo of Alafair and Valerie together, and take back all my words about her bravery. My eardrums were creaking, as though I were underwater and a great pressure was about to crush my head.

"I'd better go," I said.

"Don't," she replied.

"There's no fix for this, Valerie. You had to know that poor girl was in your drama class. Why did you hide something like that—you, a detective?"

Her eyes were damp, her nose sniffling. She rubbed it with her wrist. "I'm not sure."

"Stop it."

"Stop what?"

"Lying. You lied to me. You lied to Helen and you lied to Alafair. Worse, you violated your sacred oath as a police officer."

"At least I backed up your ass last night."

"Yeah, you did, and that's why I'm not going to dime you. But you've got to do it yourself."

"I feel like mailing my badge to the office and not returning. That's not an idle thought."

"Suit yourself."

"You're a son of a bitch, Dave Robicheaux."

"It's the opposite. I trust people when I shouldn't and other people get hurt. That's weakness. I feel like kicking your butt."

That last statement was egregious and a cruel cut of the sword. She openly wept. It wasn't feigned, either. I put my hands on her upper shoulders and squeezed as hard as I could. Her muscles were as hard as softballs.

"That's a lousy thing I just said, and you can kick the crap out of me if you like. If you want to get this behind you, tell me the truth and I'll be with you all the way down the track. But if you lie to me again, I'll see that you go to jail."

I could see the swollen hardness in her chest, see the pain and humiliation in her eyes, and smell the heat and adrenaline in her body.

"Look at my guitar up on the wall," she said.

"What about it?"

"It's a Korean knockoff. I was never good at it. Not far back from when Clemmy died, I saw her playing with a street band in Breaux Bridge. She broke a 'D' string and didn't have a replacement. Then she saw me in the crowd."

"I'm not following you," I said.

"She asked me if I had one. I told her I did. She asked if she could have it. So I gave it to her."

"Does this have to do with the guitar string that was wrapped about her throat?"

"I don't know. She was playing a Gibson. But I don't know if she was using Gibson strings or not. What kind of string was around her throat?"

"One of our techs said it was a foreign one," I replied.

Her face went gray. "I think I'm gonna be sick," she said.

I believed her. Her breath was bilious; her teeth starting to chatter.

"Better sit down," I said.

I went into the kitchen and came back with a glass of water. She was sitting on the edge of the bed.

"Are you gonna ask me the rest of it?" she said.

"Whose band was Clemmy playing in?"

"It was a pickup group, mostly Cajun. They hang at Jerry Carlucci's joint."

"That's why you busted him, didn't you?"

I was referring to her handcuffing Jerry after I had already beaten him up for throwing pool balls at the handyman Boone Hendrix.

"Yeah, I guess so," she replied.

What a mess.

I patted her on the shoulder and took the water glass back into the kitchen. I wanted to pull the plug on Valerie and all her troubles.

However, they were small compared to some I have seen in law enforcement, including cold-blooded murder.

The cat was eating on the floor. I picked him up and finished drying him with a towel that was on the counter. He kept trying to walk back and forth as I rubbed his fur up and down.

"It looks like we have a big pile of doodoo on our hands, don't we, fellow?" I said.

He gave me a power-shove with his head.

"That's what I thought you would say. Do you have any suggestions?"

He scratched himself with one paw, sprinkling me in the face, then gave me a huge yawn.

"Yes, I think the same as you," I replied. "You've got it, podna. You couldn't have said it better."

I stuck my head in Valerie's bedroom doorway. She was sitting on the bed again, looking at the floor. "I'll see you at 0800 Monday, Loot," I said. "Stomp butt and take names."

Then I walked out the door and drove down the road and didn't look back.

Chapter Sixteen

On Monday Helen and I got a search warrant on the chainsaw in the trailer supposedly owned by Elton Foot's redheaded girlfriend. Our best forensic tech Felix Babineau went right to work on it. He called me late that night.

"I'm not done yet, Dave, but I don't want you to have high expectations," he said.

I could have gotten a better booster of my spirits. "So what have you got?" I asked.

"It's not wiped down with any kind of cleanser. There aren't many prints on it, either. In other words, it looks brand-new."

"You think it's stolen?" I said.

"Probably. Foot or his girlfriend didn't give you a receipt, did they?"

"Nope."

"Dave, I'll give you this straight-up. I don't think this chainsaw ever cut anything. It was started a few times, but that's it."

I didn't reply.

"You still here?" he said.

"I'm not buying Foot's innocence on this," I said. "There's too much coincidence involved. What's he doing with a chainsaw, anyway? A chainsaw that he acquires right after someone he knows has been torn up by one."

"He knew the victim?"

"Yeah," I said.

"What if I hold on to my report and let Foot and the redhead sweat for a while?"

"That's not a bad idea."

"Can I ask you something?" he said.

"Go ahead."

"You know much about this guy, I mean Foot? Like what goes on in his head?"

"I couldn't guess. Why do you ask?"

"I got kids. The thought of a guy like that just a few miles from our house creeps me out."

I didn't want to talk about Foot anymore. The chainsaw we took from the storage room was not the one that killed Tommy Driscoll. That's all that mattered. The injustices of the world would go on being the injustices of the world. Is that cynicism? I don't think so. The real problem is the lizard that still lurks in us, unacknowledged, the gills still pulsating.

"I appreciate your help, Felix," I said.

"Sorry to bring you bad news."

"Hey, we're the good guys," I said.

"Yeah?" he said, waiting for the rest of it.

But there was nothing else to say. Tommy Driscoll, who had lost his own daughter, probably tried to help Clemmy Benoit before she overdosed, as his daughter may have. Now Driscoll was going to be packaged and shipped to a swampy reservation on the Canadian border. I wanted to jerk the starter cord on the chainsaw and shove it up Elton Foot's nether parts.

I was in the living room when I had the conversation with Felix. Alafair had been in the kitchen, but had heard most of it. I heard her walk behind me. It was dark outside, and the lamp over my head probably gave me an unpleasant look.

"Bad news, huh?" she said.

"Yep."

"You still think Foot did it?"

"How many people in one area would do something like this?"

"I think you're going about this the wrong way, Dave."

"For some reason I think I've heard that before."

"There were three women in that trailer," she said. "They all got a pass. That stinks."

"You didn't see them."

"Skanks are skanks."

"Don't talk about them like that, Alf."

"They can get clean and sober and get a job, just by walking into a meeting. You know that, Dave. Iranian women would beg to have their problems."

Alafair could be a hard case on occasion, but I learned long ago not to criticize her. She saw atrocities in El Sal that are unthinkable, literally. Both Clete and I have known survivors of the Holocaust who are similar. Neither of us ever makes a comment about any opinion they have on anything, lest we feel like fools.

"Knock knock," she said, making a fist, tapping the air.

"What?" I said.

"All three of those women knew that shotgun was aimed under the table at your loins. They also know Foot's history. All they had to do was step in front of you. If you don't care about yourself, Dave, care a little more about your family. To put it another way, get your fucking act together."

My chair was a stuffed one, the kind that's deep and soft with a plain cloth cover on it. I pulled the chain on the reading lamp and waited for my eyes to adjust to the lack of light, then took my bomber jacket from a hook on the wall and my fedora from another hook and put on both the jacket and the hat and placed my hand on the front-door handle, then casually turned around.

"It's drizzling a bit, but it's still a nice night," I said. "I think I'll take a ride and get some fresh air. See you later, Alfie."

"I didn't mean it, Dave," she said.

"It's not a big deal."

"Are you going out with Clete?"

I didn't answer.

"Don't you blow me off, Dave. I don't like that look in your eye."

But I kept going and got in the pickup and headed for the wild side of life, otherwise known as Jerry's Landing.

I could see the saloon lights against the black clouds above the bay and marshlands that bled into the Gulf. Undoubtedly there were duck hunters in the saloon, and a few fishermen, and maybe a deer or alligator poacher, but the main interest, no matter what the patrons claimed, were the prostitutes.

What's the *raison d'etre* for that kind of culture? Yeah, I know, it's a strange question. But the world of people who sell themselves or purchase others is far more complex than you think. Its members beckon from the shade, seemingly free of degradation and self-abasement. The paleness in their faces, the weakness in their smiles, could be interpreted as a sign of harmlessness or a kind offer from someone who is just like you.

However, I believe that in the unconscious there is a disorder like a pink ether that charms the body and spirit and is cool to the touch, benign to the senses, and biding its time. Ultimately the issue is about power and not sexuality. Watch out for vice cops, and watch out for grifters, and watch out for those who will take your soul and lick their lips when they do it.

I do not mean to sound like Cotton Mather. There is nothing more repugnant than a Puritan judge when it comes to spreading misery among the innocent.

* * *

The clouds were purple and black, rippling with electricity over the Gulf when I walked into the saloon. It was Monday night, and half empty, a five-piece band playing country music, the same girls working the bar every day of the week, except Friday, which was family night: when Jerry put a plastic sheet over the pool table and served boiled shrimp or crawfish free to everyone in the swampland community.

I took a seat in a dark place at the end of the bar and watched the band. They were good, and I wondered if Clemmy Benoit had sung or played guitar with them. I also wondered if one of them knew who wrapped the "D" string around Clemmy's throat. My guess was they stayed among themselves, as most musicians do.

Three minutes later I heard somebody's cowboy boots behind me, then a stool scrape roughly across the floor. I knew who it was, but pretended not to.

"You got some nerve," Jerry said.

"I wanted to see if your face had healed up," I said. "I feel bad about that, Jerry."

Actually I did, but he would never believe me. "Did you ever hear about some Confederate gold being buried in the marsh?"

"Oh yeah, that's why their money wasn't worth used toilet paper at the end of the war. Where do you get your ideas, Dave? You should go to Hollywood and be a screenwriter."

"Can I have a Dr Pepper?"

"Quit playing games. You want a girl?"

"How about I knock you down again?" I said.

"You're no different than every guy who comes in here. Except you won't admit it."

"Maybe not," I said. "But here's the difference between me and you, Jerry. I believe every person in here is a better person than I am. And that's because I spent half my life as a lush."

He looked into space. For just a moment he reminded me of photographs of Wyatt Earp, who in reality managed brothels and saloons. Jerry went behind the bar and put some ice in a glass, then some cherries, poured some Dr Pepper, dropped an orange slice in it, and pushed the glass toward me.

"We used to do the same things together, Dave," he said. "Remember when you pitched a perfect game against me? How about the Golden Gloves? How about the same fucking war we fought? Why do you always try to hurt me?"

"You sell dope. That's worse than a pimp."

"Everybody in my places of business has got free will. If they don't like the job, I give them a sack lunch and a fifty-dollar bill. Guess what. Nobody takes the offer."

"When your business partner Tommy Driscoll got dismembered, was he acting with free will?"

"Ex–business partner."

"He sent your girls home. He also tried to help Clemmy Benoit. Her body was dumped in my backyard. How old was she? Twenty? Twenty-two? You're a bum, Jerry."

"What if I clean you off that stool?" he said.

The band had taken a break, and the girls at the bar could hear us. Some were drunk; some looked crazy. None looked normal. They made me think of kids who got on a Greyhound and didn't know what to do next.

"You said you let me kick your ass," I replied.

"That's right."

"Because you were paying for your sins in 'Nam?" I said.

"You saw and did the same things I did, you self-righteous cocksucker," he said.

I picked up my glass of crushed ice and Dr Pepper and cherries and an orange slice and threw it on his clothes. I thought for sure he would swing on me. But he hooked his arm around the back of my neck, as though we had just won the American Legion all-star game we pitched when we were seventeen. I could smell the heat of his skin, his breath on the side of my face, his thigh against mine. The girls dropped their eyes. He tightened his arm.

"I didn't mean that about putting your feet in buckets of concrete," he said. "I don't know why I said some dumb fucking thing like that. Your old man was okay. I was always sorry how he got killed on that drilling rig."

Remember what he said about my father and mother before I almost disfigured him? Was he actually contrite? Or was he afraid? No, Jerry was lots of bad things, but fearful wasn't one of them. But neither could I accept him as a teenage grunt who stumbled into the war and who was more victim than villain.

His face was six inches from mine. In his eyes I saw a soldier in a helmet that was strapped under his chin, a black plexiglass shield covering half his face, his M60 pointed downward from the Huey, the shells jacking from the chamber faster than you could count, the carbon buildup on his skin as black as soot.

I pushed him away from me.

"What'd you do that for?" he said.

I got entangled in the stool and kicked it loose from my shoe. "Don't ask," I said.

I felt drunk. Maybe I was. Some AAs say there's a reservoir of alcohol at the bottom of every alcoholic's spine. The band was playing again, hiding the scene I had created at the bar. The girls looked at me dumbly, their hair in disarray, their eyes crossed. Then I realized why I had come to Jerry's Landing. I wanted to find the human race. And that's what I had done.

"What did I do to you, Dave?" Jerry said.

You're in me and I'm in you, I thought. But I refused to say it out loud.

"Fuck, man," he said. "I'm done with you. Don't come around here again."

I went out the front door. There were pools of lightning in the clouds, like liquid gold, as though they were a reflection from the swamps and the marshes, waiting to be found. A single drop of rain hit my eye as hard as a BB from an air gun. The band was playing "*La Jolie Blon*," the song that always broke my heart.

Chapter Seventeen

It was eleven P.M. and raining hard on East Main when I pulled into Clete's 1930s motor court on Bayou Teche. I ran from my pickup and banged on the door. His porch light went on, then he opened the door in his skivvies. "Why don't you wake me up?" he said as I brushed past him.

"I got into it with Jerry Carlucci," I said.

"Where?" he said, shutting the door.

"At that slop trough of his on the Gulf."

"You shot him?"

"No, but I wanted to. He offered me a girl."

"I get the feeling you're leaving out something, big mon."

"You got a towel?"

"Yeah, in the bathroom where towels are kept."

"Forget it," I said, and picked up a paper napkin from the breakfast table and blotted my face with it. "I did something that was chickenshit. Jerry was trying to make amends. I threw a Dr Pepper on his chest, one he gave me. Then he tried to hug me. My stomach started flip-flopping. I wanted to puke. But the guy was trying. He doesn't do that often."

"This definitely does not sound like Jerry Carlucci," Clete said.

"His old man was in the rackets, but Jerry wasn't a bad guy. When did you have your last nightmares?"

"About 'Nam? I don't remember."

But I knew better. The Shitsville Film Company knew how to supply monstrous images behind your eyelids night and day, admission free. "I wanted to believe I wasn't like Jerry," I said. "I wanted to be better than he was."

"You are, Dave. Both here and in Shitsville. You got that?"

"I still see that kid who got caught in our wire. The one with the can of beans. The same day I called in the 105s on our own position. How many times can you fuck up in one day?"

"Y'all would have died if you hadn't," he said. "You get all that guilt out of your head."

He didn't give me a chance to answer. He opened the icebox and tossed an ice-cold can of Dr Pepper at me, almost braining me.

"I've got another problem, too," I said.

He rolled his eyes. "She doesn't have gold streaks in her hair, does she? Like maybe Valerie Benoit."

"How'd you know?" I said.

"Oh, just a wild, crazy guess. How bad is the problem?"

"She lied about knowing Clemmy Benoit."

"Valerie Benoit lied about a possible murder victim whose death she was investigating?"

"Yeah," I said.

"Boy, you can pick 'em, Streak. Why don't you dig up Ma Barker or get it on with the Bride of Frankenstein? How about Tokyo Rose?"

"Will you stop that?"

"I can't," he replied. "Nobody would believe it. Why didn't Valerie Benoit want a fellow investigator, namely you, to know she knew Clemmy Benoit, who she was probably related to?"

"She was ashamed."

"Sell that somewhere else, noble mon."

"Remember when you were a kid and a lady up St. Charles Avenue invited you to a party in her backyard?"

He looked at the rain hitting the window, and at the blackness in the sky and the lightning striking the water down the bayou.

"When you came back in your Easter suit, you found out the kids were all black. Later that night you broke all the glass in the lady's greenhouse."

He opened the icebox again and this time ripped a beer tab for himself. He drank almost all of it in one swallow. "Time rolls by, doesn't it?" he said.

I waited for him to finish, but he didn't. He simply walked to his television set and activated his copy of *Shane*. "I can never get enough of this film," he said. "That little boy's voice echoing in the Grand Tetons makes me want to cry."

The next day I went immediately to Helen's office and told her about Valerie. She was silent when I finished. The rain was still falling, and across the bayou in the park the leaves were shredding from the trees. She propped her elbows on her desk and knitted her fingers, her eyes empty. But she said nothing.

"Should I walk back out, then come back in?" I said.

"Don't be a smart-ass."

"The problem is one of immaturity more than anything else," I said.

"Tell that to the white guys like Lloyd D'Anjou who hate her guts and the guts of every black person they see."

"Screw the white guys."

She put down her hands, as though she had no other place to put them. "It doesn't work that way, bwana, and don't pretend otherwise."

"Maybe not, but I still say give her another chance."

"Don't tell me y'all are getting it on."

"No," I replied. "She's much younger than I am. Number two, she's very vulnerable, and number three, that's a shitty thing to say."

She blew a strand of hair off her eyes. "There're times I want to hit you, bwana."

"I'm sorry I can't change that."

"We didn't have this conversation," she said.

"Fine with me."

I started to leave.

"I didn't say you could go," she said. "We've got a dead nude girl in your backyard who was either murdered or died of an overdose. We have almost zero information about her life, except that she probably wanted to be an actress or a singer and ended up naked and dead in a garbage bag with a guitar string wrapped around her throat. The latter alone and her exposed body make me sick. That's why I'm a little angry. I don't want a goddamn melodrama in my department."

I was standing between her door and her desk. Helen seldom showed her emotions. But the abuse of minority people, particularly women, tended to open up memories of her own, all bad.

"Copy that," I said.

"I've got another problem, too. I'm pissed at our citizenry. Not one person has come forward with a drop of information. The same with the chainsaw murder, for God's sake. It's like the whole area took a nap."

"It's denial," I said. "Good people don't want to believe what their neighbors are capable of."

"Yeah, they're good people. But I got another feeling, bwana. I think the enemy is already inside the castle."

Helen had many personalities, all of them damaged in some fashion. Clete said a former SS officer in St. Mary Parish molested her when she was a child. I trusted Clete. And I also trusted Helen. But when she was my plainclothes partner she sometimes used a baton on dealers and pimps and I had to step in front of her.

"Lloyd D'Anjou is a homophobe and misogynist from his dick to his eyebrows," she said. "So are the asswipes he hangs with. I think they plan to get me removed."

"Over Valerie?" I asked.

"I think it's bigger than them and bigger than her or you or me," she said. "I just don't know what it is."

"Alafair just told me D'Anjou put his hand on her breast when she was sixteen."

"Why didn't she tell you?"

"Fear I would kill him."

I could see her nostrils swelling. "That's why you busted him up in the men's room?"

"No," I said.

Which meant I would be after him again. I cut her off. "Let's talk about something else. I'll tell you what I think about the Clemmy Benoit homicide. I think it's about money. And also about young women, all over this country and the world. I think they've been fucked from the beginning of time."

"Who wound you up?" she said.

"Nobody. It's just the way it is."

"How is Clemmy Benoit connected with money?" Helen asked.

"She knew something she wasn't supposed to know."

"You don't think she died of an overdose?"

"No, I think she was tortured, then shot full of junk."

"Why didn't you tell anyone this?"

"Because it hurts too damn much to think about it," I said.

Let me explain something about police work. It isn't a science; it's a culture. We change nothing. We don't even stop crime; we punish it on occasion. Rich people seldom do time; none I know of have ever ridden the bolt or the needle. Most recidivists like the joint; outside, they're required to work and take care of themselves. For-profit prisons are usually run by rednecks whose faces look like the back of your thumb. Guess how tenderly they shepherd their sheep?

So a good cop has to be a light-bearer and carry the grace of a medieval knight from a stained glass window into a subterranean world? I suspect this may seem an elevated characterization of an underpaid police officer, but there are many brave men and women in law enforcement, and they proved that at the start of the century when they went inside the Towers, knowing they would probably not come out.

At noon, with these thoughts in mind, I drove the ten miles on the two-lane to St. Martinville where I knew Lloyd D'Anjou ate his lunch and downed two or three shots with a beer back. I can't say he was a drunk, but neither could I say he was completely sober. He was one of the guys who hovered between two identities, one of those who rose throbbing at sunrise, his breath hot, a target in his eyes, wondering who it would be on this fine day.

He liked the black district in St. Martinville. Standing at a bar, never sitting down, with one glance he could literally make a black man wither into a pool of urine. He was proud of it. I saw his unmarked car in an alley and walked through the door into a barroom where he was eating a crab burger and using three fingers to swig from a long-neck beer, watching a soap opera on the TV, simultaneously wiping crumbs dropping from his mouth. If he knew I was behind him, he gave no notice.

"What's the haps, Robo?" he said. "You keeping a cool stool?"

"No haps, Lloyd," I said. "Although I'm not too cool on the name 'Robo.' "

"I can understand that," he replied. "Particularly when somebody is spreading a rumor you've been out at Jerry's snatch-patch again. You got to raise your standards, Robo."

"Who told you that?"

"I think it was your daughter in Bojangles. She was with some college girls. The kind who think their shit don't stink."

I looked at the back of his head. He looked at me in the bar mirror's reflection.

"Hey, I'm telling you the troot'," he said. "Cross my heart."

"My daughter told me you groped her when she was sixteen."

He chewed slowly, his eyes lazy. He resembled a turtle with its head extended from its shell. "Must be somebody else. I don't do t'ings like that."

Lloyd had a way of shifting linguistic gears and becoming an innocent Cajun.

"I'm not trying to jam you, Lloyd. Maybe you tripped and bumped against her. Maybe you were drunk."

"You're saying shit happens?"

"No, I'm saying my daughter doesn't lie. But accidents happen."

"I got no memory on that, Robo." He tilted up his beer bottle.

"I'll call her on my phone. All you need to do is apologize. Less than five words."

"I'll give you two words. One starts with 'F' and the other starts with 'Y'."

"Okay, podna," I said. Then I looked up at the TV screen. Lloyd had been watching a medical soap opera. "Who's the patient being operated on?"

"How should I know?" he said.

"The patient looks like a mummy," I said.

He set down the crab burger and picked up a bar rag and wiped his hands. "I heard you got clap of the brain in Saigon."

"No, I tried to kill an M.P. in Bring Cash Alley. He was a guy like you. An embarrassment to the uniform."

"What?"

"You're corrupt, Lloyd. Call the DEA. They've got you in their bombsights. I'd make a deal if I were you."

His eyes were clicking back and forth. I had fabricated the DEA accusation, although I always believed D'Anjou was on a pad. His left hand was trembling next to his burger. He took a drink from his beer bottle, the foam sliding down in a large bubble inside the bottle neck. I felt myself swallow, an old craving rising again, a longing greater than sexual desire.

"What'd I ever do to you?" he said.

"Nothing," I said. "You're just a bum. Don't get near my daughter. If you do, I'll take you down in public and you won't want to live around here anymore."

I started to walk away. He grabbed me by my left arm. I'd had my hand on my chain and medal to keep myself from bashing his face into the bar.

"What you got there?" he asked. "Is that a wire? You been setting me up?"

"It's nothing you'd be interested in."

"A neck chain? What the fuck are you doin'?"

"That's right." I opened my palm to let him see the medal that was attached to it.

"You gonna beat me up wit' a church medal? Have you gone crazy? Because that's the word. You're fuckin' crazy."

"It's the reason I didn't leave you stuffed in the toilet. Count your blessings, podjo."

"*Podjo*? What's *podjo*?"

"Ask Clete Purcel."

"Come back here. Hey, you hear me? I'm talking, here."

Chapter Eighteen

I walked home at dusk. The days were short now, the air damp and smelling of stone and moldy pecan husks pressed into the soil under the trees, the last of sunlight like a cool fire burning brightly inside the clouds. I suppose I was reckless in my taunting of Lloyd D'Anjou, but if he came after anyone, it would be me, and I gave up long ago worrying about the future. The things we regret are not the things we do; real remorse comes when we realize the things we didn't do.

Plus, if you want to scare the bad guys, roll the dice in their faces and ask if they're willing to do the same. It's like grinning and walking through the cannon smoke. It drives them up the wall.

That of course is part of the credo of Clete Purcel, which might make you think twice.

I went inside the house and turned on the lights and saw a note on the kitchen table. It read,

> *Hi, Dave,*
> *I'm at Red's Gym. I'll see you later tonight.*
> *Love,*
> *Alafair*

I was disappointed. She usually made supper, or if she didn't, she always asked if I wanted to play tennis or eat out or go to a movie. The fact that she said "later tonight" instead of "later this evening" was troubling, too. That meant she would not be home until bedtime, because Alafair rarely stayed up late and always rose early to work on her novel.

I put a frozen dinner in the microwave, fed all the pets, and delicately placed my Jimmie Rodgers LP on the spindle of my phonograph and eased down the needle. His voice was one of the most melodic I've ever heard, and I will always believe he took something pure and good and achingly plaintive out of the South, even if it was a little salacious, and left it for the rest of us to be proud of.

I was hoping that Alafair did not think of her visit as an obligation. But I'm afraid it was. I could feel her flashes of irritability, her long phone conversations with her friends in Oregon, her attention to small maintenance deeds in the house, as though she could satisfy her conscience and then leave.

I couldn't blame her, considering the emotional internment that my vocation had imposed on my family. At the same time, I needed to explain some things I never talked about. It's like the expression "It's Vietnam, man."

In *la belle Louisiane*, the same applies. *It's Louisiana, man. What do you expect?*

She came home at 10:44 P.M. I was reading in my stuffed chair under the lamp. I shut the book and set it on the little round wood table next to my chair. It was *House of Sand and Fog* by Andre Dubus III, one of the best novels I ever read about neocolonialism. "How you doin', Alafair?"

I did not call her by any of her nicknames.

"I was running a little late," she said. "Red said to tell you hello."

Red was the owner of Red Lerille's Health & Racquet Club.

"Got a second?" I asked.

She looked through the hallway into the kitchen. "I'd better get into the shower first."

"There's something I've never told you about the life I've chosen, Alafair," I said. "I should have, because those choices had a big influence on you, for bad or good."

"I understand, Dave. You don't have to worry."

"No, I don't think you do. Nobody does. And that's because the choice is not really about police work. It's about whether you want to join the morality plays of the Middle Ages or just wait to die and see if anyone shows up. In other words, kind of like letting a cigarette burn out in an ashtray."

"Dave, I'm tired. How about tomorrow?"

I pulled the chain on the overhead lamp. "Yeah, it's late. That's because it's a workday. And tomorrow will be a workday, too, with little time for talking. Goodnight."

I went into my bedroom, closed the door, and turned out the light, my pillow clamped over my head, hoping to seal out the world. A half hour later she came into the room with a chair in her hand, put it by the bed, and sat down in it without turning on the light.

"What did you want to talk about?" she asked.

"This is the way I see it, Alafair. All life is a mystery," I said. "We come from the dark, then have a few years to walk around on the Big Blue Marble, then we go out the back exit and into the dark again. Or do we? *That's* the issue; that's the Big Mystery. The very fact that it exists means that there is probably a metaphysical reality surrounding us. That means we get to be players. And what better way to be a player than place yourself on the ragged edges of humanity?"

"I know I've been a grump," she said. "But it's not about you, Dave. At least not directly. I've had bad dreams about my mother."

When I pulled Alafair from the submerged plane at South Pass, her mother had already drowned. Most of Alafair's bad dreams had been about the soldiers who massacred the peasants in her village. The soldiers used machetes to cut open the women who were visibly pregnant.

"Can I help in any way?" I said.

"Nobody cares. They don't care about the Jesuits or the Maryknoll women or the Mennonites. Not a word is mentioned in a church or a political speech or a school. It's like all that bloodshed in Central America meant nothing at all."

I couldn't see her face in the dark, but I could hear her starting to cry. "In the dream I see the plane sliding down the continental shelf into the ocean. She's trying to reach out to me. Her dress is floating up, and her mouth is open and bubbles are coming out of it."

"It's okay, Alf. Your mom is safe now."

"How do you know that?"

"I feel it. I believe it. I think it was her prayers that brought me to you, Alfie."

"I've been mad at you because I think you're getting yourself into something much bigger than you think. I don't know what it is. It's like the world is ending; the sun is red and sinking into a black lake."

Her description jerked at my heart, because as a child I had the same nightmare repeatedly.

"Here's the rest of my problem, Dave," she said. "I have to make a choice. I've been offered a scholarship to Stanford law. If I take it, I'll have to leave New Iberia again, and I'll force you to keep working."

"No, you won't," I said.

"Do you know what it costs to live in Palo Alto?"

"Not really," I said.

She stood up from the chair. "I think I'm going to stay here."

"What would your mom tell you? To give up an opportunity like this, one that can help the world be a much better place?"

She was silhouetted against the window, one of the most beautiful young women I ever saw. Behind her, I could see the stars over City Park, cold and white against a sky that was like black velvet.

"Goodnight, Dave," she said. Then she leaned over and kissed me on the forehead. I could have sworn it burned right into my soul.

The next day was Wednesday. The air was balmy, the sun golden above the live oaks, the azaleas beginning to bloom, and I decided to walk home from the department and have lunch with Alafair. Up the street I thought I saw the truck of Boone Hendrix parked by the Shadows, but I couldn't be sure. I walked across my yard and went inside and into the kitchen and looked out the back screen. Guess who was sitting on the steps and eating a bowl of corn bread and dirty rice.

A brand-new rabbit hutch had been built under the pecan tree. The doors were unlatched. Our current pet raccoon and our giant tabby cat Cannon Ball were sitting on top of it, their tails hanging over the sides, enjoying the breeze.

I lowered my voice. "What is Boone Hendrix doing here?"

"He was halfway through making the hutch before I could stop him. So I gave him something to eat."

"We'll never get rid of him."

"So what?"

"If you haven't noticed, Mr. Hendrix has an obsession with this house or this family. He needs to find a new planet. Somewhere on the other side of Pluto."

"You want a ham-and-onion sandwich?" she said.

"Please. You didn't make one for him?"

"He doesn't eat meat," she said.

Alafair's virtues could be a pain in the neck, but if you have to be compulsive, I guess charity isn't a bad way to go.

I took a pitcher of sun tea from the icebox and two paper cups, and sat down next to Mr. Hendrix. "Sir, would you mind telling me who ordered the hutch for our yard, since we don't have any rabbits and our other pets don't need latching up?"

"Sir, do you read the Book of Genesis?" he asked.

"On occasion," I replied.

"Have you noticed what the voice of Yahweh has to say about the fifth day of Creation and the role of the animals and birds? Will you tell me what that is?"

"That God's kingdom is one of peace. A place where His creatures will be protected, I suspect."

"What food was man to eat?"

"God called it 'meat.' But it was not the meat of birds and animals," I said. "Mr. Hendrix—"

"That's in Genesis 1:29, correct?"

"Something like that," I said.

"*Something like that?*"

"Yes, you are correct, sir. But I think the rule got modified after the Flood. I'm not sure."

"You're a gentleman, Detective Robicheaux. But beware."

"Of what?"

He was sitting no farther than six inches from me, bent forward, his eyes on the bayou. He was wearing a denim shirt and jeans and a denim coat, cleaned and pressed, his leather work boots oiled, hobnailed, and steel-toed. But there was a feature about him I had never seen in someone else. He looked old and young at the same time, his eyes cups of sorrow, as though his glands never aged but his soul did.

Then I took a chance. "What troubles you, sir?" I said.

It was an invasive question, at best a condescending one. If he struck me, I would not have blamed him. But he remained stone-still, his bowl perched on his knees, his face as sun-browned as a tobacco leaf, fixed on the children playing in the park across Bayou Teche.

"Did you hear me, sir?" I said.

"The predeath of a child is wrong. It goes against nature. Don't let this happen to you, Detective Robicheaux."

"What are you saying, partner?" I asked.

He dipped his spoon in his dirty rice and lifted it to his mouth, not one kernel dropping from the spoon. Then he chewed slowly, his mouth closed, his eyes vacant.

"Mr. Hendrix, I need an answer from you."

He picked up the paper cup I had given him and drank half of it without blinking or seeming to hear my voice.

I got to my feet. "How much do I owe you, sir?"

"Nothing."

"We're cash-and-carry here," I said. "Are you listening? Don't talk craziness about my family."

"Three is a magical number," he said. "It runs through religions, in works of art, in dramas, in all forms of unity. Except one."

"I don't want to hear this, Mr. Hendrix. Over and out, you got it?"

"You have to listen to me. They steal our youth. They take their young hearts and plant them in cemeteries before they ever had a chance to know love."

I took the paper cup from his hand and threw the iced tea in the flowerbed. "I'm sorry, but you need to leave."

He set the bowl of corn bread and dirty rice on the step and rose to his feet. He seemed taller and bigger than he had been. I waited for him to speak, but he didn't. He reached out and lowered his hand on my shoulder and squeezed it.

"Get your hand off me, please," I said.

"Thank you for your food. Thank you for your manners, and for your daughter, and for all the animals you protect."

"Is that why you don't eat meat?" I asked.

"The animals protect us, Detective. But we do not do that in turn. We're destroying the Earth, sir, and you know it."

I went inside the house, wrote a check for fifty dollars, and went back outside to give it to him. Of course he was gone.

* * *

After I ate lunch with Alafair, I went to Clete's office on Main by the old Evangeline Theatre and the drawbridge next to Burke Street. By afternoon his waiting room was littered with orange peelings, soiled Kleenex, candy-bar wrappers, spit cups, greasy lunch sacks, and even fingernail parings. I'll let the reader imagine what the restroom looked like.

I went into his office and asked for five minutes.

"Close the door," he said.

I told him about Boone Hendrix's visit.

"What can I say, big mon?" he replied. "He's probably a decent guy who left his bread in the oven too long."

Then I told him what Alafair had said the previous night, her angst about her drowned mother and visions of a red sun descending into a black lake.

"Yeah, what do psychiatrists call that, world destruction fantasies or something?"

"Except the Cuban Missile Crisis wasn't a fantasy."

"Yeah," he said, sticking a lollipop in his mouth.

"Yeah, what?"

"Shit stinks," he said.

"Take that out of your mouth, will you, please?"

"Come on, Dave. How about what happened to Tommy Driscoll? I feel I should have popped Elton Foot a long time ago. Instead, he killed Driscoll with a chainsaw. What am I supposed to do about that? Put carpet tacks in my shoes?"

"We don't know Foot did it," I said.

"Count on it," he said.

"Thanks for the feedback. Enjoy your lollipop. Did you get it at the bank? Grab one for me the next time you're there."

He pressed the heels of his hands to his temples. "You're about to give me an aneurysm."

"Here," I said. "I happen to have some aspirin."

"Come on, mon, that really hurts."

I had made a mistake. On Lake Pontchartrain Clete bulldozed a gangster's mansion into the swimming pool, but he was not only a kind man, he wept over photos of children taken at Auschwitz.

"Sorry, Clete. I get frustrated sometimes."

"Forget it," he said.

Fat chance.

Chapter Nineteen

You don't wire up Clete Purcel. In this case Clete had already had two beefs with Elton Foot, both involving Foot's former wife. One confrontation ended with buckshot in the panel of Clete's Caddy and a slight bullet wound in Foot's foot, and the second with Clete bashing a rubber machine across the side of Foot's head, then taking his switchblade from him.

After I was gone, Clete closed down his office early, and drove down to St. Mary Parish, the sky as blue as silk, the clouds like buttermilk, wearing shades and his porkpie hat and his best sports coat, wondering if maybe Scarlett O'Hara could be watching from the homes across the bayou where Elton Foot lived.

The following events were narrated to me by Clete. That takes on a special meaning. As always, he tried to be honest, I'm sure. However, as you probably have noticed, there is a glitch in Clete's cognitive powers, like kryptonite radiating a green glow in a dark room. Or his brain might be compared to the barrel on a concrete truck, or a tornado that has vacuumed up a junkyard, or a firehose blowing out a New Orleans casino, which he did, or the flinging of three pimps and porn vendors off a two-story roof. (They crashed through a tree, or otherwise Clete would have been doing life in Angola.)

As he approached the Jeanerette drawbridge, he pulled in front of the antebellum homes under the live oaks and cut his engine and got out his Japanese binoculars and focused them on the trailer slum across the bayou.

It was a school day, and most of the children were gone, which was good if things got out of hand. But clothes and bedsheets were hanging from wash lines all over the trailer park, impeding his vision. He thought he saw an outboard boat and an expensive new car, maybe a Chrysler, parked in front of a trailer that had a wooden porch attached to it. Yep, that had to be Elton Foot's crib.

Clete got out his phone and dialed Erma Poche's number. Erma was Foot's ex.

"Clete?" she answered.

"How you doin', darlin'?" he said.

"Where are you?" she said.

"Across Bayou Teche from the trailer where Elton lives."

"*Oh*, shit," she replied.

"Does he drive a Chrysler?"

"Go back home. Right now."

"I need a favor, baby," he said.

"You don't know how much that man hates you. Nobody else ever took him down. Sometimes he ain't human."

Her voice started to crack.

"That's why he has to go," Clete says.

"To go? My God, what you t'inking about?"

"I mean he needs to leave and go somewhere else. Give me some credit, Erma."

"I got a chance to go to night school. I just don't want to have no mo' trouble like this."

How could he blame her? The sun was shining through the oaks on the plantation yards. Small children were playing croquet on the grass, and black women in lacy housemaid dresses were watching over them, no differently than they would have done generations ago.

"I won't put either of us at risk," Clete said, then felt instantly guilty for the lie he had told.

She knew it, too. He could hear her breathing, and thought she was going to hang up. A child was crying in the background.

"What do you want, Clete?"

"Tell me about the girls he's living with."

"They spend a lot of time on their backs."

"I know that. What else do you know?"

"Check their eyeballs. They jitter. Like pinballs in a skillet."

The noise in the background was intensifying. "Whose kid is that?"

"Maybe his. I don't know. He raped the neighbor. I he'p her sometime. Sometimes she pays me."

"What are the names of the women in the trailer?"

"The one with red hair is Flo."

"The others?"

"That's it. They're junkies. They're sitting on the railroad track, and it doesn't bother them."

"Are you willing to get Elton out of the trailer?" he said.

There was a long pause. "I cain't. I ain't that brave. I know what he can do to me, 'cause he already done it."

"I understand, Erma."

There was another long pause. "This is Wednesday. On Wednesdays Elton goes to a doctor for his foot treatment, the one you shot. It got infected. He goes at t'ree-t'irty. Don't ever give me away, Clete. You won't let that happen, huh?"

He looked at his watch. It was 2:47. He put his binoculars back in the glove box. He had no plan, at least not for Elton Foot. Foot was a psychopath, and as such was unknowable. The women were different. The peculiarity of addiction is the guilt that goes with it. Five A.M. can be purgatory for both the drunk and the hype, and he meant curling up in a ball of pain that is like a hot coal sinking through your entrails. Right or wrong?

The sunlight was spangled on Clete's Caddy, the windows cracked so he could smell the bayou and the four-o'clocks that were beginning to open. As a little boy Clete had always loved the spring because his alcoholic father sometimes took him on the St. Charles streetcar and then to a ball game. The two of them would hop off the car onto the neutral ground, where a white-jacketed black man sold sno'cones out of a cart that had an umbrella. When they hopped off the car, his father always held Clete's hand, the only time he ever did.

His father had been gone a long time, but on an afternoon like this, Clete would remember the good moments of his childhood and almost reach out with the tips of his fingers and touch two people, a milkman and a little boy, just as though they were standing inside a soap bubble.

Then it would pop and be gone, and he would feel a pang he never wanted to feel again.

Suddenly someone knocked on the driver's window glass. He had fallen asleep. What a foolish thing to do, sleeping on the side of the road, when tractors and cane wagons were rumbling to the sugar mill. In fact, he could see the thick white curds of smoke billowing above Jeanerette, the columns from the chimneys so high in the sky they made him dizzy.

The woman at the window knocked again. She was beautiful, to the degree that he fumbled rolling down the window and probably looked stupid trying to get the sleep out of his face. "Sorry, ma'am," he said. "Am I bothering somebody?"

She had chestnut hair that hung in ringlets on her cheeks. "Oh, no suh," she said. "I was afraid one of the cane wagons might hit you. Are you all right?"

"Yes, ma'am, I'm Clete Purcel. I was taking a little nap."

"Well, I didn't want you to get hurt, that's all."

Her voice was melodic. But she didn't give her name.

"Y'all surely have nice homes here," he said.

"Thank you. Are you from New Iberia?"

"Yes, ma'am, New Iberia and New Orleans," he said.

"It's been very nice meeting you, Mr. Purcel."

"Well, you, too, ma'am."

But still she had not given her name. She smiled and nodded and crossed the road and walked up the lawn of a plantation home that looked soft as a wedding cake. Then she was gone. But where? Not inside. Or in back. Or in the front. He wondered if he had taken a shot from the pint of vodka he kept in his glove box.

He turned the ignition and felt the engine start, but could not hear it. A horn was blowing loudly on a riverboat, a solitary roar that was deafening. But he saw no boat.

The Chrysler drove out of the trailer park into Jeanerette and took the highway to Morgan City in the opposite direction of Clete and his Caddy. He dropped the transmission into low and creeped across the drawbridge, staring in the rearview mirror, unable to take his eyes off the plantation home and the woman trapped inside time.

He didn't stop at the trailer park, though. He found a small floral shop on Main Street in Jeanerette and bought twenty dollars of pink and red roses, then drove back to the trailer that was headquarters of probably the most depraved man he had ever encountered.

He cut the engine, then stepped out and closed the door with one hand while holding the roses with the other. Then something happened, a drop in the barometer, a darkening of the sun, a coolness blowing off the bayou, the Spanish moss lifting in the trees on the other side of the drawbridge. He walked up on the wooden porch and tapped on the aluminum-framed screen door. A woman with dark red, perhaps dyed hair opened it. She wore a summer dress with a long-sleeve knit sweater; freckles seemed powdered on every inch of her exposed skin.

Clete took off his hat and bowed slightly. "My name is Clete Purcel," he said. "I'm a private investigator. I wondered if you could talk to me for a few minutes."

"Your name is *what*?" she said.

"I get the sense you've heard it before. Are you Flo?"

"What about it?" She turned her head. "Hey, you guys. Get this."

"Y'all aren't gonna beat me up, are you?" Clete said.

"Buddy, you'd better get your fat ass down the road before a certain party comes back."

"You mean, Elton?" Clete said. "I'm sorry I missed him. I've got a gig as location scout for a film company, and I thought I might bury the hatchet and give you guys a break at the same time. How about it?"

"Good try, bubba," the woman named Flo said.

"Bubba?"

"Or Fatso."

Clete smiled at her, his green eyes sparkling. "You don't take in wayfaring strangers?"

"You'd better hoof it, slick," she said. "We don't want trouble. And neither do you."

Clete put his hat back on. "You look like a smart lady," he said. "I'm telling you the truth. I know people who are shooting two films in this area. I can probably get you a little place in it. Or maybe not. But I'll try."

The sky was darkening, and it was hard to see her features through the screen. "Yeah?" she said.

"What's to lose?" he said. "You'd be surprised."

She pushed the door open. "Wipe your feet and come in. Don't stay too long."

"You got it," he said.

The other two women also wore long sleeves, which meant the veins in their arms were still usable and they hadn't started shooting between their toes. The two women were younger, with a disjointed look, a flare lighting intermittently behind their eyes, as though they were locked permanently in a haunted building. The shorter of the two younger women had a black eye.

"How y'all doin'?" Clete said.

But the younger women did not acknowledge him.

"Do y'all know that lady who lives across the bridge?" he said. "She was on the side of the road. I've never seen her hereabouts."

"Better get your business done, Mr. Private Investigator," the woman named Flo said.

Clete grinned. "Y'all don't have that shotgun under the table, do you?"

"What shotgun?" Flo said.

"Want to put these flowers in some water?" he said.

"Honey, I hate to hurt your feelings, but as a working girl might say, it's trick, trade, or travel, okay?"

He lay the flowers on the wood table, one that could be rigged to blow his genitalia out the door. "Can I be on the square with y'all?"

"You didn't come here to fuck, that's obvious," Flo said. "But your time is running out, honey-bunny. Do yourself a favor. Go back home."

"I've seen people stacked like burned logs," he said. "I still dream about people I killed with my hands. Elton Foot isn't a human being, he's a bucket of pus. What are y'all doing with this guy? Listen, I can help you get good jobs in New Orleans. I've got a two-story house with a patio two blocks from Jackson Square. You can stay there rent-free, and with no personal obligations. NOPD hates my guts, but they leave me alone. Do you *diggez-vous* on that?"

The woman named Flo smiled. The other two looked at her, then at each other, then seemed not to know what to think or what to do, which was a big step forward.

"Maybe we'll look you up," Flo said. "But now it's time for you to boogie."

"No, I don't do things that way, Miss Flo," he said.

"Then what are you here for?" she asked. "And stop fucking with me."

"The Iberia Parish Sheriff's Department couldn't find any evidence Foot's chainsaw was used in the murder of a guy named Tommy Driscoll, but we held on to the chainsaw just the same. I think Dick Head, pardon me, Elton Foot, is the right guy and somewhere has left shit prints all over the hit, and that's what it was, a hit, except Dick Head likes to take his time."

No one responded. Hail was clicking on top of the trailer.

"The boat," the short woman with a black eye said.

"What about it?" Clete asked.

The short woman's head was lowered. Clete thought Flo was about to shut her up, but she didn't. "He went to the swamp. He took the chainsaw wit' it. It's out there."

Bingo.

Flo raised a finger at Clete. "That's it. Beat it."

"Nobody will know where this comes from," he said.

"My ass," she said.

"You got my word, ladies. I was never here. Adios." There was a small yellow notepad on top of the table. He clicked his ballpoint and wrote on it, then handed it to Flo. "That's my phone number and my address in the Quarter."

He started to add something, then stopped.

"What is it?" Flo said.

"Watch yourselves, okay?" he said.

"Oh, why should we do that?" Flo said.

As he walked outside, he began to feel he had taken the working girls across a line. But what was he supposed to do? Let the memory of Tommy Driscoll just be a memory. *Don't hang yourself on a cross every time you do a good deed*, he told himself. Right? Fucking A, don't do that.

The sky was black, veins of lightning pulsing in the clouds, a vaporous haze rising from the hail on the lawns of the plantation-era homes across the bayou. He did not expect to see the lady who had worried about him when he fell asleep in his Caddy. But there she was, among the columns on her wide porch, wearing a scarlet dress, the hem touching the tops of her small feet, her skin as white as ivory, lifting her hand, saying goodbye with her fingers. Then she was still.

She was like a figurine, the face heart-shaped, perfect in its lines. He wanted to drive onto her lawn. He had to grasp at his throat, and almost plowed into a tree; he was shaking all over when he got home. He wondered if he had caught a cold or the flu or the old malaria-mosquito blues. Yeah, that was it, he thought. He was just a little sick. He hadn't fallen through a fissure in time. He had to get those kinds of thoughts out of his head, lest he find himself under the wrong flag and a burst of cannon shells in an orange sky, his heart thumping, a woman beside him who could be Varina Davis.

Chapter Twenty

Clete told me all this that night. It was cold, the stars bright over the bayou, and I put some old blankets inside the new hutch Mr. Hendrix built and draped a tarp over the roof for any of the animals who wanted to use it. After Clete finished talking, he and Alafair and I made hot chocolate, sliced up an angel food cake, and sat by the space heater in the kitchen.

It's strange how those simple moments can be the best ones in your life, isn't it? But Clete began to brood and take on once again the guilt he felt for good deeds that went bad.

"You tried to help those women, Clete," Alafair said. "Any alternative to their lives is better than what they have now. Did Foot give the black eye to the small woman?"

"I didn't ask, but I suspect he did," Clete said. "She was the only one who spoke up about the chainsaw. It's out there in the Atchafalaya Swamp, God only knows where, though."

"It's a start," I said.

"Yeah, it is," he replied, kneading his forehead.

I wanted to change the subject, but changing the subject was difficult with Clete, because every subject in his life was a cautionary tale.

"Tell us about the lady in the scarlet dress," I said.

I stepped in it. Clete has an expansive imagination. Ofttimes his head was full of frolicking baby elephants and pink unicorns and dancing peppermint canes, then he would plunge over the abyss. He also claimed contact with Joan of Arc. I didn't argue with him about any of it. There was a time when I had conversations with the Confederate general John Bell Hood, but only after somebody dropped hallucinogens in my glass and made my head radioactive for weeks.

"Yeah, she was real nice," he said. "She was about forty or so, and had these ringlets, see. They were hanging in her eyes, and she had this accent that's not from around here. It sounded more like Georgia or South Carolina. I just don't know why she didn't give me her name."

"She was probably standing in the road and didn't want y'all to get hurt, Clete," Alafair said.

"Yeah, that's probably it, huh?" he said.

"Sure," I said. "How about some more cake?"

"I'm ready for that," he replied. He had already eaten two big pieces. He looked through the window and at the raindrops running down the glass and the blackness outside and the electric flickers in the clouds that contradicted the season, as though nature could not abide itself.

"We have to stop them," he said.

"Stop who?" I said.

"*Them.*"

Alafair looked at me with a cautious eye.

"We're the Bobbsey Twins from Homicide, Cletus," I said.

"Yeah, that's us, isn't it?" he said.

But his heart was not in it.

Valerie Benoit came into my office early the next morning while I was buried arms-deep in a file drawer. "Helen talk to you yet?" she said.

I looked at her. "What happened?"

"An ambulance brought one of the Foot girls to Iberia General about an hour ago. The short one. She got the shit beat out of her."

"Fuck," I said. Then I let out my breath and said, "Excuse me."

"Forget the manners. That kid looks like an eggplant."

"Who did it?" I asked, already knowing. Or at least thinking that.

"She won't say."

"I gather you've seen her," I said.

She nodded.

"What are you holding back, Valerie?"

"She wanted to whisper to me. I held her hand and put my ear to her mouth. She tried to make a sound. A 'P' sound. You hearing me, boss man?"

This was the first time she called me *boss man*.

"You mean 'P' as in 'Purcel'?" I said.

"Fuckin' A and fuck, fuck, fuck."

Valerie was right. The victim was probably asking for help from Clete or she was going to stab him in the back and exonerate Elton Foot to save her life. None of it was good news.

"Did you call Clete?" I asked.

"I'll leave that to you," she said.

"Where's Foot?"

"Sitting in his trailer. Watching television."

"You saw him?" I said.

"Yeah, he was a confident man. He said she probably fell down the steps."

"I don't believe this."

"The only way to get rid of that guy is a bullet between the eyes," she said.

"Did you have a little too much caffeine this morning?" I asked.

"I'm just tired of taking other people's shit."

"Okay –"

"Okay, what?" she said.

"Clete is going to blame himself for this."

"If you want, I can tell him. I have a feeling he listens to a woman more than a man."

"Yeah, usually the wrong woman," I said.

"I'm not the wrong woman," she replied.

A half hour later Lloyd D'Anjou was in my office. "You got a problem, Robo," he said.

"Really?" I said from behind my desk, my reading glasses down on my nose.

"Yeah, that cunt you call your partner."

"You don't get to talk that way in my office, Lloyd."

"Don't tell me you're not in her pants. It's all over the department."

"First I've heard, Lloyd. Maybe you can spread it around. Have you notified the *Daily Iberian*?"

"Always the smart-ass."

"What did she do to you?"

"I was eating breakfast at Victor's. She pushed my tray in my lap. Splat, right on my dick."

"That's terrible. On a level of the *Titanic* sinking."

"The what?" he said.

I took off my glasses and placed them on my blotter and got out of my chair and walked within three feet of D'Anjou. "I've never lied to you, have I, Lloyd?"

His face was frozen, his eyelids stitched to his brow, his chest barely rising. "No," he said.

"I think you carry a succubus."

"You mean a demon or something?"

"Yeah, that's what it's called."

He swallowed. "Why would you say that to me?"

"Because I believe it. Now leave."

He started to speak, but couldn't find the words he needed. In truth I felt sorry for him. But I also had no doubt what he would like to do to Alafair and Valerie Benoit and me.

Two hours later I called Clete at his office. He had already spoken with Valerie regarding the short woman who only yesterday was perhaps thinking about getting out of the life. I said I would meet him for lunch at Victor's.

"I'm extremely cool," he said before hanging up. "You don't have to worry about your old podjo, noble mon."

Right.

He loaded up on pork chops and yams and gumbo and dirty rice, then paused and shook two vitamin C tablets out of a plastic bottle.

"Aren't you afraid those vitamins will burn your stomach?" I said.

"That's why I'm taking them with food," he said. "I'm pretty careful about that."

Then he began eating. But it was an act. He knew I knew what was on his mind. When Clete shifted into a destructive mood, it didn't go away, no matter what I or others said to him. "You think I'm gonna get out of control, huh?"

"Both of us have a bad record with guys like Foot," I said.

He put a fork-load of dirty rice and meat in his mouth, then chewed it for a long time. "Have you seen her?"

"The girl who got beat up?" I said.

"Yeah."

"Not yet. Valerie has."

"I wasn't allowed in," he said. "Her name is Carmela LeBlanc. I ran her sheet. She's been hustling since she was eleven years old."

"Clete, Helen and I will put an unmarked car on Foot when we have to."

"You never give me any credit," he said.

"You want to stack Foot's time? You're smarter than that."

He looked at my food tray. "You're gonna eat toast and a soft-boiled egg? That's it?"

"Yeah, because I think I'm getting an ulcer," I said.

"Because of me?"

"It's possible."

"Thanks," he said, and resumed eating and talking at the same time. "What am I supposed to do? I brought those women flowers. I gave them my word. Everything was gonna be jake, right as rain, in like Flynn. Then Foot turns a tiny girl into a speedbag. I'm gonna square what he did, Dave."

"No matter what happens to you?"

"That bastard is gonna keep killing and torturing people. You know it, too. You want that on our consciences?"

"The issue is latitude," I said. "It doesn't have to be 'either-or.' "

"For Foot it does," he said. "For Foot it means hoeing soybeans at Angola or trying to sleep in a cell on death row."

Clete would never change. His virtues were his character defects, and his character defects were his virtues. I hated the thought of him stacking time in a place like Angola, where he would probably stay in twenty-three-hour lockdown.

He put his hand on my shoulder. "Don't worry, big mon," he said. "On the Foot situation I'll probably just do a little recon right now. You know, easy-does-it, S&S, subdued and serene. That's me."

The following is what happened that evening.

In a drizzling rain Clete followed Elton Foot's deep-blue Chrysler to Lafayette and a place called the Underpass. Not far away was an old two-story brick building that contained a pool hall and a bar and a café reminiscent of an earlier time, with glowing yellow shades on the upstairs windows and buzzing neon signs down below. The building was not an acknowledgement of the past, but a necessity giving temporary license to the corrupt and the depraved, lest they bring their ways among the rest of us.

With his binoculars Clete saw Foot park his Chrysler in an alley, then put a newspaper over his head and walk to the back door of the brick building, a single bulb briefly lighting his profile, as ragged as the ripped top of a sardine can, his skin yellow in the rain. Then he was inside.

For the next three hours Clete kept himself awake with a thermos of coffee, twice getting out to urinate. At 1:56 A.M. he got out of his Caddy and walked through the alley, past six garbage cans and a dumpster. The owners of the building made sure the garbage was tightly bagged and picked up regularly, so as not to bother others. The building's secrets were the building's secrets. Live and let live.

Yeah, but maybe Clete might make an alteration or two, he told himself. Nothing big. So he carried an aluminum baseball bat? What the hell? There was no law against it. In fact, he was letting Elton Foot off easy from what the old-school NOPD cops would do, back in the days when they threw jackrollers from squad cars at high speeds near the Huey Long Bridge.

Yeah, it was actually outrageous. Fuck that, he told himself, then opened his utility knife and cut the valves on all four tires on the Chrysler.

The hallway inside the building was dim and decrepit but clean. At the far end was a room with men sitting around a table. Clete could hear men talking and see clouds of cigarette smoke swirling on the ceiling and hear poker chips clicking on the felt. He went up a staircase and eased down on a step and waited. The top of the staircase was boarded up, which meant nobody would bother him from above.

He actually fell asleep, then awoke at 2:27 A.M., almost unaware of where he was. The card game was breaking up downstairs. He climbed up higher, to the top of the stairs, his back against the boarded door, holding the aluminum bat as quietly as possible. He could see the legs of the players filing out, but did not know if Foot was among them. He heard the alley door open and close, open and close. Some of the voices were loud; others were not. He did not hear Foot. Most of the players were gone now. Then another man shouted out, "Hey, Elton, you coming for that steak or not?"

"I got a li'l date here," Foot said. "Another time."

"You're the man," the other player said.

The alley door slammed; the building went silent. Clete stood up at the top of the stairs, completely covered in darkness.

"You ready, girl?" Foot yelled.

Clete could hear a door open and someone else walking, someone who was not large, someone who was light and maybe wearing slippers or moccasins, the bottoms dragging.

"I ain't gonna hurt you, girl," Foot said.

"I want the money first," a girl's voice said.

"You don't trust me?"

"I'm supposed to ax for it."

"Of all the silliness," he said. "Let's go in your li'l place back here. What'd you say your name was? Dixie? I love the name Dixie, yes, ma'am, I do."

Then Clete heard them walking into another room, then a thud, one heavy enough to shake the staircase wall. Clete went down the stairs as fast as he could, the steps fairly visible, the bat in his right hand, the rail in his left. He heard the girl's voice cry out. Then his foot slipped and his ankle folded under him. The pain was as sharp as a dry twig breaking, one that went all the way to his groin. The bat clanged down the stairs.

Clete held the rail and hopped down the stairs to retrieve the bat before Foot, who was standing in front of a small bedroom. Through a door on the far side of the card table, Clete saw a girl sitting on the edge of a bunk bed, bent over, obviously in shock, weeping, unable to stop hiccupping, her arms clasped across her stomach, vomit on the lap of her dress.

Foot grinned at Clete. "Well, look who's here," he said.

* * *

Foot got the bat and swung it against Clete's upper arm, just as Clete collided against him. A normal man would have gone down with the weight and strength of the blow. But Clete clinched both Foot's arms and smashed him against the wall, then on the table, then on the doorjamb, then used Foot's body like a walking cane to work his way down the hallway to the back door and exit into the alley to get the Chrysler.

Foot's arms were pinned to his sides, his scalp and shoulder-length hair wet with blood. He tried to bite Clete's ear, but Clete whirled him around and smashed the driver's door window with Foot's head, then pulled him out of the glass and dropped him on the concrete.

He could hear a siren not far away, a screeching one, then saw emergency lights flash by the alley. He propped himself up on the Chrysler's hood, his weight on one foot, as though he were stretching his back. Then a Lafayette police car came around the corner, the siren echoing on the bricks of the building, the tires streaking the wetness on the asphalt.

"How's it hangin', you guys?" Clete said. "Long time no see. What's the haps?"

Chapter Twenty-One

Helen called Valerie Benoit and me into her office at 8:17 the same morning. She was sitting behind her desk, her hands splayed on her blotter. The sun was barely up, gaseous in the fog on the bayou, the glass in the windows cold, like someone had just breathed on them. Helen didn't offer either of us a chair. She didn't speak, either.

"You want something?" I said.

"I just got a call from Lafayette P.D.," she said. "Clete Purcel is in jail, and Elton Foot is in Our Lady of Lourdes Hospital. Foot's face looks like it was worked on with a garden rake. A heavy one, the kind you break clods with. Did either of you know this shit was coming?"

Valerie shook her head.

"You're gonna stand there, Dave?" Helen said.

"That *what* was coming?" I replied.

"Bwana not cute. Bwana gonna have his badge in the toilet again."

"Maybe Clete defended himself," I said. "Maybe he defended someone else. Foot has it coming."

She bit on a fingernail. "I can't tell you how angry I am."

"Yeah, and I don't get it," I said. "You think Lafayette P.D. is going to buddy-up with Elton Foot? Clete is probably already bonding out."

"This is not about Clete. It's about the prostitute, Carmela LeBlanc, who was beat up in the trailer park."

"What does she have to do with this?" I said.

"It wasn't Foot who tore her up," she replied.

Valerie and I looked at each other.

"Say again?"

"Foot's lawyer has seven witnesses, including the mayor of Jeanerette and a Baptist minister," Helen said. "Foot was at a wedding and the party afterward. Once again, we have seriously fucked ourselves."

She was right. Clete had blown it. Foot was probably laughing at us. We also strengthened Foot's claims of innocence and harassment in the chainsaw murder of Tommy Driscoll.

"Foot might file assault charges against Clete?" I said.

"Duh."

"How about it, Helen?" I said. "Just yes or no."

"I'm not gonna take that, Dave."

"I tried to caution Clete yesterday," I said. "No matter what you think, he's not a stupid man. If he took down Foot, he had a reason. Maybe not the best, but still a reason. Like protecting someone else. Right or wrong?"

"He put Foot's head through the car window," she said.

"You didn't answer my question, Helen."

"Foot broke the arm and two ribs of a retarded girl named Dixie Wydell in that hot pillow joint by the Underpass."

"Why didn't you just say that?" I asked.

"Sheriff, I'm as much to blame as anyone," Valerie said. "I've visited Carmela LeBlanc in Iberia General two times now. If I had my way, I'd put my gun in Foot's mouth and blow out the back of his head, while he was on his knees."

I stared at the side of her face. Cops do not say that to anyone, not for any reason, particularly to administrators.

"Detective Benoit has been diligent all the way, Helen," I said. "I think she's a little stressed right now.

Helen took a Kleenex out of a drawer and blew her nose slightly in it, then dropped it in the wastebasket, then put her elbows on her blotter and the heels of her hands on her forehead and looked at nothing.

"You okay, Sheriff?" Valerie said.

"I'm not quite sure," she said. "The FBI gave us a heads-up yesterday. We've got some New Jersey visitors down at Cypremort Point. Guess who was with them?"

"Jerry Carlucci?" Valerie said.

"While we're messing with Clete Purcel's vendettas with Foot," she said.

"Maybe they're all the same bunch, Helen," I said.

"Gee, could that be the case?" she said. "Please don't take this as an affront, bwana, but get out of my office."

She didn't mean it. In fact, she would probably give her life for either Clete or me. No one understood Helen because her separate personalities were not modifications of one another. They had their own voices, thought patterns, facial features, and way of dressing. On the job she was a bull, in slacks, her arms pumped. Toward evening, her face sharpened, her eyes narrowed; she put on lipstick just before five. At a sheriffs' convention in Baton Rouge, a racist piece of shit from North Louisiana put a dildo on her place mat at the main table in the hotel dining room. She placed her mat over it, then waited until the dinner was over and followed the North Louisiana sheriff into the hotel bar, then shoved the dildo halfway down his throat and kicked his shin, then broke a bottle on his head.

Go, Helen.

Anyway, I never get mad at her.

I thought about calling Lafayette P.D. to see about Clete's status, then thought better of it. My own record with Lafayette P.D. was not good, and my father's history with them was legend. People still talk about Big Aldous Robicheaux and how he wiped out six Lafayette cops with a pool cue in Antlers Bar. He almost went to Angola, except the warden called the mayor of Lafayette and said if he sent Big Aldous to the Farm, the warden would ensure that every Lafayette con in lockdown would immediately be paroled and on his way home.

Just before lunch, I went to Valerie's office. "Want to take a ride to Old Louisiana?" I said. "We'll pick up some po'boys on the way."

"You twisted my arm," she said.

We checked out an unmarked vehicle and stopped by Bon Creole and ordered two huge deep-fried oyster po'boy sandwiches, then headed south down a two-lane peninsular that jutted into the beginnings of the Gulf of Mexico. Once again the day was spring-like, the sun shining on the palm trees and fish camps and boat docks on each side of us, the mullet flying above the waves in the bay, the air fresh with salt and the smell of shrimp nets drying and kelp or seaweed washed up on the sand. For whatever reason, I always associated it with Creation.

"You like it here, huh?" Valerie said.

"My father and I shrimped here for years," I said. "We had a duck blind here, too."

"You still do that?"

"No."

"Why'd you quit?"

"I couldn't justify it anymore. Others might, but I don't feel good about it."

She looked a long time at the bay. "If you found Confederate gold out there, would you keep it?"

"I don't know."

"What if you found Confederate-stamped gold and all kinds of jewelry and silverware and watches and chains in an iron box? I didn't see it. But I saw pictures."

"Good luck to you, Valerie. I think you're about to get into a mess of trouble."

"I guess I had to get something off my conscience, that's all. Remember those two gold coins I showed you?"

"The ones in your drawer, yeah, I do."

"You weren't interested in them because they weren't minted by the Confederacy. They weren't supposed to be. They came from Pennsylvania. The Confederates threatened to burn a place named Chambersburg. They rounded up black people and sent them to the auction in Richmond, Virginia, free-born people as well as slaves. Robert Lee approved it."

"I'll say it just once, Valerie. Don't be caught up by people who claim to do justice when in reality they seek only wealth."

"I see," she said.

"What do you mean you 'see'?" I asked.

"Don't go probing the past," she said. "That's what you're saying?"

"No, I did not say that. I just don't want you to get hurt. You're my partner."

"Yeah?" she said.

I pulled to the side of the road. Up ahead were several expensive houses built up on pilings, with St. Augustine lawns and television discs on the balconies and yachts rocking in the slips. I tried to remember where my father's shrimp boat used to moor. But I couldn't.

"Why you stopping?" Valerie said.

"Oh, I was just looking around."

"Dave?" she said.

"Yeah?"

"Except for Helen, you were the only person in the department who stood up for me. You also endangered your career and maybe your life. I'll never forget that."

She started to put her hand on me, then took it away. A squadron of pelicans was flying in formation at the end of the road. I could see a restaurant and a number of uptown automobiles parked outside. The pelicans flew past a faded American flag popping on a metal pole in the parking lot, and waves the color of pennies and frothy with foam breaking on the rocks below. I didn't know why, but I felt that somehow, something iconic was taking place, and it wasn't good.

"You think those are our boys from Jersey?" Valerie said.

"Take it to the bank," I replied.

Louisiana has had a long history with the Mafia, or the Black Hand, as it was originally called. In 1891 a mob broke into the New Orleans city prison and lynched eleven Italian men on lampposts. Decades later, Huey Long, the former governor and then current United States Senator, gave Louisiana to Frank Costello. Slots were everywhere. So was prostitution. And all the other attendant vices. Our sisters in sin were in Florida and Cuba. The assassination of John Kennedy may have had strong ties to New Orleans. We'll never know. The Warren investigation was not meant to clarify; it was meant to distract.

Regardless, as Exodus states, the sins of the fathers are borne by the sons unto the third and fourth generations. Our group of time-traveling sinners had arrived in five high-powered, immaculately-painted, hand-waxed, white-walled, chrome-grilled, tinted-window automobiles that no one would dare put a hand on.

Valerie and I got out of our unmarked car at the same time, which with cops is never coincidental, both of us visibly armed at the waist, both with our badge holders on our belts. We went inside and walked past the cashier and the maître-d' without stopping.

But the maître d' caught up with us. "Could I help you, sir?" he said.

I held up my badge. “Go back to the front and stay there, please,” I said.

“Is there a problem?” he said.

The New Jersey crowd was in a red-leather booth at the back of the dining room. I did not look at the maître d’. “Did you hear what I said?”

“Yes, sir,” he replied.

“Everything is all right,” I said.

“Yes, sir, I understand that.”

He walked away, his face disjointed, his menus held to his chest. I did not like the way I was forced to speak to him. But bad manners often save lives.

Six men were sitting in the booth. Five of them looked too large for their clothes, as if no size would fit them. They were eating shrimp cocktails with small forks that made them bend their wrists down for each shrimp. They paid no attention to Valerie or me.

The sixth man was older and smaller, and wore a tie and a stiff tan suit and round glasses as dark as a blind man’s. His short-brim hat looked made of plastic. His skin was colorless and his stomach sagged like a hot-water bottle.

“This is a private table, here,” he said.

“How are you doing, Mr. Ludlow?” I said. “You remember me?”

“No,” he said. “My full name is Sidney Ludlow. But you did right calling me Mr. Ludlow. Whadda you want?”

“I met you in Montana. You and Sally Ducks were trying to build a casino on Flathead Lake.

Mr. Ludlow touched the big man next to him with one finger. “Go up front and take care of this.”

The big man rose and pulled his napkin from his throat and dropped it on the table. His eyes swept over my face as he stood up. His hostility was palpable. I looked at Mr. Ludlow. “This is Detective Benoit. Sheriff Soileau wanted to know how long you would be staying with us. In case we can help you in any way.”

"We don't know who you're talking about," he said. "Now get out of here."

"I'm sorry, we can't do that," I said. "One of the New Jersey vehicles parked in a handicap zone with no permit. Is that yours, sir?"

He looked at one of the other men. "See what he's talking about, Benny."

"I'm afraid the wrecker guy is on his way," I said.

Ludlow took a Kleenex from a tiny pack in his shirt pocket and blew his nose softly, looking at Valerie from behind his black glasses. "What's your name again?"

"Detective Benoit."

"Tell them to box our order and bring it to my car. Make sure everything on the bill is there."

"You were part of the casino wars in Las Vegas," Valerie said. "You murdered five or six people. You buried people in the desert."

He was breathing through his mouth now, his face tilted up, as smooth as rubber, as though he were not capable of emotion. "This is why your people got a problem," he said. "We give you an inch, you want a mile."

Valerie's eyes were glistening. "Shut your mouth, you old fart. Who do you think you are?"

I touched her on the arm. "Detective, we'll both walk Mr. Ludlow to his vehicle. These other men will follow us. Right, Mr. Ludlow?"

"No, you're not 'right' about anything," he said. "I remember you now. You were with an ex-cop named Purcel. He put sand in the engines of Sally Duck's plane."

"What are you doing in Cypremort Point, Mr. Ludlow?"

He stood up from the booth, his hands shaking on the silverware. He looked at me. "You put a muzzle on the smart mouth, here. You're lucky I'm old."

"We've got a problem, Mr. Ludlow," I said. "You need to apologize to Detective Benoit."

Valerie pushed me aside. I thought she was going to insult him again. She didn't. She slapped him across the face so hard his glasses flew against the wall. Everyone at the table froze. Then one of Ludlow's men picked up the glasses, but remained standing and motionless. Ludlow put his napkin in his waterglass and wiped the side of his face that had been slapped, then took the glasses from his bodyguard and put them back on and looked at me, as though nothing had happened.

"I'm not Sally Ducks," he said.

"No, sir, you're not," I replied.

"I'm a businessman. An old one, with a family. That's lucky for yous."

"I understand," I said.

"Good," he said.

Then he picked up a walking cane that was propped under the table, and began working his way out of the restaurant, his dark glasses back on, looking at the sky as though searching for the sunlight.

Chapter Twenty-Two

Valerie slammed the passenger door in our car. "You're gonna take that shit?"

"Don't let your enemy choose your battlefield," I said.

"What kind of crap is that?" she replied.

"He's slick. Handcuff him and he'll have people weeping for him."

I drove out of the parking lot onto the two-lane. The car was buffeted by the wind, the flag popping on the pole. Valerie's face was smoldering. "So I almost had people in tears?"

"You've got to ease up on the batter sometimes."

"Fuck. That. Shit."

"How about it on the language, Valerie?"

"Tell me if I'm wrong. In his old neighborhood in New Jersey, any black kid caught wearing tennis shoes got thrown off the closest roof."

"That's the rumor," I said. "What I'm trying to say is don't give these guys the upper hand. Ludlow is loved in his hometown. They think he's a great guy. They have a fireworks celebration on his birthday. Elderly women kiss his hands."

"Pull over. I'm gonna be sick."

She wasn't exaggerating. As soon as I turned into some palm trees, she fell out of the door and propped herself against a tree trunk and couldn't stop retching. I got out and put my hand on her back. It felt as hard as iron.

"The bad guys all go down, Valerie, even though it takes a while," I said.

She twisted her head around, her hands propped on her knees now. "Yeah, just like the people who kept my ancestors enslaved. Sell that shit to someone else, Dave."

On Sunday morning Alafair and I went to Mass at St. Edwards, then played tennis in City Park. I hoped she would stay with me in New Iberia a while, but I vowed I would not try to keep her if she wished to leave. As you might know, a daughter-father relationship is a strange one. Some of the dormant passions are probably better not discussed. Fear and covetousness are involved. In other words, it's not a rational state of mind.

But that's not my point. As Alafair glided back and forth on the court, whacking the ball with all her might, I thought about the meaning of the word "destiny." Is there such a thing? In her case, she went down in a plane that may have had a bomb on it; her mother drowned; and an alcoholic off-duty cop happened to be fishing on the continental shelf where the plane filled with water in less than three minutes.

A five-year-old Indian girl was saved from a massacre in a stone-age village and from drowning in a plane crash. There's more. My scuba tank ran out of air when I dived on the cabin. Alafair was treading water in a bubble of air no bigger than a pillow. You cannot come close to death without suddenly realizing the enormity of Creation and the plan that's at the end of your fingertips. To deny this is to deny infinity or the frozen magnitude of the Milky Way.

I'm not just talking about Alafair. I'm talking about this story. The events in it started with the discovery of Clemmy Benoit, a young Creole woman with blue eyes and roses tattooed on her breasts and a guitar string wrapped around her throat, a garbage bag for a winding sheet, dragged into my yard by a macabre figure who looked like he had escaped from the grave himself.

Now the cast of characters had grown, like actors from the medieval morality plays: Boone Hendrix, a handyman obsessed with repairing the houses of others; Elton Foot, a gargoyle who worked for the Mob; Tommy Driscoll, a good-hearted trucker tormented by the death of his daughter on an Indian reservation; Jerry Carlucci, who every night probably stood inside a helicopter, his M60 vibrating and spitting flame above a rice paddy while his targets ran for their lives.

But there were others, too, friends who should not have been on the list: Valerie Benoit, whose determination to achieve racial justice seemed to have become her own Golgotha; and Clete Purcel, who talked to Joan of Arc, never talked about Shitsville, and forgave the drunken milkman who forced him to kneel on rice grains from sundown to sunrise.

Why all of this? At a certain age you have premonitions. Call it the dwindling down of the days, a coldness that replaces the sunlight, the sound of leaves crunching under your feet, a bitter brassy taste as you lean down and take a drink from a water fountain, a terrible sense that life is not complex, it's simple: The human race's survival is because of individuals—the wheel, a spark from two rocks, a hollowed-out tree trunk that popped over the waves and became a boat, the women and children who gathered.

This was our history, our discovery of ourselves. And we learned that the human family could be loving and kind. But there was another seed at work, too, and I had a great fear that their time would one day come round.

As we walked home, I could not get these thoughts out of my mind. Was it February or March? I really didn't care. The day was grand, but I couldn't convince myself of my own perceptions. As we stepped up on the drawbridge, the vibration of the cars seemed to go up through my knees and inside my body, the rattling of the steel grid like a breach in the surface of Eden.

"What are you thinking about, Dave?" Alafair said.

"I'm not sure," I replied. "The times. The mood of the country. The anger that seems to have no source."

"Maybe it's aways been that way," she replied.

"This is different. You can feel it. There are huge numbers of people waiting for a leader."

"Like Hitler?"

"Yes, just like Hitler."

"Let's stop here for a minute," she said.

"Sure," I said.

We leaned on the railing and looked down the long, brown ribbon of the Teche and the live oaks and cypress trees and bamboo on the banks and the sloping green yards with their gazebos and flowerbeds and verandas and screened porches on the houses. It seemed a perfect place, one that did not have to abide the laws of mortality.

"Are you worried about Clete?"

"No," I said. "He's out of the can and soaking his ankle. He'll be all right."

"What is it, then?"

"It's not an emotional condition," I said. "It's what is occurring in our times. It's real."

"If that's true, why let it take us down?"

"That's my feeling, too, Alf."

"I'm not going to leave. No matter what you say or what you think or what you do. You're my father and friend and I will never desert you."

How do you deal with that? I rubbed my eyes as the cars drove by.

"Are you all right?" she said.

"It's just dust. Let's stop at Bojangles and have a bite to eat."

I couldn't clear my throat until we got there.

* * *

That evening I told Alafair I was going to straighten up the attic. In part that was true. I kept good care of the memorabilia from Alafair's childhood—her Baby Squanto and Curious George books, her Baby Orca T-shirt, her quacking Donald Duck cap, her tennis shoes whose rubber tips were embossed with the words "left" and "right." I will never give away or lose any of those things.

But I had another purpose, one I had not fully thought through. In fact, I didn't allow myself to think about what I was doing. Every few years Clete gave me weapons he took off people who should have never possessed them. One of those was an army-issue Thompson machine gun. I sat in a stiff-back chair with a lamp on the floor, and oiled and wiped down the Thompson, then thumbed the magazines almost full of .45 rounds, not loading the full capacity so the springs in the magazines would not be weakened.

From down below I could hear Alafair listening to CNN. I rolled the boxed rounds and the magazines and the Tommy gun in a blanket and put them on the floor behind a bookcase. What was I doing when I loaded a fully automatic weapon like a Thompson? I kept my mind blank. Yes, indeedy.

I heard Alafair turn off the television, then heard her talking with someone at the door. Sunday night in New Iberia is not a time to visit. Why? I'm not sure. I think Cajuns look upon Sunday night as a beginning or an ending. They're very aware of mutability, though, and I think it is because of the cruel way they have been forced from several nations.

I went down the ladder into the hallway. Alafair was headed toward me. Lloyd D'Anjou was already inside the house.

"He's drunk," she whispered. "I told him you were busy, but he won't leave."

"It's all right," I said. "Work on your book and keep the door shut. Don't open it for any reason."

"This is half my house,"

"Stay in half of the house."

"He's really lit, Dave."

"Okay, I got the message."

I walked into the living room. D'Anjou had taken off his hat and was holding it with both hands. Alafair was right; D'Anjou was boiled and had the moldy odor of a football dressing room after the game; his armpits reeked with a stench that was like cat urine in a litter box.

"You got a beer?" he said.

"No."

"Yeah, I know you're not drinking, but I thought your daughter might have something for guests. Robo, I'm in the shitter."

"Don't use profanity in my house, Lloyd."

"Can I sit down?"

"No, let's work it out tomorrow. Want me to call a cab?"

When he swallowed, a lump as big as a walnut slid down his throat.

"Dave, I know we had our differences, but I got my dork in the light socket." He tried to smile but couldn't pull it off. His voice was quavering. "Look, I feel like a fool. Them people ain't like us, Robo. Shit, I got family. Not much of one, but I take care of them just the same."

"Are you on a pad?"

"At first that's all it was. A case of whiskey at Christmas, a freebee with a couple of working girls. No big deal."

He stopped and waited to see my reaction. So far I had not shown one. "Then it got more serious," he said. "Like a Murphy gig, except when the husband busts in on the whore and the John don't give up his money. He gives up his life."

"You did a contract murder?"

"We set one up, but the John jumped out the window." He laughed. "Anyway, no score, no harm, right?"

He waited for me to speak. But I didn't. He was a pitiful man, and had always been one, and would die one. If he had ever owned a soul, I think he used it up.

"Come into the kitchen," I said. "I've got coffee on the stove."

"Thanks."

"Do yourself a favor," I said.

"What?"

"Don't lie, don't try to jerk me around."

"You don't think I know that?"

He sat at the kitchen table, unshaved all the way down his throat into his collar, his hands spread on the surface like an amphibian.

"Who else is on the pad?" I said.

"I cain't give other names. I can just give my own, Robo."

He had already started another ruse. He was the man of honor, the altruist in a damaged world, a cop who grew up chopping cotton and breaking corn. The truth was he wanted to cut a deal before his confederates did. He would disappear in the Witness Protection Program, with a house and a monthly check, and his corrupt colleagues would be left swinging in the wind. I took a notepad from a drawer and put it in front of him with a ballpoint. "Write down their names," I said.

"Just their names?" he said. "Write nothing else? Like we just work together? I'm not sayin' they done anything?"

I nodded but didn't speak.

He started to write, then stopped. "Look, I'm confessing about the pad. About confiscated coke or weed disappearing. I ain't even sayin' I did it, okay?"

I kept my face flat. "I think we can work with you on that."

"And if some rich guys are about to steal them coastal marshlands, I just say what I know and leave out personalities?"

"I need their names, Lloyd."

His hand started rattling on the ballpoint. "I cain't do it."

"Then why are you here?"

"You got influence wit' the FBI. They know you."

"Why don't you contact them yourself?" I said.

His hand was shaking out of control now. He threw the ballpoint across the kitchen. "'Contact' is what I got! They caught me in a sting." He was breathing with his mouth open.

"Porn?" I said.

"Yeah."

"Child porn?" I said.

"Yeah, but I'm innocent. I swear."

"You groped my daughter, Lloyd. Why would you not do it to some other child?"

"I told you I never did that. You're fixing to t'row me to them people, aren't you? The same people are gonna kill me that killed the blue-eyed colored girl."

"Clemmy Benoit?"

"They did it slow."

I got up from the table. "Repeat that?"

"Fuck you, Robicheaux. I'm going to New Orleans to get drunk and get laid until my dick falls off. I'll see you in hell, you rotten cocksucker."

Then he went out the front door, tearing the screen door off one hinge. I followed him into the yard, but he backed his car over the curb, crushing his exhaust pipe, then gave it the gas, his tires squealing rubber and smoke, a hubcap rolling down the street with him.

Chapter Twenty-Three

I went to Clete's office early Monday morning. It was cold, the streets puffing with fog, the green and red lights on the drawbridge barely visible. The waiting room was empty, but Clete was behind his desk reading the *Daily Iberian*, his sprained ankle resting on a pillow stuffed in a deep drawer, a pair of aluminum crutches propped against the wall. "What's the haps, big mon?"

"No haps except Lloyd D'Anjou was at my house last night," I replied.

"That's like saying 'no haps' except a walking human turd sat on all your furniture," Clete said.

"Thanks," I said. "But he's not a funny guy. He said Clemmy Benoit's killers 'did it slow.'"

"What?"

"Yeah, you heard me right."

"Where's that dickwad now?" he asked.

"I don't know. He had a load on. He wasn't at roll call this morning."

"You think he's trying to slip you a slider?" Clete said.

"It's hard to tell. He was spotting his Fruit of the Looms. I think it's probably the real deal."

"An Iberia Parish Sheriff's Detective is hiding information in a torture-murder case? Helen's not gonna allow this."

"The autopsy seemed to indicate otherwise."

"Autopsies are wrong all the time," he said. "That's why bodies are always getting dug up."

"How's your ankle?" I asked.

"Stay on the subject. What are y'all gonna do about fuckhead?"

" 'Fuckhead' is D'Anjou?"

"Who else?"

"Helen will open an investigation," I said.

"I think I just shortened my recovery. I already feel much better."

"Stay out of it, Clete."

"No way. I've always wanted to use Lloyd D'Anjou's head for a bowling ball."

"D'Anjou is a pinhead. Just like Ludlow's crowd. If they didn't have their B.O. and garlic, they wouldn't have jobs."

"You call Ludlow a pinhead?" Clete said. "The guy probably owns half of Atlantic City."

"I hate to tell you this, Clete, but you have the same fixations as Valerie Benoit. The people who run real crime in America are untouchable. Wake up."

"I'm not the problem," he replied. "But you've got one, and it's the same one you've always had."

He stopped and breathed through his nose, as though he couldn't bear to tell the truth to me.

"Go on, please," I said.

"You love Louisiana, but it doesn't love you."

I felt something flinch in me, but tried not to show it. "There's a line in *From Here to Eternity* I always liked. 'A man loves a thing, it don't mean it gotta love him back.' "

He folded the newspaper and set it on top of his desk and stared at it without seeing the content.

"Something wrong?" I said.

"What you said about real crime being untouchable? You were talking about the corporations and the military-industrial complex, like Eisenhower was talking about?"

"Yeah, what else did you think?"

"I don't argue with that, big mon. I'm talking about your faith in your state and your culture and law enforcement and the court system. It's a huge scarecrow blowing in the wind. Why do you think I bounced Elton Foot's head off his car a couple of times?"

"You ran his face through a glass window in his car," I said.

"Whatever," he said.

"Clete, will you take the mashed potatoes out of your mouth?"

"I'm saying the real war is fought by the little people," he said.

"Like who?"

"You know who: that poor, beautiful, olive-skinned, tattooed girl who might have been tortured to death after all because she had something these assholes wanted," he said. "A girl not over one hundred and twenty pounds against degenerates who couldn't get laid in Tijuana with the Hope Diamond. My own words make me mad, Streak. Do you copy that, big mon?"

I took a big breath. "Loud and clear, Cletus. How about we go across the street and have some breakfast?"

I know my attitude seemed cavalier, but Clete was right. We were entering the twenty-first century, and both he and I had a sense we would be among the last to see what was called traditional America. We also shared a feeling that the new century did not bode well for us. The indifference to the melting of the Arctic, the rising of the oceans, the sands of war blowing in the Mideast, the possible return of an evil man in the Kremlin.

Clete and I ate quietly at Victor's Cafeteria, perhaps because of our mood, perhaps because of the white density and coldness of the fog in the street. The steel workboats headed for the Gulf had turned on all their lights, but we could barely make them out. The other patrons were quiet, too, as though a solemn occasion were taking place, a funeral perhaps, or an apocryphal warning had been given to the citizenry, as happened during the Cuban Missile Crisis.

"Kind of weird this morning, huh?" Clete said.

"Yeah," I said.

"Like corpses propped up at the tables."

"Lower your voice, would you?" I said.

"I was just making an observation. On the subject of Sidney Ludlow, when I met him up in Montana he told me he voted for John Kennedy, then said, 'They should have killed Robert. Robert was the troublemaker.'"

"Come on, Clete. This stuff is too dark."

"I'm just telling you. He's been using up the supply of adult diapers too long. I think he'd make a nice bucket of fish chum."

Someone at another table gagged.

"Hey, sorry!" Clete said. "I got logorrhea! I should wear a hazmat suit or get a mop! In fact, I'll dummy-up! Hey, that breakfast is on me!"

I've acquired little wisdom in life. But one thing I know for sure: Clete Purcel will never change.

The fog didn't leave that day. I had never seen it like that, or at least that long in duration. The moisture in the fog dripped from the trees like rainwater. The bayou rose all the way to Burke Street and the back of the Evangeline Theatre, running into the storm gutters, which returned it to the bayou.

I had a long talk with the coroner, a difficult one, both for him and me. Supposedly Clemmy Benoit died of an overdose, and the guitar string embedded in the skin around her neck was cosmetic in terms of pain or mortality. There was no physical evidence proving that she suffered, only Lloyd D'Anjou's statement "They went slow." In the coroner's office I made three calls to D'Anjou's house up the bayou on the St. Martin Parish line. No answer, and no answer at the department.

Here was the problem. There are many ways to make people suffer before they die. Psychic pain is just one example. I will not go on. It was obvious the coroner didn't wish to go on, either. He was a kind and genteel man, who had adopted three impoverished children.

"Thanks for your time, doc," I said as I was going out.

"Dave?" he said.

"Yes, sir?"

"If I find evidence that this girl was tortured—"

I waited for him to continue. He cleared his throat. "I'll call you," he said. "Yes, that's what I'll do."

"You're a good guy, doc," I said.

"Get out of here," he said.

I did not know where Lloyd D'Anjou was. Neither did Helen. "Got any ideas?" she said.

"D'Anjou said he was going to get laid in New Orleans," I replied.

"Because his ass is grass with the Mob or whoever?"

The fog was hanging so densely in the trees I couldn't see the bayou through Helen's window. "I believe he's planning on eating his gun," I said.

She shook her head. "No, D'Anjou likes himself too well. He didn't mention any names? The other guys on the pad, the grease-balls, whoever has got him wetting his pants?"

"No."

"Okay, fuck him. He'll come in on his knees. In the meantime, I've got a shitstorm going on with our legislature."

"What about?"

"Iberia Parish is one of the few that voted down casino gambling. The reps in the legislature are having a fit."

"They don't believe in elections?" I asked.

"Not when they lose."

"Tell them to get lost," I said.

"That's what I said to four or five of them. They're not the problem though. There's something going on about land boundaries and ownership along the southwest parishes."

"Is Jerry Carlucci involved?"

"Not that I heard," she said. "You know something I don't?"

"After I beat him up, he offered me a job as a resort developer. He said it would be as big as Reno. He called it a 'giant, neon toilet.'"

"He's proud of developing a toilet?" she said.

"Yeah, I thought that was a little strange."

"It's a crazy world, isn't it, bwana?"

I shrugged.

She turned around and looked out the window. "Take me to an early supper?"

"If Alafair can go."

Once committed to a principle or his word, Clete Purcel was the most undaunted man I ever knew. Nothing could stop him. As long as there was breath in his lungs and blood in his veins and a heart that was still beating, he would persevere. But what made him unique were the causes he served, not the violent or comedic way he went about the solution. Clete had no peace, no sleep, and no happiness if he saw cruelty taking place before his eyes. The perpetrators would be lucky to survive. Clete out of control was like a steel ball with spikes on it swinging through a building. He was literally capable of ripping off a neo-Nazi's arms and using them to beat him to death.

The following is not fiction: Years ago, he saw a photo in a magazine of a Polish woman walking with her three children to the showers at Auschwitz. He tore the picture from the magazine and carried it in his wallet until he found an antisemite who had defrauded millions in Europe and the U.K. and the United States. I'll let Clete tell you what happened, but he got justice for the mother and her children and created a monument for them in a little graveyard among the oaks on Bayou Teche. You can see it there, in the shade, and from time to time there are flowers scattered on the stone, and I know he has put them there, although he will not talk of it.

After Helen and Alafair and I went to supper, Clete put on a warm wool shirt, a rain jacket, a cap with earflaps, gloves, disposable rubber swamp boots, and loaded the Caddy with his crutches, a thermos of coffee, two hamburgers with fried onions, his handcuffs and binoculars and a slapjack and his cut-down double-barrel. Then he motored on up the two-lane to the home of Lloyd D'Anjou on the St. Martin Parish line, the trees still draped with fog, the stubble fields still burning in the darkness, choked with smoke, the air as acrid as syrup spilled on a woodstove.

Chapter Twenty-Four

D'Anjou's home was a strange place, and it was strange because it was a fine-looking two-story farmhouse with an attic and a wide verandah and a swing and dormers and a barn with two or three cows. Not far away was the ever-present Bayou Teche. Why should he be such an angry man, convinced that he had been cheated by God and Man and the very elements around him? I'll venture a guess: Giving the Black Man access to the same world D'Anjou lived in was the unforgivable sin, and the people he hated most were the whites who gave away D'Anjou's racial superiority.

Clete pulled the Caddy to the side of the road and cut his lights. The fog was so heavy D'Anjou's yard was completely covered, the veranda as well. The first and second floors were dark, but a light was on in the attic. D'Anjou was not in New Orleans. Or if he had gone there, he had returned. Clete guessed D'Anjou had sobered up and regretted his confession to me, and now was trying to find a way to get rid of Clete and me and Helen.

But this was all guesswork. The real issue, both legal and moral, was the murder of Clemmy Benoit, and the way in which she was killed. The kinds of death to which she may have been subjected made Clete's eyes film and his heart shrink. He was not going to let Lloyd D'Anjou get away, either in the Witness Protection Program or inside the Iberia Parish Sheriff's Department. D'Anjou and his friends had already degraded and tormented black inmates in the parish stockade and gotten away with it, at least so far. Also, they would never quit their harassment of Valerie Benoit. No, this time around D'Anjou was going to dime himself, with Clete listening, or do the rhumba boogie down the South American way, as Hank Snow would say.

Clete was looking forward to it.

He crossed the yard, clanking with his aluminum crutches, the fog up to his waist, as though the lower half of his body had disappeared, then thumped his way up on the veranda and opened the screen door and cupped his hand on the brass knob. It was locked. He propped his crutches and kept the screen door open with his butt, got out his Swiss Army pocketknife, and opened one of the blades and edged it into the jamb, deep enough to get behind the screws and prize them loose.

Then he cupped both hands under the knob and raised the door and put all his weight against it at the same time. The jamb splintered and the door swung open. He stepped inside with his crutches and shut the door.

The inside of the house smelled like a grave, devoid of sunshine, lacking house pets or a freshly cut pie on a kitchen counter. Better said, lacking humanity.

He was carrying his .38 Special and his titanium hideaway, but had left the cut-down double-barrel in the Caddy because of his crutches. Besides, he had a concealed-carry license for the .38 Special, but cut-downs were touchy when it came to legality. He had already committed what is known as breaking-and-entering; he didn't need any more technical trouble. *Oh*, what was his plan? He didn't have one.

That's the way his life had always been, he told himself. The upside of being a private investigator or a bondsman is its legal vagueness. The laws governing a bondsman go back to medieval Britain, a surrogate the court employed to shuttle petty criminals around and give them a bath before they were brought to court. Some of them did scutwork in the castle's dungeon. The forms of torture were inhuman and unthinkable. As a P.I. and a hump for bondsmen, Clete spent 90 percent of the time renouncing and keeping his mind clean of what he was doing.

He closed the front door and got on his crutches and looked up the stairs. He could see a drop-door and ladder that had been pulled from the second-story ceiling. A lightbulb on a cord was hanging from a beam. Someone was walking back and forth in front of it, casting his shadow across the opening in the ceiling.

Clete wished he had brought the cut-down. It had a strap and he could put his arm through it and go up the ladder with both hands free. There was no guarantee that D'Anjou was the only person in the attic, either. In fact, the only knowable certainty about D'Anjou was his penis envy, hunger for all women, a special hatred of educated black men, and Jews of any kind, although he probably never knew one.

He carried a hideaway twenty-four hours a day, and not just as a drop. Lloyd D'Anjou could be infantile, particularly after a few drinks. One Sunday afternoon he blew up the propane tank on his sister-in-law's trailer, and made her take the blame when the cops came out.

Clete tried to think his way out of the situation he had just created. Over the years most of his plans led to ruin. But he didn't care, not really. Clete was never envious, because he never wanted to be anybody except Clete. But that's too simple. I'll give you the real gen. He was a thunderstorm with a conscience, the blue-collar knight-errant, wearing chainmail, solitary on one knee atop a green hill, his sword and shield on the grass while lightning splintered around him. That's what he was and that's what he still is. Because of the times we live in maybe that seems a foolish characterization.

I think it's right on the money. Ask a marine what it takes to earn the Navy Cross. Just don't ask Clete. He'll run away.

Hailstones were pinging on the roof and the barn. Now was the time. Clete lay down his crutches on a couch and worked his way up the stairs to the landing, then got on the ladder, his weight and swamp boots banging on each step, knowing he would be heard, his .38 Special strapped in his shoulder holster, his eardrums about to burst with the pounding of his heart.

Then he was inside the attic, standing up, although off-balance, staring straight into D'Anjou's face. D'Anjou was holding a screw-can of dynamite in his left hand. His mouth had dropped open.

"What the hell are you doing in my house?" he said.

"I'm glad you asked that," Clete said. "What are you doing with those cans? Those are old-time explosives for offshore oil exploration, right?"

"Yeah, and blowing up assholes like you."

"Is that more of them over there?" Clete said.

"Yeah," D'Anjou said. "And the primers and the nitro-caps that go with them. I've also got both a primer and a cap in my pocket, asshole. How would you like me to blow my own fucking house down with you in it? What do you say to that, you fat shit?"

"Tell you what, Lloyd," Clete replied. "I'm easing my .38 snub out of its holster because it rubs a blister on my nipple and drives me nuts. Here, you want to hold it? I'm here on a peace mission. In fact, you got any snacks?"

"You break into my house and call that a peace mission?"

"That's what I'm trying to tell you," Clete said. "Take my snub. I got nothing to hide. I just want to find out what happened to Clemmy Benoit."

"What happened is she got herself killed."

"How?" Clete said.

"What do I get out of this?" D'Anjou said.

"Maybe you get to keep your job. Maybe you don't go to jail."

"Hey, I told Robicheaux some shit 'cause I was coked and drunk. If you want to know what I've been doing, this is it. I've been running a little undercover myself. I got in with some guineas, real greaseballs. Guys wit' no respect and no morals. What did they want to know from the dead girl? Fuck if I know. You gonna give me that gun?"

"Yeah, I can do that." Clete flipped the cylinder out of the frame, then dumped the shells on the floor, each of them bouncing on the planks, then threw the gun to D'Anjou.

"You're kind of dumb, Purcel."

"I hear that a lot."

"I have my own piece. It's loaded, too. Not good for you."

"What are you gonna do with all that dynamite? That's some lethal stuff."

The cans were made to be screwed into each other, and used on offshore seismograph rigs. Six dynamite cans were screwed together, then a primer was screwed to what was called "the stick," which was eighteen cans of dynamite. Then a nitro-cap was attached to the last can and slid down the drill hole with a wire that led to a detonator. The explosion could dramatically jar the iron hull and pilings of the drill barge and break coffee cups in the wheelhouse.

"You ax me what I'm gonna do wit' it?" D'Anjou said. "What do you t'ink?"

"You're gonna blow yourself up?"

"You wish."

"You're gonna blow me up?"

"I haven't made up my mind."

"Where did you go wrong, Lloyd?" This night was the first time Clete could remember using D'Anjou's given name.

"I never did go wrong," D'Anjou said. "It's you people that's done it. Like Robicheaux and that dyke Helen Soileau. Now we got Goldilocks filing charges against people who've had their badges for decades."

"To my knowledge, that's a lie, Lloyd."

"Stop calling me by first name, asshole. We're not friends. We never were. I think you're a traitor. Yeah, you got your medals, but when you came home, you became a rat."

"How about I throw you through that window?" Clete replied.

"You seem to have a reality problem, here. I've got your gun. You got dick."

"I think you know more about Clemmy Benoit than you're telling me, Lloyd."

"Yeah, she gave good head. How's that?"

"You're starting to piss me off, Lloyd."

D'Anjou tossed Clete's .38 Special in the corner. "What if I just kick the shit out of you? And when I get finished wit' that, I'll have a visit wit' Robo and his nigger girlfriend. It looks like you got a problem wit' your ankle or your foot."

Clete eased his titanium five-chamber snub revolver out of the back of his belt and cocked the hammer. It felt like a feather in his hand. "Toss the can," he said.

"Toss the can, he says. What I'm holding is a primer wit' a nitro-cap. How fuckin' dumb can you get?"

"I'll give you to three."

"I hate you, Purcel. Everything about you. You and Robo. If I had my way, I would make this last a long time. Then we'd see who has the real courage."

He threw the primer with the nitro-cap at Clete's head. The can exploded against the wall. The effect was like a flash grenade, a snapping sound inside the eardrums, a blinding light, images that distorted the entire attic, his feet going out from under him, the pain in his ankle doubling.

D'Anjou was on his hands and knees picking up bullets to load in Clete's gun. Clete fell backward, through the drop-door in the floor, down the ladder, crashing on the second floor. He stumbled to his feet and fired one round from the titanium snub at the hole in the attic, then ducked as D'Anjou began shooting. Clete dragged and pulled himself down the stairs to the first floor, then aimed at the attic and squeezed the trigger on the snub until the hammer snapped dead on every shell in the cylinder.

He went out the front door on his crutches, then down the steps and into the wind and yard and the flecks of ice and snow, the yellow flames in the attic leaping to the ceiling, the hailstones stinging Clete's face.

The cows were bellowing in the darkness, a calf wailing for its mother. Clete was throwing his legs ahead of the crutches as fast as he could, the hailstones evaporating in the grass. He wondered if he was going to catch a bullet between his shoulder wings or through his spine and become a quadriplegic, his greatest fear when he was in Shitsville. What a laugh. He had come all the way back home in order to be a giant caterpillar squirming around on somebody's floor. What a sick joke.

But as always with Clete, the unexpected happened. D'Anjou burst out of the screen door, lit with flames from his head to his feet, his mouth a black hole, filled with such pain and ferocity it could make no sound.

D'Anjou raced across the yard, a human torch, then plunged into a tangle of barbed-wire and cedar posts, flailing his arms and struggling in the darkness, ripping his clothes and skin, winnowing down to what looked like a carbonized mannequin.

Clete had stopped running, traumatized with shock or disbelief, his aluminum crutches like spears in his armpits. The flames were spreading through the house now, creeping up the wallpaper and flattening on the ceiling, while overhead the stars were twinkling between the clouds. Clete remained stupefied on his crutches, wondering what all this meant. What should he do? He couldn't think, nor did he want to.

He worked his way back to his Caddy and got inside and drove away, as though he were leaving an outdoor movie theater of decades ago.

He could hear sirens now and even see one coming from New Iberia; he thought that some form of order would somehow be imposed on all the violence and chaos he had just witnessed. Then he gave up thinking and clicked on his car radio and concluded that nothing in this world was predictable, and that age brought no wisdom, and that even the worst of men deserved a teaspoon of mercy.

Chapter Twenty-Five

At 8:47 the next morning Valerie Benoit came to my office. She closed the door and looked back through the door glass into the corridor, then at me. "Did you get a report on the D'Anjou fire?"

"I drove out there and came back at three A.M. The fire was out by then."

"You saw D'Anjou?"

"Yeah," I said. "You want some coffee?"

"No," she answered. "Was the fire inspector out there?"

"Yeah, he said D'Anjou was dead and his house was burned to the ground. He also said the fire was caused by an explosion."

"A propane explosion?"

"If D'Anjou kept propane tanks in his attic."

She nodded, her eyes blinking. "I heard the explosion and saw the light in the sky from my house. I got in my car and went there."

"You did?"

"It was too late for me to do anything," she said.

"I see. What are you trying to say, Valerie?"

"I saw a Cadillac convertible headed up the two-lane to New Iberia."

"Get a tag number?"

"No."

"Color?"

"Orange or maybe yellow."

"Nobody has been assigned to the investigation," I said. "If you feel a need, you might talk to Helen."

"Might?"

"I saw D'Anjou's body," I replied. "I couldn't go back to sleep."

"Stop acting like a stupe, Dave. The neighbor said he heard either firecrackers or gunfire. Is it possible we're protecting somebody here?"

"You really know how to say it, Valerie."

"What am I supposed to do?" she said. "Clete Purcel promised he would keep out of our investigations. Now he's like an octopus."

"I saw Clete early this morning. This is what he got from D'Anjou before D'Anjou lit up his own house: Clemmy Benoit was tortured and murdered by the greaseballs. She had some kind of information they wanted. But they didn't get it."

"They tortured her?" she said.

"That's what D'Anjou said."

"You got a Kleenex?" she asked. "My hay fever kicked in."

"No, I'm out."

She turned away and rubbed the back of her wrist on her nose. Then she sniffed and cleared her throat.

"Who do we get in the box?" she said.

"What?"

"D'Anjou's buddies. The trash that's been trying to make my life miserable."

"You won't get anything from them," I said. "Their secrets died with D'Anjou."

"Shit," she said, wiping her eyes on her forearm. "Shit, shit, and shit."

"We're going to get justice for Clemmy, Valerie," I said. "One way or another."

"Say it again," she said.

"Let me rephrase. We'll do our best. Guilt is a cancer. God help the bastard who did this."

"That's it?"

"No, my thermos is empty," I said. "How about treating an elderly man to a cup of coffee and a donut?"

She picked a gold ringlet out of her eye. "Elderly man, my butt," she said.

I really didn't need that.

Then Helen swung open my door. "In my fucking office, you two, and I mean now!"

I hadn't had time to report to Helen, and was sure she was in a rage for my not having done so. However, I was wrong.

"I've had four peckerwoods in the legislature asking me what I'm going to do about the 'terrorist' attack on 'Homicide Detective' D'Anjou's home,'" she said. "Every one of those bastards sounds like he has a clothespin clamped on his nose."

"Why are they talking about 'terrorists'?" I said.

"Because of their mediocrity."

"I don't see the connection between the legislators and Detective D'Anjou, Sheriff," Valerie said.

"D'Anjou was a part-time snoop for the racetracks and the casinos," Helen said. "They've got churches, teachers, school principals, and newspaper people kissing their asses. I'm tired of this shit."

"So how about toning it down?" I said.

Mistake.

"When did you start telling me how I should talk?" she replied. Am I surrounded by lunatics? Am I the crazy person in this room? Both of you smell like ashtrays. Go down to the locker room and take a shower."

I looked casually out the window. The sun was pink, the clouds white. Valerie looked at the floor. I promised myself I would not say another word until I was out of Helen's office.

"I didn't tell you everything the peckerwoods had to say," Helen said. "They're in with the insurance companies. They asked if Clete Purcel was in New Iberia now."

"They think Clete is a terrorist?" I asked.

"They make it up as they go, bwana, and they're real good at it."

The light started blinking on her telephone. She picked it up, then made a motion to stay where we were. "Yes, I'm sure you have the background for that," she said into the telephone. "I'll tell the dispatcher to escort you upstairs . . . Yes, the pleasure is all mine. Mr. Hendrix . . . Pardon me . . . Call you Boo? Got it. Thank you."

She put the phone back in the cradle.

"Was that Boone Hendrix, the handyman?" I said.

"Absolutely," she replied. "And I want you here for every minute of it. He went inside the burned remains of D'Anjou's house."

"And you're letting him inside your office?" I said.

"Yes, and I want you here."

"Why?"

"I want you to see the kind of people who you bring into my life, Streak. I'll just listen and let you take notes."

"That's cruel," I said.

"No, it's not. This man has an obsession. It has something to do with you, and people connected with your life, starting with Clemmy Benoit and your beef with Jerry Carlucci. I'm tired of dealing with mind-fucks, bwana."

"Should Valerie stay?" I said.

"That's up to her."

"I'd like to," Valerie said.

"Good," Helen said. "Maybe I can have five minutes of peace."

Boone Hendrix entered the room dressed in his usual starched, stonewashed denims, his cheeks freshly shaved, a dent in his chin, his brunette hair tightly clipped. "I hope not to waste your time."

"Don't worry about that, Mr. Boo," Helen said. "Take a seat."

"Boo is just fine without the 'mister,'" he said. "Detective D'Anjou's home was blown up by dynamite. The explosion was in the attic. There was probably turpentine and gasoline and kerosene and paint stored on the floor and on the shelves. There were also elements to make narcotics."

Helen had been chewing gum. Her jaw slowed as Mr. Hendrix talked.

"The building had been infested with rats, both in the walls and under the floors. Usually there are not that many rats here'bouts, because the alligators consider them a delicacy. Pardon me if I am making your stomachs sick. That is not my intention."

The only person I ever heard speak like Mr. Hendrix was a character in the radio show "The Life of Riley." The character was called Digger O'Dell. His voice sounded like a talking burial chamber.

"Mr. Hendrix, we're not sure what your message is," I said.

"Your curiosity is justified, Detective Robicheaux," he said.

"It's 'Dave,' sir,'" I said.

My words could have been butterflies bouncing off his face.

"I'm here because of the man who died in the flames," Mr. Hendrix said. "He found the place he had always been searching for. But it was a far more grievous one than he had expected."

"Let's hold off on that, sir, and keep our discussion within earthly bounds," I said. "Okay?"

"I understand," he replied. "I'm not here about this man. He furthered the drug trade while he pretended to be its enemy. Many young people have died as a consequence. Now he is a piece of burnt cork, and rightly so. My message is about your friend, the light-bearer."

"Dave, we'd better wrap this one up," Helen said.

"All of you know who I'm talking about. His enemies now have the power to lock him in a prison that has no light. I don't know where it is, but I've seen it in a dream and I know that it's real."

His eyes were recessed, filled with brightness, like the eyes of people who have fallen into dementia. The silence in the room was deafening.

I cleared my throat. "I think you're a fine gentleman, sir, and we appreciate your coming here. Right now we have to go a number of places, but we'll always welcome your visits."

He stood up stiffly. "There's something I have to say."

"Go ahead, Mr. Hendrix," I said.

"We must watch out for the children."

"We agree with that, sir," I said.

"The man named Carlucci, he's one of them, isn't he?" he said.

"One of what?" I asked.

"The killing of the children, sir."

"No one is sure about that, Mr. Hendrix, so let's get rid of that right now," I said.

"I see it in your eyes, Detective," he replied. "You know the truth. Why are you defending this man?"

"I am not defending him. We were friends as boys. He was not a killer."

"How do you know?" he said.

He headed for the door. I tried to catch him by the shoulders. "Did you hear me, Mr. Hendrix? Sir, please! Stay here so we can straighten this out!"

"You don't know what grief is!" he said.

He jerked the door and walked into the corridor, leaving the door open. I went after him. The stairs were forty feet away. I looked both ways in the corridor. It was empty. I went back into the office. Helen and Valerie waited for me to speak.

"He's gone," I said.

"Gone?" Valerie said.

"My new glasses aren't too good."

"You only wear reading glasses," Helen said.

"Yeah, I'd better get that long-distance kind," I said.

"This scares the shit out of me," Helen said.

It rained that afternoon. When I got home from work, Clete's Caddy was in the driveway, but there was no Clete. Long ago I had given him a key to the house, but he had never used it. I walked through the porte-cochere and around the back of the house. He was sitting on the back steps, wearing a slicker and his porkpie hat, a stainless-steel container balanced on his right knee, a bottle of Jack by his left foot. The container had a strawberry or cherry milkshake in it. Our cat Cannon Ball and a beautiful, thick-furred raccoon named Lady Godiva were inside the rabbit hutch watching Clete, the door unlatched, a tarp on the roof.

Clete looked up at me. He was a wreck. And it wasn't from the explosion and gunfight with Lloyd D'Anjou.

"Why didn't you go inside?" I said.

"I didn't feel like it," he replied.

"How much Jack do you have in the milkshake?"

"Four fingers."

"That's it?" I asked.

"Four fingers each time I pour. That way I don't let things get out of control. I'm very mellow, big mon. Sit down."

"I've got to talk to you, Clete, and that Jack Daniels is not going to help us."

"So talk." He started to reach for the bottle. I lifted it up and set it on the hutch.

"Why'd you do that?" he said.

"Some guys in the legislature are coming after you. They're calling you a terrorist."

"Because D'Anjou blew up his house?"

"They're going to put all the heat they can on you, Clete, and they've got the bastards to do it."

"Really?" he said, looking up at me, the raindrops tapping his face, his eyes unblinking. "I don't see how they can do that. That sounds silly to me."

I eased the stainless-steel milkshaker out of his hand and set it inside the back screen door. "You got to quit killing yourself, podna."

"That's no fun."

"I'm getting mad now," I said. "That handyman, Boone Hendrix, came to the department. He called you a light-bearer. He seemed to be saying the guys in the legislature planned to bury you in a prison cell or a dungeon. He scared the hell out of Helen. I went after him in the hallway and he disappeared. Right in front of me."

Clete reached inside his slicker and took a clean handkerchief out and wiped his face with it. "I let you down, noble mon. I just got creepy in the head and thought I was in a rainforest, and for a while I wanted to sail off to Tahiti and never think of Vietnam again."

"You never let me down, Clete. Never. Not once."

"I think I got 'The Re-Enlistment Blues.' Remember that song in *From Here to Eternity*? God, that's a sad movie."

"There's another thing," I said, ignoring his attempts at distraction. "The handyman thinks Jerry Carlucci is a murderer of children. I think he might try to take Jerry out."

Clete tried to get up, then fell back down. The flowerbeds on each side of him were in full bloom, the scarlet and pink petals denting when the rain ran off the roof. He wiped off his face again, this time with a bare hand; for a moment his eyes seemed to clear. "If I had to go after D'Anjou again, I'd do it," he said. "I think he had fentanyl in his attic. I wonder if Jerry Carlucci is in on it. If those cocksuckers in the legislature want to come after me, let them come."

That was the old Clete coming alive again, but I didn't want to encourage him. I helped him up and gave him his crutches and straightened his porkpie hat on his forehead, then held the doors open.

"I thought I was on fire when explosive cans went off," he said. "It was just like the night that navy corpsman dragged me down the hillside on a poncho liner. I felt all my blood leave me. Just like the earth sucked it out of my body. I told the corpsman, 'Don't let me die.'"

"You're going to be all right, Cletus," I said.

"No, you don't get it. I died. Then I came back. I'm telling you the truth, Dave. It wasn't a fantasy."

"Come on, we're almost inside."

Then Clete crashed through the mudroom and landed on the linoleum. A bag of dry cat food fell off the top of the icebox and burst on the floor. Clete was in a daze. He looked at the cat food scattered all over the floor. "Hey, I was gonna feed the little guys," he said. "Can you bring them in?"

That was Clete.

Chapter Twenty-Six

Clete ate a half pecan pie, with a scoop of ice cream on it, and drank a full pot of coffee with hot milk, then asked if I had any sandwich meat.

"No, you ate it all the last time you were here," I said.

"Oh," he said. "That's all right. I could knock off a pound or two."

I nodded, trying to keep my face empty. "What do you want to do about the handyman and his attitude toward Jerry Carlucci?" I said.

"You mean him wanting to take Carlucci out?"

"Who knows?" I said. "I think he's a schizophrenic."

"Maybe Carlucci has it coming,"

"Think about what you just said, Clete."

"You mean about having Jerry Carlucci on my conscience?"

"Yeah, not counting the handyman," I said.

"You always mess me up, big mon. As soon as I get a little psychological rest, you stick a fork in my head."

"It's your choice," I said.

"All right, let's go see the son of a bitch."

"I want to take Valerie Benoit," I said.

"Fine with me," he said.

"I've got to have a promise, though."

"What?" he said.

"Jerry is a trafficker. Your feelings about him are justified. But let the DEA handle him."

"I told you, I'm serene and meditative and completely under control," he said. "I don't start trouble."

"Glad to know that. I almost forgot."

Alafair walked through the front door, two bags of groceries in her hands. The rain had stopped, the fog and mist had not. Her hair and face were wet. "Thanks for leaving your car in the driveway, Clete," she said.

"Oh, Jez, I wasn't thinking," he replied.

"What happened to the floor?" she said.

Clete looked under the table. "I think Cannon Ball or Lady Godiva had an accident."

We took Clete's Caddy and met Valerie at the edge of town and headed for Jerry's Landing. I wanted her to go with me for several reasons. I believed she was brave and intelligent and would eventually become a good homicide cop, or what we used to call a "homicide roach." You had to have brains and class and stomp-butt guts to be a roach. She had dignity, and she showed it when D'Anjou and his thugs were as cruel as possible to her. If I had been in her place, I would have been tempted to shoot them. You may not believe this, but a Catholic priest friend of mine in Baton Rouge said if I ever wanted to shoot drug dealers on Baton Rouge street corners, he would come along to give them the last rites.

Lastly I felt bad about her confrontation with the mobster Sidney Ludlow, when he said her people would take a mile if they were given a foot. Plus, and I hate to say this, Valerie's gold-and-brown ringlets and her swan neck and trim figure and Indian profile made their impression on my unconscious whether I liked it or not. Get my drift?

It was seven P.M. when we got to Jerry's Landing. It's strange how things work out, at least in my life. Whether in a tragedy or comedy, there seems to be a plan at work. The great irony is that no matter how many times the story is performed on the stage, neither the audience nor the players see the last act coming. The same plots and themes are in Chaucer and the Bible and the Greek myths and Elizabethan theater. But so far little if any wisdom has been passed on to the multitudes. If anything, they seem best at banning or burning what they can't understand.

Check out the French National Assembly under Robespierre.

"How do you want to play this?" Clete said.

Clete's convertible top was up, the sun a molten, dull red on the horizon, Clete behind the wheel, Valerie in the passenger seat, with me in back. The fog in the swamp looked like dirty rags drifting above the ponds and lily pads and cattails. In fact, I thought of death and Matthew Arnold's shingles sliding down the edge of the earth and a patch of pinkish-blue sky in the west that one day might prove to be the last light we will ever see. Oh, I know this is a macabre depiction of the Earth, but the natural world does not die. It re-creates itself. That's a hard standard to beat.

Clete had asked how we should play it. We never had a chance to decide. "That's Sidney Ludlow's car," Valerie said.

"Where?" I said.

"In the shadow of the saloon," she replied. "He's wearing an overcoat and a fedora and shades. There're three or four other greaseballs with him."

Clete pulled the Caddy to the side of the dirt road and cut the headlights. "Get my binoculars from the glove box, please," Clete said.

There were two or three shacks between the dirt road and the marsh. The shacks had electricity but not plumbing. The adults and children on porches or dirt yards saw us and went inside. Clete put the binoculars to his eyes. "Dig this," he said.

"Dig what?" I said.

"The guy next to Sidney Ludlow. That's his son."

"How do you know?"

"I've seen his photos," he said. "He's supposed to be impaired in some way. What's he doing in a shithole like Carlucci's Landing?"

"Can I see?" Valerie asked.

"Sure, sorry," Clete said and handed them to her. Then he looked at the floor behind the seat. "What's in the duffle bag, Dave?"

"Odds and ends," I said.

"I'm not supposed to know what I'm allowing in my own car?"

"It's backup," I said.

Clete's eyes narrowed.

"It's all right," I said.

"I've heard that one before," he said, and turned forward. "Let's ramble, children."

We rolled down toward the saloon, tires clicking, the board sidewalk and the lights and tinkling music like a leftover from another century.

Ludlow's entourage went inside the saloon without acknowledging us, except for Ludlow's son. He must have been twenty-five. He was tall and wore a golf cap and loafers and a sweater with buttons and had a caved-in chest. He looked straight at us, then smiled as though we were friendly creatures from another dimension. Valerie got out of the car and slammed the door, tucking in her shirt with her thumbs, her handcuffs hanging from the back of her jeans, her presence in the sheriff's department becoming stronger and stronger, and a little threatening. Clete twisted around in the seat. "What's in that damn bag?" he said.

"The chopper and three mags."

"Are you crazy?" he said.

"Why'd you give it to me?"

Clete raised his arms and pressed his fists on his temples.

"If it ever goes down with Jerry or Ludlow, you'll wish we brought a flamethrower," I said.

"The day you start acting like me is the day you've gone nuts, big mon. Anyway, *c'est la vie.*"

He got out of the car with his crutches and porkpie hat, then smelled the air. "Lordy, Lordy, isn't the world a fine place to be? In that spirit, I can surely go for a bowl of crawfish gumbo."

We lined up at the bar. It was a weekday night, but a crowd was building—rounders and bounders and gamblers and midnight ramblers. Ludlow and his fellow greaseballs were farther down the bar from us. Look, let's get something out of the way here. The word "greaseball" is not ethnic. It's a state of mind. The greaseballs call themselves greaseballs. "Greaser" is another matter. Jerry Carlucci was among the greaseballs, but looking at us and clearly perturbed. Clete hammered on the bar. "How about some service, Jerry?" he said. "You got your head up your ass again?"

This was the man who five minutes ago accused me of starting trouble.

Jerry walked the length of the bar, wearing his black suit and sequined shirt, his mustache a pencil-line. He ignored Clete and me and let his eyes settle on Valerie. "Welcome to my club, officer," he said. "What can I help you with?"

"She's Detective Valerie Benoit, Jerry," I said.

"I'm sure she is," he said, his gaze on her. "You're from the Benoit family?"

"My family is none of your business," she said. "We want to talk to some of your musicians."

"Can you tell me why?" he said. "Did they commit a crime? Are they planning to commit one?"

"You cut that shit out, Jerry," I said.

"She can speak for herself, can't she?" he asked.

Valerie was between Jerry and me. "Let me handle this, Dave," she said.

I raised up my hands in mock surrender. She turned back to Jerry. "We'd like to talk to any of your guitar pickers, particularly if they play Gibsons."

"Sure, Detective, but if you don't mind, can we wait until they take a break?" he said.

"You've got it, Mr. Carlucci," she said.

"Y'all want a drink on the house?" Jerry said.

"A glass of water for me," she said.

Clete was chewing gum, his gaze sliding around the building. "Hey, bartender!" he called out. "We need a diet Dr Pepper and a gumbo and a draft beer in a frosted mug!"

"Coming up," the bartender said.

It looked like things might go okay. The dangerous moment had passed. Jerry was a wise guy but not a racist, and Clete had gone back to being Clete.

But in the time we had been talking to Jerry, Ludlow and a couple of his greaseballs had gone to the restroom and Ludlow's son had wandered over to us.

"Hi, I'm Bedford," he said. His face was childlike, his cheeks rosy, his bones probably as frail as a bird's. "You're here about the music, aren't you? I play the mandolin. I'm going to hunt for treasure, too."

Clete looked at me and raised his eyebrows. Why would Bedford Ludlow know about our interest in the musicians? Now two of the greaseballs were coming after the Bedford boy. There was no doubt about the intensity of their mission, either. Valerie stepped in their way. "Your friend here is fine. He was just introducing himself," she said. "So get the broom out of your ass."

"Is that right, Bedford?" one of the greaseballs said. "They weren't asking you questions about your father?"

"I told them about the treasure."

The greaseball had close-set eyes and wide shoulders, his maroon flannel sleeves rolled tight, his biceps as round and big as softballs, his chest coated with black hair, his skin like whipcord, the kind of man who tears apart wood boxes for fuel.

"Step back," Valerie told him.

"Who you think you're talking to, *schvartze*?" the short greaseball said.

"What'd you call me?" she said.

"It means 'nigger.' You didn't know that?"

The short man's companion was over six feet and probably weighed three-fifty and had a stomach like a sack of wet concrete. He grinned. "But you're cute."

"That's it," Valerie said. "Both of you assholes are busted. Turn around and put your hands behind your neck."

She'd blown it. We went there to find the killer of Clemmy Benoit, and instead we were going to bust a couple of throwbacks who would be out of the can in a half hour.

"Look at me, you two pieces of shit," I said. "Get your asses out the back door and stay out or I'll slapjack every bone in your head. Are you hearing me? If I have to, I'll kneecap both of you. I've done it before. Look at me and tell me I'm lying."

Valerie started to speak, but I stepped in front of her and put my hand on Bedford's shoulder and kept my back to the greaseballs, hoping they'd believe my rhetoric. "You doing all right, pal?" I said. "How about you and me walk up by the bandstand?"

"I'd like that," he said.

I started walking just as Ludlow came out of the restroom. He snapped his fingers at another pair of greaseballs, then headed for us. I felt like I was in a dirigible and someone had just lit a cigarette.

"Don't get the wrong idea, Mr. Ludlow," I said. "We don't make use of people's families. You've got a fine son. He has our respect."

Ludlow lifted his chin. His eyes were hidden behind his dark glasses, his tie and collar so tight I thought he was about to choke. "None of yous knows what it takes to be a success. You! Yeah, I said you! You could be somebody. The African woman, same thing. Youd got brains, but no courage. If my son had a couple of your physical gifts, he'd own this whole parish. Yous couldn't clean his toilet."

"I'm going to move on, Mr. Ludlow," I said. "But we'll be talking again."

I slipped my hand under Valerie's elbow and walked her across the dance floor, gesturing for Clete to follow.

"Are you just gonna let this happen?" Valerie said.

"Yes," I said.

"Everybody within a radius of twenty yards heard everything that bastard said to you," she replied. "Don't let him get away with it."

"Lose the dog shit."

"*What did you say?*" she said.

"Clemmy Benoit deserves better than a quarrel with a man who hides behind dark glasses at night and can't speak his own language. Now show me the musicians who might have known Clemmy."

But she had lit the fuse, even though it was a long one.

We didn't get anywhere with the musicians. They shook their heads and looked into space and sucked their teeth and tapped their feet nervously or admitted they knew her but only "slightly" or "a long time ago." I didn't hold it against them. Throughout America there are witnesses to heinous crimes, or even minor ones, who have the protective security of fish chum. Actually it's worse. A claimant's name and address are automatically given to a defendant's attorney, and when the defendant gets out of the slammer, the claimant or witness is seldom notified. Think I'm jerking you around? Have a fling at the system and see how you feel. The maniac knows where you live, but you don't know where he is. Isn't that fine?

Bedford stayed close to his father during the interview of the musicians, but all the while he kept looking at me and Clete. His mention of "treasure" had given us information that probably troubled his father, but Ludlow didn't take his son to task. The Mob might be depraved, but most of them are kind and protective with their children. Go figure.

Clete gave up talking to the musicians and went to the bar to order a cup of coffee. Valerie and I followed him.

"Let's wrap it up," I said.

"Yeah," he said. "I've got a bad feeling. Like this really stinks."

"Yeah," I said. "Like somebody spit in my ear."

Valerie's eyes were downcast. She remained silent.

"I'm going to talk to Ludlow," I said. "I'll be right back."

"What's the deal?" Clete asked.

"I really don't know," I said. "I'll tell you when I figure it out."

I walked to Ludlow's table at the back of the saloon. The band was playing Jerry Lee Lewis's "Boogie Woogie Man from Tennessee."

I suddenly realized what had been bothering me all evening. It was the world in which we found ourselves, as opposed to the world represented by the murdered girl. She was delivered to my yard in the nude, but really not in the nude at all. It was the world that was lewd; the girl was angelic, her breast decorated with roses, her eyes looking straight into mine, with a message from the spheres to which we give little thought. The ancient Greeks would recognize Clemmy, and so would Tennessee Williams and William Shakespeare. It's us who are blind and deaf.

"Can I have a word with you, Mr. Ludlow?" I said.

"You again?" he said.

"One of your men racially insulted Detective Benoit," I said. "That's the second time it's happened. How about sending your messenger over to the bar and let him say he's sorry."

He raised his chin. "You got something buggin' you. Problems of conscience or something. Maybe you and Jerry Carlucci can be a team. Call yourselves the 'Weeping Brothers' or something."

"Leave Jerry out of this."

"Get out of here," he replied.

"I'll think about it," I said. "Okay."

"Okay, what?"

"Just okay."

Then I started walking away, just as the short man who was made like a steel trap laughed. No, he didn't just laugh; he hawked up a gob of phlegm and drained it from his mouth into a napkin and tied the corners and bounced it off the back of my head. I cannot quite describe what that felt like.

Regardless, my old enemy kicked into overdrive, a nameless rage I have never been able to conquer. I heard a click, then a whooshing sound, then I was in a room roaring with smoke and flame, and I gripped the short man around his thighs, like you would a dangling dummy, and smashed him cleanly through a tabletop.

But I didn't stop there. I knocked him down each time he tried to get up, then stomped the side of his head and knotted his coat in my fingers and flung him into the wall. In the meantime, the greaseball who had the waistline of a whale was coming at me. I knew this time my luck had run out. The red-black inferno had been temporary, and I was on my own. I had my .45 auto but I would not draw it. I pressed my palm around my gold medal and waited for whatever was going to happen.

Then Clete Purcel, without his crutches, came from the edge of my vision and split a chair on the whale's head, then smacked another chair across his face. The whale keeled over just like a whale.

What happened next is hard to remember. The building was pandemonium. Somebody yelled "Fire!" People were screaming; some went through the windows; Clete was flinging beer bottles and beer mugs at the greaseballs. "Come on, Dave!" he shouted. "This is great!"

I got Valerie out the front door. People were running in all directions or driving down the road as fast as they could. The sun had not set but was little more than a dreamy yellow-red flame descending into the bay; while the backs of alligators slid through the froth, the tide was pushing into the marsh.

Valerie was shaking inside my arm. "I never saw anything like this," she said. "It's like civilization died."

"That's well put," I said. "You should contact the Department of Tourism."

I walked her to Clete's Caddy before someone discovered the Thompson .45 machine gun Clete gave me.

Chapter Twenty-Seven

One evening later, on Wednesday, Alafair and I went bowling. Nothing was made of the riot at Jerry Carlucci's saloon. In fact, no one knew in which parish it legally existed. Plus, the keepers of hot pillow joints rarely dialed 911 on themselves.

I picked up a bowling ball and was just about to address the pins when I saw Alafair's eyes suddenly go past me. I eased down the ball and turned around. Somehow I wasn't surprised to see Jerry Carlucci; I felt that one way or another our personal war would never be over, at least not until one of us gave up this earth.

"How about giving me ten minutes, Dave?" Jerry said.

"Another time, okay?" I said.

"I'm not asking much," he said. "Quit being a hardnose, huh?"

"Go ahead, Dave," Alafair said.

I set down my ball and went into the lounge with Jerry. He ordered for both of us without asking what I wanted. It was an offensive gesture, but I let it slide.

"Pretty crazy last night," he said.

"I don't remember it," I said.

The bartender put a diet Doc in front of me and a Vodka Collins in front of Jerry. "Can I have your word you won't talk about some private things I got on my mind?"

"No, I can't do that," I said.

"A hard-ass to the end," he said.

"I'm an officer of the law, Jerry. What do you expect?"

"It's not legal stuff."

"I'm not a psychiatrist or a minister," I said.

"All right, fuck it then."

"Lower your voice."

"Do you tell Purcel that?"

"Yeah, I do."

He rubbed his forehead. "It's about 'Nam. Two days ago I was stopped at the train track and the bells and the crossing guards went off and I was trapped inside maybe one foot from the tracks. I just sat there looking at these images inside my head."

"What were the images?"

"I saw a giant praying mantis going across the land. It was eating all the people. I tried to make it stop, but it wouldn't listen. It's still going on."

"Have you talked to a shrink? Maybe someone at the V.A.?"

"Yeah, they're good guys. But it didn't help. Hey, you know what I'm talking about, here. The stamp is on your soul, not your brain."

"What does the praying mantis represent, Jerry?"

He rotated his neck and dug his fingers into the back of it. "It's me, isn't it? That means I'm not gonna get any rest, huh?"

He drank from his glass, then looked at the mirror behind the bar. Some loud bowlers came and left. Jerry's expression never changed. Know the term the "thousand-yard stare"? Jerry had it. I shook his shoulder.

"What?" he said, blinking.

"You just owned up," I said. "You got to flush Shitsville, Jerry. The world is a grand place."

"You don't get it, Dave. I've owned up to what? I don't know what I did over there. I stayed chemically zoned on anything I could get my hands on. My head glowed in the dark. The guy we called 'Pappy' was one year older than me. We were just kids."

"You have no memory of shooting people?"

His face twitched. "Yeah, I do. But I don't know what I shot. The warrant officer said I was a Section Eight. He didn't want me on his Huey."

Misery comes in many ways. But I don't think I ever saw more misery in a man's face than I did in his.

"Remember that night we fought in the finals in Shreveport?" I said.

"At the Gloves, you mean?"

Yeah," I said. "You bounced me off the ropes. I thought you were going to rip my head off."

"Yeah, but in the second round you split my eyebrow. I still think you had concrete inside your gloves. What'd you put in them?"

"You know that's not true, Jerry."

"Yeah, I know. Did you ever think you could have become me and I could have become you?"

I let my gaze follow a group of high school kids going out the door. "I never thought about that, Jerry. A guy just does the best he can. I think that's about all we're supposed to do."

"I kind of got off the track after my old man got mobbed-up, and your old man got blown up on that derrick. I think that was a rotten deal, huh?"

I took a sip from my glass and looked straight ahead. I didn't like the comparison Jerry was making. Aldous Robicheaux never complained; he was brave and honest to the end of his life. The same with my mother. She was driven to her death because of poverty and desperation and the machinations of an evil man.

"You came home in seventy-three," I said. "Why don't you let it go? It's time, isn't it?"

"You think so? I haven't offended you or anything or messed up worse than I already have?"

"No," I said. "Of course not."

"But there's something you're not saying, right?"

"Yeah, the company you're keeping," I said.

"You're talking about Ludlow?"

I shrugged and looked at the bowlers smacking the pins in the alley.

"Maybe Ludlow's got some virtues," he said.

" 'The prince of darkness is a gentleman.' That's from William Shakespeare."

"That's a pretty good line. But I got obligations, meaning 'debts.' "

"Tell Ludlow to eat shit," I said.

"You're not a fan?"

"You're a stand-up guy, Jerry. You always were. Why do you hang around with guys like Ludlow?"

"You mean that about me being a stand-up guy?"

"Yeah, that last three rounds at the Gloves was the worst fight I was ever in," I said. "You swallowed your blood and never showed your pain. That's class, podna."

"Lower your voice," he said, grinning, the first time I had seen him do so in years. There was also a tear in the corner of his eye.

"How'd it go?" Alafair said.

I was back at our seats in the lanes. Alafair had continued by herself. She was very good, just as she was at tennis and swimming, and I suspected Jerry regretted that he never married and had a daughter like Alafair. Also, I did not want Jerry around her.

"I think Jerry is a tragedy, and I think that's because our country is a tragedy."

She stopped, with a ball cupped in her hands, her fingers inserted in the holes. "What do you mean?"

"Our politicians send young people to wars they don't fight themselves, and let the same young people carry the guilt when they come back home. The guys who do this are what Dwight Eisenhower called 'the Military-Industrial Complex.' No one pays attention to that statement anymore."

"You do," she said.

She bent her knees, advanced on the lane, and hit a strike. "You're up," she said.

On Thursday morning Helen called Valerie Benoit into her office. Through her window I could see the sunlight on the park and the live oaks and what seemed like all the good things of the Earth.

"I got an anonymous phone call about twenty minutes ago," Helen said. "Y'all's visit to Carlucci's Landing wasn't a total waste."

"You're kidding?" I said.

"A guy called and said he overheard y'all questioning the members of the band."

"He wasn't one of them?" I asked.

"I can't be sure," she replied. "He sounded on the square." She looked down at a piece of notebook paper on her blotter. "He said, 'Miss Clemmy was a good girl and it ain't right what's been done to her. It's that criminal that's got hair all over his body, the one that smells bad and likes to bust up people. He's the one you want.'"

Helen looked up from her blotter. "You know who he's talking about?" she asked.

Valerie looked at me, too.

"Yeah, I do," I said. "I smashed him through a table and stepped on his head and threw him into a wall."

"At Carlucci's Landing?" she said.

"Yeah, I'm pretty sure that's the guy."

"How do you get into these things, Dave?" she said.

"Just a knack I have."

"Pull that son of a bitch in no matter what you have to do," she said.

"Copy that."

"And bwana not screw this up unless bwana want to change vocation. Like cutting city lawns."

"Wouldn't think of it."

"Dave, we can't mess this up. Our whole of life is in the balance."

"You mean the casinos?"

"I think that's for starters."

This was a strange thing for Helen to say. Her eyes were unfocused, and there was no heat or force in her voice. I started to say something, but I didn't, and if I had, I think she would have chosen not to hear me.

I went back to my office and called Jerry's saloon. I was surprised. Jerry answered.

"How about getting on the sunny side for a change?" I said.

"What do you mean?"

"I need your help. Who's the dude who spat in a napkin and threw it on my head? In my hair, to be specific."

"The guy you used to break a table in half?"

"I didn't remember the details, actually. You know me. Blackouts and all that jazz."

"Why you wanna know?"

"I thought he'd like to join our book club."

"Dave, I'm not in the business of handing over the names of Sidney Ludlow's employees."

"Are you going to front points for a geek who spits on your friends?"

"Sorry, Dave, No-can-do. I'm saying that from the heart." He hung up.

Valerie Benoit had been sitting in my office while I talked to Jerry. "Let me try," she said.

"Have at it."

She dialed Jerry's number. When he picked up, she immediately went to work. "I'm putting us on speakerphone, Mr. Carlucci. Sir,

Dave Robicheaux has enormous respect for you. He's told me about all your good times, too. He could have capped the hairball who spit on him and got away with it. But he didn't. Are you gonna side-up with a creep who smells worse than GAPO . . . ? What's GAPO? The acronym for 'gorilla armpit odor.'"

There was a pause, then Jerry said, "That's Jack Raider. When it comes to women, he's got a dork for a brain. He also plugs it into the lamp socket occasionally. Be careful."

"Where can we find him?"

"There's a shithole or two around Breaux Bridge. I'm talking about dogfights, bottom of the barrel stuff."

"You're a gentleman and a scholar, Mr. Carlucci," she said, and eased the receiver into the receptacle.

"Pretty good," I said.

"Have you been to one of those places in Breaux Bridge?"

"I'm not sure," I said. I didn't want to say anything else. That's where my mother turned her first trick. It's funny how things work out, huh?

I made two or three calls, then that evening told Alafair where I was going and with Valerie drove an unmarked car down the old two-lane outside Breaux Bridge into St. Martin Parish and passed the old gambling joints and red-light houses and barns where cockfights were once held regularly and dogs ripped each other apart for the amusement of people who called themselves Christians. However, that was not the only activity that went on there.

"You're kind of quiet," Valerie said.

"The Breaux Bridge Highway doesn't bring back warm memories for me," I said.

"Something happen?"

"A pimp named Mack got my mother on the spike when my father was in the parish jail. Then Mack told her she could make good money as a dance-girl, 'a hostess,' he said, at one of those shitholes."

"What happened to your mother?"

"A couple of gangsters swarmed on her like crabs."

"Jesus," she replied. "What happened to Mack?"

I was driving, the left tire on the other side of the yellow stripe. A car swerved away from my fender, its horn blowing, its headlights bouncing inside the interior of our car. "I'd rather talk about it another time."

"Yeah, I think that's a good idea," she said, her hands braced on the dashboard.

I turned off on a road and went up a dirt levee that extended for miles into the Atchafalaya Basin, a full moon high in the sky, under it a flooded woods with ponds that were as silvery as mercury, dotted with dead tupelos that were hollow and flanged at the waterline, rotted as teeth, perhaps gators sleeping amidst them, waiting to be pounded like Congo drums.

It was not difficult to find Jack Raider. The South may love John Calvin during the day, but from the Mason-Dixon to the Gulf of Mexico the darkest creatures of the Middle Ages are still alive and well in Dear Old Dixie.

The levee descended into a flat strip of land next to a channel and a chain of small islands. On it was a paintless wood building with a peaked, rusty tin roof and two lightning rods. The lights inside were powered by a generator, and several cars and trucks were parked in front and a half dozen boats dragged up on a sandy beach streaked with oil. I pulled behind a cane break and sump full of willows and cut the engine.

Through the front windows I could see two men stripped to the waist in a boxing ring, smeared with blood, eye-gouging, kicking, aiming at the genitals. There was a light over our heads, but no one seemed to care. The referee served no purpose, either, other than to pour water on a split eyebrow or a mashed nose or ask the fighter if he wanted to stop.

One of them was Jack Raider. I thought I had put him out of action. I had to hand it to him. His upper body was bright with sweat, the muscles in his back as pronounced as rope.

He saw me through the window glass and lowered his gloves, grinning, his teeth red with blood. Then he spat in his opponent's face and right-crossed him, shaking a halo of sweat from his hair.

Then he pointed one glove at me, either as a greeting or notification I was next.

There were no women in the crowd, at least that I saw.

"Ready?" I said.

Valerie looked at the ring. "Yeah," she said. "Sure. Let's do it."

"Maybe you should stay here and back me up."

"I can't handle it?"

"We don't have any legal status here, Val," I said. "The people who come to these fights are morally insane."

Her gold ringlets hung over her forehead, her skin was dusty and smooth and beautiful in the moonlight. She pushed the ringlets out of her eyes, then looked up at me.

"Sometimes when I'm afraid, I think about Willie Francis," she said. "He was a child, electrocuted and burned twice, once by drunkards. In the last photo taken of him, he was smiling. How can anyone have that much courage, particularly a child? Could I ever be that brave?"

That was a hard question to answer.

"Let's hit and get it," I said.

We went through the front door and closed it behind us. Every set of eyes in the building was staring at us, but mostly at Valerie. The referee put his hands on each fighter, stopping the fight. No one in the building moved or spoke.

"My name is Detective Dave Robicheaux." I said, raising my badge. "This is my partner Detective Benoit. We are not here to interrupt your sporting event. We just need to have a brief moment with Mr. Raider."

Raider kept dancing on the canvas, his gloves in front of him. The air was full of sweat and cigarette smoke and the stink of urinated beer and expectorated chewing tobacco in Styrofoam cups. A barbecued pig was laid out on a table where a man was cutting meat.

"Did anyone hear me?" I said. "Who's in charge?"

Still no response.

"You're out of your territory, slick," Raider said.

Slick? Don't you like people who give other people names?

Valerie stepped in front of me and held up her badge. "I grew up in St. Martin Parish and know some of you gentlemen," she said. "You're better than this. You go to church, you own businesses, you make sure your children get a good education. Do you really want to associate with a man like Jack Raider?"

She paused for a few seconds. A few men looked down at the floor.

"This is not an exaggeration," she said. "Jack Raider kills people for hire. He doesn't have a soul. Ask yourself if you want him walking the streets beside your children."

At first there was no sound. Then someone coughed. Another man blew his nose in his handkerchief. Someone popped a tab on a beer. Then someone else said, "I don't know about you boys, but I'm getting me some fresh air. What about y'all?"

That did it. They filed into the dark, under the stars, the moon cold and clean, woodsmoke drifting above the channel, getting into their cars and trucks and outboards, leaving behind the barbecued pig.

Valerie and I stayed in the building. "You want to get ahead of your situation, Jack?" I said.

He smelled himself. "What situation?" he asked.

"The murder of Clemmy Benoit," Valerie said.

"Nobody is talking to you, bitch," he said.

Valerie looked at me. "Should we tell him?"

I had no idea what she was talking about. "That's up to you, Detective," I said.

"Tell me what?" Raider said.

"It's this way, Mr. Raider," she said. "Sidney Ludlow says you're not only psychotic but a German who can never be a made guy, because that's the same as being a Nazi."

Raider's eyes were bulging. He pulled his laces off his gloves with his teeth. His opponent went out the back door. Raider threw his gloves one at a time back in the ring. "I ain't a Nazi and I ain't stupid," he said. "In fact, I'm out of here. But the old man is gonna hang yous from meat hooks. If you don't believe me, I've seen him do it."

"Who's the old man?" I said.

"Who is he? What's with you, man?" he replied. "You got some brain disease? You got some kind of guilt about niggers? What is it?"

"I killed innocent people," I said.

"Well, I think you're nuts. And with that I'm leaving."

Raider picked a towel off a ring rope and wiped his armpits. "Except one other thing. I think she wants a sniff."

He lifted the towel in Valerie's face.

I knocked his hand down. "You're under arrest, Raider," I said.

He turned around and stuck out his wrists. "That's great," he said. "It'll be part of my civil suit."

"Let it go, Dave," Valerie said.

"No."

"Come on," she said. 'I don't blame him for being upset. He was probably strapped on the pot days at a time."

"What?" Raider said.

She was right. I had already gotten into it with Raider at Carlucci's Landing and anything I did now was fuel for a shyster. Plus, I had no authority in that parish. "Okay," I said. "Let's go. As for you, Mr. Raider, we'll see you down the track."

He blew his nose in the towel and threw it in the ring. "Yeah, right," he said. "Yeah."

I didn't know what he meant, but I was too tired to care. Actually the evening had a moment that was special, one I had never witnessed in the South or anywhere: I had watched a black woman correct a testosterone-laced crowd of white men who listened to her every word. It wasn't a grand moment in history, but it was certainly a good one. It reminded me of the night I listened to Joan Baez sing "The Night They Drove Old Dixie Down" at Ole Miss. I cried.

We began walking to the car. The sky was like black velvet, and I started to point out the constellations to Valerie. Then she did something I knew would happen at some point in our relationship. I guess those things are just human. But an old man cannot afford the luxury of being a fool, because for him the title is forever.

She let her hand go down my arm and touch the tops of my knuckles. A tingle went all the way to my feet.

I scratched at my hand as if a lone mosquito had bitten it.

"Sorry," she said.

How do you get out of embarrassing situations like this? Answer: You forgive others. You forgive yourself, and most importantly you don't weigh yourself down with the frailties of the heart.

"Excuse me, Valerie," I said. "That speech to these guys was beautiful. They're not bad people. NAFTA took away their jobs, and they started looking around for a leader and found the worst in themselves and others. That's what gave us Huey Long. There'll be more like him, too."

"Can we get to a bathroom?" she said.

"Pardon?"

"I'm about to wet my pants. There's a gas stop about three miles from here. I'm not sure I can make it though."

So much for spiritual abstractions. We got to the cane break where I had parked the car. "Okay," I said. "I'll get you there as fast as I can."

I unlocked the passenger door and waited for her to get in. She was making a groaning sound and obviously she was very uncomfortable. I was no longer thinking about anything else. That was a mistake. I heard feet splashing and someone huffing through the willows and breaking bamboo that was as sharp as board splinters, a wired-to-the-eyes guy chugging with a purpose, one he was determined to achieve, loving his pain, not fazed by broken glass or shellfish in his shoes, reaching a peak not unlike a climax, delighted at the prospect of peeling off the skin of a fellow human being.

I turned and saw Jack Raider coming right at me, his right hand curved inside the knuckle guard of a 1918 Marine Corps trench knife. I had carried my badge but because I was out of my jurisdiction, I had left my firearm under the car seat. Now I was on the passenger side of the car. I figured I had about five seconds before Raider would stab me in the chest, then everywhere else.

Have you ever had this moment? You know your time is up, and in all probability it's because you made an innocent mistake; however, you cannot undo it. Oddly, the primary emotion, fear, which you have fought for a lifetime, is not there. Then you realize a much greater enemy has been waiting for you. It's loneliness. I think that's why men call out for their mothers. But I think the mother figure is also a surrogate for everyone you ever knew, and you want to go back in time and buy them candy canes and balloons and sno'cones and be kind to every creature on Earth, as though they're all God's children.

A Bouncing Betty that tried to tear my hip off gave me that perspective, or what I call "the Edge"—the stepping off place, know what I mean? I also believe I spent thirty seconds in a place I call the Other Side. But who knows? Or cares? At least that was what I thought when I saw Jack Raider cock his trench knife above his head in preparation for splitting my face from my brow to my nose down to my chin.

That's when Clete Purcel stepped out of the cane between me and Raider and swung a long-shaft shovel across Jack Raider's kneecaps, sending him screaming to the ground, then knocked the trench knife out of his hand.

"Where'd you come from?" I said.

"I was behind the building," he said. He picked up the knife and threw it into the channel. "What do you want to do with this guy?"

"I don't know," I said. Raider was rolled into a ball, holding his knees. "What about it, pal? Want to cooperate and dump the greaseballs who call you a Nazi?"

"Blow me, bacon," Raider said.

"What do you say, Valerie?" I asked.

"I say cut him loose. I say spread it around he's a snitch."

"Hey, you can't do that," Raider said.

"Watch me," I said.

Clete drove away in his Caddy, and Valerie and I got in our car and followed him. When I looked in the mirror, I saw Raider standing knee-deep in the saw grass. He looked like the loneliest man in the world. I did not know how correct I was.

Chapter Twenty-Eight

It happened several hours later, early in the A.M. on Friday, in a trailer not far from the levee where he had almost opened me up with the trench knife. A hooker had just left, evidently terrified by the john she had just booked. I almost felt sorry for Jack Raider, as I did with Lloyd D'Anjou. They traded off their lives in service to people who used them for a spit cup. Anyway, Jack Raider went out in spectacular fashion, one that even got the FBI's attention.

The shooter set up his weapon on the hood of a rusted-out car about forty yards from Raider's trailer; the weapon was a German MG-42 machine gun; in the trenches of Russia and France, it was called "the bone saw."

Helen and Valerie and I went to the site at 6:14 A.M. The shooter left the MG on top of the rusted car hood. The belt had jammed in the bolt, but not before more than two dozen shells had been ejected and the trailer had been pocked with holes and the glass blown out of the windows. I went in first; I won't describe the interior. But the big question was the weapon's continued presence at the crime scene. Its stream-like visual lethality made it a dream for collectors and auctioneers. One with the original parts would sell for twenty thousand dollars. Why dump it?

Helen and Valerie had gone into the trailer together and come back out. Their faces were empty, or maybe just tired. The sun was barely above the trees, like a broken egg in the morning steam. Helen had a coffee thermos under her arm. She opened it and offered it to both me and Valerie. Valerie blinked as though she had not understood, then said, 'No, thank you." I shook my head.

"That's the shits, isn't it?" Helen said, nodding at the trailer.

"Did y'all notice something about the angle of fire?" I said.

"Yeah, any round that went long hit that old Airstream that's full of hay bales," Helen replied. "If you want to be imaginative."

"I know what you mean, Sheriff," Valerie said. "But I had a different take on it. I think the guy left us a message. I think by leaving the gun he's saying *adios* to something."

Helen rubbed her face. "Know anybody around here who would fit that profile?"

Valerie hunched her shoulders. "Maybe I'm full of it."

The coroner and sheriff and more emergency vehicles and personnel from St. Martin Parish were arriving. "Where's Purcel?" Helen said.

"Asleep," I said.

"Let me talk to my counterpart and I'll buy y'all breakfast," Helen said, meaning the sheriff from St. Martin.

"Thank you, ma'am," I said.

Sometimes that's the only way you deal with death, and by that I mean you don't deal with it at all; the fucker is just *there*, excuse my language. You can't get rid of it; you can't disremember it; you can't stand its touch or its smell; and most of all don't disrespect it. For good or bad, Old Death knows how to throw a slider.

So we drove to the truck stop down the road, and scarfed up all the ham and scrambled eggs and pancakes we could eat, and tried not to think about mortality, and drank coffee and more coffee, not speaking, staring at the images inside our heads we had just witnessed, wondering when they would appear in our sleep, wondering when and how we would be called.

* * *

On Saturday morning I got up early and put on my old fedora, got in my old black pickup, and drove to a secret place east of Avery Island, down on the Gulf, where my father Big Aldous and I used to bobber-fish for goggle-eye perch with the black people. I was only nine or ten years old back then, and Jerry Carlucci and his father came with us, and we all spoke Acadian French and cleaned and deep-fried the goggle-eye with the black people and had a wonderful time. Mr. Carlucci even brought a fiddle and played "*La Jolie Blon.*" Of course back then Mr. Carlucci was wending his way into the criminal world, which has been the way of many people in our corrupt state. Nonetheless, *la belle Louisiane* was a wonderful place to grow up in, a place that was safe from the rest of world, even though Nazi submarines torpedoed our oil tankers on the southern horizon and we watched them sink in a curl of yellow and red flame.

Mr. Carlucci wasn't all bad, either. He was a master builder of pirogues, and for a gift he carved small models for both Jerry and me. From time to time Jerry would still come to our secret place, and carve small pirogues and give them to any children who wanted them. I hadn't been to our spot in years, but for whatever reason I believed Jerry would be there this particular Saturday. Lordy, Lordy, that's the way it was back then.

I drove down the levee through a bay full of empty duck blinds, blue herons pecking among the shallows, the tide sliding through the cane, a squadron of pelicans high above, hiding in the sun, cocking their wings and diving like aerial bombs into the waves, rising with baitfish in their pouches.

Jerry was sitting in a folding canvas chair at the end of the levee, his Jeep parked next to him, carving a piece of balsa wood. He glanced over his shoulder, then continued his work. I parked behind his Jeep and got out and closed my door.

"How did you know where I was?" he said, not turning around.

"This is our secret place."

"Yeah, but I don't come to it that often," he said.

"You believe in Karma?"

"I can't even spell it."

"Who you kidding, partner?" I said. "You're one of the smartest men I've ever known."

"Lose it, Dave."

"Jerry, why don't you examine what you just said?"

"What do you mean?"

"You consider a compliment an insult," I said. "You think only a con man would think you're intelligent. You should find someplace like Jonestown and sign up."

"Why are you here, Dave?"

"You know about Jack Raider, don't you?"

"Sidney Ludlow told me."

"Have you thought about ordering the newspaper so you don't have to depend on the Mafia to see if it's going to rain?"

"Why do you always figure out a way to make me feel small?" he said.

"Back to the subject, Jerry. The shooter used a German machine gun. Then left it there."

"So?"

"He was a pro, but maybe one who wanted to hang it up."

"You saying it was me?" he asked.

"It crossed my mind. A couple of other authorities had the same feeling."

"Like Helen Soileau and Valerie Benoit?"

"Leave them out of this," I said.

"Leave them out? Valerie Benoit can't wait to cause shit-piles of trouble for lots of people."

"In what way?" I said.

"Claiming that historical artifacts are all over every parish in Southwest Louisiana."

"That's her right."

"The people Valerie Benoit runs with have even gotten Ludlow's autistic kid hyped up. You'd better tell her to knock it off, Dave."

"Would you look at me?" I said.

"Why?"

"Did you pop Raider? Don't look away from me. Did you or didn't you?"

"I don't 'pop' people."

"So who did?"

"I don't know and I don't care," he said. He got up from his chair and dusted the shavings from the carving. "I got to say something."

"Go ahead."

"You think that's what I am?" he said. "A nutcase blowing up people's shit?"

"No."

"You're lying," he said.

"You're the one who's got the reality problem," I said. "You're hooked up with the cartels and maybe white slavery, but you don't hurt people? Do you know how dumb that sounds?"

"I saw your truck coming through my binoculars," he said. "I thought we might catch some goggle-eye."

"I didn't say we couldn't," I said.

"I'm gonna put away my things and let you be, Dave."

"Don't be like that, Jerry."

"You can't say anything you want, then just walk away, Dave."

"Hey, come on, your father and my father are probably looking down on us now," I said.

He folded his chair and threw it in the backseat of his Jeep, them slammed the door and gave me a dirty look.

"Say what you got to say, Jerry."

But he didn't. Instead he opened the Jeep again and took out his carving-in-progress and flung it in the bay.

* * *

On Sunday afternoon the quick-stop service station that served as our Greyhound station made a 911 call to the Department. Sidney Ludlow's son had gotten on the bus with a lunch box and an army e-tool in a drawstring bag and asked to be dropped off "where the treasure hunt is going on."

The dispatcher called Helen at her home, and Helen called me. "His name is Bedford," she said.

"I know his name. Why did you call me, Helen?"

"He gave your name to the bus driver."

"This goes under the title 'social services.' I don't want any connection with Sidney Ludlow."

"Well, Bedford is eating right now. Take him down to Carlucci's Landing or that greaseball condo by Cypremort Point."

"I've had all of Carlucci's Landing I can take, and the greaseballs, too."

"Dave, why do you think I called you? The poor guy probably has an IQ of fifty or so. Who else is gonna handle him?"

"His father?"

She hung up. I took a quart of ice cream out of the icebox, wrapped it in a towel, picked up two bowls and two spoons, and was at the quick-stop in ten minutes. Bedford Ludlow was waiting outside, wearing a long-sleeved candy-striped shirt, a clip-on bowtie, and a gold-and-purple Mike the Tiger cap. He grinned when he saw me, and jumped in my pickup before I could speak.

"I know where the gold bars are, Mr. Robicheaux," Bedford said, his eyes shimmering with light.

"How'd you get my name, partner?"

"You were nice to me when all the fighting started at Jerry's house."

"That's not actually 'Jerry's house.' That's where Jerry works."

I pulled into the traffic and headed toward Cypremort Point.

"Are we gonna hunt for the gold bars?" he said.

"I'm not sure they're out there, Bedford."

"Oh, yes, I've seen them. The dead girl told me all about them."

"The dead girl?"

"Yes, her name is Clemmy. I think she's a colored lady, but she has blue eyes."

I almost hit the curb. "What's the colored lady's last name?"

"That's easy—Benoit. It's French. She told me."

"When did she show you the gold bars, Bedford?"

"I can't remember. That's why I bought an army shovel so I could help dig. My father says always to be ready."

"Does your father know where you are?"

"I'm going to surprise him. He doesn't want to spend time digging. He builds casinos."

"Are you sure you didn't see Clemmy in a dream?"

"No," he said sharply. "You should know better. She was at your house."

"You mean she was found dead at my house?"

"No, she listened to your records."

I pulled into the front of a bait shop and turned off the engine.

"Why are we stopping?" Bedford asked.

"What records are you talking about?"

"The ones with the yodeling songs on them. His name is Jimmie Rodgers."

I couldn't compile the thoughts and confusion going through my head. My right hand was trembling on the gear shift. "Where did you hear the name Jimmie Rodgers?"

"Clemmy told me about him. Clemmy was your daughter's friend."

My heart turned to a kettledrum. "You knew Clemmy Benoit, Bedford?"

He seemed to look inside his own mind. He started to speak again, then his eyes went blank.

"You can talk about her," I said.

"About who?"

"Clemmy," I said.

He pulled on his fingers with one hand, then the other, as though he were cleaning them. "I don't remember some things. I go to sleep instead."

I was losing the thread. Sometimes you let go with impaired people, then later return to the subject. But the mystery usually remains a mystery. Then I remembered the ice cream. I unrolled the towel I had wrapped around the quart of ice cream, spooned it into the two bowls I had brought, and set the bowls on the dashboard. "How about we eat up, Bedford?"

"Yes, sir, I surely like ice cream, Mr. Robicheaux. But we're still gonna go hunting for treasure, aren't we?"

"There are people in your father's business who do not want historical items discovered in Southwestern Louisiana."

"Why?"

"Historical areas are sometimes treated like graveyards. They stop construction. That can mean no more casinos."

"Oh," he said.

"How do you like the ice cream?"

"It's melting. It's gooey all over my pants. I don't like it."

I started the engine and rolled back on the two-lane. The air was warm and the late-afternoon sky pink, and seagulls were cawing over the bait shop and the bay. A man on a shrimp boat was stringing up an alligator gar that must have been five feet long, then he inserted a knife in the white place between the gills and split the stomach all the way to the tail. The gar's guts flopped out on the deck.

I had a problem of conscience. I wanted as much information as I could get about Clemmy, but Bedford could end up dead if it went to the wrong people.

"Bedford, I think it's better that you not talk about Clemmy, unless maybe it's me," I said. "Can you do that?"

His forehead filled with wrinkles. "I already told them."

"Who did you tell?"

"Jack," he replied.

"Jack Raider?"

"Yes, he wanted to help Clemmy and your daughter."

"My daughter?"

"Her name is Alafair. She and Clemmy were friends. That's why I told my father about them. He can protect them."

I felt sick to my stomach. Not just a passing moment, either. Have you ever had food poisoning? Maybe a dose from a cow that died of anthrax?

"You don't look good, Mr. Robicheaux," Bedford said.

"I see your father's condo up ahead," I said. "I think the sheriff has already notified your father about your safety, so I'll walk up to your door and make sure you get inside. Then I'll be on my way."

"You said you were gonna take me to the treasure area."

"No, I did not," I said.

"But you acted like you did. I'm gonna tell."

"Tell what?"

"You tricked me." He threw the ice cream container and his bowl and spoon and the towel out the passenger window, then stuck his head outside to watch them bounce along the roadside. "That's funny, isn't it?" he said. "You think everything is good, then it falls apart. Clemmy was good to me. She touched her hand to my forehead and kissed my eyes."

He started stomping his feet on the floor mat, his eyes teary, his mouth like an enfant's, stiff and trembling with uncertainty. "When is she gonna come back?" he said.

Then he fell asleep, his eyes half-lidded.

Thanks, Helen.

Chapter Twenty-Nine

Alafair was waiting for me when I got back home. It was still Sunday, and like all Sundays, the sun seemed to resist sinking in the trees, or on the horizon, or on the ocean, as though the source of our warmth did not want to desert us.

"Sorry I'm late for supper," I said.

"It's okay," she said. "Sit down. I've made Mexican food."

She told the truth. She made it from scratch, and probably with a fair amount of trouble. Alafair did not like to cook. I hated to tell her about my experience with Bedford Ludlow.

"Sidney Ludlow's son got lost and I had to take him back to his father," I said.

"Yeah?"

"I guess he's what's called an 'autistic savant.' But with a nasty edge."

"Go ahead."

"He said he saw Clemmy Benoit two nights ago. He knew about your friendship with Clemmy, and he knew about my Jimmie Rodgers records."

Alafair stopped eating and looked out the window. The oak trees were full of robins, starting their long haul back to the north, the bottom of the sky raining, the pinkness in the clouds dimming, turning green.

"He must have known Clemmy," she said. "But that means he knew her when she was in the hands of Ludlow's goons, if that's who killed her."

"But he seems to think his father was protecting her."

"Well, don't worry about it," she said. "You did a good deed. That's all that matters."

She knew better though. If Ludlow's people knew that Alafair and Clemmy were friends, even if only through a drama class or a visit to our home, they probably would try to get the information from Alafair they could not torture out of Clemmy.

I wanted to load up the .45 Thompson Clete gave me and wipe Ludlow's lowlifes off the map.

"Cheer up, Dave," Alafair said, and restarted eating. "You want some iced tea?"

"No, that's all right," I replied.

"You like sun tea. I'll get it."

She scraped back the chair and opened the icebox and lifted out the pitcher of tea and let the door swing shut on its weight. Then she looked through the window and down the slope and dropped the pitcher, breaking and splattering it all over the linoleum.

"Oh, Jesus," she said.

"What is it?" I said, getting up.

She crossed her arms across the top of her stomach, as though she had been punched. "It's the shaggy guy. I just saw him. He's running toward the Shadows."

I got a flashlight from a drawer and went outside into the gloaming of the day and walked along the bayou's edge until I reached the back lawn of the Shadows. I saw no footprints. However, our unwanted visitor had been there, I had no doubt. This time he left an odor that was like offal in an incinerator. What's more, I swore I saw the backyard of the 1834 plantation home shake, then become still again.

I told Alafair none of this when I returned to our kitchen and our lighted windows and the comfort of our simple but fine home.

* * *

I've had many losses in my life, as I'm sure you have. And I'm also sure you faced them with courage and the ability to bear a terrible burden without transferring your pain to others. I suspect, too, that these particular virtues define you, as I hope they define me. Why? Because in our darkest hours we can take solace in the knowledge that we share what is best in the human family.

However, I think there's a flaw in the gene pool that I don't understand, other than to say it makes me ashamed of my kindred. I'm talking about the indifference to foreign wars. Oh yes, we have the politicians who love war, although they do not attend them, and the lobbyists who kneel before the weapons industry, but I'm talking about those who watch napalm sliding through a Third World village or a two-thousand-pound bomb bringing down ten-story apartment buildings filled with civilians in the middle of a Middle Eastern city, and walk away from their television sets unphased.

To this day Alafair does not know her original name. Or the names of her father and mother. Or the names of the soldiers who murdered almost all the adults in her village and left the children to find their way. The issue, of course, is neocolonialism. But is anyone bothered? You know the answer to that. So I ask myself why I killed those people in Southeast Asia. Do you know what happened almost immediately after the Vietnam war? The Chrysler Company built a factory there, and the others followed.

The point is I wasn't going to lose Alafair. There are contracts you make with yourself and never break. You can't even call it brave. You go to a place inside your heart and listen to a tiny voice that tells you it will never let you down. You do not know if the voice is a man's or a woman's or a child's. In fact, you don't care. Nor do you feel extraordinary. Nor do you ever tell anyone about the conversation.

It's called character. Tell me I'm wrong.

* * *

After work Monday I asked Valerie Benoit to walk with me and sit on a stone bench between the library and the grotto of Jesus's mother and the home where Joel Chandler Harris, a former Confederate who after the war became an advocate for the rights of black people, lived in a two-story house among the live oaks and created Uncle Remus.

"I need your confidence, Valerie. If things go wrong, the same people who tortured Clemmy Benoit are going to get their hands on Alafair."

Her face drained. "How? Or why? I don't get it."

We were in deep shade, and the stone was damp and cold and hard through my slacks. I felt irritated because she did not understand. "Bedford Ludlow says he has seen gold bars. That's obviously a fantasy, but that doesn't matter. Sidney Ludlow doesn't want anyone digging up historical objects that will give his enemies the legal means of shutting him down."

"His casino plans?" she asked.

"What do you think?"

Her face flinched. "I know you're upset, but getting angry isn't going to make things better."

This is the kind of rhetoric that causes a popsicle stick to snap inside older people's heads. "I want to see justice for Willie Francis and I want to see the casinos blown off the planet, but I don't want my daughter hurt in the meantime," I said.

"We're not going to let that happen."

"Don't even breathe a sentence like that. It shows arrogance, non-experience, and plain stupidity," I said. "The bad guys always have the upper hand. We don't know where they are, but they can put bombs under our cars or mail them to our houses. We have to get a warrant to use their bathroom. The average lunatic can buy a bump-stock equivalent of a fully automatic rifle with his credit card."

She was nodding her head as I spoke, looking at the ground, obviously hiding the injury I was doing. When I stopped, she said, "May I speak now?"

"Yes," I said.

"There's another way the system works. It has categories. I'm in two or three. I'm black, I'm a woman, and I'm dumb enough to think you might be different."

"I apologize, Valerie. I can't mess this one up. These people will kill my daughter. It's the kind of situation you can't undo."

There was a long moment while she stared at the leaves and new grass coming in. She was wearing jeans and tennis shoes and a jersey with her gun belt and her handcuffs pulled through the belt. "Will you look at me?"

"Sure."

"What do you see?"

"A fine lady. A good cop. A woman with great courage."

She got up and ran down the horseshoe driveway crying, winter's leftover leaves scattering like desiccated butterflies all around her.

I went right over to Clete's 1930 motor court on the bayou. He was in his skivvies, doing push-ups and leg-lifts in front of his television set. I didn't see his crutches anywhere. Just as I closed the door hailstones began clicking on the roof. His purchased video of the 1928 silent film *The Passion of Joan of Arc* was playing on his TV screen. I was always cautious when Clete went back into the fifteenth century, either in his head or while watching the film. As you know, Cletus had many personalities. The one to watch out for was Joan's medieval knight errant escort, Sir Clete.

"What's going on, noble mon?" he said.

"Sidney Ludlow probably knows that Alafair was a friend of Clemmy Benoit."

Clete froze the video. "How'd that happen?"

I told him.

"That's not good." He looked at the television screen. The actress who played Joan, Renée Falconetti, had just tilted her head, and a soulful expression seemed captured on her face in a way that would never leave her, not out of fear for herself but for the benighted world that could impose such cruelty on a young, illiterate girl set upon by wolves.

"Have the Feds given y'all any help with the Raider homicide?" Clete said.

"Just about the machine gun," I said. "No prints, not even on a shell, no collector paperwork, no history of any kind."

"The Feds think it's a hit?"

"They know button men don't leave behind their machine guns."

"You talk to Jerry Carlucci?" he asked.

"Of course."

"He told you to get lost or worse?" he said.

"That's close."

He got up from the rug and started to turn off the television, but paused and looked at the sorrow in Joan's face. These were the kinds of moments Clete never shared. He went somewhere that didn't have clocks or horizons and waited until the light went out of his eyes, then he would walk off. But this time he remained fixed on Joan's image.

"Hey, Cletus," I said. "You got a cold diet Doc?"

"Did you know that carbonated water can give you gallstones? That's right, the cocksuckers who make it know that and don't care as long as they can get their money. So it's over the gunwales with carbonated water."

"I feel relieved already."

"What are you so touchy about?" he said.

"I tried to explain to Valerie Benoit why Alafair was in jeopardy. I sent her down the library driveway in tears."

"*Dave*, what's the real problem?"

"I just told you."

"No, you didn't. The real problem is you're lonely. You also never got over Annie's murder and you keep blaming yourself for it."

"Knock it off, Clete."

"I know you, noble mon. You went into the Garden a long time ago and still have one foot in it. You got to shake it, Streak."

"Just lay off me, will you?"

"Hey, I'll tell you what your other problem is, too. Valerie Benoit is lookie-lookie and ready to boogie. Except you're not gonna take advantage of her, so you walk around with your Johnson in lockdown and wonder why you feel miserable, night and day, and particularly night, *diggez-vous*?"

"If you say one more word on this subject, I'm going to leave. By the way, where are your crutches?"

"I gave them to the trash man."

"Isn't that a little early?"

"I have friends in high places," he said.

I looked at the frozen image of Joan on the television screen, then back at Clete. There was nothing comic in his expression. "Yeah, you got it," he said.

I knew better than to ask what "it' was.

"I'll see you later, Clete." I put on my fedora and walked out among the hailstones, which were bouncing all over the cottage lawn and driveway. Then I heard Clete behind me. He had on his porkpie hat and was trying to get his slicker on while limping toward me. "Where you going, noble mon?" he said. "I gotta have something to eat. I lost three pounds today. My pants are sliding off."

We ended up at Popeyes. I ordered a salad. Clete ordered enough cholesterol to plug a storm drain, his own cloth napkin tied under his chin, his face beaming.

"Hey," he said.

"What is it?"

"I shoot off my mouth," he replied. "I can't help it."

"I had it coming. I feel bad about Valerie. She's a good kid."

"Kid?"

"Yeah, how old do you think we are?" I said.

"I say blow off that age stuff."

"Yeah, that'll keep you young," I said. "How about adding on another hundred pounds?"

"No, listen to me. There's two sides of the human race. One wants to hang around the Garden of Eden, see, before it got screwed up. And there're others who would jump at a chance to work at Auschwitz."

"Don't say that."

"It's the truth. You know it. I bet at least thirty percent of the population would go along with it."

"Yeah, you're right," I replied. "All that's depressing. But right now we haven't made a case on Elton Foot who probably ripped a man apart with a chainsaw and still works as a pimp and probably does torture jobs for the greaseballs. Also we're no closer to solving the murder of Clemmy Benoit than we were on day one."

"No, what's really depressing is the Willie Francis issue," he said. "How could Jimmie Davis turn down a plea for mercy after the kid had already been electrocuted? How could anybody live with himself?"

Clete's voice was breaking. This was the side of Clete Purcel no one saw. He was carrying someone else's pain from decades ago. And oddly this was the side of him that made him lethally unpredictable.

"Say a prayer for Willie Francis," I said.

"I already did. And I talked to Joan about him, too."

Oops. I kept my eyes flat, my face neutral. But he waited me out. "What did Joan say?" I asked.

"That she's already seen Willie. That he's all right."

I nodded gently. "Could I have some of your fries?"

"Yeah," he said. "Try the mashed potatoes and gravy and biscuits, too. I got to take a drain."

There he went, squeezing between the tables, his napkin hanging over his chest, transitioning from the fifteenth to the twentieth century without anyone noticing.

That night I had the worst dream of my life. Alafair was five years old and standing under a cottonwood tree on the edge of a bluff next to a wheat field somewhere in west Kansas, late in the summer, the wheat seeming to stretch into infinity. She was barefoot and pulling the petals off a sunflower and blowing them with her fingers so they floated off the bluff into a sandy red river below. Alafair was humming to herself, the wind blowing her dress across her knees, a dust devil curling in the distance. Then I heard the thropping of helicopter blades, and out of an orange sun I saw a Huey coming like a giant insect, its shadow streaking across the wheat, Jerry Carlucci hanging in the door, his M60 bursting alight, the rounds gouging a straight dirty-gray line through the field toward Alafair.

She began running, but she didn't have a chance. I went crazy inside the dream. I could not allow it to reach its end. I leaped out of the bed and knocked over my desk lamp and tore the door open and went down the short hallway into Alafair's room and sat on her mattress and covered her with my arms and chest, sure that Carlucci had reached all the way from Vietnam to her bedroom.

"Dave, you're having a nightmare," she said. "It's Alafair. Wake up. I'm all right. Can you hear me?"

Then the little girl grew into a woman whose eyes were filled with pity. I stumbled out of the room into the kitchen, afraid to turn on the light, lest I find one of the bottles I hid in the toolshed or the boathouse years ago.

Chapter Thirty

I walked to work the following morning, trying to shut the dream out of my mind. It was a fine day for it. The hydrangeas and bougainvillea were beaded with moisture in the shade, the bugle vine dripping as bright as gold in the sunlight. I walked up the stairs to my office. The time was 7:56 A.M. A note on the door read: *See me, H.*

I went down the corridor to Helen's office and opened the door without knocking. Why? I was tired of running errands.

"What's up?"

"Oh, just your regular shitstorm. Have a seat."

"Clete did something?" I said.

"Valerie Benoit took a promised day off. I just got a call from Jerry Carlucci. She brought a busload of hippies and farmworkers on his property, with mattocks and rakes and a tractor. Or at least he claims that's his property. Do you mind going out there?"

"Yeah, I do."

"You're fed up with Carlucci?"

"You could say that."

I didn't want to tell her about the dream. I'm one of those people who believes that dreams have a purpose. Or maybe they don't. What did Shakespeare say? All power lies in the world of dreams.

"Jerry's a toxic guy," I said.

"Most of our clientele are."

"He's one of those guys who smells like death," I replied.

"That's pretty rough."

"Some people have the touch for it."

"It's up to you," she said. "How about Valerie? What she's doing may be legal, or may not be, but either way it's a pile of shit for the department."

"They're digging for artifacts?" I said.

"Ask them."

"Come on, Helen, what kind of crap is this? Do you want me to go out there or not?"

"Bwana not in good mood."

I let her remark pass, but it was hard. "I'll drive out there."

"I appreciate it."

"No problem," I said.

"No, it's a big problem. Louisiana is floating away while the worst people in the country wipe their feet on us. Call me if you need me, Streak. You're the best."

How do you respond to that?

I caught a back road to Carlucci's Landing and approached his property from the south. The bus of hippies and Mexican farmworkers were working in a long marshy stretch of land behind Jerry's saloon and whorehouse, screening buckets of sand for artifacts. The sun was bright, the sky pale blue, like Clemmy Benoit's eyes, the bay the color of bronze, the clouds on the horizon pulsing with what looked like bits of electric wire. Except that wasn't the whole story. A couple of Jerry's hot-pillow shacks had obviously burned down during the early hours, the tin roofs already fallen into the smoke and ashes.

Valerie was amidst her workers, wearing rubber boots and a floppy straw hat, her fists on her hips. I parked my unmarked car and walked toward her, my loafers sinking in mud. "Good morning," she said.

"Yes, isn't it?" I said.

She gave me a look. "Helen send you out?"

"I wouldn't put it that way. What happened to the buildings?"

"Probably lightning last night," she said.

"Yeah, dual bolts of lightning hit cathouses simultaneously a lot. No one called the fire department?"

"Don't know."

"What's going on here, Val?"

"We pulled in here just after sunrise. That's all I can tell you." She coughed into her hand. Valerie was a miserable liar, which I guess was a good sign.

"Y'all find anything?" I asked.

"No, but we will," she said.

I looked at the long sweep of the wetlands and the saline channels that cut through living marsh, and the bay winking in the distance, and the oil wells stenciled against the sky, not far from where my father died. "Where's your point of reference?" I said.

"Pardon?"

"What you're doing is like searching for a cigarette butt on the moon," I said.

"You've got to have faith."

"Right," I said.

I saw Jerry Carlucci come out the back door of his saloon and look at us through a pair of binoculars. Valerie looked back at him, then at me. "Pay no attention to that asshole. If he comes out here, I'm gonna rip him a new one."

"Val, I would not have those thoughts about Jerry."

"Okay, I'll tell you what we're doing. In 1865 General Kirby Smith would not surrender, and he and his soldiers tried to make a run for Mexico," she said. "They had a huge amount of gold and jewelry from New Orleans. It's supposed to be out here."

"Who told you that?"

"An old family in New Iberia," she replied.

I asked her which family. She gave me their name, and then I knew where the legend came from. At Spanish Lake in 1863 a plantation owner filled a barrel with gold and silver dinnerware and candelabras and rolled it into the lake before the Yankees got their hands on it. It was obviously the same legend.

"Where did you get the Mexicans?" I said.

"A donor who wants to see us save our state," she replied.

"I'm bothered about what you're telling me," I said.

"I beg your pardon?"

"People like to dream, Val. But you're smarter than most people. You're asking me to believe that an Act of God struck those two buildings while the owner watched and didn't call the fire department, the same guy you busted."

"*C'est la vie*," she said. "Maybe Carlucci got religion."

"I don't think you know who your friends are."

But she wasn't listening now. Maybe she had found herself. You know what I mean? Three or four people are running around inside you, then one day you forgive yourself for your frailties and mistakes, and accept the world for the fine place it is and go about your way.

However, Valerie Benoit's maturation was not on my mind. I stared at a thin, tubercular-looking man raking piles of dirt and sand that others were putting on the screens.

"I can't believe my eyes," I said. "Or maybe I've lost my mind."

"Are you talking about Bedford Ludlow?" she replied.

"Did his father bring him out here?"

"No, he knew some of the volunteers and wanted to come. What, he shouldn't be allowed?"

"You have no idea what you've done, Valerie."

"So explain it to me."

"Bedford gives people the impression that my daughter was a friend of Clemmy Benoit," I said. "Do you know what that means? The people who killed Clemmy and Jack Raider might set their sights on Alafair. How could you do this?"

"I'm sorry you feel that way," she said.

"How else could I feel?"

"Well, I'm sorry. I don't know what to say. I thought I was doing a good deed."

"Say you'll take him back home," I replied.

She took a breath. "All right."

"Do it now."

"I promised him he could come with us. Look, Dave, the damage is done. Let him enjoy himself and he'll forget it. Why exacerbate the situation?"

"Did you burn down those two buildings?"

She made a stupid face. "Me no remember."

"That's what I thought. Shame on you."

I knew she had burnt the buildings, and I knew that Jerry knew. He wasn't far away, watching, imperious, casual, maybe a smirk on his face, I couldn't tell. I pointed one finger at him and started walking toward him.

Jerry stuck a cigarillo in his mouth and scratched a match on a wood post and cupped his hands around the flame on the cigar's tip, all the while looking at me as I approached him. He flipped the dead match past my shoulder. "Got something to say?" he asked.

"Too bad about your buildings," I said.

"I think it was an electric short. I didn't pay it much mind. I'd already told my girls to beat it."

"That's supposed to be funny?" I replied.

"Pull the broom out of your ass."

"Your insurance carrier must really like you," I said.

"I don't believe in insurance."

"You're getting out of the life?"

"I quit a long time ago."

"Are you working with Valerie? Leading the good life?"

"Dave, you need a therapist. I saw Bedford Ludlow through my binocs. He shouldn't be here."

"You don't have to tell me."

"See you around, Dave," he said. "We've both got better things to do. A man can build an empire or live the life of a pauper."

He turned his back to me.

I reached out and put my hand on his arm. "Don't blow me off, Jerry. I fear for you."

"Fear for me? A planet is gonna crash on my head?"

"You've got blood all over you, partner. I think you're about to shed some more, too."

He was standing on a higher level of ground than I, his cheeks and throat unshaved, his eyes luminous, the size of dimes, under the brim of his black Stetson. He looked truly like a western gunman from the nineteenth century. "Take that back," he said.

"It has something to do with my daughter."

"You're crazy, Dave."

"I can smell it on you," I said.

"I don't hurt people. I empower them. I give them a way out of this shithole."

"Who cut up Tommy Driscoll with a chainsaw? Who killed Clemmy Benoit with a hotshot?"

"I don't know."

"But you know every dope dealer from here to Mexico City?"

"I've let you slide many times because you were my podna when we played ball and fought in the Gloves," he said. "Now I'm gonna do it again. But that's it. No more free fucking passes."

I stepped back from him. His cigarillo was gripped tight in the corner of his mouth, and one eye was bigger than the other.

"Leave Alafair alone," I said. "That's a one-warning deal, Jerry."

"You've made up a fantasy. Shove it up your nose."

"One other thing," I said. "I was never your podna. You were just a guy I used to know."

I didn't mean to say it, but I did. He looked like I slapped his face.

I walked back down to the bus where the diggers were rubbing the dirt on the screens, and tossing bottle caps and broken glass into a garbage can. I didn't see Valerie and assumed she was driving Bedford to his home. I was convinced that Valerie or her friends had burned the two buildings. But the real issue was Jerry Carlucci's indifference. When Jerry made a move, it was for a reason. But what was the move? I had no idea.

The sky was as blue and flawless as ceramic, the earth greening before my eyes, as though it wanted to heal a wound that had been caused for no purpose.

I got in my vehicle and drove back to New Iberia, then went to Victor's Cafeteria and nursed a cup of coffee until noon; I didn't go into my office until there were only a few people left.

I had a sense or a premonition like I had never experienced before. I believed something was changing in the world, but I knew not what. It wasn't just an era; it wasn't the dying of the light. It was a vibration, a grinding of the tectonic plates, an invisible snapping of steel cables underneath the continents, none of which was supposed to happen.

Valerie called on my cell and said she had taken Bedford home to his father, without any trouble. In fact, she said the father was "gentlemanly." In that frame of mind, I cleaned out the paperwork in the wire basket on my desk, then asked Helen Soileau if I could no longer work with Valerie Benoit.

"What happened?" she said sitting behind her desk, wearing her navy blue slacks and starched white short-sleeve shirt.

I told her about Bedford and the burning of the two buildings.

"By your own admission, nobody cares, so drop it," she said. "Bringing Ludlow's autistic kid to the dig, that's dumb. But she's young and she apologized and took the kid back home, right?"

"Bedford isn't just a kid," I replied. "He has a gift. He knows that Clemmy was friends with Alafair, and he knows she was in my house and he knows I own some Jimmie Rodgers records. How do you like that?"

"Okay, you got a point," she replied. "I'll talk to her. But I still think you're being too tough on her."

I was standing by Helen's desk. Through the window I saw our handyman across the bayou pedaling his ice cream cart.

"You don't get it, Helen. All of this emphasis on treasure and artifacts doesn't slide down the pipe. People like Jerry Carlucci and Sidney Ludlow and Elton Foot don't care about Jubal Early's gold teeth."

"Who is Jubal Early?"

"He was one of the idiots who invented the 'Lost Cause.'"

"That stuff is over my head, bwana. What about Valerie? Does she go or do you go? Or do both you go, or do I have an aneurysm?"

"She stays and I stray," I replied. "But I think we need to remember something. It's on the subject of causes. Clemmy died for a 'cause,' and a noble one, even though we don't know what it was. Follow me?"

"Go ahead."

"The people who killed her didn't want information about Confederate artifacts. Clemmy would have given them up in a second. Instead she probably died a terrible death. Or maybe she killed herself."

"I understand what you're saying—"

"No, you don't," I said. "Saints in the arena or patriots in the torture chamber have one commonality. They look as plain and average as people in a grocery line. They also enrage their tormentors."

"Okay," she said. "I get it. You really think Alafair might have something they want?"

"Who knows? But I think Elton Foot needs to get his ticket punched."

"I didn't hear that," she said.

"It's a metaphor."

"I bet."

I turned to go. "Anything else?"

"Be good to Valerie."

"You don't think I will?" I said.

"Now it's you who doesn't get it. She's in love with you."

"Wait a minute," I said. "You're talking about paternal feelings, right?"

"Women aren't the same as men, bwana. Their feelings are directed at the whole man. You guys have never caught on very well."

That evening I took Alafair and Clete to supper in Lafayette, and pretended I never heard those words. Fat chance.

Chapter Thirty-One

At noon the next day I caught our handyman Boone Hendrix in the park, by the seesaws and the jungle gym, handing out popsicles for ten cents apiece. He was dressed in whites, like a naval officer, including the hat with the shiny black brim.

"You look sharp today, Mr. Hendrix," I said.

"The same to you, sir," he replied. "You want a popsicle?"

"I wouldn't mind."

His hair and eyes made me think of a comic character, maybe Superman, a man who was funny but of depth and conscience. The popsicle was cold in my hand. After I gave him the dime, his eyes drifted to the children, all of whom were below school-age.

"You giving up your handywork business?"

"No, sir, I am not. I work afternoons and nights. Have you had more dry rot problems?"

"No, no, we have no problems with dry rot," I said. "Mr. Hendrix, I was wondering about your accent. Are you from New England?"

His eyes roved over my face. I became more and more uncomfortable. "You seem to have a bit of the pilgrim in you," I said.

"They were a wicked breed."

"I don't know if I would go that far."

"They hanged their neighbors, Detective Robicheaux. They put people's wrists and ankles in the stocks. They burned out the Indians. They pressed an old man with stones."

"Who are you, Mr. Hendrix?"

He looked at three little girls coming down the slide. "Why do you ask?"

"You seem like you might need a friend."

"I can't bear what is real, sir, nor can I find release from what is unreal. How would you like to trade places with me? Just for one day?"

I never heard a solitary statement that held such misery in it. He pedaled away, after running over my foot.

That evening I was reading the newspaper and Alafair was playing tennis in Lafayette when Valerie Benoit rang my doorbell. She was wearing a silk-like purple dress, and holding a white cake.

"Hello," I said. I was still holding the newspaper in my hands.

"Can I drop off this cake for you and Alafair?"

"She's not here now."

"I'll put it in the kitchen. It'll just take a moment."

"I can take it."

"It's no problem."

She opened the screen door and stepped in. Her hair was freshly cut and blow-dried, and smelled like strawberries when she walked past me, a fixed smile in her eyes. "There," she said, coming out of the kitchen. "I need to tell you something. Boone Hendrix was at my house this afternoon."

"About what?"

"May I sit down?"

"Yeah, sure," I said, then realized I had just lost possession of my living room.

"He went to our dig on Carlucci's Landing. He found the frame of an old pistol. I have it in my car."

"In 1863 there were a lot of skirmishes down that way, Valerie. British arms smugglers came through there, also."

"He found a coin, too. It's hard to read, but the date looks like 1850."

"That's all interesting, but I want you to tell me the truth about something. Did you set fire to Jerry Carlucci's buildings?"

"No, I did not," she said.

"Did any of your diggers?"

"No, they don't do that kind of thing."

"I see. That leaves us with a big question mark. Jerry is known as a tightwad. Why would he let his buildings burn?"

"Insurance money?" she said.

"He said he doesn't carry insurance."

"Maybe it's an accident. Who cares? You're not interested in Boone Hendrix's findings?"

"Yes, I'd like to see them," I lied. "Please."

She went out to her car, then came back in. But I could tell her heart was no longer in it. She unwrapped an oily rag that contained a cap-and-ball revolver encased in rust; the cylinder and grips were gone.

"Yeah, that's interesting, Valerie," I said. "But we're losing our emphasis here. We have some dead people on our hands, and we're not making much progress about who killed them."

I could see the glow going out of her face. I tried to get her attention back. "Hey," I said.

"What?"

"You've done a good job. You've backed me up whenever I needed help. You stood up to the bullies and racists like Lloyd D'Anjou, and even Sidney Ludlow, and you're just getting started in your career. That's not bad."

She shook her head.

"But that's not why you're here?" he said.

"No, it isn't."

I knew what was on her mind. I did not want to talk about it. It was embarrassing, dumb, awkward, foolish, and guaranteed to cause more trouble. Why is that? I'll tell you why. It's the kind of thing you absolutely hate, because age is supposed to relieve you of certain kinds of discomfort. In other words, I wanted to run out of my own house. "I'm old, Valerie. And I mean *old*."

"You're also white," she said.

"I'm not sure about that. Nor do I care. Anyway, I think you're a great person, and the right guy is waiting for you down the track."

She looked at me a long time. Then she gave me a sad smile. "Maybe one day on the other side of morning, huh?"

I fiddled with a ballpoint in a ceramic ashtray on the lamp table. "I've heard that expression. But I've yet to figure it out."

She got up from the couch. "Hope y'all like the cake."

I saw her shadow fall over me, then she pushed open the door and walked across the square of light on the porch and was suddenly out in the darkness on the lawn. Then I realized she had left her artifacts. I grabbed them and ran after her, waving them in the air, but her taillights were already passing the Shadows, even though I wasn't far from her and sure that she must have seen me in her rearview mirror.

An hour later Alafair came in from her tennis game, and went immediately into the shower. After she was in the stall and the room was clouded with steam, I went inside. "It's just me," I said. "I'm placing a clean washcloth on the counter and leaving a .25 auto on it. I'm also removing the magazine and clearing the chamber and leaving you a box of shells. I'm almost certain that bad people are convinced you have the same information they killed Clemmy Benoit to get."

"I can't hear you!" she yelled.

"I'll wait outside," I said.

Fifteen minutes later she came into the kitchen wearing jeans and a jersey and rubbing her hair with a towel. "So what about the gun?"

I told her again.

"Okay," she said.

"Okay, what?"

"I'll put it under my bed."

"Let's get you licensed tomorrow."

"Dave, try to relax. Just this once. This collection of shitheads have no interest in me. If that happens, I'll throw away the twenty-five auto and buy a shotgun."

"I can't lose you, Alfie."

She looked at me a long time. Then sat down and looked into space, her batteries drained. "Okay, whatever you want," she said.

"How about some hot chocolate?" I said.

"No, I'm pretty tired," she replied. "I think I'll go straight to sleep."

Normally we watched the late news together.

"Goodnight," she said.

"Yeah, goodnight, Alafair."

I didn't call her "Little Guy" or "Alfie" or "Alfenheimer." I felt like a stranger in my own home.

The next morning I knew I had to make a move. Small-town law enforcement does not have the technology and financial support of large cities or the federal government. It's far closer to the medieval world. The term "sheriff" comes from "shire" (a section of land, and "reeve," a leader). Since the ninth century, the Anglo-Saxon world has had an enormous influence on our villages, and particularly on the criminals. Their vocabulary has changed very little, the same with the courts, and the attitudes as well. Most criminals convince themselves they are the victims and they work hard for what they steal. Read what is thought to be the autobiography of Butch Cassidy.

Butch considered himself "a socialist" and the capitalistic enemy of the railroad barons. Of course, Butch and Jesse James and Pretty Boy Floyd robbed the rich because the poor have no money.

Anyway, you get the point. People like Bonnie and Clyde and other small-town criminals are easy to round up. But we were dealing with something far more powerful than country boys with a twang and holes in their trousers or a twenty-one-year-old Dallas waitress who wrote pretty good poetry and got a rotten deal.

Yeah, we were dealing with an organism, something that was mindless and ubiquitous, a festering form of greed and cruelty and desire, and I don't mean sexual desire, either; it was something that wanted to literally grind away the earth, to destroy the animals on it and crack the roots in the forests and leave the ocean a littered desert.

I believe this nameless force wrote the history of my family. Others can disagree with me. Or they can disagree with the bodies I lowered in the ground. I've looked in the face of evil.

That night we had a thunderstorm, the kind that splits the heavens and crashes oak limbs across powerlines and floods East Main and darkens the town. If I was going to make a move, this was the time. I took my duffle bag from the attic and drove to Clete's motor court and ran up the stoop to the cottage door and pounded on it until the room inside shook. He jerked open the door in his skivvies, the electricity in the clouds lighting his body, the rain pelting his face.

"What's shakin' bacon," he said. "Better come in. I hear there's a bad moon rising."

I went inside and threw my duffle on his bed.

"That bag is starting to make me nervous," Clete said.

"I brought my laundry in case we pass a washateria."

"Cut the doodah, Dave. All our electricity is out. An oak tree went through the top of my Caddy. This is not a happy night."

"We've got to bring a few guys down," I said.

"Which guys?" he said.

"Elton Foot for starters."

"When did you get this change of heart?" he asked.

"When I realized my daughter was endangered."

Three candles were burning in beer bottles on his breakfast table, the wicks distorting Clete's features, as if he were someone else and the humanity had gone out of his face.

"Go on," he said.

"This is what I want to do. I'm convinced Foot dismembered Tommy Driscoll with a chainsaw, then dumped it in the Atchafalaya. However, he kept one in his trailer that tested out clean. So far, so good for him. Except we didn't give the chainsaw back."

I stopped talking and watched Clete's face. "You'll tell him y'all found the murder weapon, but you don't tell him where?"

"Think he'll buy it?" I said.

"Yeah, maybe. He's not that smart. He's still in that trailer on the bayou."

"You're in for this, Clete?"

"Yeah, sure. I'll get dressed."

There was a big Houston telephone book on a shelf by the bathroom door. It was long outdated. "Can I borrow this?" I said.

"Help yourself."

I picked up the phone book and stuffed it in my duffle bag. "Why are you looking at me," I asked.

"I don't know," he said. "I really don't. Must be the weather."

We got in the pickup and were at the trailer park in ten minutes. The power outage evidently was in play all over St. Mary Parish as well as Iberia. But as in all perilous situations, the distinction between the poor and the rich became quickly apparent. The carriage lamps and candelabras and kerosene lamps in the plantation houses on the bayou were as brightly lit as Christmas trees, while the trailers across the drawbridge were as dark as the inside of a chamber pot.

I cut my headlights when we crossed the drawbridge. The wind must have been forty knots, the bayou at high tide, the waves capping a soapy-yellow froth from the glow in the clouds. I cut the engine before we reached Foot's trailer, then coasted to a stop so the brake lights wouldn't come on. A piece of tin was flapping in the background.

"How do you want to play it?" Clete said.

"It's up to him."

Clete gave me another strange look. "Maybe I should go in first."

"Nope," I said. I dug the Houston phone directory out of my duffle. "Let's get on it."

I went up the wood steps and kicked open the door, then plunged inside the trailer and into the instant smell of gymnasium sweat. Elton Foot was sleeping on a couch in front of his television set. Two fifty-pound dumbbells lay on the floor. I saw the malevolence in his eyes as soon as we burst through the door.

"What the fuck?" he said.

"Shut up and we'll tell you," I said.

He put up his hands. "I got nothing to do wit' you, Robicheaux," he said. "That's the word from the Mob. The greaseballs don't kill cops. They don't kill judges. They might pop a dingleberry like Purcel, but usually they don't waste their time."

"How would you like your head on a pike?" Clete said.

"I'd say 'bite me,' but you're not a cop. That's because you took juice and everybody knows it. Plus, you killed a federal witness."

I hit him across the face with the phone book. Then I did it again, harder. Something was pulling loose in my viscera, like the locked door on a basement, or better said, a medieval dungeon that smelled of feces and sweat and an iron rod and red-hot coals.

"Listen real close, Elton," I said. "We found the chainsaw you used on Tommy Driscoll. You're going to ride the needle, partner.

If you don't believe me, I'll show you the report in the truck. DNA doesn't lie, Foot."

"The tech said you must have wiped your ass with it," Clete said. "Cross my heart."

"Yeah?" Foot said. "Where'd you find the chainsaw?"

"In the Atchafalaya, you stupid mutt," Clete said. "You dumped it right where a friend of ours runs a catfish line."

"So bust me."

I pinched my eyes, then rubbed them with my wrist. I did not know why I felt the way I did. I take that back. I was tired of people such as Elton Foot.

"Would you try to hurt my family, Elton?" I said.

"I don't do that," he said. "At least not now. I changed my ways."

"You're serious?" I said.

"I did contracts," he replied. "Everybody had an understanding. That's the way it is in the life. I'm talking past tense, here."

"You killed a living human being with a chainsaw," I said.

Clete clicked a flashlight in Foot's face. "Answer him, fuck-face."

Foot was sitting up on the couch. He dropped his eyes to avoid the light. His head looked like it was carved from polished mahogany, his neck long, deeply tanned, like brown leather. He smiled to himself.

"What's funny?" Clete said.

"Nothing," Foot said.

"You were smiling, bub," I said. "What's the joke?"

"Okay," he said. "So I'm smiling. What do you make? Thirty-five, forty grand? Worrying over this Clemmy Benoit bitch?"

Then something very strange happened. I could no longer see or hear Elton Foot, but I could see Clete. His mouth was moving in slow-motion, the sound dragging like words in a cave. Then his mouth was forming the words "No, no, no," his hands trying to push me back.

Then I saw Foot again, but not in the present. Or maybe I saw things associated with him: tools flecked with blood, an animal shaking with fear, a naked fat man chained to a chair, a blowtorch. I know I hit him, and not with a phone book. My fists shuddered when they landed on his bones. I knew I was about to take his life.

Then I saw an enfant in a microwave, and I saw the silent agony in the baby's face and realized I had just seen the unbelievable, and the pain of the child would go on and on in the body and the mind of the adult, until the adult was taken off the earth.

I felt Clete hit me between the shoulder blades, knocking my breath out of my lungs, then grab me by the arms and wrestle me to the passenger side of the pickup, hitting me with his fists now, tearing my clothes, pushing me on the seat, slamming the door in my face.

Then I blacked out and didn't become conscious until we were on the far end of the LSU Agricultural Experimental Farm just outside New Iberia, the pastures green and lush, the windshield wipers flapping, crushed ice on the windshield, the plantation houses swallowed in fog.

"Did I kill someone?" I said.

"No."

"Where's Foot?"

"Yelling at the sky," Clete said. "Forget him."

"Was that him I hit?"

He stared at me, a wheel banging in a pothole. "You're the best guy I've ever known, Dave. That's who you are. Don't ever forget who you are."

"What's that supposed to mean?"

"What it says."

He didn't speak again until we were at his motor court. Then he went straight to a cabinet and took a bottle from it and lifted it at a forty-five-degree angle and drank and drank, an amber brilliance glowing from the bottle neck while an ache burned inside my heart.

Chapter Thirty-Two

Early the next morning, the sun was bright and the trees dripping, the Teche high over the banks and up to the lawn furniture in our backyard, just past the place we found Clemmy Benoit's body. That aside, it should have been a grand spring day. But I felt sick, like I had gone on a drunk after a long abstinence. That's how the metabolism of an alcoholic works. If you kick the flack juice for a while, then re-up, you think your odometer is where you put it down, then it hits you like a baseball bat and you realize that re-upping automatically puts you on the dirty boogie for the whole slide, Clyde. Talk about a lousy deal. I don't know if it's worse or better than food poisoning, but at least ptomaine doesn't guarantee clinical depression, psychoneurotic anxiety, suicidal thoughts, and levels of guilt that make you want to guillotine your own head and toss it into the ocean.

You like Jerry Lee Lewis? He was from Ferriday, Louisiana, right on the Mississippi. If he were still with us, he'd tell you about the Hadacol Boogie. He and Buddy Guy.

I fed our animals, and invited the neighbor's pets as well. That's why I quit hunting. I don't mean other people should, but I thought I should. I love animals and birds, and actually fish, too, and I feel I have no right to harm them. In fact, I know hunters I would like to shoot.

I scared Clete last night, and frightened myself as well. But right or wrong, the die was cast. So I fixed breakfast, then tapped on Alafair's door. When she didn't respond, I peaked inside. She had her pillow pulled over her face, one eye behind the pillow slip. "Is that you?" she said.

"Who else would it be?"

"The handyman?" she replied.

"What would he be doing here?"

"He was in the backyard at five this morning."

"No."

"Yes, inside big clouds of white fog. I went outside."

"That's not smart."

"Should I have shot him instead? Or maybe dialed 911 and let a cop shoot him?"

"What'd he say?"

"Nothing, he ran away," she said. "Where did you go last night? You look like a truck ran over you."

"Had some trouble with Elton Foot. Come on in the kitchen. I made breakfast for us."

"Elton Foot?" she said.

I didn't answer.

She swung her bare feet over the mattress and tugged on her slippers, her eyes lifting to mine. "You got mixed up with that sadist?"

"Yeah, that's why you have to be careful, Alafair."

"Thanks for talking to me like I'm five years old. Oh, look out the window. Why don't you handle things now?"

I couldn't believe it. Boone Hendrix was standing under an oak tree, spangled with sunlight, his face as somber as a prune. He must have seen me, because he raised one hand as though he were recognizing a long-lost companion. I asked Alafair to put our breakfast in the oven, and walked down the slope.

* * *

"Good morning to you, sir," I said.

"I need to build you better animal quarters," he replied. "I don't know how they didn't drown last night."

"They were in my house. I've got doggie-doors for anyone who wants to get out of the storm."

"You do that for your critters?"

"It's not a big deal. My daughter said you were here at five this morning."

He cleared his throat and began tucking his shirt inside his belt with his thumbs, scanning the tree limbs overhead, gazing up the green slope, avoiding my eyes. "Have you had great loss, Detective Robicheaux?" he said.

"I think that's fair to say," I replied.

His gaze lingered on my face. "The kind that gives you no rest?"

"The kind that you hope will turn from an open wound into a scar," I said. "You want to have breakfast with us, Mr. Hendrix?"

He ignored what I had just said. "You've killed people, haven't you?" he said. "In Vietnam or in your work?"

"I don't talk about it," I said.

He raised his chin, as though examining each word I had just spoken. "Do they follow you?" he asked.

"Does who follow me?" I said, although I knew the answer to my question.

"There are different kinds of people out there. Some seek justice. Some seek you."

"Who do you mean by 'you'?"

"The 'you' who is loved by them," he said. "Have you learned nothing, Detective Robicheaux?"

"How about turning down your burner, Mr. Hendrix?"

"I've got a confession to make," he said.

"Wrong party," I said.

"No, you're not. Remember when I dug your dry rot out of your roof?"

"I will never forget your discussion on the perils of dry rot," I said.

"When I fell through your attic, I saw a Thompson submachine gun. You had multiple magazines for it. My guess is you do not have a permit for it."

"I'm going to break off our conversation, Mr. Hendrix."

"The only reason I'm telling you this is I don't want to be accused of voyeurism. Do you understand? I am not of that ilk."

"You're about to get pitched in the bayou, Mr. Hendrix."

"Have you used that weapon, Detective Robicheaux? Will you use it again?"

"Get off my property, sir."

He was breathing hard now, his eyes glassy. "This is almost the spot, isn't it?"

"What spot?" I asked, although I knew the answer to my question.

"Where the colored girl was laid down. This should be a hallowed place. Why isn't there a small monument?"

"Why don't you put one there?"

I turned and walked away, my mouth dry, my fingernails curled into the heels of my hands.

In the kitchen I sat down with Alafair to eat breakfast, but I couldn't swallow my food. Was my anger justified? Or should I have been harder on him? I'll never know. Sometimes I believe there's a reason for madness in oneself and in others, and it's better in both cases to leave it alone.

It was Saturday and so I began raking and burning leaves, stacks of them, heavy and wet, curls of smoke rising from the leaf barrel. I preferred it to any more of Mr. Hendrix. Then Helen turned her cruiser into the driveway, cut the engine, and stepped out in the shade, her badge on her belt. She seldom drove her cruiser or wore her badge when she was off the clock. "Did bwana have a hard day's night?" she asked.

I leaned on the rake handle and gazed down the street at the Shadows. A tourist bus was stopped in front of it. Every time I saw that bus, I thought about the wasted lives embedded beneath us. "No, I'm very contained," I said. I took out my handkerchief to hide the rawness on the knuckles of my right hand.

"Didn't you and Clete Purcel visit Elton Foot last night?"

"I'd call it a chat," I said.

"Foot turned himself in at seven o'clock this morning."

"*He did what?*"

"He's in a holding cell as we speak. He's also scared shitless."

"Of what?"

"He said, 'Tell Robicheaux I'll work wit' y'all about that chainsaw.' What'd you and Clete do to him?"

"It was minor. Clete pulled my plug."

"Want to talk to Foot now or Monday?"

The holding cell was just that: a wood bench, strings of dried yellow urine on the floor drain, and religious crosses and profanity and male and female genitalia scratched deep into the walls. Elton had thrown his breakfast tray against the bars and splattered oatmeal and black coffee all over the cell and corridor.

"You prefer decaf and toast?" I said.

He ran at me, banging with his hands curved against the bars, then tried to shake them. "Get me out of here!" he said.

"I understand you want to talk about the murder of Tommy Driscoll."

"I didn't say anything about a murder. I said maybe I know who belongs to that chainsaw!"

"I think this is another waste of time."

"Okay," he said, his breath rife. "Whatever you want to write up! But you gotta get me away from that guy!"

"Which guy?"

"Hendrix, that handyman! Who the fuck you think I mean? He's hounded me. He came to my trailer. After you guys. Then he followed me here."

"When did he come here?" I asked.

"An hour ago!"

"I checked your visitor list in case your shyster was already here. You've had no visitors except me."

He squeezed his cheeks between the bars, his long greasy hair hanging on his shoulders. "He told me he was dead," he said, his voice rasping.

"Here? Where I'm standing?"

"Yeah," he replied. "He said I'm gonna be dead, too. He said it was gonna be hell. He smelled like he'd been digging in fresh dirt."

I looked back over my shoulder. No one was in the corridor. "This is the way I see it. I believe you have a lot on your conscience, Elton, and you've manufactured a figure who is, in effect, yourself."

"I knew you'd do that, you bastard," he said. "The handyman told me things about gigs he had no way of seeing."

"What things?"

"Serious ones. Jobs I did for the Sicilians. Details nobody could know."

"See you around," I said, and started to walk away. He tried to press his face deeper between the bars, then began beating his head against them. "You gotta listen, man. This ain't right. I didn't get a square shake when I was a kid. Even that motherfucker knows that."

"Which motherfucker?"

"Hendrix or whatever his name is. He said he knew everything about me. He said he knew everything about you."

"In what way?" I asked.

He let go of the bars and rubbed his forehead. His eyes were pink-rimmed with fatigue, one eyebrow cut. "He said you listen all the time to hillbilly songs. He called it shit. There was one record you can't even listen to yourself. He told me to write it down. I got it back here. He gave me the pencil to write it wit'."

"Not interested," I said.

"Oh, yeah?" he said. He went to the back of the cell and picked up a newspaper from the bench. "Here, I'll read it to you," he said.

"When it rained down sorrow, it rained all over me,
When it rained down sorrow, it rained all over me,
Cause my body rattles like a train on that old S.P."

It was "T.B. Blues" by Jimmie Rodgers. I had not played it in years.

I wet my lips. "Hendrix has done work at our house, Elton," I said. "He must have gotten into my records."

"And you didn't notice while he was walking around your house?"

"Could be," I said.

"When's the last time you listened to it?"

"That doesn't mean anything. Someone probably told him I didn't play that particular recording."

"You and Purcel are gonna hang me out to dry, aren't you?" he said. "Or somebody is gonna do a hit on me?"

"I think you're talking yourself into the East Feliciana unit for the criminally insane. In the meantime, you'll be transferred to the Iberia Parish Prison. Three or four screws in there were buds of Lloyd D'Anjou, real shitasses."

"Come on, man, don't do that."

"I'm sorry. I don't make the rules."

"It ain't right. You can't put me in there wit' them guys. Take me up to Angola. I can request twenty-three-hour lockdown, then we'll work things out. I liked it there. They got good food. It's clean."

"Look, you're not charged with anything, except throwing your breakfast tray and being obnoxious," I said. "Call your attorney. I'll talk with Helen. She'll probably cut you loose."

"I ain't going to do it. Y'all setting me up. I'll confess. I took the truck driver apart wit' the chainsaw. You got to protect me."

Elton Foot was con-wise and knew the holding cell was not wired. After he got what he wanted, he would deny his confession and probably claim that other cops and I beat it out of him.

"I'm going to recommend we turn you loose," I said.

Just then Helen walked up to the bars. "Your lawyer is outside, Mr. Foot," she said. "You're a lucky man."

"Could you say that a little louder?" he asked.

She stepped closer to the bars. "Your lawyer has contacted the judge. On weekends most people have to wait until Monday."

Foot spat between the bars. Most of his spittle didn't hit her. But it was enough.

"We'll try to find a solitary cell at the Parish Prison, Mr. Foot," Helen said, mopping at her shirt with a handkerchief. "Have a good day."

The next week I tried to forget about Elton Foot. I also wanted to forget about his claim of seeing Boone Hendrix and Hendrix's stories about his being dead and his knowledge about my record of Jimmie Rodgers's song "T.B. Blues." Louisiana is a haunted place. Maybe it has to do with our guilt. Confederate dead lie in almost every nineteenth-century cemetery in the state. I believe the weight of those stones is to keep the boys in butternut under the ground, because they were lied to in the worst way and fought a rich man's war in poor-man's rags and often without shoes.

You think I'm jumping you over the hurdles? Try this on for size. The Confederate secession was a hard sale. Initially only South Carolina was unhinged enough to commit suicide. So a powerful group of newspaper publishers and plantation owners gathered in

Atlanta and found the theme that would strike fear in the hearts of Dixie when arguments about cotton prices would not. Editorials appeared all over the South about the supposed lust of black males and how the ferocity of their emancipation would be imposed on white women. It worked. It was the Willie Horton campaign of 1862.

What am I saying? I was full of guilt, and the guilt was about Elton Foot. I know, he was the scum of the earth, the kind that has triple-A batteries for a brain and has to stay in lockdown for his own protection. But any decent prison guard, like any decent cop, knows the challenge is not the psychopath; the challenge is to yourself. The day his methods become yours is the day he owns you. He knows it, too. He'll grin and howl at the moon.

I told these things to Alafair in her bedroom where she was finishing her novel, and I didn't want to bother her, but she was the only person besides Clete in whom I confided.

"Think of it this way, Dave," she said. "If you had wanted to kill Foot, you would have done it, and Clete wouldn't have been able to stop you. You know who told me that?"

"No."

"Clete."

"Really?"

"Yeah."

"On the other stuff about Boone Hendrix creeping our house and playing your Jimmie Rodgers records, I believe that happened."

"Why?"

"It's too detailed to be a fantasy. I think he wants to be a musician or a man like you."

"He already told me he that he didn't look at things in our attic when he was working on the roof. In fact, he used the term 'voyeur' as he would 'degenerate.'"

"Exactly. He doesn't want you to know he has a compulsion he can't control."

"But Foot says the handyman told him about the Jimmie Rodgers song in the holding cell. Nobody saw the handyman there. There was no name on the visitor's sign-in. Usually only attorneys get as far as a holding cell, and a deputy walks with him."

"So somebody wasn't doing his job. Is that somebody going to be anxious to tell you that?"

"Well, I appreciate your listening to me," I said. "I hope I don't slow up your novel."

She shook her head good-naturedly. But I knew better. From what I've heard, every writer's enemy is the telephone and the postman. I got up to go.

"One thing though," she said. "This case is different. It has to do with a crossroads. We're just small figures running around on it."

"Helen said that, too," I said.

Alafair started typing again, no longer listening to anything I had to say.

Chapter Thirty-Three

It was Wednesday night, and you could smell the honeysuckle and see a star or two drop off the edge of the horizon, which doesn't happen too much down South because of the humidity. Alafair and I played ping-pong in the basketball gym at the park, then walked back home through the oaks and over the drawbridge, the reflection of the full moon wobbling in the current on the bayou, a big alligator in the cattails on the banks of the Shadows.

It's strange how much of my life has been lived among symbols I didn't create: the scorched pillars on a courthouse burned by Union soldiers in 1863; a gator killed by a plantation owner that would have eaten some small Acadian children had not the owner saved them, which had a great deal to do with the creation of the McIlhenny Company and Tabasco and the founding of company towns across the South. The Episcopalian Church on Main was a battalion aide station for Confederate wounded, then the Yankees took the town and looted it and pushed the pews together and filled them with hay for their horses.

The nuns lived in a convent among the live oaks across the drawbridge. The angelus rang three times a day. A vendor sold po'boy sandwiches in a wagon under an umbrella in front of the home where the slave overseer had once lived across the street from the Shadows.

I never saw the future. There was no such thing. The present was the past, and the past was the present. The brothels were on Railroad Avenue. The Sunset Limited went by every day, going either to Miami or Los Angeles, and the prostitutes sat on their small galleries and dipped draft beer from a bucket and watched the train go by.

The bars and the saloons were also gambling places, with slot and racehorse machines and punch cards and, on Saturday, football betting, blackboards on the walls, and ticker-tape machines clicking out piles of paper on the floor. I never saw one underage kid refused a drink or a go at gambling. The bourrée and domino tables were in back, and often a colored man would shine your shoes for a dime. Police officers in uniform worked behind the bar in every southern parish in the state of Louisiana.

For good or bad, that world is largely gone. It could be found perhaps in the paintings of Toulouse-Lautrec or Edgar Degas or Van Gogh in his madness, but that's it. How do I feel? I won't say. If the Bible is to be believed, Jesus kept company with drunkards, thieves, and prostitutes. So thank you, God, for the state of Louisiana, the place that will always offer refuge for the likes of people such as me.

Alafair and I stopped at the center of the drawbridge and leaned on the rail. The tide was coming in and the moonlight's reflection looked like a broken mirror on the bayou's surface. "Something on your mind?" she said.

"Nostalgia is better left alone," I replied.

"You'll always love Louisiana, Dave. You could no more leave it than give up people like Clete and all the eccentrics in the French Quarter. It's no accident that Tennessee Williams's greatest work was about a streetcar named desire. He lived it, and so did you. You're not a cop. You never were. That's why you're always in trouble."

My phone buzzed in my pocket. It was Helen. For some reason I didn't want to answer it.

"Dave?" she said.

"Yeah."

"Get your ass to the parish prison. Call Clete, too. I need every swinging dick I can get. Out."

Her call went dead.

I picked up Clete at his motor court and drove out of the city limits to the Iberia Parish Prison. Before we got there, we saw the sparks streaming in a black sky, a pasture filled with firetrucks, ambulances, squad cars, and inmates in orange jumpsuits who had been taken from the facility on wrist or ankle-and-waist chains. The firetrucks were concentrating their hoses on a fire in back, one that had started in a cell and obviously had spread.

Helen saw my pickup and started waving her flashlight at me. I pulled up to her and rolled down the window. "What happened?" I said.

"I had Foot in isolation," Helen said. "A deputy said he heard an explosion in the cell, then flames spread under the door. He heard Foot screaming, then there was another explosion. He said Foot was beating on the door."

"Where's Foot now?" I said.

"He's still in there. The lock's jammed. It's an old cell. I think somebody might have broken off a screwdriver in the keyhole."

"He's alive?" Clete said.

"One of the firemen said he heard a voice inside before he got his hose on the flames."

"Jesus Christ," Clete said.

I looked around. "Where's Valerie?"

"On the way from St. Martinville," Helen said.

We got back in the pickup and drove behind the building while Helen temporarily took over custody of the prisoners, all of them sitting in jumpsuits in the grass, their faces turned up at the sky, filled with awe.

The firemen were using two pump trucks, the arcs of water crisscrossing in the holes burned in the roof. A big man named Dee Dee

Blanchard walked toward us, and raised his plexiglass shield. His face was red and dilated and running with sweat and soot. A *whumping* sound came from the building. "That's the third time that's happened," he said.

"What's it mean?" Clete said.

"We're dealing with impaired explosives of some kind," he replied. "It's probably wet or decayed."

"How did anybody get explosives in a jail cell?" I said.

"There was an old vent above the cell," Dee Dee said. "My guess is somebody stuffed a charge down it, then poured gasoline on it."

"Gasoline?" I said.

"I smelled it when I first got here," Dee Dee said. "I think the bomber soaked the place before he lit it up."

"Did Helen tell you somebody might have jammed the keyhole?" I said.

"Yeah, she did," he said. "Hey, this is what I think. Somebody with old dynamite dropped a bunch of cans down the air vent onto the ceiling of the cell, followed by gasoline and some fulminate caps or a handful of cartridges. Kind of like the fire Lloyd D'Anjou set off in his attic. You were there, weren't you, Purcel?"

"Yeah," Clete said. "What about it?"

"I was just axing."

"What'd you leave out?" Clete asked.

Dee Dee's eyes roved over Clete's face. "The guy who did this doesn't know shit about explosives, except how to make somebody go out as miserable as it gets. That's all I was saying."

Clete put a cigarette in his mouth, but didn't light it. "Here comes Helen," he said.

She had a pair of pliers wrapped with a cloth in her hand. She lifted it up. "It's a Phillips screwdriver."

"Have you got the door open?" I said.

"The firemen have the jaws-of-life on it," she said. "Y'all want to follow me?"

* * *

Firehoses were strung through the front door of the building and down the corridor to Elton Foot's cell. The door was not of a conventional jailhouse kind. Rather than bars, the door was solid and made of one piece of steel except for a peephole and a boxlike apron through which a trusty pushed a Styrofoam cup and paper plate and metal spoon twice a day.

The amount of fuel was so great flames had climbed through the food slit, and the heat so great the ceiling had sagged and crushed the doorframe, wedging it as tight as a weld. The fireman overseeing the jaws-of-life stopped and looked at us. "You guys ready for this?" he said.

I don't think he was worried about our safety, either. He tore the door out of the jamb, the metal screeching.

Clete knotted a handkerchief and held it to his face. "Whoa!" he said.

I turned away so I wouldn't gag. So did Helen and so did the other firemen. A trusty bent over, his arms gripped across his stomach. Elton Foot's body was curled next to the toilet bowl, encrusted, like burned tree bark, his hair gone, his mouth in rictus, his teeth immaculate white against his skin, which was as black as tar.

"Clear the hall and get the body bag and gurney down here on the double!" Helen yelled.

Then she looked at me and Clete. Her expression was like a peeled hard-boiled egg. "Could Boone Hendrix do this?"

"He had to have a man on the inside," Clete said. "A trusty or a deputy to break off the screwdriver in the keyhole. The guy pedaling popsicles in the park is probably a whack-job but doesn't look like your regular jailhouse crowd."

"Then who should we be lookin' at?" I said.

"A guy who's been hurt bad," Clete said. "Or a guy who wants us to think that way. Maybe a guy like Sidney Ludlow. He made his bones by popping a shoeshine man who tried to run numbers in the wrong neighborhood. What a guy."

We had been standing too long next to the cell. The odor had collected now. It's funny about the dead. It's hard to walk away from them. Somehow we feel rude, as though we're showing off our independence from them. When Clete and I were walking a beat on Canal, a drunk ran a light and killed a Catholic nun. A dirty vice cop made an ugly remark close to the nun's body and Clete dropped him right in the middle of the street. Later, the same cop got his brains splattered over his pasta in an Italian restaurant one block away. Reckonings seem to find their way.

Just as Clete and I got in my pickup we saw Valerie Benoit's car coming down the two-lane. She pulled aside when she recognized my pickup and rolled down her window.

"Sorry I'm late. I blew a tire," she said.

"Helen is still there," I said. "She'll fill you in."

"Tell me now," she said.

"Elton Foot is dead."

"He was killed in the prison?"

"Yeah, Valerie. That's exactly what happened."

"Shit," she said, staring through her windshield.

"Shit, what?" I said.

"I saw Boone Hendrix tearing ass about twenty-five minutes ago. I know his truck."

"Call it in, Valerie."

"You're sure you want to do that?"

"Yes, I am sure. Indeed I am sure."

"Why don't we go after him?"

Clete looked at me "She's got a point."

We drove until midnight and saw nothing of Boone Hendrix. I didn't even know where he lived. I was so tired I didn't even care. I told Valerie to buy new tires and I would pay for them. I also felt like blowing up her car. Outside of that and Elton Foot's incineration, Alafair and I had a lovely evening.

Chapter Thirty-Four

The next morning, Thursday, Valerie looked out her office window and picked up her phone and buzzed my office.

"Hendrix is in the park," she said.

I went to my window. "Roger that," I said.

Ten minutes later we pulled up to his popsicle and ice cream cart by the jungle gym. The day was warm and sunny, and small children were everywhere. Valerie was driving. Hendrix was wearing his white navy-style hat and starched uniform. He paid no attention to us.

"How about a minute or two of your time, handsome?" Valerie said.

I thought that was a little brash. The handyman showed no expression. I got out of the cruiser, keeping it between him and me, with my hands visible and empty. It's a simple maneuver that can save lives, particularly when you're dealing with the mentally impaired. "How you doing, sir? I said. "Did you hear Detective Benoit?"

"I did," he replied. "I do not like to be addressed in a condescending fashion."

Good for you, I thought. But I didn't say it.

"Last night you seemed in a hurry in your truck," I said. "Maybe an emergency of some kind?"

"I might have. But I broke no law."

Then the wind shifted and I smelled an odor I had just smelled last night. "You weren't on your way to a fire, were you?" I smiled when I said it.

"I was burning leaves and they got out of hand. I had to borrow a neighbor's hose."

"You know about Elton Foot?" Valerie said.

"I'm not interested."

"What have you heard?" I said.

"I know he's a dangerous man who has no business among decent people."

This was the moment. He had spoken in the present tense. "He said you threatened him," I said.

"I don't have any memory of that."

"You're an intelligent man," I said. "You threatened him or you didn't. Which is it?"

"I watch out for children," he said. "If I see an evil man around children, I straighten out the situation. Why are you asking me these questions? I don't like it."

Have you ever talked to recidivists who could stare at the side of a battleship and tell you they didn't know what it was? That was Boone Hendrix.

"We're on your side, Mr. Hendrix," Valerie said. "I was worried about you when I saw you driving too fast. That doesn't seem your way. You wouldn't know where Elton Foot is, would you?"

"I don't associate with people such as that."

She nodded and looked at a squirrel running across a limb above our heads.

"Could we have a couple of popsicles?" she said.

Wonderful, Valerie, I thought.

He opened the lid of his cold box just as Bedford Ludlow came roller-skating down the asphalt path through the live oaks that covered most of the park. Skating behind him was one of Ludlow's gunsels, the tub of guts we had trouble with at Jerry Carlucci's Landing, who was now obviously acting as a bodyguard.

Bedford whizzed past us, then spun around and skated back. "Hi, hi," he said. "You're Detective Valerie and Detective Robicheaux. Do you like skating, too?"

"We're kind of busy right now, Bedford," I said. "Can we talk to you later?"

He wore freshly ironed khakis and a pink shirt and gray vest and a striped cap a locomotive engineer would wear. His face seemed feverish rather than pale, like a dying flower, the way a disease clings to the cheeks or the throat.

"Did you hear about the bad thing that happened last night?" he said.

Bedford was just about to blow our situation.

"We're on top of that, Bedford," Valerie said. Then she looked at the bodyguard. "Hey, big guy, you know the drill. We need some space here, okay?"

"Yeah," he said. His throat sounded corroded, as though a raw oyster were caught in it.

Valerie started to turn back to Hendrix.

"We're buying a popsicle, here," the bodyguard said.

"Another time," Valerie said.

"Who the fuck are you?" he said.

"What did you say?" she said.

"You can't tell people to get out of the park for no reason," the big man said.

"You need to step way back, sir," she said.

"*Fuck* you," he said.

I stepped toward him and raised my hand. "You heard her, partner," I said.

"Yeah, I did," the bodyguard said. "We're not supposed to skate in the park? We're not supposed to eat a popsicle?"

"Have you visited the parish prison?" Valerie said.

Don't do this, Valerie, I thought. *Don't, don't, don't, please.*

But it was too late. "Turn around," she said, pulling her handcuffs from the back of her belt.

"What's wrong?" Bedford interjected. "Why is everybody arguing?"

The big fat man grabbed Valerie's face with his fingers like a grapefruit and crunched it, squeezing her eyes shut, mashing her nose, then shoving her backward as though he were contemptuous of her touch. In fact, he wiped his hand on his pants.

She pulled a blackjack from her slacks, and beat him to his knees, slashing the leaded top into his head, giving no mercy. I think she would have killed him if I had not locked my arms around her body and lifted her in the air and gotten her between the cruiser and the fat man, who was now on his hands and knees, trying to get up, his skates slipping out from under him.

The children in the park and the mothers with them seemed frozen in time. So were the handyman and the robins that had been descending on the trees and the bodyguard splayed on the asphalt. Even Valerie seemed painted on the air, her face stricken at what she had done.

But not only had time stopped, so had sound. The silence was so intense I could hear my ears ringing, as though I were sitting at the bottom of the ocean. Then I heard Bedford Ludlow weeping. No, not just weeping. He was moaning as though an invisible umbilical cord had been severed from his body and he had drifted away inside infinity, with no one to care for him.

I put my arm around his shoulders and pulled him as tight as I could. "Hey, it's okay, partner," I said. "We'll get some help for your friend, and everything will be fine. I bet you have lots of friends, Bedford. Why, look, Mr. Hendrix has already gotten us a popsicle or two."

"Clemmy," he said, his face as pale as bone. "They did things to Clemmy."

"Who did you say?" I asked. "Bedford! Look at me! Tell me again."

He had almost admitted to witnessing Clemmy Benoit's death. But Bedford went dead silent and stayed that way until he rode with the ambulance crew to Iberia General.

Back at the department Valerie and I went immediately to Helen's office. She listened first to Valerie, then to me. I said little of nothing. Why is that? In police work you keep it short and impersonal, even if it's not. Secondly, Helen was a good administrator and protected her people. But a mean cop is a mean cop, and they come in all colors. They also have secret lockboxes, chain-wrapped and welded to the floor of the unconscious. What is the greatest source of their rage? Yeah, you got it: control, physical constraint, constant stress, domination, and probably sexual abuse. Put all these together and you've got a cop who is always digging his nails into his hands.

I knew what Helen was thinking. Valerie Benoit was too easily provoked. Better put, Valerie was too easily tempted when it came to stomping ass.

"You're lucky," Helen said to her.

"You'll have to explain that to me, Sheriff," Valerie said.

See what I mean about stress?

"The guy is in Iberia General," Helen said. "I heard his head looks like a broken flowerpot."

"I ran his sheet," Valerie said. "He hung a guy by his rectum in a freezer."

"Thanks for the image," Helen replied. "But that's not the point. We do our jobs and that's all. You could have maced him, or called for backup or swarmed him or popped him behind the knee with your baton. Instead, I think you wanted to kill him."

I could see it coming. Valerie was about to shift into four-four time, which would probably end her career in the Iberia Parish Sheriff's Department.

"Pardon me, Helen, there's something we haven't discussed," I said.

She was sitting behind her desk. Valerie and I were standing. Helen was angry and not going to change the subject.

"Ludlow's kid opened up," I said.

"What?" she replied.

"After the bodyguard went down, Bedford said, 'They did things to Clemmy.' "

Helen's eyes never blinked, but her pulse was visibly beating in her neck. "Say that again."

I repeated Bedford's statement.

"They witnessed Clemmy Benoit's death?" she said.

"Or torture," I said. "Or both."

"He could put his own father in jail," she said. "Or on the injection table."

"Yeah, he could," I said.

"Where's Bedford now?" she said.

"He *was* at Iberia General," Valerie said.

"For his own good we need to get that kid in a psychiatric ward," Helen said. "I don't think the old man would kill him. A lobotomy is another matter."

"UL and LSU are the closest," Valerie said.

"You know somebody there?" Helen said.

"Yeah, I had some great fun there," Valerie said. "That was after I was raped in the army."

Helen's jaw tightened, but not in a sympathetic way. "I've had about as much as I can take of this," she said.

"It wasn't meant toward you, Sheriff," Valerie said.

"I don't care if it was meant for me or not," Helen said. "You've got a chip on your shoulder. Now the two of you get the hell out of my office."

Valerie walked out the door first. I paused in the doorway and waited until Valerie couldn't hear me. Helen lifted her eyes. "What?" she said.

"She admires you," I said. "Ease up."

"My ass. I've been too lenient on her."

"Remember when you were a meter maid at NOPD. She's got the same kind of guts. She's more like you than you think, Helen."

"She's gonna kill somebody," Helen said. "*I* fucked up."

"Let's get some coffee."

She flung her ballpoint past my ear, then slumped in her swivel chair, her face empty.

I took Clete to lunch at Victor's and made sure we got a quiet table in the corner. He had already heard about Valerie Benoit beating the bodyguard almost to death. "It's not going anywhere with Ludlow, if that's what you're worried about," he said.

"No?" I said.

"When it comes to cops, Sidney Ludlow's boys eat their pain," he said. "What I can't process is the kid, what's-his-name, Bedford. He talks like he was there when Clemmy Benoit was killed."

"Yeah, earlier he acted like he knew her, and from what he said I believed him. But this is different. How else can you interpret 'They did things to Clemmy'? It gives me chills."

Clete set down his fork, releasing it onto the plate. "Yeah, it puts images in your head. It makes you want to do something. I also wonder why Sidney Ludlow lets his son hang around here when the kid has information that can put the old man in jail."

"The project here, whatever it is, is too profitable for him to go back to Jersey and he doesn't want to leave his kid?" I said.

"That's probably it," Clete replied. He picked up his fork again and slipped it into a ball of dirty rice. But he didn't put it in his mouth.

"What's wrong?" I said.

"The images in my head. That girl nude, the guitar string around her throat, degenerates putting their hands on her. Just thinking about that gives me a gallstone. I'm not kidding. My bladder feels like somebody put out a cigarette on it."

This was not a good sign. Clete was winding up. Like a tectonic shelf starting to rumble.

"You think Foot did it?"

"Yeah, he was a cash-and-carry guy," he said. "But you can't put it in the bank. Look, noble mon, there's something a lot bigger than us going on. It's like a war. The cocksuckers who start them never fight them. It's the same with battlefields. Nobody gives a shit about a straw village."

"Hey, cool that language," somebody said forty feet away.

"Shut up," Clete said.

"What's your take on Hendrix, the handyman?" I said.

"You mean is he crazy or maybe a little spooky?"

"Foot swore that Hendrix was going to kill him. He also swore Hendrix came to Foot's holding cell. Hendrix denies all this."

"So?" Clete said.

"Hendrix seems like he's on the square. But he also says he was never in my house. I think he was. He played my records."

Clete blew out his breath. "I hate to break your faith in people, Dave. I've got a bail-jumper who was in the holding cell next to Foot's. He told me Hendrix was a visitor. He's not a spirit. He's a meltdown."

"Who said he's a spirit?" I asked.

"You know what's wrong with both of us? We just don't want to accept liars and shitheads for being liars and shitheads."

"What about that language, fella?" said the man forty feet from us. "I got my lady here."

He was lithe and wore a three-piece neon-blue suit and had fingers like a piano player and hair that was as shiny as patent leather. I had seen him with Jerry Carlucci and guessed he was a button man.

"Yeah, whatever," Clete said. "Sorry about that. I got logorrhea. You look familiar. Were you in the dollar store the other day?"

Clete's aggravation had the same source as mine. The autistic boy, or man, Bedford, who may have witnessed Clemmy's murder was going to be guarded night and day or gotten out of the state, while we sat in Victor's making remarks with somebody in the life.

Then Alafair walked in, spoke to some people, and continued on to our table. She always lit up a room, no matter where she went. I think it was because of her childhood years in Central America. The death squads there made anything else a paradise. The man with piano-player fingers couldn't keep his eyes off her. Across the street was a maroon Malibu with a Florida tag. I had an idea it was his.

"Can I join you?" she said.

We both stood up for her. That's the way we still do it in dear old Dixie. "I just talked to Valerie about the incident this morning," she said.

"Valerie told you?" I said.

"Yeah," she said.

I could not believe Valerie had breached Helen's order to not discuss anything about this morning in City Park.

"I'll have some pie, and we'll talk later, huh?" she said.

"Why don't we go outside now?"

I was too late. The man with the long fingers was heading for our table. Clete stared into neutral space. I took out my badge holder and flopped it open.

"Goodbye," I said.

He was grinning. "You won't have trouble from me. I just wanted to let you know you have a nice town here. Lovely, in fact. The kind of place where people live and let live."

"I'll pass on the news," I said.

"No gossip, know what I mean?" he said.

"Yeah, I think so," I said. "That's why we eat at Victor's. No riffraff. See you."

"You're a card, Jack," he said. He slapped me hard in the middle of my back, then walked away.

Clete huffed air out of his nose. "You gonna take that?" he said.

"Let it slide, Clete."

He nodded, his face serene. "I'll be right back."

"Don't do it," I said. "Please."

"I'm very composed, big mon. I'll pay up and meet y'all outside."

He put on his porkpie hat and went to the cashier's counter, passing the man in the electrified blue suit and the lady with him. I got up with Alafair and walked toward the front door. In ten more seconds we would be out of the building and hopefully Clete would be right behind us.

Of course, that did not happen. Clete folded a crisp bill longways and stuck it in his shirt pocket, then calmly walked to the table of the man who was affronted by Clete's profanity. He grabbed the man at the table by the shoulder and neck and slammed his face in the middle of his plate not once or twice but probably four times. Then he held up the twenty-dollar bill from his shirt pocket, showed it to the cashier, dropped it on the table, and walked outside into the sunshine.

Chapter Thirty-Five

Clete had made a mistake, but not because he mashed a button man's face in a plate of grits. Clete's mistake was letting the button man know we understood him when he said "live and let live." The warning was not meant for us; it was for Alafair.

After the scene in Victor's Cafeteria, I went back to the house with Alafair rather than to the office.

"I want you to go back to Portland," I said.

"Why?"

"I fear for you."

"You shouldn't."

"The people we're dealing with have no boundaries."

"That's why I should be here. With my father."

"They know where you are, but you don't know where *they* are."

"You want me to run away? You raised me to be a coward?"

"You don't fight your enemy on his terms, Alafair."

"I don't stay out late. I'm usually with friends. And I have the gun you gave me."

We were in the kitchen. My head was swimming. "Before you came into Victor's, Clete was talking about the way Clemmy probably died. And the kind of guys who did it. Clete couldn't handle his own thoughts. That's why he pounded that guy's face into his lunch."

"Good for Clete," she said.

"No, good for the bad guys. Clete tipped our hand."

"The man was both mocking and threatening you," she replied. "Clete thought he was standing up for you."

"We're talking about your life, Alafair. We're talking about a level of evil that most people can't imagine."

"I've studied autism. Valerie Benoit has a relationship with Bedford Ludlow."

"She drove him home," I said. "That's not a relationship."

"The old man appreciated it."

"I bet he loved his mother, if he had one," I said.

She waited a long time before she spoke again. "From what you've told me, Bedford has suppressed memories that are probably intolerable. Autistic people are extremely sensitive and caring. Frankly I don't how he has survived if he was there when Clemmy died. As you said, even Clete couldn't take it."

What does a man learn if he raises a daughter, particularly by himself? Answer: He never lets her down; he's always by her side; he never ridicules her because the damage is a stone bruise she will carry to the grave. But the big one is about puberty and marriage. One day she will see a man who does not see her, one who reminds her of her father or the father she should have had, and inside a random situation he will commit an act that is both kind and strong at the same time. At that moment a little voice inside her will say, "That's the one."

But I told none of this to Alafair.

"You make a point," I said. "If we can get Bedford in an environment where you can talk to him, he might give us the whole package, huh?"

"Could be," she said. "Tell me the truth, did you think I would leave you here at a time like this?"

"You'd open your veins first, Alafair."

* * *

I went back to the office at 1:27 P.M. and tapped on Valerie Benoit's door. "Come on in," she said.

She was writing on a yellow legal pad and didn't look up. I had a feeling Helen had been pretty hard on her. "Busy?" I said.

"A little bit."

I took a guess. "You're resigning?"

"I'm afraid so."

"When the world hurts you, why hurt yourself on top of it? Tell me who's the best cop you ever knew?"

"Clete Purcel," she said.

"Second question," I said. "Who will never be hired by any police department in the United States or Canada or even the South Pole?"

"Good try, Dave."

I pulled up a chair to the side of her desk. Behind her I could see the tops of the oak trees by the bayou and a lone pelican gliding close to the water. "Have the good sense to know who your friends are," I said. 'You're brave, you're smart, and you stand up for the downtrodden, just like Clete and Alafair. The combination is rare."

"Alafair was the most talented in our drama class in St. Martinville. She and Clemmy. I was jealous."

"I need you to get to Bedford Ludlow," I said. "He obviously likes you. He's worked with you at the archeological site. He senses you have a kind heart. He probably hasn't known many people like you."

She slowly pulled loose the top page of the legal pad, tore it into strips, then cross-stripped them into the waste basket.

"I give you my word I'll try my best not to cause trouble again," she said. "Particularly knocking people down."

"That's no fun," I replied.

She smiled, but not at my joke. There was a sadness about her, and I knew why. She never had a father, and I promised myself that I would never exploit her. It's funny about the dead. They have great control over us. Sometimes on a rainy afternoon I saw my parents looking at me from the edge of a cane field stricken by drought, beckoning in the mist, telling me that it's all right to join them. But I never know if it's a trick, and for that reason I flee their presence and feel a great guilt for doing so.

"Are you okay?" she said.

"Sure."

"I think we need to come down on the handyman before we do anything else," she said. "He told you he didn't have anything to do with Elton Foot going to jail, right?"

"Yeah."

"But Clete said he was lying?"

"That's what Clete's jailhouse snitch said. You know where he is?"

"The handyman is renting a little farmhouse up on the bayou just before you go into St. Martin Parish."

"What's to lose?" I said, and winked.

Why did I wink? For the same reason most jerks do when they want to cover their own inadequacy.

The farmhouse she mentioned was next to a cane field not far from the place where I often saw my parents. I looked at the sky. A rain shower was just starting to fall in St. Martin Parish.

The house was small and stained with smoke from stubble fires, the gallery, window screens, and tin roof rusted, with chickens in the yard and the handyman's ice-cream-and-popsicle cart parked by his truck. There was also a stench from a cracked brick barbecue pit that smelled like burned garbage or chitlins or a rat caught in a chimney.

I told Valerie Benoit to drive the cruiser, primarily because Valerie made a promise to me but not to Helen and I wanted Valerie to feel she was on board. I suspect that sounds foolish. But small things mean a great deal to a class and culture that has been demeaned for over four hundred years. During my lifetime, including my adulthood, the Klan blew up colored churches and blinded and killed children and castrated and hanged and sawed-in-half black males, and I knew lawmen who thought these events were hilarious. They weren't in a whorehouse, either. I listened to them roar in the bar of the Evangeline Hotel in downtown Lafayette when I came home from Shitsville.

By the way, Willie Francis, twice electrocuted, had lived a short distance from the farmhouse rented by Boone Hendrix.

I stepped up on the gallery and knocked on the screen door. Hendrix came from the back of the house dressed in his denims and eating a slice of ham and onions and pickles and tomatoes inside a chunk of French bread. He tilted his head to see past me. "Is that the woman who clubbed that man half to death?"

"I wouldn't phrase it that way, Mr. Hendrix," I said.

"So what do you want?"

"We have a witness who says you visited Elton Foot before he got transferred to the stockade and cooked in a box," I replied. "But you weren't there?"

"I did not say that," he said. "I don't associate with people like that. He was burned up?"

"Did you or did you not talk to Elton Foot in a holding cell?"

"I prefer not to say." He looked at the ceiling. The rain was hitting the roof as hard as pecans.

"Look at me, please," I said.

"All of this will be gone."

"What will?" I said.

He wrapped a napkin around his sandwich and put it in the pocket of a denim jacket on the back of a chair. Then he snapped the flap on the pocket and looked at it. "Everything is gonna be burned or washed away," he said.

"When I hear that kind of talk, I believe the people saying it want it to happen. I think you're a better man than that, Mr. Hendrix."

His face went out of shape. It was obvious he was a man not often corrected. "I got carpenter work to do. That's my real work. I come from shipwrights."

"I believe you, Mr. Hendrix," I said. "That's why you vex me. You're an honest man. But I think you might have told at least one lie to me."

His nostrils whitened around the edges. "About what?"

"Not going in my house. Not listening to my Jimmie Rodgers records."

He coughed like he had a small fishhook in his throat. I felt sorrow for him. If he was a liar, he had little practice at it.

"You went to extremes to assure me you were not a voyeur, remember?" I said. "You accidentally punched through the roof into the attic, and told me you saw a Thompson machine gun. You were trying to be honest."

I thought he was going to have a nervous breakdown. "I listened to your records, Detective Robicheaux. Yes, sir, I did it and I'm ashamed. You can arrest me if you want."

"That's not exactly on a level with the Brinks Robbery," I said. "You can listen to my records anytime you want. But I need to know if you had something to do with scaring Elton Foot out of his skin."

"I don't have anything to say on that, Detective Robicheaux," he said.

"We're trying to help you, Mr. Hendrix," Valerie said.

He shook his head before the words were out of Val's mouth. "You don't know me," he said. "You don't know the things I've done. You don't know what has been done to me."

"We've run you through every computer in the country, Mr. Hendrix," I said. "Who are you?"

He took a thermos out of his icebox. "I'm helping the man who runs the bird and wild animal shelter in Loreauville. Lock up for me, will you?"

* * *

Valerie was silent as we drove back to the sheriff's department. Outside of New Iberia we went through a tunnel of trees that was whirling with rain. On one side of the road was an old antebellum plantation home, one made of wood, not stone or brick or Spanish ironwork. It had been built by a free black man who owned slaves and a brick factory.

"What are you thinking about?" I said.

"The mention he made of what had been done to him," she replied. "He didn't say exactly what or who. There's nothing on him in the computer?"

"There're places where people still disappear. The Washington rainforest, Northwest Montana, the Glades, the Atchafalaya Basin. There're places in Canada that are like the first day of Creation."

She went silent again, a frown on her brow.

"Something is bothering you, Valerie," I said. "You want to tell me what it is?"

"You said he accidentally found a Thompson machine gun in your attic. Did he mention the name 'Thompson' or did you make the reference?"

"He identified it."

"How many civilians would know what a Thompson is?" she asked.

"They've been around since 1918."

"No, no," she said. "There were just a few of them used in Vietnam. He obviously wasn't in the service or he would be in the computer. What does that say to you?"

"I haven't thought about it."

She made a murmuring sound and looked in the rearview mirror. I think she was looking at the desiccated plantation house and its grayness in the rain and the emptiness in its windows, or the fallow acreage that might have contained her ancestors, all of which could have iconic meaning for her and none for a white man.

Then she looked straight at me, as though she read my mind. "You think he might be a collector?" she said.

"You never can tell," I replied.

"One who would know about German machine guns?"

"You got me."

"Maybe a MG-42, the kind that shredded Jack Raider into shit."

"Where did you get the image?"

"Dave, have you talked with the FBI about this?"

"They're smarter than I. I don't want to bother them."

"How generous," she said.

"Forget the Feds," I said. "They've got their own grief. We're going to be dealing with Sidney Ludlow and his autistic son. You thought the greaseballs in the Quarter were bad? Sidney Ludlow is not a criminal. He's a vapor, an ugly thought, a bad dream you had when you were a kid. He's the guy who steals your faith in your fellow man."

"I think that's all wrong," she said.

"How?"

"Ludlow is a racist, but he tipped his hat to me because I drove his son home. Before the Civil War, right here in New Iberia, a vicious white lady branded and blinded a black woman. The ex-slave woman would have starved to death if she hadn't begged food from Willie Burke's house right there by the drawbridge. I know that because that black lady was my great-great grandmother. Don't talk to me about evil, Dave."

We were in the beginning of a strange era, one that saw statues torn down and films censored with insane unintended consequences. Nobody would know of the injustices done to people of color, just like the Taliban at work. Oh, well, if Valerie Benoit kept flying the flag and blowing the bullhorn, our history would not sink in the sand, and for that reason I said nothing and closed my eyes and slept briefly before I heard the tires hit the grid on the drawbridge over the bayou, then pull in behind Clete Purcel's detective agency.

Clete opened the back door. We ran inside, an umbrella over our heads.

"What's the haps?" he said.

"No haps, no ideas, no plans," I said, folding the umbrella, shaking it off.

"That bad, huh?" he said.

"Yeah, you got something in mind?" I asked.

He looked at an empty yellow bus go over the drawbridge, then looked at Valerie. "Today's Thursday?" he said. "Think your archeological group could borrow a school bus or two on Saturday?"

Chapter Thirty-Six

As I said earlier, time gets away, doesn't it? Janus, the two-faced Roman god who gave us our first month on the calendar, seems to devour the past in a wink while disallowing us the future that we feel should be ours. Why, it seems only a few days ago I told you of the young people who saw a creature dragging the poor body of Clemmy Benoit along the bayou while fireworks popped in the sky. In no time, we discovered how fragile our Acadian world was and how easily it sifts between our fingers.

That's why the two buses loaded with young people were such a balm to the soul as they arrived early Saturday morning on the possible edges of Jerry Carlucci's property. The sunrise was the color of a broken peach; the light seemed to race across the miles of green marshland and then drop into the Gulf of Mexico. It was a magical place, one that could have floated away from Eden, one that had its own metamorphosis. You could feel a tension in the sky, like it was made of silk and easily torn, but for reasons we would not understand. In the distance I saw a black bear and her cub splash through a chain of ponds, then the mother stopped and slapped a fish on the sand, as though demonstrating that the antediluvian world was still with us and still aborning.

* * *

Yes, it was a grand morning. The young people were happy, in the way that young people are. But not everyone there was of a glad heart. Valerie had gotten Sidney Ludlow's phone number and called him and asked if he and his son would like to join their dig. It worked, except Ludlow brought a half dozen gangsters with him, including the man whose face Clete flattened in a plate of grits. Also, I saw Jerry Carlucci coming toward us in his Jeep, although this area seemed too far from his saloon to claim ownership, which made me wonder why he was about to join us.

Clete and Alafair were standing next to me. "I really don't like that guy," Clete said.

"No kidding?" I said.

"He gave the rest of us a bad name," he said.

Of course, Clete was talking about Shitsville and the lost sleep that many of us brought home. "Forget him," I said. "Let him hump his own pack."

Clete screwed a cigarette in his mouth but didn't light it. "It's pretty out here. But I think those greaseballs need to go somewhere else."

Alafair frowned. "Clete, that's not why we're here."

"So what do I know?" he said, and lit his cigarette with his Zippo. I could smell last night's beer on him. I took the cigarette out of his mouth and flipped it into a hole full of water.

"Dave, will you stop turning with my dials?" he said. "I can't stand it."

"Sorry," I said.

Jerry parked his Jeep and got out. He was wearing a black suit and a six-star Stetson hat with a purple vest and needle-nose Lucchese boots. He could have been the twin brother of Wyatt Earp. He tipped his hat to Alafair, but looked right through Clete and me.

"Y'all still looking for Confederates on their way to Mexico, Miss Alafair?" he said.

She smiled but didn't speak.

"You're not going to say hello to Clete and me?" I said.

"Sure," he replied. "What the hell are you doing here again?"

"Enjoying life," I replied.

"No, you're not," he said. "You're here because you're on the wrong side of history. So are you, Purcel. You think a casino is going to ruin the earth. You know how many jobs a casino will create around here? Why don't you ask the Indians? They can't wait to get started."

Clete's eyes went flat, the way they do when he goes away to a private place.

"Sell your doodah to someone else, Jerry," I said. "How's it feel to be a hump for Sidney Ludlow?"

"I work for myself, not for anybody else," Jerry said. "Maybe sometimes I jiggle the law, but this is Louisiana. People want it that way. We had a governor who said he could only lose an election if he got caught in bed with a dead girl or a live boy."

"Yeah, and he went to the pen," I replied.

Jerry turned back to Alafair. "I got some food coming out, Miss Alafair, just a little show of goodwill."

"I think you might check with Valerie," Alafair replied.

"Valerie Benoit is here?" Jerry asked.

"Yeah, what do you think?" Clete said, like an elephant emerging from a nap.

"I got no grief with you, Purcel, even though you wrecked my property and you've got a toxic personality."

"Well, I've got a beef with you," Clete said. "You're not wanted. So how about climbing into your shit-machine and going back to your squirrel-hole and taking out the garbage and cleaning the toilets; they're known for their stink. While you're at it, get rid of the Henry Fonda costume."

"What do you mean?" Jerry said.

"Henry Fonda was a war hero," Clete said.

Jerry stared at Clete, his face a study in confusion, as though he couldn't understand the emotions taking place inside himself.

Clete had robbed Jerry of his icons—both the great actor and the clothes he wore in *My Darling Clementine*—and used them to debase Jerry. Even though Clete bore Jerry a great animus, I don't think he intended for the blow to go so deep. But it was there on Jerry's face and in his body, like a boxer who had taken a right hook right under the heart, the kind of punch that turns your viscera to water.

However, Jerry was Jerry. I had to hand it to him. He caught himself and lifted his hat to Alafair.

"I've heard you were Phi Beta Kappa at your college in Portland," he said. "I hear that's quite an honor. Best of everything to you, Miss Alafair. I was always one of your greatest admirers."

Rhett Butler couldn't have said it better. Jerry got in his Jeep and turned around carefully so as not to splash mud or water on us.

I don't know why I used a boxing metaphor to describe his humiliation. Maybe it was because Jerry had been a true champ when he was in the Golden Gloves finals, then the nationals, and should have gone up north and stayed in the ring. He probably could have had a career. Jerry would let you break your fists on his face. How many guys can go fifteen rounds and keep telling the referee the blood in their eyes is from the other guy?

Or maybe I was just being a sap. Clete knew what I was thinking. He always did. He was twitching a matchstick up and down between his teeth.

"*What?*" I said.

"Don't let him fool you, noble mon," Clete said. "That guy would put the Statue of Liberty on the stroll if he could," he said.

Sometimes it was hard to argue with Clete.

The young people had spread from the buses with their rakes and shovels and sifting screens, finding more beer cans than any object that resembled a nineteenth-century artifact. Their equipment was certainly not professional, nor were their methods, and like most young people, their desires were of an innocent nature that they masked with foolishness they would eventually give up as the day warmed and the sun climbed. By noon the grills were lit and the franks and hamburgers were streaming smoke, and no one was paying much attention to the year 1865 and an army that planned to cross the Rio Grande and sign on with Maximilian and lose another war.

However, I do not mean our young group was like any other. Not at all. The piece of terrain on which we were standing seemed to have a strange ambiance, a defect in the sunlight, a connection to past events, as though it floated loose from an earlier time when Man made choices that for good or bad still had their consequences.

The wind was from the south, and the salt air and the kelp and the fish roe were like human birth. But it was more than that. The swamp was full of flooded trees and birds in the limbs, hundreds or thousands of them, and the levees were green and had yellow wildflowers on them and flocks of grasshoppers that were as long and thick as my index finger. A rain cloud blocked the sun, then broke with a scattering of raindrops that were like coins, just as though it were a small part of something much bigger than itself.

I guess my description here is more like a stage play than a depiction of young people on an outing on Saturday morning in spring. But that's how I felt. Clete already said it. Sidney Ludlow and his thugs didn't belong here. No, sir. Or at least in our opinion they didn't. The only decent member among them was the boy-like autistic Bedford, who had a metal detector now and was letting other members of the dig use it.

About noon Boone Hendrix showed up in his truck, wearing pressed denims and rubber boots and a brilliant yellow straw hat with a black band. He had also brought two welding rods that were bent at ninety-degree angles and could be used to search for minerals or metals under the ground. Beyond the swamp, I could hear the muffled sound of thunder, although I could see no storm clouds.

Clete bit into a hot dog, a wad of bread and wiener in his jaw. "What do you think the handyman is up to?" he said.

"Maybe nothing. He likes kids."

"Will you stop it?"

"Stop what?"

"Pretending that crazy people are normal. That guy was not born. He was shot out of a cannon."

"Clete, will you quit all these pessimistic statements? You remind me of Digger O'Dell."

"The friendly undertaker?" he replied, pointing to his sternum. "Me?"

"Yeah, in a word."

"That deeply insults me. Could you at least use a contemporary insult?" He bit into his hot dog again. "People don't even know who Digger O'Dell was. Know why that is?"

"Tell me," I said.

"They're dumb shits. I hate them all. With their fucking phones grafted to the sides of their heads. Know what the problem really is? It's not the phone. It's what they do with it. Nothing. They should have them buried in their coffins."

"Do you know that sounds a little unhinged?" I said.

He was about to answer, then his gaze went past me, toward the south, where a black bear with her cub was walking along the edge of the swamp.

"Jesus Christ," he said.

"What is it?" I replied. "They won't hurt anybody."

"You got your binocs?"

What Clete called my "binocs" were a pair of opera glasses. I handed them to him. He lifted them to his face. "Oh, shit, I knew it, I knew it, I knew it."

"Will you tell me what you're talking about?"

He shoved the glasses in my hands. "Button man at two o'clock. That cocksucker."

I put the glasses to my eyes. It was the man whose face Clete had grinded into the table at Victor's, the one who we guessed was a hitter for the Mob. He held a chrome-plated revolver with two hands and was raising it to a firing position. It was probably a .357. Clete must have seen it flash in the sunlight.

"Get in the pickup," I said.

Before I could reach the driver's door, I heard two pops, like wet Chinese firecrackers in the wind. I got behind the wheel and floored the accelerator, jolting over a patch of dry ground, both doors hardly shut. But the damage was done.

The button man without a name was among his friends, dressed in a suit and wearing shades, an ignorant, half-twisted grin on his mouth. Clete sprinted out of my pickup before I could stop. "You motherfucker!" he said. "Why did you do that?"

"They were headed our way," the shooter said. "They're dangerous when they got a cub."

Clete twisted the revolver, a .357, from the button man's hand and hit him in the face with it, then lifted him in the air by his clothes and threw him over the hood of a Chrysler. He picked up the revolver and flicked the cylinder out of the frame and shook the bullets out of the chambers.

Five of the button man's friends were walking toward us. I pulled back my coat and exposed my shield and gun. "Detective Dave Robicheaux, Iberia Parish Sheriff's Department," I said. "Step back or go to jail."

The button man was on the ground, his back propped against the right-front hubcap of the Chrysler, his sunglasses crooked on his face, a rivulet of blood from one nostril. Clete loaded one round into a chamber of the .357, and snapped the cylinder back in the frame, then half-cocked the hammer and spun the cylinder and kneeled down in the saw grass.

"What's your name?" Clete said, breathing hard, the back of his neck as hard as boiler plate, the pockmarks in it as deep as cigar burns.

"Did you hear me?" Clete said.

"John Smith," the man on the ground said. He wiped the blood from his nose.

"You don't look like a John Smith. You look like a button man. You push the buttons, people disappear."

"I'm who I say, wiseass. You know whose Chrysler that is?"

"Shut up and give me your wallet."

"I think I got a broken tailbone. I can't get up."

"Good, I've got an excuse to chain-drag you."

"I got witnesses," the man on the ground said. "Go fuck yourself."

Clete's face was as flat as a bread pan, and not putting on a performance. In fact, he was scaring me.

"Why did you do it?" he said. "Why would anyone do it? You don't deserve to live."

The button man, or the man on the ground, knew it, too. "Wait a minute," he said. "Maybe I went a little wrong. Maybe I can fix it. Maybe bring some veterinarians out here."

Clete shoved the snub nose of the .357's barrel into the button man's mouth, raking his teeth, sticking the sight into the roof of his mouth and the back of his throat. Then he pulled the trigger. The hammer snapped on an empty chamber. The button man jerked against the hubcap and fender, sweat breaking as bright as ice water on his face.

"That's just a mommy bear raising her baby," Clete said. "Tell me why you did it, you piece of shit. Why'd you *fucking* do that?"

In situations like this I had seen Clete palm a bullet and fake loading a revolver with it, but this time I was sure I saw it go into the chamber.

"Clete," I said, my voice as low as I could speak. "We need to get the veterinary guys out here."

He looked at me as though I were a stranger. "Yeah, let's get that started."

"So let's do that," I said. I reached toward his right hand.

"You want the piece?" he said.

"Right, we don't need it now," I said.

"Yeah," he replied. But he didn't put down the .357.

"Clete, I can see the mama bear," I said. "She's limping with the cub, but she's alive. First things first, right? We want to get the docs out here."

"Yeah, you get on that, Streak. In the meantime I'll get this guy's identity," he said. "I think he's trying to coordinate with us here. Right, John Smith? You're doing a real solid for the Earth? You wouldn't put me on the slide, would you, Clyde?"

Clete pulled the button man to his feet by one hand and started to raise the barrel of the .357. Then he lowered it. "Throw your wallet on the ground," he said.

"Sure," the button man said. "You're not gonna do that again, huh? Look, man—"

"Shut up," Clete said. He picked up the wallet and shook everything out of it. "I see four names here, none of them John Smith."

"Well, I've got different names," the button man said. "I can work with you on that. If you'll give me a—"

Clete threw the wallet in the button man's face. "If I see you in town, you'd better cross the street. It would really be the smart thing to do."

Then Clete walked away, his cell phone pressed to his ear, his lips moving in the wind.

I could feel my heart slowing, the air going out of my lungs. The friends of the button man looked at the ground and said nothing.

Chapter Thirty-Seven

Few or any of the people who came on the buses knew what the button man had done. I suspect that like all gentle and innocent people they could not process an aberration like the button man without traumatizing themselves. Truth be known, I had the same problem. I had been worried about Clete, my fellow member of the Bobbsey Twins from Homicide. Clete was the benevolent warrior who casually mentioned his relationship with Joan of Arc, and the fact that she called him Sir Clete. When people stared at him, he smiled back at them, his green eyes bright, his little-boy haircut wet-combed, without a drop of booze on his breath.

I caught up with him at the pickup. "Tell me you knew where the loaded chamber was," I said.

He looked past the swamp at the brassy sunglow rising off the Gulf. "Yeah, I think it had a heft to the right."

"You were pretty sure of that, huh?" I said.

"Yeah, I asked Joan about it."

"Why didn't you say that?"

"Joan didn't answer," he said. "But when she doesn't answer, she means 'Stomp-ass, whatever you do will be fine.'"

He nodded energetically to make sure I got the message.

"Yeah, I can see how you'd be assured on that," I said, then took a large gulp of air. "Did you get the veterinarians?"

"Yeah, both of them," he replied. "They promised to be here this afternoon. Dave?"

"What?"

"No matter how this comes out, I'm gonna get Sidney Ludlow. He brought that button man down here."

"Let him alone. He'll fall in his own shit."

"No, he's a killer. I can smell it on him. All hitters have it. It smells like birth. They hate the world, and they get as many of us as they can. And they don't all carry guns, either."

I walked back toward the buses and the cookout grills looking for Alafair, then saw her up on higher ground, her back to me. She was watching Bedford Ludlow, who was now by himself and swinging his metal detector on a dry piece of land that was not far from Jerry Carlucci's property, or what Jerry would deem his property.

"What's going on?" I said.

"Bedford seems to have found something," she replied. "I thought this would be an opportunity to talk with him. Did you and Clete have a problem with those gangsters?"

I told her what had happened. Her face turned pale, her dark hair blowing in her eyes. "Dave, you need to get Clete out of here. All this may be a big mistake."

"It's okay now," I said.

"Think so?" she said. "Isn't that Jerry Carlucci coming in his Jeep?"

"Jerry could have had a real life," I said. "He still might have a run at it."

"You've never learned a lesson from your own experience, Dave."

"What's that?"

"When I was thirteen you told me the difference between good and evil. You said, 'There are people who deliberately erase God's thumbprint from their souls. You'll see it in their eyes. They will never change. They will take you down to their level, but you will never bring them up to yours. Leave them forever.'"

"I haven't seen that in Jerry," I said.

"You might have a chance. He just stopped to peel the skin off an autistic savant. Unless I'm mistaken, there's spit flying from his mouth."

She wasn't exaggerating. The wind was up, loud enough to hear, strong enough to ripple the water in the ponds and blow a green haze above the flooded grass in the marsh. But Jerry was surmounting it all, waving outside his Jeep, his mouth a dark hole. Poor Bedford was obviously terrified.

I hooked my arm in Alafair's and walked toward him. He seemed not to notice either of us. Why did I hook her arm? When you get into it with a rageaholic, you do not indicate that your companion is less than you or him.

"Dial it down, Jerry, or I'll do it for you," I said.

"I'm trying to help this man, Dave, so beat feet and for once mind your own fucking business."

Here's another tip. When your enemy is compelled to swear, he's afraid.

"This *is* my business," I said. "I'm a police officer. We protect innocent people who are being harassed or in this case terrorized."

"I was protecting him from himself," he said. "His metal detector went crazy because we're all standing on top of an oil dump. We're talking about hundreds of barrels."

"How do you know that?" I asked.

"I dug down to it one year ago."

"And didn't tell anybody?" I said.

"There's no question about the ownership of this property. It's mine. I'm planning to build a casino here. I didn't want to start a panic."

"You can sue," I said.

"Are you serious? Louisiana encourages out-of-state companies to dump their waste in open ditches in black towns from Baton Rouge to New Orleans. That's why they call it Cancer or Death Alley. Their kids go to school with vomit bags. Do I have to explain that to you, Dave?"

It sounded like a comic book tale. It wasn't. The governor even stopped pro-bono attorneys at Tulane from filing class action suits against the waste companies. I knew people personally who died moaning from the steady infection of the drinking water they trusted for years. Yes, Jerry was telling the truth about our history. But that didn't mean we were standing on it.

"I'd like to take Bedford back to the bus," Alafair said.

"That's what I was trying to do," he replied.

"Stop lying, Jerry," I said.

"You always want to push it, don't you, Dave?"

"In your case, yeah, I would like that."

"Anytime, pal."

"I think for the first time I see the real you, Jerry," I said. "You could have come home and been humble and asked people to forgive whatever you may have or have not done. But instead you had to be a mystery man. Why is that? I'm not sure. But my guess is your old man kicked you out when you came home."

He pulled a shovel out of his Jeep. "I'll count to five before I take your head off," he said.

"I'll save you the trouble," I said. "Do it now."

Then the sun went behind a dark cloud, dropping a shadow across the entirety of the terrain. Bedford had stepped between Jerry and me, as though he were just waking up. "I know who took Clemmy away from the bad men," he said. "He wears parts of animals. I don't want to play anymore. I want to find the treasure. I want to go somewhere else."

Then he swept his metal detector back and forth, wobbling with its weight, like a drunk man, dialing up the volume, the static crackling like an electric storm.

* * *

That night we had fifty-mile-an-hour winds that blew garbage cans down East Main Street and broke windows in the downtown area, including Clete's agency. Clete boarded-up the window, bought a bucket of fried chicken and buttermilk biscuits and dirty rice, and came to the house for supper. By the way, in Louisiana people eat supper at night and dinner at noon. I know of no other group that practices this custom. I do know, however, that Louisiana has the highest rate of coronary and arterial disease in the United States. "Yeah, that's because of the obesity," Clete says. "Louisiana is packed with baby hippos." But he doesn't include himself.

We finished supper a little after eight P.M., after the storm and the light had drained from the sky and the rainfrogs began throbbing, the clouds purple and black and flickering with electricity. The backyard was soggy and green, the bayou over the bank, flooding the mudflats, the surface rippling like spoons of pewter, almost like the night our Saturnalian tale began.

Can I confess something to you? I believe there is a beginning and an end to all things, with a caveat: The end can be the beginning. Circularity is the nature of the world and the universe. It's Man who imposes the square and the rectangle under our feet, even though our bodies wish to be round.

In other words, I realized that evening I had returned to the place where I began when Clemmy Benoit's body was dropped on my property. The creature who had dragged her body in a garbage sack was still out there, rife with the permanence of the grave, investing his faith in a legal system that was shoddy at best, and Clete and Alafair and Helen and Valerie and I had changed nothing and remained witnesses and not participants in the long slog to provide justice for those who have no voice.

As I stood in the doorway of our small screen porch, breathing the wet coolness of the evening, the rain dripping from the trees, I knew I would never have peace unless we gave justice to the killers of Clemmy Benoit. And I knew that the struggle was not just about her either, and I knew that wherever she was she would understand my feelings, because when you stack time in the Garden of Gethsemane, your ticket is punched, and you have brothers and sisters forever.

That said, Alafair had not spoken about her conversation with Bedford Ludlow, who had swung his metal detector in an apparent panic.

"You're worrying about me again?" Alafair said behind me.

"Yes, I am," I replied.

"Why?"

"Because when you don't talk, you're hiding something. Worse, you're hiding it because it's really bad and you don't want to leave some ugly images with your listener."

"That's pretty close," she replied.

"What did Bedford say?"

"He said 'Bad people hurt Clemmy to find a treasure. Then a monster man took her away.'"

"That's the guy who dropped her here?" I said.

"Sounds like it."

"Bedford saw Clemmy tortured?" I said.

"I didn't ask. I think he's pretty fragile. I'm not an analyst, but I fear for him."

"He's going to have a psychotic break?"

"I would not want him around firearms," she said.

"Did he mention any names besides Clemmy's?"

"No."

"Did you mention Elton Foot's name?"

"No," she said. "I won't either."

"That's all right. You did a good job, Alfie."

"But you think the man who tortured or killed Clemmy was Elton Foot?" she said.

"He worked for the Mob in New Orleans and Florida."

"Which means Sidney Ludlow might have employed him here?"

"Yeah, the old-time dons kept their distance from their own dirty work. There aren't many of them around anymore."

"Who set Foot on fire in the parish jail?" she said.

"Someone just like himself," I said. "A guy who's depraved and hides it well."

We went back inside the kitchen and made *café au lait*, then took the tray into the living room and joined Clete where he was watching a baseball game. Clete claimed he loved baseball, but I think his love was for the few games his father took him to as a boy, the drunken milkman with the leather strop and the scattered rice grains on the floor.

"Everything all right?" he said, picking up a cup from the tray.

"Yeah, sure," I said.

But he wanted to know if Alafair had gotten any information from Bedford Ludlow about Clemmy Benoit. Why should he not? We had all come to a dead end.

"We didn't learn much today, Clete," Alafair said. "Sorry."

"Another day, then," he said, lifting his cup to his mouth.

Rough as he was, Clete was always a gentleman with women.

Do you have premonitions? I think I've had a few. I've probably already described the twang of a wire stretched between two tree trunks in a rainforest, or a psychopath in a strap undershirt lowering his newspaper with a smile and popping two .25-caliber rounds into my back. Just before each incident the clock stopped and the world went silent and the molecules or atoms that make up the universe became a patina of stillness.

I wanted to speak but couldn't. I also wanted to run, but my nervous system was useless, the way spinal anesthesia robs you of sensation and the ability to move.

Clete's coffee cup was below his chin, his mouth open with a word that never came out. Alafair seemed to be looking through the hallway and into the kitchen and maybe through the back window into the rabbit hutches Boone Hendrix made for our animals.

But what I saw most was myself, as though I had floated out of my body, and I knew what was coming and could do nothing about it. I wanted to die, and to ensure that Alafair and Clete did not. I was the oldest of our three and if a tragedy was about to happen, it should be on me, not others, because long ago I was spared while others fell by the wayside, and I was not worthy then or now. Wasted days and wasted nights were my bane. Were the people I loved most on earth about to be taken from me while I watched their deaths?

I heard the tinkle of glass and a thropping sound, and saw the curtain on the front window jump, with no report behind it. But I couldn't keep the images in sequence and couldn't be sure if one or two projectiles had been fired at the house. I was not hit, but I wanted to be. What was happening was not fair. Clete had three Purple Hearts. Was it right for him to come home and be shot by a piece of shit? How about Alafair? She escaped the massacres in El Salvador and drowning in a plane crash only to be murdered on an oak-shaded street in southern Louisiana?

I saw Clete's cup shatter and Alafair's hands jerk in the air, as though someone had jumped at her from behind a door. Outside a car sped away.

"Clete!" I said. "Clete! Oh, Alfie! Alfie! Alfie! Oh, please, God, not this! God, not this! God, not this!"

That's all I could say. Then I thought I was going to go crazy.

Chapter Thirty-Eight

The ceramic had exploded in Clete's hand, cutting his fingers and his upper right breast and Alafair's cheek. I grabbed Alafair and pushed her to the floor, then pulled the .45 auto I kept sometimes under a cushion on the couch. Clete was already unstrapping his hideaway from his ankle, his face as taut as a drum, staying lower than the windowsill, his eyelids stapled to his brow. "I'm going out the side window," he said. "I'll call in the shots-fired."

"Roger that," I said. I clicked off the ceiling light and the television and pushed down the reading lamp and pulled the chain, then looked at Alafair. "Are you okay, Alfie?" I said.

"Yes," she said, her voice hoarse.

"Look at me," I said.

She started to stand up. I pulled her back down. She was obviously traumatized. "Stay where you are," I said.

"I heard the bullet go by," she said. "There was only one."

"Yeah," I said, not sure what she meant.

"The bullet didn't hit a wall or glass," she said. "It must have exited through a back screen."

Her eyes were filled with fear. "The animals," she said, and got up and ran through the hall and kitchen and out the back.

I pulled back the slide on the .45 and chambered a round, then went out the front door and down the steps, half-crouched, both hands gripped on the .45 auto, both arms extended. The street was empty. Most of our neighbors must have heard the shot and turned off their lights. The trees and scrubs were drenched, the rain gutters clogged with leaves. I saw Clete's silhouette behind a magnolia tree.

"You okay?" I said.

"Yeah," he said. "But stay where you are. There may be a backup shooter across the street. Three o'clock, by the old bank."

"You saw him?"

"Maybe," he said. "At least a shadow. Behind the pillars."

"You're not sure?" I said.

"No, I'm not sure. Just wind it down. That's what I'm saying. You're wired."

Maybe I was. But them's the breaks. I crossed the street even though the streetlamps were on. The old bank dated from Reconstruction. I walked all the way around it, then crossed the street back to the house. "Clear," I said.

"That was dumb," Clete said.

I looked up and down East Main. A fresh set of tire tracks went from our curb to the Shadows and into the business district. "You didn't get a good look at a possible backup shooter, huh?" I asked.

"Are you listening to me, Dave?"

"Yeah, you said I'm dumb."

"You want to kick ass, big mon. That's not cool."

"My daughter was almost killed and you were inches from having your face blown off. What am I supposed to feel?"

"Serenity."

"There's a first aid kit in the bathroom," I replied. "Use it, then soak your head."

I walked up the driveway and under the porte-cochere and into the backyard. Alafair had our long-hair cat named Cannon Ball nestled in her arms. She nuzzled his head, then kissed him between his ears. Lady Godiva, our raccoon, was perched on top of the hutch, her fat tail hanging over the side, her nose twitching in the breeze.

Clete told me to wind it down. I thought I had. But he was right. I was on a dry drunk, what Clete calls "stoned, zoned, and shit-blown" without the flak juice. Something was seriously loose in my head, and I'll tell you what it was. When I saw Alafair's arms jerk in the air and Clete's blood fly on her skin, I thought she had been hit and was going down. I cannot describe the momentary sense of loss I experienced. I do know how human beings can watch their family members murdered. I do not know how the surviving Jews of the camps in Hitler's Europe kept their sanity.

"Did you see anything out front?" Alafair said. "Brass or a cigarette butt maybe?"

"I haven't looked," I said. I released the .45's magazine and pulled back the slide and tipped the round out of the chamber.

"You don't look right, Dave."

"That's because I don't feel right."

"Don't tell me to go back to Portland," she said.

"I won't."

"So what are you planning to do?"

"Talk to Helen. Throw a wider net. Maybe cooperate with the Feds."

"No, you're not. You and Clete are going to run up a black flag and get yourselves killed or sent to prison. In Angola."

"Give me some credit, Alfie."

"I do. Each of you," she said. "Every day. You don't listen."

I could see the red and blue and orange flashes and reflections and pulses of emergency lights on the drawbridge and out on Main and in the front yard and driveway. Valerie Benoit came up the driveway first, in a cruiser and in uniform. I could see the silhouette of a man in the backseat, behind the grill. Valerie got out with a six-battery flashlight and walked toward me. The man behind the grill was cuffed and made me think of an animal in a cage.

"How's Clete and your daughter?" she said.

"Okay," I said.

"You're not gonna believe this," Valerie said.

"Believe what?" I said.

"Boone Hendrix was in City Park. In his truck. Right by a stolen car."

So why didn't you just tell me that? I thought.

Hendrix was cuffed with his wrists behind him, his neck and spine obviously hurting. "Why did you hook him up?" I asked.

"He sat down on the ground and refused to speak."

"Speak about what?" I asked.

"What was he doing around a stolen car, one that somebody had just abandoned."

"You put your hand on the hood?" I said.

"What do you think, Dave? It was stolen in the early hours this morning. Now it ends up minutes away from a shooting at your house. Then the popsicle guy shows up in the middle of everything, and tells me in effect to go fuck myself. Why would I cuff him? Gee, I don't know."

"You think he's a racist?"

"No, I think he's nuts. The guy who runs the McDonald's says Hendrix drapes paper towels all over the toilet seat, then flushes the towels and floods the building, usually during lunchtime."

"Why are you in uniform?"

"I need the overtime."

She was angry. I couldn't blame her. I was taking her inventory. But I was bothered. She bounced off the wall too many times. Maybe I lived in one world and she lived in a half dozen. I had all the latitude in life I wanted. A shift in the electorate could have her cleaning toilets.

I looked down the street. The canopy of live oaks was bending in the wind, the reflection of the moon and lamps as bright as pearls on the asphalt.

"Is there still a camera on the fence at the Shadows?" I said.

"Yeah, but I don't know if it's pointed at the sidewalk or the street though," she replied.

"Let's take a ride."

"What about the handyman?"

I had to think about that one. "Unhook him."

"You're sure about that?"

I opened the back door of the cruiser. "Do you promise to behave, Mr. Hendrix?"

"I don't promise anything."

"I was almost killed tonight, sir. So were my daughter and my best friend. I would appreciate your help."

His eyes held on mine. "I won't lie to you. That does not mean I'll use the truth to injure."

I gazed at him a long time. His self-imposed righteousness was hard to take, but my adrenaline was burned out and I was running on cinders. "You're an eccentric man, sir," I said. "But God bless you for it. Lean forward and poke your wrists out and don't give me any more of your trash."

"Run that by me again?"

I didn't answer. When you're in a throw-down, no matter what kind, silence is always louder than noise.

We drove down to the Shadows and stopped in front of the entrance and got out on the sidewalk. The bamboo was clattering along the pike fence, the Spanish moss swaying overhead. Valerie went straight to the security camera. "It looks like it's been vandalized," she said.

"When's the last time you saw it?" I said.

"I passed by a couple of days ago," she said. "It looked all right."

Mr. Hendrix was staring through the bamboo at the moonlight on the veranda and the twin chimneys and the flower gardens and the ancient brass sundial by a rain pool that had camelias floating on it. "Look out there," he said to me.

"Yeah?" I replied.

"You don't see anything?"

"Nothing that I don't see every day," I said.

"That's because you don't want to," he replied.

"Would you care to explain that?"

"There are dead people all over these grounds, Detective Robicheaux."

"That might be, Mr. Hendrix. But I don't see them. Right now I want to find out who shot a bullet through my house. Have any members of your family died at the hands of criminals?"

It wasn't a good question to ask. His face sharpened. "Say that again."

"I think you heard me the first time," I said.

"I might break your jaw," he said.

"I do not advise you to do that, sir."

His face was as flat as a shingle.

"I'm waiting, sir," I said.

But he didn't move or even open his lips. Behind him Valerie shook her head, an indication for caution.

"It's the worst burden in the world, Mr. Hendrix," I said. "You might close up the wound, but the scar is for life."

"I'm not interested in your descriptions."

"Why did you pull over to the stolen car?" I asked.

"I heard a *pop* and knew it came from across the bayou and by your house."

"Why did you not dismiss the *pop* as a firecracker?"

"Because I'm not a fool."

"You know something about firearms?"

"Enough to stay away from them. I'm tired of this. I want to go home."

"I'm afraid you can't do that right now," I said.

"Why not?"

"You seem to carry a smell like animals and leaves and smoke, Mr. Hendrix. Why is that?"

"Maybe if you had been to hell, you wouldn't ask that question. It's right close to you. Put your arm through that fence. You'll see."

"Good try, Mr. Hendrix," I said. "Get back in the cruiser."

Valerie drove us over to City Park, where Hendrix's truck and the stolen car, a dark Buick as glossy as a shield, were parked by an asphalt bike trail that threaded through the trees. The Buick was new, the key on the dashboard, the wax-job fresh, pine needles on the roof and windshield. I borrowed Valerie's flashlight and shined it inside. Then I shook out my handkerchief and pulled open the driver's door. The interior light didn't come on. I swept the inside with the flashlight. It was immaculate. I closed the door.

"What's your opinion?" Valerie said.

"It's too neat for the kinds of kids who boost cars. Kids don't think to turn off the interior lights, either. Who owns it?"

"A rich guy and big duck hunter down by Morgan City. Writes for sports magazines. No record for anything."

"You know him?"

"I've seen him around St. Martinville. He's just a fat guy who likes to shoot things."

"Would you ask Mr. Hendrix to get out of the cruiser?"

"What's going on, Dave?"

"To be honest, I don't know."

"That's helpful," she said, her back to me, opening the rear door of the cruiser for the handyman. "Step out, sir. Detective Robicheaux wants to speak with you. I don't have any idea about what."

Chapter Thirty-Nine

He stepped out in the moonlight. It was like a net on his face. I was irritable and didn't want to be mean to him, but the twentieth century was the most violent in human history, and I was tired of being a participant in it.

"This vehicle we're looking at is probably a 'drop car,' Mr. Hendrix," I said. "Hitters or button men leave one at the scene or they drop it later if the package is in the trunk or if the package and the car are going into a crunching machine. Are you with me, sir?"

"No," he said.

"I thought you might say that," I replied. "Let me put it this way: You show up where you shouldn't be. Or where you might have been. I think maybe you burned Elton Foot to death."

"I don't like you saying that to me," he replied.

"Too bad. Tell that to Foot. Frying in lockdown must be a nightmare. Evidently the explosives went slow."

He stepped toward me. "Why are you treating me like this?"

"Because I have the feeling someone else is about to die," I said.

He was within ten inches now, his shoulders and neck as tight as a stump. "You're like them," he said.

"Like who?"

"The pilgrims. They loved the creak of the lynch rope."

He was shorter than I, closer now, his breath on my skin.

"Step back, sir."

"I've taken human life."

"Don't push it, Mr. Hendrix," I said.

"It haunts me."

"We'll talk about it," I said.

I saw Valerie moving toward my right side, her feet quiet on a pad of wet pine needles.

"No, they'll be no talk," Hendrix said.

I could see Valerie only on the edge of my vision now. Her palm was resting on the grip of her sidearm.

"I think you have a great love for children, Mr. Hendrix," I said.

"They can't be brought back," he said. "So sometimes a man has to do justice for them."

"Who are you speaking about, sir?"

His eyes were lidless, staring straight into mine, his breath hot but without any odor. "Are you trying to take me to a hospital?"

"I have no intention of that."

Valerie was stone-still, the breeze ruffling the leaves overhead.

Hendrix stepped back and looked at the ground, the moonlight on his head, his heavy, lace-up, steel-toed work shoes motionless in the shadows. I put my hand on his shoulder, then walked away from him, although I was sure he had just confessed to a homicide.

Valerie was silent as she drove back across the bridge to my house.

"You think I let him slide?" I said.

"That part about 'justice'?" she replied. "Maybe he was in the service. Maybe he was a Section Eight. I wouldn't make any judgments yet, Dave."

She made a turn at Burke Street and circled back on East Main, which is a one-way street and of course where I live. The ambulances were gone, but the cruisers were still there, so was the yellow crime-scene tape, and Clete, drinking a beer someone must have given him. The tape stretched through the trees and around the corners of the house, vibrating in the wind, taking me back to the night my wife Annie was murdered alone in our bed when we owned a boat-rental farther down the Teche many years ago.

Clete tilted his beer bottle and almost drank it empty, then looked at me. "I didn't mean to drink inside your house," he said.

"Don't worry about it," I replied. "How do you feel?"

We were in the kitchen with Valerie and Helen. Clete widened his eyes, the skin around them the color of a toadstool, but didn't answer. Alafair was in the backyard with the uniforms and the technicians looking for the bullet that had passed through two windows or one window and one wall.

"Did the handyman help you any?" Helen said.

"Not really," I said.

"He was just passing by?" she said.

"He said he had 'taken human life.'"

"Anyone we know?" she said.

"I believe him, Helen," I said.

"So do I," she said. She was standing in the middle of the room, in her navy blue suit and starched white shirt, her hands on her hips. "Okay, this is what we've put together so far. Interrupt or tell me when I'm wrong. We've got a shooter who fired through the glass, and we've got a stolen car in City Park. We also have a car that burned rubber after the shot was fired. We also have a shadowy figure who was hiding on the property of the old bank. How am I doing so far?"

"Fine," I said.

Clete crunched his beer can and dropped it in the waste bucket next to my reading lamp. He glanced at the kitchen.

"Need something, Clete?" Helen said.

"No, go on."

"Thank you," she said. "How much do you know about the stolen car, Valerie?"

"Not much," Valerie said. She was sitting at the breakfast table, tired like the rest of us. "The owner says it was taken from outside a restaurant about three A.M. in Morgan City."

"Something bother you about that?" Helen said.

"That restaurant closes at eleven P.M. The owner also left the key inside the vehicle. For a rich guy he seems pretty carefree with his automobile."

"Did you try to get to him?" Helen said.

"No, ma'am," Valerie said.

"You don't need to call me 'ma'am,'" Helen said.

Valerie's eyes gazed into neutral space, a place I think she had probably spent a lot of time.

"Good work," Helen said.

But the injury had been done. Helen caught it, too, namely being corrected in front of her peers. Way to go, Helen. "All right, let's start over tomorrow," she said.

Alafair came back into the house, and Valerie and Helen and the uniforms and technicians rolled up their search without finding the lost bullet, and Clete sat down heavily in the living room, the pieces of his coffee mug still on the rug.

"You want to sleep here tonight?" I said.

"Yeah, I might do that," he said. But that was not on his mind. He looked at his watch. "You think that mama bear made it?"

"She's probably a tough gal, Cletus."

"Think so, huh?"

"You bet."

"The Winn-Dixie is open to eleven on Saturday," he said. "I think I got a low sugar level. I might run over to get a couple of candy bars."

Alafair was standing in the door to the hallway. "You really want to do that, Clete?"

"It's a thought," he replied.

I dropped my eyes. I knew his pain. For an alcoholic, one is too many and ten thousand not enough.

"Maybe I should have some coffee and pecan pie and all that kind of stuff," Clete said.

"I think that's grand," Alafair said.

What would I do without Alfie?

Actually I had my own problem, one that bordered on another kind of addiction, but produced the same madness, in fact maybe even worse, the Full-Tilt Boogie on overdrive.

We ate some pie and drank some coffee, then Alafair went to bed and Clete clicked off the light in the living room and lay down on the couch with a pillow for his head and a quilt for his body, although I doubted he slept at all.

In the meantime I pulled down the ladder from the ceiling in the hallway and went up the steps to the attic and turned on the light and sat down on a cane chair and unwrapped the oil cloth I had left the gun in. Just as I had done previously, I loaded the shells in the three magazines, but this time I was more dedicated because I knew the killers who had failed once would not fail again, lest they lose their own lives.

Who were they? No matter whose umbrella they were under, they were professionals, without conscience, willing to kill their own family members. If ordered, they cracked a victim's skull in a vise. This is not the exception; it's the norm in the world of psychopaths. But I had another problem. I didn't know who the target was. Clete had a coffee cup blown out of his hand. That did not mean he was the target. It could have been Alafair or me. The shooter fired only once. This left all kinds of possibilities.

I moved the tips of my fingers over the Thompson's steel-and-wood stock, wondering who carried it at Guadalcanal or Normandy or Iwo Jima, touching the oil or body-grease or volcanic dirt the wood had absorbed, the burnt powder that was perhaps still inside the chamber. It was possible.

Then I realized the serial number has been disfigured with acid and probably ground with an emery wheel. Clete had given me the Thompson in good faith, but the disfiguration meant at least one previous owner was not a collector or G.I. but part of the American Underworld. The disfigurement felt like a secular sacrilege.

But I didn't let that stop me. My home had been violated, my daughter almost killed with a high-caliber bullet, one that cut clean holes in an obstacle and kept going. In my venomous mood, my mind was only on my daughter, not Clete, not me. The man who fired into my house must have seen her, and made a conscious decision to take off her face if he had to. The idea sickened me. I felt my hand squeezing the grip next to the trigger guard, my knuckles whitening.

I had a long list of who might have shot at us. But the only lead we had was a non-lead, the reporting of the stolen vehicle I called the "drop car." The owner said it was stolen from a restaurant that had closed four hours before he called in the theft. The next day was Sunday, a good day to find people at home and unawares. I called Valerie in the morning.

"I need the name of the Buick owner and his telephone number."

"Yeah, sure, what's up?" she replied.

That was a question I didn't want to answer. There were too many people who had motivation to commit serious crimes since we had opened a file on the Clemmy Benoit homicide. Valerie, I hate to say, was one of them, including lying when she denied her relationship with Clemmy. Also, she was dead serious about finding Confederate gold that could tie up thousands of acres in litigation, a situation that could give her and her group political power.

"I need to talk to the Buick's owner, that's all," I said.

"What are you not telling me, Dave?"

"I just want to double-check the times of the restaurant closing and the man discovering the loss of his car."

"I was gonna do that myself," she said.

"There's probably an explanation. Maybe the restaurant was hosting a private party. It's probably not a big deal."

"Want me to go with you? You don't even know what the guy looks like."

My ear was starting to perspire against the phone receiver. "It's Sunday. Why not relax?"

"Sure, while some fuckhead plants another .357 or a Magnum .44 revolver round in my partner's house."

"Can you hold down the profanity?"

"Sorry," she said.

"How do you know what the shooter used?" I said.

"Because there was no brass at the scene. As to the second part of the question, the shooter probably fired only one round because a heavy recoil made him lose his aim for a second shot, so he decided to haul butt. That's when you heard the car burn rubber."

"Meet me at my house and we'll go in my pickup," I said.

"Why not take a cruiser?"

"We arrive as friends, not as adversaries," I said. "What's this guy's name?"

"Lester Rhoads. Sometimes he calls himself Lonesome Rhoads."

"Oh, yeah, he rings a bell or two," I said.

Chapter Forty

I didn't know Lonesome Rhoads, but I knew his kind, one of those who in their innocence longed for the American West and rather than let it pass by on the Sunset Limited they decided to become a self-mocking icon of what in fact was the extermination of a race and their culture and their animals from 1866 to 1891.

I wasn't sure how he got wind of us, but I suspected the restaurateur dropped the dime on us right after confirming that his restaurant closed at eleven P.M. every night except Sundays. Regardless, Rhoads was on his gallery to greet us, in the midst of Morgan City, which is like a village in the Caribbean full of windmill palms and banana fronds and huge elephant ears and bougainvillea, the small paintless houses lined up and down the Atchafalaya, which in spring is choked with mud and overflows its banks all the way to the Gulf of Mexico.

Lonesome Rhoads's house was an 1890s Victorian with a veranda, on which he was standing red-faced with white whiskers and loaded to the gills, a German mug in his hand, a jolly man wearing a silver-and-gold buckle and cowboy straw hat tilted back on his head, his upper body the size of a beer keg.

"There's our man," I said, looking through the windshield.

"Yeah, one who shoots animals and birds."

What do you say to that?

"Can I make a suggestion?" I asked.

"Why not?"

"Give the guy some slack. You can always take it away."

"Like he does the deer?"

"You've made your point. But hostility isn't going to get us anywhere."

She nodded slowly, as though she were taking in everything I said.

"Our host is waiting," I said.

"Yep," she said.

She had brought a clipboard and placed it on the dashboard. I picked it up and handed it to her. "Ready?" I said.

"Not quite," she said. "I already know Rhoads, but you don't. However, you know everything about him."

"Yeah, I guess I sounded that way."

"Here's the message, Dave. I've known his kind all my life. Sugar wouldn't melt in their mouths. Yuck! Look at that bastard. I think he's about to piss in his pants."

There are times when you say nothing. This was definitely one of them. I opened the door and stepped out on the pebbled driveway and walked side by side with Valerie up the steps to the veranda. "Hello, Mr. Rhoads," I said. "This is Detective Valerie Benoit and I'm Detective Dave Robicheaux from the Iberia Parish Sheriff's Department. You certainly have a lovely house. How you doing, sir?"

He was a gentleman and held the screen door while Valerie walked in first. "Y'all want a drink or cold beer or julep or something?" he said.

"No, thank you," I said. "We'll just get some information about the theft of your vehicle, then we'll be gone."

"Any way I can he'p," he said.

The woodwork in the living room was done with submerged cypress, some of it probably two hundred years old, the sun glowing on the entire interior like warm butter. At the bottom of the staircase was a wheelchair. A bouquet of roses in a green vase was propped in the seat.

Valerie and I both sat on the couch. Rhoads stood by the fireplace, holding his mug, smiling. His teeth were all slanted, as though he were leaning inside the room.

I looked at the clipboard, then scratched at my forehead. "You were at the Pink Pelican Friday night and left about what time?"

I had just pulled a trick on him. I made both a declarative and an interrogative statement in the same sentence. It's underhanded, cheap, and meant to confuse. What a way to start.

"Well, I don't rightly remember," he said. "What's it say on that clipboard you got there?"

"We're a bit confounded," I said. "I think we may have made a mistake. I'd like to get your perspective, if you don't mind."

"To be honest, I was on the grog," he replied.

"Take a guess," I said. "It doesn't have to be right. Give it a shot."

"To tell the truth, I don't know anything."

"Mr. Rhoads, your call came in at three in the morning," I said. "The Pelican closed at eleven the previous night. That's a four-hour gap."

"Well, I'm sure that's right. I probably fell asleep somewhere."

I smiled and nodded. "Sir, do you have a receipt that shows you were at the Pelican?"

"Why do I have to prove that I was at the Pelican?"

"It's kind of complicated," I said. "Val, would you help me here? I don't think I got a lot of sleep last night."

I surprised her. But it was she who found the handyman and the Buick and saw the holes in Rhoads's story, and now she was forced to listen to me talk and get nowhere.

In fact, I thought Mr. Rhoads may have been more slick and less drunk than he had seemed. I have also, since childhood, hated the presence of white, male authority figures. Hand on the Bible, I have never known more obnoxious human beings in my life.

Valerie paused, her eyes on his until he blinked. Then she said, "Mr. Rhoads, we think your vehicle was used in an attempt to kill Detective Robicheaux or his daughter and a friend of his."

"Now wait a minute," Rhoads said.

"No, no, Mr. Rhoads, listen to what I'm saying," she said. "Late Friday evening your vehicle was lubricated at a filling station in Abbeville. There's a sticker on the windshield that gives the date and the mileage. The distance between Abbeville and New Iberia is twenty-one miles. The distance between Morgan City and New Iberia is forty-eight miles. The mileage on your odometer is less than the miles the auto thief would have to drive your vehicle from the Pink Pelican to New Iberia."

Mr. Rhoads looked like an icicle had pierced his entrails. "Well, I guess I'm just an old fool."

"We're on your side, sir," Valerie said. "But you have to help us. Where was the Buick when it was stolen at around three A.M. Saturday?"

He put down his German mug on the mantel and stared at the stairs. A thought or a decision hovered inside his eyes, then froze, like a camera lens shuttering, not to be disturbed again.

"You want to tell us something, sir?" I said.

"The insurance company told me to make a report," he said. "I've done that. I'm done."

"That's not the smart way to go, Mr. Rhoads," Valerie said.

"I need to call my attorney, Miss," he said.

"I'm not a 'miss.' I'm a detective, Mr. Rhoads," she said. "The people we are dealing with have no mercy. Do not underestimate them."

His eyes were starting to glisten. "You make it hard on an old man. I don't care about my car. Y'all can keep it or run it into the Gulf of Mexico."

A woman in a nightgown appeared at the top of the stairs. Her bones looked like bamboo. She was holding on to a walker. "Who is that, Lonesome?" she said. "Is that Harold? You know what day this is."

"It's just some friends," Rhoads called. Then he waited for her to speak. But she didn't.

Rhoads looked at us. "Harold was our son. He died in a car accident. Today is his birthday. Y'all gonna have to leave now."

Valerie and I stood up from the couch. Our interview was over. We might have dragged it on, but there was no point. The man would probably go to his grave with his lies, and his wife would talk to a son who was not there. If anything, I felt sorry for them, but I also thought their grief was about to get worse.

"I'll leave you my business card," I said.

"I have no use for it," Rhoads said.

I dropped it on the coffee table. "You know where we are, sir," I said.

"Don't come here again," he said.

"You've chosen the wrong team, sir," I said.

"I'll be just a few minutes, Harold," the elderly lady called from the top of the stairs. "Just let me find my purse. I declare, when will that darky stop losing my things?"

Rhoads bolt-locked the door when we left his house. I didn't feel this was our finest hour. We walked to the pickup without speaking, the pebbles crunching under our shoes. I opened the driver's door but didn't get inside.

"You feel bad about the dementia lady and her son?" Valerie said.

"Yeah," I said.

"But maybe we got jobbed, too?"

"You got that right."

"What do you want to do?"

The breeze was cool, the sunlight dancing on the river, working-class families barbecuing in their backyards. It should have been a grand afternoon. But there was a falsity in the conversation with Lonesome Rhoads, a calculated willingness to risk the lives of others in order to hide a difficulty of his own. Rhoads knew I might lose my daughter, but he was not bothered in the least, even though he had lost an adult child.

"We can bang on his door again," Valerie said.

"No."

"Then let's go home."

"You know what he's hiding, right?" I said.

"About where he was? Yeah, he was probably in a hot-pillow joint."

"You're pretty smart."

"I hear that a lot," she said.

We got into the cab of my pickup, and I backed out of the driveway onto the asphalt, the western sun in my eyes. Then I realized its brilliance was not just from the sun. In a vacant lot across the river someone was flashing a reflective object, maybe a telescope or binoculars. I stopped my pickup and got out again just as I saw a man walk fast between two houses and disappear.

"What is it, Dave?"

"Maybe somebody looking at the river."

"Or maybe not?" she said.

"Yeah, that too," I said. "Son of a bitch."

"Want to warn Lonesome Asshole in there?"

"No, it's probably nothing," I said.

We got two blocks down the street, then I swung a U-turn and went back to the Victorian home of Rhoads and his wife. I went up the steps and hammered on the door with the flat of my fist. He jerked open the door, his face twisted in anger.

"Somebody might have you in his crosshairs, Mr. Rhoads," I said. "If you don't care about your own life, you might think about your wife."

When we got back to my home on East Main, Alafair had gone to get some ice cream and Clete was barbecuing a chicken in the backyard, grease flaring on the coals, the smoke rising in the oaks and Spanish moss, our pets Cannon Ball and Lady Godiva looking on, Clete wearing his porkpie hat and a Tulane jersey, the sleeves chopped off at the pits, his croquet-ball-size muscles dusted with sunburn.

"I thought you guys might need a snack when you got back from questioning that sportswriter fraud in Morgan City," he said.

"You know him?" I said.

"Yeah, he's a fraud," Clete said. "He writes hunting pieces that mention various gun companies, and in turn they give him the guns and his camping equipment and pay all his travel costs."

"What else do you know about him?" I said.

He looked at Valerie.

"Say it, Clete," she said.

"Who am I to judge?" he replied.

"Come on, Clete," I said.

"He gets his ashes hauled."

"Where?" I said.

"I don't know," Clete said. "He went down to Mexico and shot over four hundred ducks in one day."

"What's that have to do with his romantic life?" I said.

"He's that kind of guy," Clete replied.

"Is Rhoads a patron of Jerry Carlucci's hot-pillow joint?" Valerie said.

"It's a possibility," Clete said.

"A possibility?" she said.

I thought Clete's nerves had healed since the bullet had blown up a coffee cup in his hand, but I was wrong. He was wired.

"Forget about all that crap," he said. "Hey, I made this food for you guys. I got a tossed salad and some French bread and some dirty rice that'll break your heart."

"Thank you," I said.

"Just relax," he said. He looked at his watch. "Where's Alafair with the ice cream?"

"When did she leave?" I asked.

"A while ago," he said. "Fifteen minutes. I don't know. Paint the chickens for me. I'll be back."

He dropped his barbecue brush in the sauce bowl and headed for the front of the house. I went after him. "Get a couple of diet Docs and cool down," I said. "We've got everything under control."

"No, we haven't. Not in the least. I know you, Dave. You never got over Annie. Where's the Thompson?"

"Forget about the Thompson."

"See," he said, jabbing his finger at me. "That's what I mean. You're ready to go back to the Shitsville boogie while you're telling me to soak my head."

"Okay, Clete, have it your way," I said, and started to walk off.

"Okay, here goes," he said at my back. "While you were in Morgan City, Sidney Ludlow came to my cottage with his kid, what's-his-name."

"Bedford?"

"Yeah," he replied. "Ludlow said he wanted you to know he had nothing to do with the bullet that went through your house."

"You believe him?" I said.

"No, I don't believe him, but I believe what he *is.* He's got no feeling if he sees a black kid thrown off the roof of an apartment building, but he'd chop off his own arm to save his son. It's a funny thing with some of these guys."

"What are you talking about?" I said.

"Maybe the guy's got a piece of humanity. Al Capone loved his kid."

"If you put yourself inside a man like Sidney Ludlow, at best it's a sewer. At worst, you don't want to think about it."

"Okay, maybe he wants you to pop Carlucci for him. I'm just trying to help." The rims of his eyes were pink, the eyes a watery green. He looked at his watch, then at the street. "You got your phone? You need to call Alafair. If something happens to her, I'm gonna go nuts. Absolutely crazy. The kind you don't come back from. You got me, Dave?"

"Sure, Clete. You're a good guy. Don't say these things about yourself."

Then I saw Alafair's small Toyota come around the corner, one I kept so she could come home more often, although she said it made no difference. Clete's face beamed as big as a streetlamp. She made a wide turn out of the street and bounced into the driveway, the oak leaves drifting down from the trees, as though the season were fall rather than spring. She lifted up a chocolate cake. "Sorry to keep you waiting," she said. "Anything going on?"

Chapter Forty-One

The next morning, Monday, at five A.M., I drove my pickup alone to the stretch of marshland south of Carlucci's Landing. The marshland was blanketed knee-deep in curds of fog, the tips of the saw grass barely visible, like a purplish haze waiting for the wind to blow or the sun to rise from an ocean that was once a dwelling place for Nazi submarines that sank our oil tankers in the year of 1942.

It happened. I saw them. I was on my father's shrimp boat when he and his deck hands pulled up a net dripping with shrimp and bodies that looked like burned cork, bait fish flipping among them on the deck. The smell caused my father, a stalwart man, to heave his breakfast over the rail.

Even though I was a child, I learned that morning that the earth is very old and had occupants of all kinds, many like the submariners who could core out the steel bottom of a tanker and drown their fellow man with the least of conscience.

So my return that Monday morning to this stretch of peninsula should not be taken as unusual. In fact, as I gazed at the bays bleeding into the Gulf and the clouds of fog rolling out of the gumtrees, I was convinced that the story of my life was right here, but not just mine. Don't we all share the stars that drop from the sky, and the sun shaping itself on the horizon, more like a red emerald than a flame? Don't we share the salt air that weighs in our lungs, and the scars in our necks that were once the gills of our ancestors, the labor they underwent working their way onto a sandbar? Isn't this a fond and grand way to think of our home?

As I had these thoughts, I did a silly thing. I twirled around and around, my arms spread, my eyes pinned on the heavens, seawater and sand sloshing in my shoes, a military plane scratching a frozen vapor trail high above, the sun finally lifting from the horizon, lighting the crustaceans and the bears and the deer and those creatures who have not yet decided what they plan to be.

"Have you lost your fucking mind?" a voice said.

I stopped and dropped my arms by my sides, so dizzy I almost fell down. "I didn't hear your Jeep, Jerry. You've been digging around, have you?"

"What does it fucking look like?" he said.

A bulldozer with a backhoe was parked next to a slot in the earth, water squeezing from its sides. I had paid no attention, even though I had been a few feet from it. In my spinning with the Earth, I didn't bloody care. I knew that both Clete and I were moving in a direction whereby you step across a line in your aging process. But it's not about age. It's the way you see the planet and the human condition. It's like throwing a switch. Hang around. You'll see.

"Hope you don't mind my having a stroll on your property," I said.

"You're drunk?"

"I don't think so," I replied. "This is your waste dump, huh?"

"None of your fucking business, Davie."

"Give me a cute name again and I'll have you in that hole, Jerry. Tell me, do most people use a backhoe to claw toxic waste from rusted-out oil barrels?"

"Last chance before I call the guys with the butterfly nets, Dave."

"Somebody almost put a large-caliber bullet in Clete Purcel's face while he was drinking coffee in my living room," I said. "It came close to my daughter, too."

Jerry's eyes didn't leave mine. "I heard about it. Purcel has got a lot of enemies. That's the other comment I have."

"It was probably a toppling round," I said. "You know how they keyhole a face. It's like a windmill. Sometimes you see a big red mist. You ever get that close to your targets, Jerry?"

"I didn't know you were this lousy a guy," he said. "I think you got brain damage. If I didn't think that, I'd tear you up." He kept nodding after he had spoken.

"What's down there, Jerry?"

"The Confederate Army," he said. "They needed a latrine. Maybe you ought to join them."

He walked away, the sky now streaked with strips of blue and pink and white, looking at the west, his profile as sharp as tin, like a great man surveying the world.

Then I heard the hoarse, deep growl of a large animal. I shaded my eyes, looked into the glare, and saw the mama bear and her cub running out of the sun, both of them tossing their heads, splashing through a chain of sandbars. I did not imagine this. Good things can happen in the world, if you let them. At least that's what I want to believe. I couldn't wait to give Clete the good news.

I was at the department at 9:47 A.M. There was a note stuck on my door. It read:

See me immediately,
Helen

I tapped with one knuckle on the frosted glass of her office door.

"Come in," she said, her voice without tone.

I went inside and closed the door behind me. She was fishing in a drawer. "Good morning," I said.

"Just a minute," she said. She took a yellow legal pad from the drawer. "Sit down."

"Is something going on?"

"Did you see Benoit?"

"No."

"I put a note on her door ten minutes ago."

"Want to tell me what's going on?"

"You and Benoit did an interview at the home of this guy, Lester Rhoads?" she said, no longer using Valerie's first name. "He calls himself Lonesome Rhoads?"

"Yes, we were at his home in Morgan City yesterday afternoon."

"His wife was there?"

"It's apparent she's in dementia. It seems pretty progressed."

"Outside of that, the two of them were all right?"

"The husband told us to leave," I replied.

"Why?"

"He knew he'd been caught in a bunch of lies about where his car was stolen. He also knew he might go down on a murder beef. What are you trying to tell me, Helen?"

"Lester Rhoads and his wife are dead," she replied. "It looks like they did it with gas and sleeping pills."

I stared at her, blankly.

"In the kitchen, with newspaper stuffed under the doors," she said.

I felt like an ulcer had flared on the lining of my stomach. "When were the bodies found?" I said.

"The maid found them this morning."

I was sitting in a chair directly in front of Helen's desk. I was leaning forward, my hands cupped on my knees, my lungs going up and down in my chest. "Has the coroner been there or made a statement?"

"He's there now. But no statement."

"Who called you?" I asked.

"A Morgan City detective. Your business card was on the coffee table."

"When we left, I thought somebody was looking at us from across the river."

"You mean with binoculars?" she said.

"Yes, I went back to the house and told Rhoads to take care of himself and his wife."

"I hope you recorded that."

"I did not." I blew out my breath and looked at the floor, my arms still stiff on my knees.

"Don't put this on yourself, bwana. Whether that man intended it or not, he was aiding and abetting a homicide. End of story."

"Did you say the maid found the bodies?" I asked.

"Yeah, why?"

"A black maid?"

"Yeah, what about it?"

"The last thing I heard the wife say was, 'When will that darky stop losing my things?'"

Helen stared into space. "Time to shake it and bake it," she said.

"What the hell does that mean?"

"It means we pick up the garbage, and nobody could care less, so don't turn this into a mountain of guilt."

I walked home for lunch. The crime-scene tape was still in place, bouncing in the wind. I felt it was an insult to my home, and I tore it down and wadded it up and stuffed it in my garbage can. I suspect my symbolic act was probably a comment on the culture I served rather than the ugliness of the tape.

Alafair came out the back door. "What are you doing?" she said. "We still haven't found the bullet."

"It's probably in the bayou," I said. "It's worthless anyway."

"Who set you off?" she said.

"Lester Rhoads and his wife were found dead early this morning. It looks like a double suicide."

"Oh, Dave, I'm sorry."

"No, this doesn't pass muster. Rhoads was an egotistical, cruel, self-serving man. He might run from a problem, but not by killing himself. Nor would he kill his wife, even though he cheated on her."

"He was killed about the Buick?"

"That's my guess."

"So why take it out on the tape?"

"I was down on the Gulf this morning, right on the edge of Jerry Carlucci's property. He's digging up what he says is a waste dump. I don't think it's a waste dump."

"You didn't answer my question."

"Whoever shot at us is a functionary. We're in somebody's way, just like Clemmy Benoit. The issues are the earth, the ocean, the air we breathe, the democracy we hold sacred. The Mob and the drug dealers and the cops and legislators on a pad are just crab lice."

"Nobody is going to listen to that."

"You've got that right."

"I worry about you, Dave."

"Don't."

"Come inside. I made your favorite sandwich."

"I've got a bad feeling about Jerry Carlucci, Alafair. He loves myths, the Earps blowing the Clantons all over the O.K. Corral, Doc Holliday's beautiful mistress. But all that was a dream, in their lives and in his. Jerry went to Vietnam and has been dragging a chain ever since. I think he's about to lay down his load."

"He'd better not do it here," she said.

It sounded good, but so did the bugles at Roncevaux and the Little Bighorn Valley.

She looked at me in a strange way. "Don't be sad, Dave. I'll never leave you."

* * *

We ate lunch at the kitchen table and washed the dishes and gave the animals a midday snack, then I made sure she was carrying the pistol I gave her.

"Come on, Dave, just ease up," she said.

"What did Ambrose Bierce say about pacifists?" I asked.

"He said a pacifist was a dead Quaker, even though I think he liked Quakers."

"See you at five," I said.

"You bet," she replied.

Then I drove away in a light rain, one that sparkled in the sunshine and the trees, like a reminder that the resilience of the Earth is forever, at least according to the promise of the Bible and Ernest Hemingway. I think they both had it right, and I think my experience on the peninsula early that morning was a valid one. The enormity of both geological and human history is beyond our comprehension. But the incomprehension of it gives us a mantle that no form of evil can violate. That's the gift of the light-bearer, in his nakedness, his feet, imprinting the clay with a message that will last for millions of years.

Other than Clete Purcel, I knew only one person who knew what I was thinking about. Most people would laugh; the kindest would be kind; the others would think me mad. Oddly, among the previous three, the closest to the truth is the third. Madness can be a conduit into the truth or at least a marvelous zoo. The man I was thinking about was only ten minutes way, on the St. Martin Parish line. Of course, we're talking about the handyman, Boone Hendrix.

Chapter Forty-Two

I caught him at lunch, eating in his small screen porch, smoke drifting from a trash fire in his brick barbecue pit. His antique truck had been washed, the tires blackened, the hubcaps buffed and shiny, two paint-splattered ladders mounted on the roof. Mr. Hendrix was obviously a utilitarian man.

I pulled into the driveway and got out. The chickens were gone, his ice cream cart half-visible in his barn. The wind changed, and a column of black smoke and sparks rose from the chimney of the barbecue pit.

"You mind if I come in?" I said through the screen.

"Please do, Detective Robicheaux," he replied.

I went inside. "Is there any chance you will ever call me 'Dave'?"

He pursed his lips. "I'll give it careful thought. The 1960s have taken away much of our civility."

He was wearing pressed denims and a clean khaki cap, eating spaghetti at a redwood table with a glob of tomato sauce but no meatballs.

"Mind if I sit down?" I said.

"No," he replied, chewing, his face vacuous.

"Where are your chickens?"

"Gave them to a black man down the road who promised not to butcher them."

"Just to lay their eggs?"

"That is correct," he replied.

"Yeah, I remember Alafair's saying something about your being a vegetarian," I said.

"Yes, sir, I have discussed that with her."

"Could I ask where you went to school?"

My question had nothing to do with the subject, but I had to get inside him. Did you ever see a man on death row? Mr. Hendrix had the same look, same twitches, the same expression and non-expression, as though he were in a room of bats.

"I didn't go to school," he said. "I grew up gyppo-logging and tapping syrup trees. You want some spaghetti?"

"No, thank you."

He bent over his food again, mopping the plate with a piece of French bread. But I believed that Mr. Hendrix was a far more complex man than he seemed. More important, I believed he had a great sadness inside him, the kind that takes the light from our eyes and the blood from the heart.

"Do you have children, Mr. Hendrix?" I asked.

He stuck his fork gingerly into his pasta, then put it down again.

"Did you hear me, sir?" I said.

"No," he said. "What did you say?"

"Are you a family man?"

"I see my children when they're able to visit, Detective Robicheaux. But they don't get to stay long."

"Can you tell me where they are?"

"Out there," he said, looking at Bayou Teche and the light tangled in the oaks and Spanish moss.

"I see."

"They come and go," he said. "They like to play with animals. I taught them the animals are always our friends."

I nodded as though I understood. He pushed his plate away slowly, his attention gone to some place I would fear to enter.

"Mr. Hendrix?"

He blinked, as if he didn't know me.

"I believe everything you say," I said. "But we don't want to see you get hurt. You reading me on this? Do me a solid. Talk to Alafair."

"I don't need to. My children are safe now. Among the trees."

Suddenly there was a glow in his face, like a man sitting before a fireplace.

"What happened to your children, sir?" I asked.

"You mustn't talk about that, Detective Robicheaux."

"I have to, sir. Were they hurt in Louisiana?"

"No, no," he said, lifting his hand.

"Are you planning to do something? Maybe go up against somebody?"

"Detective Robicheaux, you should not get involved with certain things that have to occur."

"Did you kill Elton Foot? Talk to me."

He got up from the table with his plate and silverware, and went into his kitchen, then turned on the hot water full force, splattering tomato sauce on his forearms and shirt.

"Sir, you're going to burn yourself."

"Mind your business, Detective Robicheaux."

I tried to reach for the faucet.

"Take your hands away, Detective Robicheaux." His forearms were reddening, the steam rising in his face.

"Please don't do this, sir," I said.

He spread his feet. They were booted and laced, double-soled and double-heeled. "Leave my house," he said. "And leave me with my children."

I tried to pull him aside, but his body was as hard and heavy as concrete. I got one hand on the faucet, but instead of shutting it off I sprayed water in my eyes. It was like a shower of hot BBs.

"I'm going to hit you, Mr. Hendrix," I said.

"Stay out of my way, sir. I may have saved your life already. Will you not let me have some peace of mind?"

"How did you save my life?"

"You know already, sir. You just will not admit it," he said, the backs of his hands as red as boiled lobsters.

I couldn't watch what he was doing to himself. I stepped back and lay my hands on the point of his left shoulder and drove my knee into the top of his thigh. The consequence was immediate. His mouth dropped and he hit the floor.

"I'm sorry I had to do that, Mr. Hendrix," I said. "I think you're a good man."

He remained on the floor, one knee pulled up to his chest, breathing as though he had run up a staircase. "No, I'm not good, Detective Robicheaux," he whispered. "I have been forced to take strong measures. Maybe I'll do more."

Then his voice faded and he went to sleep.

What do you do with a situation like that?

I turned off the water, eased a couch pillow under his head, locked the doors from inside, drove back to New Iberia, and checked in with Helen and Valerie. If I had been able, I probably should have avoided the appearance of due diligence.

"You put a pillow under his head?" Helen said.

"That's about it," I said.

"After you kneed a crazy person in the femur bone, you locked up the doors from inside and said 'ta-ta,' and then toggled back to the department?"

"More or less."

"Didn't think about taking him to Iberia General?" Helen said.

"I thought he was better left alone," I said, dropping my eyes, waiting until Helen got off her righteous streak.

Then she looked at Valerie, who had leaned her butt on the heater that ran along the wall. "What are *you* grinning at?"

"Sorry, I thought you were telling a joke," Valerie said.

"Do I look like I'm in a joking mood?"

"I'm sorry," Valerie said. "The stuff about the kids was sad."

"Thank you for telling us that," Helen said.

"Come on, Helen, give it a break," I said. "I didn't want the guy to end up in a restraint jacket."

"Or in a room where they throw their feces," Valerie said.

Great move, Val, I thought. *How did I get started in this? Answer: I told the truth.*

Helen wouldn't let it go. "Detective, I'm gonna ask you to go back to your office and think about your career, and I mean real hard."

Val looked like she had been slapped. "Ma'am?" she said.

"I've asked you not to call me 'ma'am.'" Helen said.

"I over-speak sometimes," Valerie said.

"No, it's not 'sometimes.' It's a habit. Or maybe a compulsion."

"Helen?" I said.

"Shut up, bwana. I'm tired of this attitude of I'll-do-whatever-I-want."

"Who are you talking about?" I said.

"Both of you," she said. "I'm sick of it."

"Are you having trouble with Baton Rouge?" I said.

"No, I'm having trouble with you."

"I started this, Sheriff," Valerie said. "I'm sorry and I won't let it happen again."

"Get out," Helen said. "You, too, Dave."

"You're the boss," I said. "Talk to you later."

"Call me 'boss' again and I'll roll your head down the stairs," she replied.

I let Valerie walk out in front of me. She tried to stop and turn around, but I put my hand on her shoulder and didn't let go until we were down the hallway and heard Helen's door shut.

"My head is ringing," Valerie said. "What happened in there?"

"I don't know," I replied. "I really don't."

"Shit!"

"Shit, what?" I said.

"I don't think things are working out," she said. "It's like a bad moon rising."

"Listen, Val, you're a good cop, and a brave and good person on top of it. I admire you, and so does everyone else in the building."

"Not everyone," she said.

"Are you talking about those deputies at the parish prison? Their IQs couldn't match your fingernail clippings."

She stopped by the watercooler. I thought she was going to take a drink. Instead she hung her head in the shadow of the little cove in the wall.

"What's wrong?" I said.

Then I heard her sniffle.

"Hey, none of that," I said.

She got a Kleenex out of her purse. "Why don't you go on?" she said.

"Okay," I said. "Call me when you need me. But don't let that bad moon get you. It always goes away."

I walked down to my office and went inside, then locked the door and called Clete Purcel at his office. I was convinced the murder of Clemmy Benoit would never be solved by ordinary means. In Louisiana the number of unsolved female homicides is stupefying. They are usually young, poor, addicted, covered with tats, laced with needle tracks, infected with venereal disease, and pulled out of bayous, sand bogs, and the trunks of junked cars. The most sanitary environment they ever find is the stainless-steel tray where their blood is drained and their viscera taken out.

Clemmy was an icon, one that had risen above a culture no one enters of his or her own volition. If we did not find justice for her soon, other crimes would warrant our full attention and eventually her case would go into a file and more time would pass and finally she would be a memory. That's how it works. And it really sucks.

Unless a guy like Clete Purcel is hanging around.

But Clete had not answered my call, and I suspected he had closed up for the day and gone down to Clementine's for a dozen on the half shell. Then one of the red lights on my desk phone lit up. I was standing up when I put the receiver to my ear, looking at my watch, ready to go home, ready to have supper with Alfie.

"Robicheaux here," I said.

"Can you come down to my office?" Helen said.

"Sure," I said. "You want Valerie, too?"

"That won't be necessary."

Oops.

I walked back down the hallway. There was no one else in it. My shoes echoed off the walls. I twisted the knob on Helen's door and opened it a few inches, unsure about what I was getting into. "Helen?" I said.

"Come in," I heard her say.

At first I didn't see her. She was in her big leather swivel chair, her back to me, looking across the bayou at the park and the softball diamond, some kids playing under the lights.

I opened the door wider and went in. "What's up?" I said.

"Close the door," she said.

Her chair squeaked when she turned to face me. She stared at me as though she wasn't sure of what she wanted to say.

"Helen, if you're worried about our earlier conversation—" I started.

"I got out of hand," she said. "But that's not what I have to say. I have a serious problem. Val Benoit is getting deeper and deeper into Louisiana politics. As soon as she gets home, she starts sticking it to someone in the legislature. I've talked to her, but it doesn't do any good. The real issue is casinos and gambling. You know that. I know that. But she does not."

"Maybe that's just the way it is. Let it go."

"I've got an ulcer and gallstones," she said. "The real deal. I may have to have surgery. I'm not dumping all this on Val Benoit, but she's pigheaded and on certain subjects she's uneducable."

"You're talking about race, the environment, the electrocution of Willie Francis?" I said.

"No, duh."

"Off the job Valerie can protest as much as she wants, as long as she's out of uniform."

"Except she's not getting her ass kicked," Helen said. "I am. The department is. And you're not helping me."

"Give me the names of the guys who are giving us a hard time," I replied.

"They are not giving 'us' a hard time. You just don't get it, Dave. You never do. My stomach just flared. So did my bladder stones. You just don't fucking get it."

Her eyes were welling. She leaned forward, her face ashen, breathing heavily, her mouth puckering.

"I'm sorry, Helen. Is there something I can do?"

"In my bottom-right drawer there's a bottle of lemon juice and a bottle of olive oil. Put a teaspoon of each in the cup and get some water from the water fountain."

"You got it," I said.

I did as she said, and came back in with the water cup full. She held it to her mouth and drank it to the bottom, the upper half of her face turned up like a carp.

"We'll get you through this, Helen," I said. "You're family."

"I forgot," she said.

I didn't understand. "Forgot what?"

"Alafair left a message for you. Your phone is evidently dead. She said she was going to a meeting with Valerie in St. Martinville and she'd left some cold chicken in the refrigerator. She also said she was taking her Toyota."

"Valerie didn't say anything about going to a meeting with Alafair," I said.

"Really?" Helen said. "I can't believe Valerie Benoit would do something like that. I'm not being ironic. I just can't believe she keeps doing this shit."

Chapter Forty-Three

I used my desk phone to call Alafair at the house and then called her cell phone, but got no answer. I caught Valerie going out the back door of the building into the department's parking lot.

"Val!" I called. "What's this about you and Alafair at a meeting tonight?"

She was almost to her car. "I thought Helen gave you the message."

"Helen did," I said. "But Alafair and I were supposed to have supper and maybe go to a movie. Or at least I thought we were."

"This is kind of an important meeting," she said. "Alafair wanted to attend."

"What does 'kind of' mean?" I said.

"We're making plans to address the legislature, or maybe march on them."

"'March on them?'" I said. "I don't want my daughter as a target."

She rubbed one finger in the middle of her forehead. "I'll call her and tell her not to come," she said. "She can come another night."

"I already have," I said. "She didn't answer."

"She didn't?" Val said, and frowned.

"I'm going to St. Martinville," I said. "Where's the meeting?"

"It's too early."

"I'm not interested in the time. I want to know where it is."

She gave me the name of a large, two-story 1870s building that had been refurbished as an art-and-drama center. "Why are you doing this, Val?"

"I believe in fighting back," she replied. "I believe in justice for Willie Francis."

"So do I," I said. "But you don't do it at the expense of others."

I saw the hurt in her face, but I'd had all I could take. There is something wrong with the human brain. We injure those whom we love the most, and do it again and again, each time poisoning our lives with guilt. Why? You tell me.

I picked up Clete Purcel at the bar in Clementine's, and headed up the two-lane. He had a po'boy in his right hand, his phone in his left, his porkpie tilted over his brow. The sun was red in the west, on the far side of the Teche, dust devils spinning in the stubble fields, the trees swelling with robins. "Call her again," I said.

"Okay, big mon, but maybe she went somewhere else and is coming to the meeting later. It's too early for the meeting now, right?"

"She knows I worry about her. It's not like her."

He punched in her number, looked at the face of the phone, then shut it.

"Dave, she's got her own car. It's still daylight. She's an intelligent woman. Give her some credit."

"Yeah, you're probably right," I said, brushing at the left side of my head, where my anxiety was tightening like a loop of piano wire.

We passed the antebellum house of the black man who owned slaves and became rich making bricks off their sweat. I had passed it hundreds of times. But this time I was bothered by it more than ever before, as though the antebellum years were not finished, only waiting to be reborn in the worst way.

"You see something in that house?" Clete asked.

"No."

"You were looking at it."

"We're still doing it."

"Doing what?"

"Everything we were doing in the past."

Clete tore his po'boy sandwich in half, wrapped one half with the foil, and handed it to me. "You need to put something in the tank, noble mon. You're starting to creep me out."

"The man who talks to Joan of Arc?"

"Because she's there," he said. "How many times have I told you?"

I didn't reply and kept driving. The sun was setting, like a smithy's forge, the top of the sky still lit with flame, roiling with black clouds. We passed an old, white farmhouse with a screened-in veranda and a pasture, an iconic Louisiana home of a kind that was dwindling by the year. Farther on was a shut-down nightclub from the 1930s, a sign with a nude woman in a martini glass still hanging above the boarded front doors. The two-lane made a bend through shadows and spangled sunlight, and as I turned into the glare I saw an automobile in the bayou, perpendicular, submerged, the current rippling over the rear bumper and an exhaust pipe and a license tag.

A mushroom of gray mud had risen around the car.

Clete threw his po'boy out the window. "It's a Toyota!" he said, slamming his fist on the dashboard. "Oh, shit! It's Alafair's!"

I was already out of the pickup and running, kicking off my loafers, then I hit the water flat on my chest, my arms slicing through the surface, a great coldness rising to greet me.

"I'm coming, Dave!" Clete yelled, wading waist-high. "I'm coming! Damn it, I knew this was coming!"

I dove down to the driver's side of the Toyota, feeling my way, the sunlight filtering through the silt. I touched the roof, the glass windows, and a door handle. I cupped the handle and jerked on it. It was locked. I hit on the glass vainly with the flat of my fist, then used my knuckles and my elbow. Each blow pushed me away from the glass. I could vaguely see the steering wheel, but there was only darkness inside, with nothing to reflect the light from above, nothing to show a body or someone suffocating in an air pocket.

I thought I was in a nightmare. I thought I had gone back to the crashed airplane from which I pulled Alafair many years ago. My lungs were on fire and about to burst. I pushed myself to the light and broke through the surface, gasping for air. Clete was wedging open the trunk with a crowbar that I always carried under the pickup's front seat. The trunk sprung open. It was empty.

"What's inside the car?" he said.

"I can't get in or see. I need the crowbar," I said, working with my hands along the car.

"Let me do it," he said. "I got the weight and a flashlight, too. Follow me down, big mon."

Then he curved like a whale down to the bottom, with me behind him. He broke the glass with the crowbar and chopped the shards out of the window frame, then flashed the light over the dashboard and the roof and the floor and the panels on the far door and in the backseat.

Alafair wasn't there.

We both rose to the surface and swam toward the bank and struggled up the incline, falling against the side of my pickup. Leeches had gotten in our clothes, and broken garbage bags twisted around our legs. Three vehicles were pulling off the bend in the road. A black man in overalls in a car full of kids got out of the first vehicle and walked toward us. His eyes kept going from us to the Toyota. "Anybody in there?" he said.

"No," I said, opening my badge. "Are you coming from St. Martinville?"

"Yes, suh."

"Did anyone go past you pretty fast?"

"Not real fast, but making sure they were getting along, know what I mean? It was a nice-looking car. Say, you okay?"

"Do you remember the color or the make?"

"It wasn't purple. There's another name for it."

"Maroon?" I said.

"Yeah, that's it."

A series of images went through my memory, my mind racing: *A maroon Malibu parked across from Victor's, the button man Clete pulverized, the button man who called himself John Smith and shot the mama bear.*

"Did you see the tag?" I asked.

"No, suh, I got my hands full with these kids."

"You said 'they.'"

"There was two people. A man at the wheel and a woman in back."

"By herself in back and no one in the passenger seat?" I said.

"Yes, suh, that about says it. Her hair was flying."

"What color was it?"

"Black and long."

"How old was she?"

"I just seen her for a few seconds. I'd say she was young. Now that I think of it, she looked through the back window when she passed by me. Yeah, that kind of bothered me. You know, a young woman in the backseat, by herself, not nobody in the passenger seat, like she didn't have no control of herself."

"That may have been my daughter."

He looked at me awkwardly. "Suh?" he said.

"Maybe an evil man kidnapped my daughter."

"*Po*," he said as Cajuns and people of color often do. "I'd tell you more if I could, but I just ain't seen a lot."

"You've helped me very much," I said, putting a soaked business card in his hand. "Please call me if you remember anything else."

He looked down at my feet. "You got a baby snake in the bottom of your pants."

I looked down at the cuff of my left trouser leg. A small cottonmouth was sliding over my loafer. I kicked it into the bayou, hardly noticing or caring about its presence or its departure, wondering if I would see my little girl again.

Chapter Forty-Four

For the next three hours we alerted every emergency and police unit in the bayou country. By dark we had come up with nothing. And we knew that was the way it was going to be. American emergency personnel are among the best-trained and bravest in the world, but they deal with "emergencies," not psychopaths, serial killers, or Mafiosi hit men. Regarding the latter, none of the drivers we interviewed along the two-lane remembered seeing a maroon car or much less a Malibu, which meant the driver had taken a back road through farmland and disappeared into the bayous and swamps to the south.

Clete and I were filthy. The mosquitoes were humming in our ears, biting our necks, clustering in our nostrils, fattening on our blood until we slapped them, reminding us of Shitsville and the deposits of eggs we brought home. The leeches had not left us, either. Clete had to take off his shirt and trousers while I burned them from his skin with a hot cigar I bummed from a motorcycle cop.

Clete was standing on the roadside in Loreauville, in his skivvies, twitching each time I touched him with the cigar while he doffed his porkpie hat to the cars passing by, their headlights blinding.

"This really blows, noble mon," he said. "Let's get showered and put on dry clothes, then start kicking serious ass, I mean ripping colon, starting with that cocksucker who probably owns the Malibu. Where's your Thompson?"

"Behind the cab," I said. "If the Feds see it, they'll have us in the can. I got a better idea."

He jerked when I touched the cigar on his lower spine. A leech fell to the ground. "Go on with what you were saying," he replied.

"I've learned some things about the handyman."

"That he's got a chamber pot for a brain?"

"He's not just a repair man," I said. "He knows about sophisticated firearms. Also, there's something on his property that gives me pause."

"What?"

"I'd rather you look at it," I said. "Or smell it."

"What kind of crap is that? Just tell me."

"I don't want to mess things up, Clete. How about a little patience? Alafair may be in the hands of a monster."

He was staring into the headlights, like they were sliding across his face, his green eyes never blinking, the skin around them as pale as a frog's stomach. "Yeah, I dig what you're saying. But you got to clean out your head. See, it's like a dream. That's all. It's not real."

But Clete knew better. A kidnapper is one of the worst people on Earth. Alafair was probably a few feet or inches from loaded weapons or instruments or tools that could turn her life into an agony. Perhaps there are those among us who are depraved from birth, and perhaps others are taught that moral insanity is acceptable if their cause is a noble one. Later an American president would again and again tell the media "the United States doesn't torture," while a chain of torture chambers worldwide was doing the dirty work for us. Don't believe me? Try Guantanamo for a warm-up, then check out some of our contract friends on the dark side of the world.

The thought of Alafair's captivity and the state of her body and mind made me tremble. I dropped my eyes and went to a place I shared with no one and said a prayer and then opened my eyes again.

Clete pulled my cigar from my hand and threw it sparking on the two-lane. "I didn't get that," he said. "What were you saying?"

"I didn't say anything."

"Yes, you did. As loud as you are now."

"Put on your clothes before we get arrested," I said.

"Roger that. Look, Dave, let's put some better thoughts in your head. Every cop from Lake Charles to New Orleans has got the APB. They know and respect you, which means they're gonna give the shithead or shitheads who kidnapped Alafair special handling. Whoever did this is gonna think twice. You *diggez-vous* on that?"

"You're a good guy, Cletus."

"But you do not *diggez-vous*? You will not let me say a positive word?"

"Sure, I understand."

"Dave, there is no one who lies as bad as you. It's like an insult to the school of liars, if there's such a thing. How fucked up in the head can anyone be?"

We showered at my house, put on fresh clothes (Clete kept some in the guest room), and filled a backpack with canned goods, such as black-eyed peas, chicken, salmon, smoked oysters, and cherries, and slung the bag in the pickup. I also put my cut-down Remington twelve-gauge pump in the big steel toolbox welded to the back of the cab. I also added a .38 special and a Beretta. Then I locked up the house and paused in the porte-cochere, the street dark now, a night-light burning in the hallway.

"What are we waiting on?" Clete said.

I really couldn't say. I had only lived in two houses in the entirety of my life: the one on East Main in New Iberia, and the ancient house down by Avery Island where my wife Annie was murdered. Houses are not necessarily homes, as you probably know. A home is part of your soul. It's the place in your mind to which you retreat until the day you close your eyes for the last time.

I didn't want to leave my home on East Main. I saw myself in the living room, looking out the front window at Alafair getting off the bus in the fall, the leaves blowing around her, waving goodbye to her classmates, promising she would see them that night at the high school football game.

"I changed my mind about the Tommy gun," I said. "Screw the Feds."

"Good choice," Clete replied. "Are we still headed to the handyman's?"

"Affirmative on that."

"What if he's not home?"

"He doesn't need to be home."

Clete's eyes clicked sideways.

The moon was rising as we approached Boone Hendrix's small farmhouse on the St. Martin Parish line. No lights were on, not even on the gallery or in the outbuildings to forewarn trespassers. I pulled up to the barn and cut the headlights and engine. I could hear the heat ticking under the hood, my heart beating. I was on the ragged edge of everything, with little confidence in my ability to think, and feared that I was running out of time.

"What do we do now?" Clete said.

"See that brick barbecue pit? I think someone has been burning waste rather than barbecue."

"Maybe Hendrix is cutting down on the overhead. It's his trash."

"Hendrix is a squared-away guy," I said.

"What are you getting at, Dave?"

"Take a walk with me."

Clete got out of the cab and closed the door behind him, his massive shadow bigger than normal because of his sports coat and porkpie hat, his shadow sliding in front of him. He screwed an unlit cigarette in his mouth. The barnyard looked empty and pale under the moon.

"Dave, I don't know what we're doing here, but I don't think we have time for this."

"Smell it."

"The barbecue pit?"

"Yeah, smell the ash. See what you think."

He gave me a look, then leaned over the pit and inhaled deeply through his nose, his nostrils rattling, like somebody with a cold. He picked up a stick and poked into the ash, layers of it, some of it blackened material that resembled the leather apron a horseshoer might wear.

Clete flipped away his unlit cigarette and wiped his nose on the back of his hand. "It stinks. Like cowhide or animal hair. Those re-bars are caked with burned fat of some kind. It's hanging in the ash. What's this guy doing?"

"I think that's bear hide," I said.

He looked at me a long time. "You're thinking about the guy who dragged Clemmy Benoit into your backyard in a garbage bag?"

"Yeah, the guy who visited me twice and smelled just like that barbecue pit."

Clete stuck another cigarette in his mouth, then started flipping the top of his Zippo back and forth, a habit that I think he deliberately designed to drive me crazy.

"Big mon, don't get me wrong, but our gyroscopes aren't in the best shape tonight. Because if what you're saying is true, Hendrix is not only a crazoid but a ghoul who might know where Alafair is."

"It's possible," I said.

"We can't bet on 'possible,' noble mon," he said, snapping the top of his Zippo harder and harder. "I feel like burning this guy's house down."

"Hendrix is on our side," I said. "He just chewed his gum too long."

"Yeah, but he may be the guy who fried Elton Foot in the parish prison. Or maybe he was the guy who blew Jack Raider apart with a German machine gun. Have you thought about that?"

"Maybe," I said. "But how many people had reason to kill Foot or Raider?"

He snapped his Zippo shut and dropped it in his pocket, then blew out his breath and stared at the moon. It was dented with blue shadows, its glow disappearing inside rain clouds over the Gulf. "'You gets no bread with one meatball,'" he said.

"Run that by me again?"

"You know, that song from the nineteen-forties. When the average guy or girl goes to a diner, they get shit on. That's how things work."

At a time like this only Clete would remember a song like "One Meat Ball."

Then my two-way radio lit up. It was Valerie Benoit. "Dave, Sidney Ludlow wants to talk to you," she said. "He calls it a 'sit-down.' In the parking lot of Popeyes. What do I tell him?"

"Hang on," I said. "First, we want to put out an APB on Boone Hendrix."

"For what?"

"We'll figure it out," I said. "Now what was this about Ludlow?"

Chapter Forty-Five

"He wants to talk to you," she said. "He says both of you are fathers. He says you'll understand what he's saying."

Clete and I were just passing the home of the black man who enslaved his own people for money, and the rain had just started clicking on the windshield, and the Spanish moss overhead looked like silver in the trees, and once again I felt that strange sense that a stricken world lay under our feet, one whose beauty was reclaimable if we would only take the time to see it.

"Tell him I need to hear a little more detail," I said.

"Hang on," she said, and went off the two-way. Then she came back on. "I took notes. He says he's a practical man and he uses practical methods. He's a businessman as well as a family man. He says to tell you also he's got all the background on Boone Hendrix, that you should have come to him first, that Hendrix should be put in a hospital."

"We're two miles away," I said. "See you there."

"You'll talk to him?"

"Copy that," I said. "Out."

I put the two-way on the floor just as a piece of hail pinged on the windshield. I had said nothing to Clete.

"You don't buy Ludlow's sit-down?" he asked.

"No, he's an anachronism, and he knows it. The casinos have the power of Third World countries. The guys who run things now have degrees from Yale."

"That's a terrible thought," Clete replied. "Ludlow say he got the gen on the handyman?"

"That's what he says."

"What do you think it is?" Clete said.

"I don't know. I think it's one of those deals you don't want to find out about. That's kind of a funny way to be, isn't it?"

"I'm totally with that, big mon." He slid his hat over his eyes. "I think you're right about Ludlow. He's not worried about his son. He's worried about himself. Wake me up when we get there."

He took his .38 snub out of his shoulder holster and put it in his lap before he closed his eyes.

The Popeyes was closed. Bits of smoking white hail were scattered over the parking lot. A black Cadillac limousine was parked in the middle of the lot, with three smaller vehicles around it. I let my pickup coast toward the front of the limo. As I got closer, at least five goons stepped out on the asphalt from the smaller cars, all of them large men, with the expressions of bowling balls. I had never seen any of them.

Valerie Benoit was parked in a cruiser one hundred feet away, the engine running, her interior lights on, a paper cup of coffee on the dashboard. She was insuring no other cops pulled off from the four-lane and broke up "the sit-down."

Sidney Ludlow rolled down a tinted rear window in the limo and leaned his head out. He was wearing dark glasses, even though it was almost midnight. Now I was parallel to him, two feet from the window. I could see a uniformed chauffeur, but no one else in the limo. Ludlow started to speak, but I cut him short.

"How do I get my daughter back?" I said.

"I can't guarantee it, but if anybody can find her, it's my people," he replied. "More are coming, too."

"Right now I'm interested in a guy who goes by the name John Smith and drives a maroon Malibu with a Florida plate and has patent-leather hair and fingers that look like a piano player's. He also likes to shoot animals."

"Yeah, I know who you mean, but he works for Jerry Carlucci and knows better to come around my employees."

"Why is it I think you're full of shit, Mr. Ludlow?" I said.

He was under a lamp, and the rain and the hail were swirling in the light. He pushed his glasses tighter on his face and raised his chin, his skin dampening from the mist. He reminded me of a blind man begging in the street. "Where'd you get your manners?" he said. "I'm here to help you. What's the matter with you?"

I glanced at my wristwatch, and made sure he saw me do it. "Detective Benoit and my friend Mr. Purcel and I are about to leave," I said.

He raised his index finger at me. "You got a nutcase on your hands. It's not his fault. But he took out that sadist Elton Foot and probably others. You know who I'm talking about, right?"

"No, I don't," I lied.

"I put some private detectives on him up in New England," Ludlow said. "His children got killed. All three of them. I'm talking about the handyman, this guy Hendrix. A kid came into the classroom and killed like I don't know how many students and teachers, the blood a quarter inch on the floor. There was a lot of television coverage of it. Most of the time it don't go anywhere. Maybe you didn't hear about it."

I remembered the slaughter of the children and the teachers who tried to save them. Who could forget evil on that level? Ludlow's voice had the passion of a metronome.

"What kind of work did Hendrix do?" I asked.

"Carpentry and gunsmithing. The latter for collectors."

That explains the German machine gun, I thought.

"Why could you find Hendrix when the Feds couldn't?" I said.

"Who says they couldn't?" he replied. "They tell you what they're doing when they feel like it. That's why I want to help you. I'm a businessman. We need to clean up some things around here. We can make this place like Atlantic City or Vegas. Believe me, you're not gonna have any kidnappers around here."

I had left my engine idling to keep the cab warm. I turned the engine off and got out, even though Clete tried to grab my arm. It was cold and I had forgotten my jacket, and the rain was spinning and I felt like I was on a piece of moonscape. "Where's my daughter?" I said.

"You need hearing aids?" Ludlow said. "The kind that looks like clamp-ons? We got mutual goals. Jerry Carlucci has turned out to be no good. He's got some kind of disease on the brain about going to war. Why go to a war if you don't kill people? He's always got some story or problem about the fucking war. I got news for him. It's not a big deal. The world don't need all these slants."

"Where is my daughter?" I said.

I heard Clete ease out the passenger door.

"I'm working on it," Ludlow said. "Give me time."

"Where's your son?" I asked.

"Leave my son out of this."

"I think your son saw Clemmy Benoit murdered," I said.

"Don't you put your dirty mouth on my boy," he replied.

I stepped closer to the limo, then leaned down into the open window, forcing Ludlow backward. "You're a liar and a fraud, Mr. Ludlow, and you're not working on anything except your greed," I said. "Right now your chauffeur and your goons are surrounding me and my friend Clete Purcel. That's because they know you're craven. You're not only sickly in body, you have a black soul. Your men feed off your fear. They suck it like the leeches Clete Purcel and I pulled off our bodies tonight."

"You're not gonna talk to me that way," he said.

"Here's the rest of it," I said. "The only family I have is my daughter. If she is not returned to me unharmed, I'll come after all of you, even if you have nothing to do with the kidnapping or any injury to her. Look at me and say I'm lying. You copy? Don't look away from me. You're an elderly man. That is the only reason I've chosen not to slap you all over this lot. I hope you enjoy the rest of the evening."

I pulled my head out of the window. Clete was standing behind me, still wearing his pale-blue sports coat flat against his chest, his arms hanging by his sides, his palms open, which meant his .38 snub was stuffed in the back of his belt.

I had just done what a cautious police officer, or even a schoolteacher, should not do, namely, shame a dangerous man in front of his underlings. Ludlow had to do something, even if it was simply to pretend he was restraining his men. He pulled the door handle and got out, raising his hand when the chauffeur tried to help him. "Take it easy, boys," he said. "Everything is all right. We're going back to the condo to have some good food. Tomorrow I'm taking yous out on the yacht, with maybe a few broads."

"What about Purcel, Mr. Ludlow?" one of his men said.

"He's cat food," Ludlow said. "He's shit. What do you do with shit? You wipe it on the curb."

I saw Clete's right hand open and close, and all the wrinkles on the sides of his face flatten and his eyes turn to green stone.

"You got something to say, Mr. Purcel?" Ludlow said.

Then Valerie Benoit roared toward the limo, her thumb on the "yelp" button, the cruiser throbbing with lights. The glare was so bright Ludlow had to wrap his arm across his eyes.

Valerie slammed on the brakes, jumped out of the seat, and pulled her .357 Magnum and spread her feet and aimed with both arms straight out, her hands on both grips.

"Good evening, gentlemen!" she said. "Who would like to catch one in his brisket?"

* * *

The parking lot was empty in five minutes. Valerie was dressed in uniform and a bomber jacket and a fur cap. I could not remember a spring night so cold in Louisiana.

"Good news," she said. "The State Police in Baton Rouge got a hit on a maroon Malibu with a Florida tag. Two weeks ago the driver was speeding across the Huey Long Bridge. His name is Cory Diamond. Nothing with the NCIC though. In fact, it looks like he's clean everywhere. Here, you want to see my camera?"

I looked at the image Baton Rouge had sent. "Yeah, that's him," I said. "His address is in Florida?"

"Tampa," she said. "You don't seem excited?"

We should have had him in the can when he shot the black bear, but Clete in his love of animals had played Russian roulette with the button man and given him the high ground.

"Thanks, Valerie," I said. "You've done a good job."

Clete and I followed Valerie to the Sheriff's Department, then parked my truck and went inside. Most of the building was dark except for Helen's office upstairs and the dispatcher's room. Clete went into the men's room. I tapped on Helen's glass. There was no answer, so I opened the door slowly. She was in her leather chair, her chin on her chest. Then she suddenly woke. I had never seen Helen fall asleep anywhere.

"Dave," she said. She looked around as though she had walked out of a dream.

"Yes," I said.

"Are you okay?" she asked.

"Fine," I said.

"No, you're not," she answered.

She was right. I was drunk on the kind of subterraneous dirty adrenaline that eats you alive and leaves your nerve endings dead to the touch, or with bumblebees in your head. It's the long night of the soul in the storm sewer.

"Did you hear me?" she said. "Go downstairs. I'll wake you up in a half hour."

Downstairs meant a holding cell that contained three clean cots for worn-out cops whose emergency hours went longer than twenty-four hours, which often happens in the hurricane season.

"We've got an APB on Cory Diamond?" I said.

"Yeah, we'll get him, Dave," she said.

Maybe. But I saw the look in her eyes. Helen was old school. Whoever kidnapped Alafair probably had no plans for her return. That thought was literally driving me mad. The level of psychic pain a parent experiences when he realizes his child is in the hands of a deviant cannot be measured. Booze, dope, injection? Forget it. You'll eventually sleep, and you'll have the worst nightmare you ever dreamed.

Valerie Benoit walked in, with Clete behind her. "The State Police picked up Boone Hendrix and are five blocks from us as I speak," she said.

"Bring him in the back door," I said. "Don't let him be seen."

"Why?" Helen asked. Then she caught her breath and her face twitched and she grabbed an eight-ounce water glass, one of eight glasses she drank a day. I had the feeling that gallstones had a special way of injuring the human body.

"Hendrix is our best clue to the location where Clemmy Benoit was murdered," I said.

"I wouldn't depend too much on this guy, bwana," she said.

"I think he's a straight arrow," I replied. "I just think he lives in another world."

"Keep talking like that and you two can share a padded cell at the state asylum," she said.

I wanted to say something clever, but I couldn't. I was used up. Maybe all of us were. Maybe we were on a great plain and walking into a wine-dark sea we never thought would be ours.

I washed my face in the lavatory, scrubbed my skin with paper towels, then looked at myself in the mirror. I did not know who I was. My face looked as tight as a skull. My eyes were sockets, not eyes. My mouth was dry, a crooked line, even though I had cupped water in it. The only part of me I recognized was the white patch in my hair.

Then I saw Clete in the mirror. "Go easy," he said.

"I'm doing all right," I said.

"Yeah, keep saying that."

"Forget me," I said. "The handyman is the key. We don't let a bondsman, a lawyer, or other cops get a hand on him.

"You got it, big mon."

I ran a comb through my hair and stuck it in my pocket. "Do I look all right?"

"No, you scare me."

"How so?"

"You think Hendrix is a spirit or something. If he burned Foot alive, he's a monster. By the way, what kind of APB did you put on him?"

"'Possibly dangerous to himself," I said, and pulled open the restroom door. "Coming?"

Chapter Forty-Six

Behind the Sheriff's Department two young State Policemen unhooked the waist and ankle chains they had hung on the handyman. The sky was black, the stars bright and cold, the oaks pale with a luminosity that seemed to have no source. "Thanks," I said. "We'll do you guys a favor one day."

"What are y'all holding him for?" the younger of the two men said.

"Primarily as a witness," I replied. "Did he give you any trouble?"

"No, but he said something strange when we crossed the drawbridge by the Shadows."

Then he paused. Both men wore blue uniforms and gold badges with blue trooper hats that had gold-and-black cords around the crown. The younger trooper had cropped, stiff blond hair and a profile that looked scissored out of tin. He stared into the distance.

"What did Mr. Hendrix say?" I asked.

"He said the children were coming," the trooper replied. "What's he talking about?"

Hendrix was staring at the moonlight on the bayou, an empty pirogue spinning in the middle of the current. I didn't want to answer the trooper's question.

"I guess there's a lot of strangeness going around," I replied. "Hope to see y'all another time."

Clete and I watched the headlights of the State Police cruiser tunnel onto East Main. Then we put Hendrix uncuffed in Valerie's backseat, with me next to him and Clete in the front passenger seat. Valerie left the engine idling. "Where we going, Dave?" she said.

I looked at Hendrix. "Did you see something unusual at the Shadows?" I asked.

"I keep my business to myself," he said.

"A lot depends on you tonight, Mr. Hendrix," I said. "If things go wrong, my daughter might never come home."

Mr. Hendrix needed a shave. That was the first time I had seen him unshaved or ungroomed. I wondered if he was entering another level in his life, one of descent, without children and popsicles and animal shelters.

"Are you listening, Mr. Hendrix?" I said. "I really need your help, partner."

No answer. Then I took a real chance. What kind? When people are hurting bad, you don't put a thumb on a bruise.

"Ludlow says your children were murdered in a school shooting," I said.

He lifted his gaze into mine. His eyes were bursting with light, then they brimmed with tears and a pink shine.

"Sir, I didn't mean to offend you or breach your privacy," I said. "I wouldn't hurt you for the world."

"I don't wish to talk about this, sir," he said.

"Do you have a wife?"

"She passed before the girls. I'm glad she did. The most dangerous places in the country are our schools."

He was staring up through the trees, squeezing one wrist, then the other, as though an invisible pair of cuffs were on him.

"Mr. Hendrix, we have no charge against you," I said. "If you wish, you can go. In fact, we'll drive you home."

He looked at me. His mouth was like a cut with a breadknife. "You'd do that?"

"It's a free country," I replied. "Tell me one thing."

"What?"

"Did you dress up in a bearskin?"

He started to rub his whiskers, then lowered his hand. "I should have shaved. A man should always shave. It's unseemly not to."

"What about the bearskin?" I said.

"I used it," he said. "I made a mask with animal fat and hair and sticks. I harmed no animal for it."

"Why did you do this?" I said.

"I scared the dope runners. That's how I found the dead girl."

Clete and Valerie were stone-still, breathing as slowly as they could so they would not miss a word of what he said.

"Where?" I said.

"I was on the south end of Carlucci's Landing, almost to the saltwater. Then I got lost in Vermilion Parish. The sinkholes were up to my knees. The girl was lying on a board—her eyes translucent-blue, harmless and beautiful, absorbing the sky, just like she was when I put her down in your backyard."

"Why didn't you call the cops?"

"You're not gonna like this," he said.

"Try me," I said.

Whatever it was, he didn't want to say it. Which convinced me more that whatever he wanted to say was true.

"Mr. Hendrix, we think you're an honorable man," I said. "But you have to put some trust in us, too."

"The dead girl told me to take her body to you and your daughter," he said.

Valerie's fingers stopped twiddling on the steering wheel. Clete looked out the window at nothing. The only sound inside the cruiser was the engine idling. "Let's start with Jerry Carlucci's place," I said.

"It's after midnight," Valerie said. "You know a judge who'll give us a warrant this late?"

"I'm calling Helen now," I said.

"You think Alafair is on Jerry Carlucci's property?" Helen said.

"I don't know," I said, looking at the handyman's face as I talked. "Mr. Hendrix is our best lead. I think he's on the square."

"Okay, I'll get the warrant and bring it out there," she said. "It might take me a while. Bluff your way as long as you can."

"Roger that. Clete and I are going out there in my pickup. Valerie and Mr. Hendrix can come in the cruiser."

"Why your truck?" she asked.

"It's tougher."

There was a pause. "Bwana?" she said.

"Yeah?"

"I don't know what Jerry Carlucci is made of. One day I think he's a vet who got a dirty deal. Then I see the teenage addicts and hookers in morning court, and I want to beat the shit out of him, I mean break bones and smear brains on the sidewalk."

"Yeah, Jerry has that kind of magic touch," I said.

"One more thing, Streak. A friendly Fed called just before you did. He said Sidney Ludlow has landed a small army of wise guys in our area."

"To do what?" I asked.

"The Feds don't know. Maybe it has to do with the traditional families breaking up. Watch your butt."

"What about Cory Diamond, the guy who probably kidnapped Alafair?"

"That's the first thing I asked. They don't have crap on him." Then her voice changed gears. "Except Diamond might be a half brother of Elton Foot. The father was a white guy."

"Diamond may be the half brother of a sadist and he's got my kid?"

"There's no confirmation on that, Dave."

"I'll talk to you when I get to Carlucci's Landing," I said. "In the meantime please get me in contact with the guy from Fart, Barf, and Itch."

"Affirmative on that," she said. "But I'm coming out there too."

"How are your gallstones?" I asked.

"A collection of lead bullets," she replied. "Actually, that's kind."

But I couldn't concentrate on her metaphor. My stomach felt like a water well a hundred feet down. My daughter could be in the hands of a depraved man. Every breath I drew was like a broken razor blade working its way through my lungs. The images are infinite.

In front of us, Valerie lit up her cruiser and hit the gas, the light bar rippling silently, the two-lane highway eating a hole in a black sky.

That's how it went down. Yeah, you've got it. You've seen movies about the Middle East, haven't you? Perhaps with Lawrence of Arabia in them? He actually understood the importance of the ocean and the desert and the tropics and the medieval-like flags that flapped over them. In the Muslim mind, the greatness of the Earth is as Genesis describes it. The Earth abideth forever, regardless of the terrors it contains. It's also alive. There's still an ocean of lava in the center of our planet and shelves of rock the size of the Andes sliding on their sides. Our paternal home has not been a tranquil one.

That's the way it was that night on the south end of Jerry Carlucci's Landing. Balls of lightning rolled across the clouds, rumbling and exploding like bowling alleys, solitary pieces of hail flying past us like snow.

To put it another way, on that night the land and the heavens were not simply momentous, they were out of the past and the future, and we were caught like stick figures between heaven and hell, with perhaps a horn echoing from the summer-green hills of Roncevaux in the year 778.

You think not? You might be right. But read Lawrence's *Seven Pillars of Wisdom*. It is probably the most prophetic book in the English language, and considering its importance it's the most ignored.

Valerie led the way down to the southern rim of Louisiana, then toward the place where Jerry Carlucci claimed barrels of oil waste were buried. The fog in the marsh was as big as thunderheads, but we could see the electric lights and dredges and bulldozers that had already excavated a giant steel cargo container, one that was painted a garish yellow dripping with moisture. Valerie's brake lights went on, then she shifted into reverse.

"What's she doing?" Clete said.

"I don't know," I said.

Clete rubbed the inside of the windshield. "It's Diamond! By the edge of the cargo container! There's some other guys, too! They're carrying, Dave!"

"You're sure it's Diamond?" I said.

"Yeah, it's him. It's got to be. He looks like an undertaker. They're all carrying."

"He could have Alafair with him," I said.

"They've got M16s or AR-15s," Clete said. "We need your Thompson, Dave. You hear me? I think we just re-created Shitsville. This is not good, big mon."

Valerie's cruiser was coming fast in reverse while she looked through the rear window. She twisted the wheel and stomped the brakes on a muddy slick, slid in a half circle, then righted the wheel and kept coming, right at us.

The sky was crawling with electricity, which meant problems with radio reception. Remember, this happened at the end of the twentieth century. Also, these were different players, with more sophisticated weapons. Out in the fog someone was firing with an automatic rifle or a "hell trigger" or "bump stock," and had loaded his magazine with tracer rounds that looked like bits of neon drifting on a background of black velvet.

I started backing up as fast as I could, wondering if this was it.

Maybe you do not know what "it" is. *It* slips up on you, and gives you no time to adjust your situation. *It* cheats, too, the bastard. Yeah, that's right. You thought you already beat *it* somewhere else and were invulnerable. If you just had a few more seconds, you could explain to *it* and make *it* understand a mistake had been made and *it* had better get down the road.

We had another problem as well. I was driving backward, banging over potholes, the springs slamming down on the frame, and Valerie coming at me with her headlights, white-hot, red rings burning inside my eyelids. I could hardly think. I had never been so tired, not even in Shitsville. The choices I had, the many wrong ones I might make, were more than I could count, and there was no e-tool for the fatigue and fear that had become my new environment, which was reborn from my old one.

The Thompson was in the iron box spot-welded behind the cab, but the key was hanging with the truck key in the ignition. The Beretta and the cut-down Remington pump were on the floor, but we needed the Thompson or we were not going to make it. Valerie and Hendrix were coming straight at us. But my greatest fear was the possibility that Cory Diamond had Alafair in his possession, and would use her for a shield or a bargaining tool. Or worse.

"I can't see," Clete said. "I feel like I have sand in my eyes. Drop me off and keep going. I'm going around their right flank with the Remington to blow the shit out of these guys."

"Negatory on that, Cletus," I said. "We do not break visual contact."

He squeezed his temples with his thumb and index finger. "Copy that," he said. "How do you want to play it?"

I had no answer. Then I saw Valerie do something that was as brave as people can be, namely, when they give up themselves, their plans, their happiness, their future, their chances of ever seeing their loved ones again. She knew she was about to crash into us. She also knew she was blinding us with her headlights. She swerved across the mud road, creating a ninety-degree angle, shoved Hendrix down on the floor, got out from behind the wheel, exposing herself to incoming fire, and ran around the front of the cruiser and stood in front of the hood and started shooting, the caps flashing in the chambers, fire bucking from the muzzle.

I stopped the pickup, jerked the keys from the ignition, and rolled out of the driver's seat onto the road, then crawled up into the truck bed and stuck the key into the lock on the toolbox, pulling out the Thompson and the duffle bag with the three extra magazines and at least one hundred .45 rounds.

Clete was kneeling by my right fender, firing the Beretta. Whoever was stringing tracers through the night was doing a good job. Six or seven rounds pocked my windshield, exiting the rear of the cab or ricocheting inside. Clete burned two magazines in the Beretta, then the chamber locked empty with no backup magazine, leaving Clete to thumb-load in the gloom one bullet at a time, sitting with his back against the fender, the tracers floating by like Sir Charles used to sail them across a rice paddy, a smell like cordite and water buffaloes.

I wanted to nail the shooter whoever he was. But where was Alafair? Should I fire without a defined target? There is no worse shooter than one who works out his mistakes with the wounded and the dead. Did you ever see what a toppling round can do to living tissue?

Then *it* got us. *It* had to. The amount of incoming rounds sounded like tap hammers. I saw Valerie silhouetted against a spotlight, then she went straight down, like a shadow that melted into a pool, the way mortally wounded or dead people do.

Then I heard Clete say, "Oh, Dave. Oh, Dave. Oh, Dave. This is not happening. You stay there." Then he said it again, "You stay there. You stay there. You bloody well stay there and cover my ass."

Clete was never coherent in a firefight. However, he never showed fear, either. After it was over he went somewhere inside himself and then returned and walked around for a few days with a look like a slap. Once I commented to him about that, and he said, "Yeah, what's the haps? I dig it. I really do."

I started running toward Valerie Benoit. She was down, and down bad, but I could not see her, nor could I see Boone Hendrix.

Alafair, Alafair, where are you, my darling Alafair?

I ran and ran, caring nothing for my life, the Thompson in both hands, waiting for Neptune's imperious and deadly net to drop on me any second.

Chapter Forty-Seven

Valerie was curled in a ball, looking up at me, her teeth white in the darkness. "Load my gun," she said.

"You need a medic," I said.

"Fuck that," she said.

Her hand was squeezed on her hip, the blood leaking through her fingers. They were red and shiny and stuck together. I lifted them off the wound. It looked clean. I inched my hand behind her. I felt an exit wound. "Ouch," she said.

"Sorry," I said. "We're going to get you some help, Val."

"I said screw that. Load my gun."

"Where's Hendrix?" I said.

"*Here*," I heard Hendrix say from the darkness, crouched low, an M1 carbine in his left hand. "She almost knocked me out."

"Who knocked you out?" I said.

"*Her*, who do you think?" Hendrix said.

"Where did you get the carbine?" I asked.

"I got it," he said. "What does it matter?" He looked up in my face, waiting for me to answer a question he had not asked, lest he frighten Valerie.

"I think the wound is clean," I said. "I can't tell for sure."

A sling bandoleer stuffed with .30-caliber clips was tied over his shoulder. He made me think of a peasant in an Ernest Hemingway story. I gripped the barrel of the carbine. It was cold. I wasn't up for Hendrix's peculiarities. "Are you going to fire that or not?" I said.

A fly walked on his face. He didn't blink.

"The question stands, Mr. Hendrix," I said.

"You got that right, podjo," Clete said. "It's us or those assholes out in the dark."

The handyman rubbed his mouth. "I don't know what I'm going to do," he said.

"You used the German machine gun on one of Ludlow's goons, didn't you?" I said.

"I cannot deny that, Detective Robicheaux. I feel great pain for that."

"Do your best, Mr. Hendrix, but do it," I said, and hit him on the arm. "Right now that means help me save some lives. You know who you remind me of? One of Hemingway's guerillas fighting in the mountains outside Segovia in 1937."

"I know nothing about Ernest Hemingway," Hendrix said.

"I'm shocked," Clete said.

I felt sorry for the handyman, even though I believed his problems of conscience might cost us our lives. I feel sorry for anyone who loses a child. Actually I didn't know how Mr. Hendrix kept his glue together.

Then he wet his tongue, and I knew that one way or another he had made a choice and would probably carry it to the grave. "Is help on the way?" he said.

"We hope," I said. "But we seem to be detached from the rest of the world, Mr. Hendrix. Nonetheless, I want my daughter back. Does that make sense to you?"

But I had lost his attention. He was staring into the darkness, the hair on the back of his neck rising.

"*There*," he said. "A man with a flamethrower."

"Mayday! Mayday!" Clete yelled, then jumped on top of both me and Valerie, spreading his arms and big shoulders over us, crushing us into the ground, ready to die as he would for two children, smothering us with his manly smell.

Simultaneously a whoosh from the flamethrower seemed to leap into the heavens and swallow the sand and patches of saw grass around us and consume itself by broiling its own heat and oxygen at the same time. Then the man in the dark with the fuel tank and wand squeezed the trigger again, strolling toward the cargo container, ignoring the velocity of the flame wrapping around the steel plates, the stench of burned diesel wet enough to drink, the heat curling the hair on our skin and eyebrows.

I clenched my holy medal on my chest, then waited for the furnace-blow that would be my last on earth.

But it didn't happen. The man with the wand and nozzle that dripped fire was no longer interested in us. The target was Jerry Carlucci's treasure, namely, enough narcotics to ruin the lives of a generation and leave hundreds of addicted babies shivering in charity wards all over Louisiana.

The flames had gotten inside the container and were melting the plastic-wrapped stacks of heroin and cocaine that poor people in the Third World considered a gift, lest they starve and their children die. How did all this make me think about Jerry Carlucci, the man whose idol was Wyatt Earp? Guess.

"Is that what I think it is?" Clete said.

"Yeah, but who's the guy with the flamethrower?" I said.

Clete started to get up, but I pushed him back down.

"We've got to get Valerie out of here, big mon," he objected.

"Wait it out," I said.

"Wait *what* out?" he said.

That was a legitimate question. I could hear cars starting and farther out see a glow under the storm waves on the bay. The glow was not a reflection of the moon or the sun. It was large and wobbling, the way a big jellyfish glows, its tentacles an electric pink, threading through the incoming tide. I had no idea what it was. I even wondered if it was a submarine. Nazi subs sank our oil tankers just a few miles to the southwest. I always believed they might come aborning again, and perhaps sooner than we thought. The Silver Shirts came once. They could come again.

But other things were happening, too. I heard a man moaning and another call for his mother and another tell him to get his shit together. Did you ever hear the sounds on a night trail after a second lieutenant called in the 105s on his own platoon? You'd hear the accents from Dixie to the Bronx. I know. Because that's what I did.

"This isn't reality, Cletus," I said.

"What is it, then?" he asked.

"It's Shitsville."

"You can't turn it on and off," he replied. "You know that."

"Okay, but just don't borrow trouble," I said. "For once in your life, listen to other people."

But he wasn't listening. He touched his finger to his lips.

"What?" I said.

"Two o'clock," he said, meaning geographic position. "Same dude. He dumped the torch. He's got something else."

"What does he have?" I said.

"I don't know," Clete said. "I don't like guessing about this guy. Call him out or let's boogie."

That was Clete. He wouldn't add *or drop him*. Even when we worked NOPD Homicide and could get away with anything, he'd rather eat a bullet than roll the dice on an uncertain shoot.

"You know who that dude looks like, don't you?" I said.

"Sir Charles?"

"So let's ride it out. Maybe we're on acid," I said. "Or he might be on our side."

"I knew you were gonna say that. I just knew it."

Actually I didn't think our man was in need of anyone's friendship. He had too much confidence. I could see him more clearly now. He was walking straight at the fire, the flames lighting him from head to toe, in dirty canvas work pants and small tennis shoes and an ancient bulletproof jacket and a Mongolian cap with earflaps tied under his chin, not strapped. He was also Asian, his features small, concentrated, like a fist. He was also carrying a satchel charge.

"Who in hell is this guy?" Clete said.

The Asian man pulled a cord from under the flap on the satchel and flung it into the fire, then walked calmly down toward the marsh, his back to us. The explosion was almost immediate. The smoke and ash fountained sixty feet high, forming a mushroom, a smaller one than Hiroshima, certainly, but its shape a reminder of mankind's potential.

Clete got to his feet, then helped up Mr. Hendrix. "Are you ready to rock, partner?" he said.

"I wouldn't say it that way," Mr. Hendrix said.

"Oh, really?" Clete asked.

"Knock it off, Clete," I said.

"Excuse me," Clete said. "I really like humping a pack for Florence Nightingale when we're about to get our sausage blown all over on a tree. I think he's a cutesy, Moxie kind of guy."

Clete didn't mean it. That was just Clete. Plus, he had a point. It was hard to think of Mr. Hendrix as a saint after he had admitted he mowed down a goon with a Nazi machine gun, then was deciding at our expense if he should give up his violent ways.

A second explosive, maybe a boobie-trapped one, blew up deep in the cargo container and lit up a car bouncing over a hard-packed dirt road that led to the next parish. My heart was hammering, my eyes burning, but I believed I saw Alafair bound in the passenger seat of an Avalon, her face stark white, her mouth taped, her body bouncing each time the Avalon slammed across a pothole.

The image lasted just seconds.

"Can you see who's in there?" Valerie said, trying to get up from the ground.

"No, I couldn't," I said.

"Don't lie," she said.

I paused. "Yeah, I'm almost sure it was Alfie," I said. "And maybe Cory Diamond at the wheel. But you're not going with me."

"I can drive if you can get me in the cruiser," she said. "Please don't argue, Dave."

"You may be bleeding inside. You need to stay here."

"Fuck you, Dave. I'm going."

We all die. Why not go out with somebody who really has class?

"Okay," I said. "You're a brave lady."

But I did not give in entirely because she asked. The clouds were crackling like cellophane, the kind of electricity that builds until it bursts across the heavens and floods the countryside and leaves cows on roofs. Secondly, I did not believe we were standing on real earth. Oh, I know, everything has an explanation. Except that hasn't been my experience. Our best science cannot create a fish. So how can a fish create itself? Forget it. That's not my point. I believed that in one way or another our lives were about to change forever. Call it destiny. Call it the graves of Shiloh or the madness of Sand Creek. I believed the die was cast, and on this forlorn piece of geography we were about to slide down the shingles of the world.

Chapter Forty-Eight

We began our slog toward the west, primarily because I believed the man in the Avalon with Alafair was Cory Diamond and that he would try to get to dry ground southwest of Lake Charles. Clete and I were in my pickup, and Valerie was driving the cruiser with Mr. Hendrix. The flames died incrementally under the edges of the cargo container, the ashes still sparking in the wind. Then I heard the thropping blades of a helicopter, one we used to call a "slick"—a Huey that had no Gatling guns mounted on it.

"Where'd that come from?" Clete said.

The Huey went right over us, drowning out my voice, pulling into the blackness of the sky. I wondered if we were about to step into a nightmare, or were we witnessing an illusion that had its origins in Southeast Asia? "Did you get a look at anybody?" I said.

"Too dark," Clete replied. "Maybe the oil guys are buying some more army-surplus stuff."

"What do they want from us?"

"Their helicopters are good for transporting their crews out to the rigs. Did you know Kristofferson used to pilot them? That's how he got the line 'Busted flat in Baton Rouge.' I'm not kidding you."

What were we both doing? You already know. We wanted to believe that the iconic helicopter of the Vietnam War was serving a peaceful purpose not far from Jerry Carlucci's saloon, that Janis Joplin and the song that was the most heartbreaking statement of an entire generation had somehow just passed by us.

"Is that guy turning around?" Clete said. "Please some guy like Kristofferson be on it. Yes, yes, fuckin' A."

My heart was racing, just like his. Valerie was driving at about twenty-five miles an hour with her headlights on, trying to stay on the road. She doused her lights, and I did the same, both of our vehicles splashing across a coulee where the bridge was washed out and saltwater was flowing into grass.

The helicopter had made a U-turn and was coming in and leveling out, a single prop acting as two blades. It made me think of a praying mantis, although I didn't know why. Maybe I was thinking about herbicides again. Yeah, I remembered the chemicals from back then. Wow, the Agent Orange? The 2, 4-D? Shitsville's rainforests were full of it. We had it all over us. Sir Charles did, too. Everyone did. Lucky us.

Fuck that.

The slick was right above our vehicles, the air swirling with grit, flattening the grass in the downwash. I wanted to get out of the truck and open up with my .45 auto, the one I bought in Saigon's Bring Cash Alley. But those were bad memories. The Stake wasn't far from Bring Cash Alley. I remembered the Stake, and I never wanted to think about it again.

Then I saw Alafair in the door. She was tied up with rope. A man was holding her. The wind and the rotors were whipping his clothes against his body, but I could not see his face. My guess was he was going to throw her from the door. The image of him covered in shadow, his hands clinched on my daughter's shoulders, made my knees weak, my body filled with rage. I wanted to kill this man.

The Huey made a wide circle, thropping across the greenery in mockery of us, headed to a saltwater bay where the waves were brassy and sliding through the root system of an island, scooping away forever the land we thought eternal. I wanted to weep.

"It's gotta be Carlucci," Clete said. "Only that shitbird would do something like this."

"He wouldn't do it to Alafair," I said. I stared into the distance, my eyes burning, hoping my words were true and not a stack of lies.

"Come on, Dave," Clete said. "Snap out of it. That bastard would do anything. He's a pimp. What's lower than that?"

"Yeah, maybe you're right," I said. "I can't think now. I've got to find a way of seeing things the way they really are."

"Kick some ass," Clete said.

"That's what every stupid person on the planet says."

"Okay, I got my shortcomings," he replied. "But we've gotta do with what we have. Right now that's the Huey. We gotta get it on the ground. This whole place looks like a bombing zone and the rest of it is a sponge."

But the Huey was gone and I was no longer looking at the southern horizon. I was watching another Iberia Parish Sheriff's Department cruiser, this one coming along a levee to the southeast. All of its lights were flashing, the outside spotlights spearing at odd angles across the landscape. It was Helen's cruiser. She never let anyone else drive it. I should have been joyous, but I was not. She was by herself.

Clete and I got out of the pickup, afraid to watch what we were seeing. Either Iberia Parish no longer existed or Helen Soileau and her vehicle had been dropped off by Martians.

Valerie stopped her vehicle and rolled her window down, but stayed inside. I had the feeling her bullet wound was more serious than she thought. I also believed she feared Helen's solitary appearance, just as I did. Helen belonged in a hospital.

Clete was staring at Helen's cruiser, obviously disappointed that she had not brought help. "Where's the cavalry?" he said.

"They must have gotten drunk or lost," I said.

"We don't need this kind of shit," Clete said. "This cannot be happening. No one is this incompetent."

"They're not, Clete," I said. "We're in a special place. I just don't know what it is."

Helen pulled up her cruiser to Valerie's window and cut her engine and lights, then got out and closed the door so the interior light would shut off. "What's going on?" she said.

"That's what we're trying to figure out," Clete said.

"I had a dozen emergency vehicles behind me," Helen said. "Then they were gone."

She was wearing a checkered wool shirt and her customary navy blue pants and dull-black shoes. The collar of her shirt was twisted under her jaw, like a teenage girl might accidentally wear it. I didn't know why I was thinking like that. I believe it may have had to do with an ending of things, although I did not mean to think in a macabre way.

"Yeah, I looked in the mirror, then they were gone," Helen said. "The wind was spitting snow, then my radio and phone went dead."

"Have you seen Jerry Carlucci?" I said.

"I saw people in cars, but not Carlucci," she said.

"Who were in the cars?" I asked.

"I couldn't tell," she said. "Probably Ludlow's greaseballs. They all have shapes like minnows."

No one laughed.

"You never saw them in Miami Beach in the winter season?" she said.

"You didn't stop at a drive-by for some hallucinogens, did you?" I asked.

"Alafair is in a helicopter, Helen," I said. "A man was holding her. I thought he was going to throw her from the door."

"I'm sorry," she said. "I didn't know."

"It's not your everyday news," I replied. "How are your gallstones?"

"Forget the gallstones. Who was the guy in the helicopter?"

"Couldn't see," I said. "We're a little beat-up here. Valerie has a wound in her side."

"How bad?" she asked.

"Probably more than she'll admit."

Helen blew out her breath. "You asked me about the gallstones. They're hard to deal with."

"That bad, huh?" I said.

"Between me and you, yeah. The worst pain I ever had. Just keep the lid on."

Valerie got out of her cruiser and limped toward us, pressing the wound on her side. Her shirt was dark with blood. "Hi, Sheriff," she said. "I've been waiting for you. You doin' okay?"

I have no great knowledge about mythology or antiquity, but I do wonder about those who are dismissive about the supernatural or perhaps the "legends" that have trickled down through the ancient world, as though they were stardust and the products of the imagination.

You know? As though the Greek Atomists of the fifth century BC knew nothing of physics?

It was after three A.M. now, and the clouds were thickly layered, as tight as an iron lid on the southern rim, the electricity striking the water like gold wires. We moved like a caravan, all of us impaired in some fashion, either in a martial way or a crippling of the mind or through the losses that we never thought would be ours.

I thought about the fourteenth century and what it must have been like, and the global heat and the rats and the Black Death. Supposedly a single Genovese ship spread the plague along the rim of occidental Europe, perhaps in places similar to the one we were now traversing, yes, us, the descendants of pilgrims who spoke of a city on a hill.

"We'll get Alafair back, Dave," Clete said, bouncing in the passenger seat of my pickup. "If the guy in the Huey wasn't Carlucci, it's Cory Diamond. They know better than to hurt her."

"What do you think they've already done?" I said.

"No, no, think about it," Clete said. "Whoever is in that Huey wants a deal. That means with you and me, not the Feds. Carlucci is a millionaire. That button man is probably rich, too. They'll give us back Alafair, then they'll be gone."

"What if Ludlow is running everything?"

"He's never done a day's time," Clete said. "He's not gonna start now."

"The deal they want is to see us in a charnel house, Clete," I said. "Plus, what we're seeing outside our windows is crazy. Even Helen agrees with that."

"I don't buy it," he replied. "How many times have planes gone down in the Bermuda Triangle? Ships, too. Same thing off Japan. Things just happen. What do you have to say about that?"

I didn't want to mention his relationship with Joan of Arc. But I didn't have to. He read me before I could speak.

"Okay, so you think I'm a little weird with ancient times," he said. "But that's what I chose. It makes me feel good. Know why? It lets Joan know that a clod like me cares about her. And if a clod like me cares about her, everybody likes her. And that means she's out there and on the side of everything that's good. I don't give a shit if anyone believes it or not. I say she's real. How do I have the proof? She saved my fucking life I don't know how many times. Can you copy that, big mon?"

"Roger that, Cletus."

"Then what is the big deal about the current weather?" he said. "We've had hurricanes with coconuts blowing inside them.

Remember when live fish rained on the concrete in front of the Café Du Monde in the Quarter? Top that."

He rubbed the moisture off the windshield. But he wasn't thinking about fish anymore. "Look there in the fog," he said.

"Yeah," I said. "I see."

"That's Carlucci's Jeep, isn't it?"

"Yeah, it's him, Clete."

"That guy gives me diarrhea. I want to say it's because he makes me sick. That's not it. It's because he's a killer. I never thought about it that way."

Jerry's Jeep banged across a row of sandbars that looked like piano keys. He passed by Valerie and Helen and stopped next to my pickup, then stepped out on the ground wearing his black Stetson and silver vest and Lucchese boots. His mustache and whiskers could have been Wyatt Earp's. I got out of my pickup and closed the door behind me. Clete stayed inside, staring into the fog. Helen got out of the cruiser and flung the door behind her.

"What are you doing here?" she said.

"What am I doing here?" Jerry said, pointing to his sternum. "Somebody set a fire close to my property. An Asian of some kind. Or some geek. I thought you might know."

"You have a phone?" Helen said.

"No," Jerry replied. "My power has been out five or six hours."

"Have you seen any helicopters?" I said.

"Yeah, I heard one," Jerry said. "But I didn't see it. Why is Purcel staring at me?"

"He's not," I said. "He's just tired."

"I've seen people all over the place," Jerry said. "I think they're Ludlow's guys. Whatever they're doing, it's got nothing to do with me."

"Let me see if I can understand what you're saying, Jerry," I replied. "You want to help Ludlow turn Louisiana into Atlantic City, but Ludlow's activities are of no interest to you?"

"I'm a businessman," he said. "What am I supposed to do? Tell the Mob to go home?"

I heard Clete open the passenger door on my pickup, then the door closing and Clete walking.

"I'm guessing a million dollars of narcotics got smoked on your property this morning," he said. "For you that's lose-lose. Either you owe the cartels, or your cash is already trash."

"Whatever got destroyed was not on my property, got it?" Jerry said. "And I still say there were barrels of waste oil in that cargo container."

"I think you've left your dork in the light socket again," Clete said.

"You were always a thug, Purcel," Jerry said. "Even your broads were dum-dums. You should read a better brand of comic books. Why don't you wise up?"

"About what?" Clete said.

"You follow Dave Robicheaux around like a child," Jerry said. "I bet he's secretly embarrassed."

"Shut up, Jerry," I said.

"Let him talk," Clete said.

"You know what y'all's real problem is?" Jerry said. "Both you and Dave and, yeah, Alafair, and everybody like you, you don't think you have to pay dues. You work the system just like I do. Blimpo gets a pass on fighting on the side of the communists in El Sal, and nobody notices. Then he kills a bunch of people in an airplane. And you, Dave? How did you send your daughter to an expensive college in Portland? You weren't on a pad, huh?"

"Who was in that Huey, Jerry?" I said.

"Don't change the subject," he said. "You got favors. I got shit. Why? Because my family is Sicilian."

"My daughter is in that Huey, Jerry," I said.

"What?"

"You heard me," I said.

"That doesn't make any sense. If that's true, I got nothing to do with anything like that."

"But you know who does," I said.

"See?" Jerry said. "That's what I was talking about. You think you're special."

"About what?"

"Everything," he said. "I won at the Golden Gloves and came home with a broken nose. You had your face on the front page of the *Daily Iberian.* You came home from 'Nam with the Silver Star. I came home with rumors I was nuts."

"Your problem isn't the war, Jerry," I said. "Your problem is your vocation. You lead young people to disease and death."

He sucked on a cherry-flavored cough drop. For just a moment he looked like an ordinary man. "Everybody dies," he said.

"What's that supposed to mean?" I asked.

"You still don't get it."

"Enlighten me."

"Why do you think you or your daughter are different? Maybe this time you messed around with the wrong people and got yourself in the shitter for good."

"You're talking about Alafair being killed?"

"Boy, aren't you the smart one?" Jerry said.

I wanted to break his neck. This time Clete had to hold me.

Chapter Forty-Nine

Sometimes a painter or perhaps a film director can have more success in describing an aberration in the elements than a writer. Most writers seek rationality, primarily because they know that madness often accompanies the gift of creativity. The coastal territory I have described is not fiction, no more so than the antediluvian or postdiluvian in the Old Testament. I doubt, however, that others see them through the same spectrum as I. But that's all right. I have never found normal people very interesting, although I realize they have their qualities, I'm sure.

The electricity bursting in the clouds overhead was explainable, and so were the tidal surges and temperature-plunges and waterspouts that wobbled like spun glass on the bay, sometimes wrecking a sailboat. However, I had no doubt something else was at work. Call it a collective pause in our lives, one we never expected, a suppressed rumble in the swamp, the earth oozing, perhaps bleeding, momentarily under our feet, filling our shoes. Hundreds, then thousands of birds were scattering in the sky. That's right, the Gulf seemed to sink under the land, then swell suddenly and become a huge purple wave traveling froth-capped inland, ripping the roots of the entire environment like wet newspaper.

But more importantly, I felt a bond growing among us, a sense that individuality is for performers and in the long run has little virtue and is more vanity than a friend. We realized we had taken on a commonality, seen and unseen, an acceptance of our fatigue and the muddy stiffness in our clothes and on our skin, a shared awareness that mortality might be at our door, and if so, it might not be so bad after all.

I've always believed that the real gladiators among us are the most nondescript, the ones who scrub floors on their knees, maybe a woman with small children and no food and no one to help her, the elderly whose best day is one that entails a change of undergarments. That was Clete's great virtue. He always thought highly of these people, and always took up their cause.

Our group was finished with Jerry Carlucci. He knew it, too. That's why he had become more and more obnoxious. But for me the worst was his indifference to Alafair's standing in the door of a Huey while a degenerate held her hundreds of feet above the ground. Yes, true, I didn't spell that out to him, but he knew what kind of man Cory Diamond was and couldn't care less. What's the term for that kind of behavior? Malignant narcissism?

"Hey, I'll take any of y'all to the saloon," he hollered out. "Maybe the power is on. How about steak and eggs for breakfast?"

No one acknowledged him. He put his hand on my arm before I could get in my pickup.

"You were the only one I ever cared about, Dave," he said.

"Care about what?" I asked, pulling his hand from my arm.

"The Golden Gloves. The Army. Stomping ass. Being somebody! We were always each other's pacing horse."

"Get my daughter back, and I'll believe you," I said.

"I can't pull a Huey out of the sky."

"Then leave and don't come back," I said. "If she dies, I'm going to make sure you ride the needle. I hear there's some suffocation involved."

He started to speak, then his voice broke. He pointed his finger at me. But whatever words were in his mind were lost.

Helen was standing close to me. She dropped her eyes and whispered, “Let the son of a bitch alone.”

“Gladly,” I said.

Jerry got in his Jeep and drove toward his saloon, his door unshut, his front wheels banging in the potholes, his windshield wipers whipping on the glass.

Earlier I said that a painter can often convey an emotion better than a writer. Maybe, maybe not. Here’s an example. In a book in the Iberia Parish Library there’s a photo of a large thirteenth-century oil painting that shows a road on which a column of carts and oxen are fleeing a walled city, inside of which the castle is in flames and the conquerors are looting the houses, raping the women, enslaving the children, and leaving some examples of cruelty that are repellent and you should not think about.

But it’s the left-hand side of the canvas that takes you away from the baseness of an army that has become depraved. It’s the carts and the animals and the peasants that restore your eye and your heart and give you hope that not all of humankind are bestowed with the worst in us. You can almost hear the wood creaking in the carts; the hand-carved wheels have no spokes and are held together with pegs. The oxen are walleyed and probably rank with fear, and the hay is piled, the women nursing their enfants in it, their chins held above their children’s heads, their eyes both fearful and angry, looking back at the smoke in their village.

The men have torsos like inverted triangles and faces of stone or broken pumpkins tossed away after Halloween. They wear skin-tight hose and tunics tied by a string as they push and pull at their wagons. Other than the oxen, their only animals are the dogs and milk cows tied to their carts; their only weapons are rakes and scythes. The cows and dogs are straining at the cords at their necks.

But in the distance a fiery sun is rising above a green river, and on a hillside friars and peasants and Knights Templar are about to welcome those who no longer possess homes. Who are they exactly? Why are they so kind? I have no idea. Perhaps the painting was a farce or Templar propaganda. But it's easy to be a cynic. Albeit the Knights Templar were a violent bunch, but at least they weren't shoddy and they didn't give in when their faith was tested, even when they burned at the stake in front of Notre Dame Cathedral.

What am I saying? The sun rises in the east and sets in the west, and it's for a purpose. That's why I love this painting, and why I always like to remember it when I feel the earth pulling on my ankles or when the wind shifts out of the north a little harder than it should. Yes, that's when I tell myself the wayfarers on that ancient road found a new home, one between a molten-red sun and a green river and a snowcapped hill, and probably that day met a tumbler or a jolly friar or a kind lady from the castle who announced that the dinner bell was calling.

I was driving my pickup, with Clete next to me, and Valerie and Mr. Hendrix and Helen in front of us, almost as laboriously as the peasants in the painting, when I saw the Huey again, backdropped by storm clouds low on the Gulf.

"What do you think that guy is doing?" I said.

"Which guy?" Clete asked.

"Whoever has got Alafair in his hands, Clete."

"He wants to keep us on the south rim of Carlucci's Landing and away from the settlements," Clete replied. "Then he wants to do some serious damage."

"To trap us with Jerry?"

"That's what I think," Clete said. "That's why I'm gonna use a baseball bat on Carlucci. I'm not using a metaphor, here."

"So you don't figure Jerry is alone?" I said.

He made a face. "I can't figure that guy, Dave," he said. "I thought I could, but I can't. I guess he's just a piece of shit. Yeah, that's it. There are no complexities in feces. Any other questions?"

* * *

A sudden shower of hailstones, as white as snow, clattered across our convoy, piling on our windshield, then it was gone, and was replaced by a black velvet sky, under it a dozen cars, all pointed at us, a gleaming Buick in front.

"Is that Ludlow's car?" Clete said.

"Yep," I said, pulling the Thompson from behind the seat.

"I pushed you on using that," Clete said.

"Yeah?"

He shrugged and wiped his nose, then said nothing.

"Something bothering you?" I said.

"Sometimes you gotta think like the AA people do. Easy does it. Most of the greaseballs are stupid. That doesn't mean they all deserve to be dog food."

"When did you start going to AA?"

"I didn't. It's common sense. We've got two injured people, Valerie and Helen. Our other partner is Hendrix, whose head probably glows in the dark. You want to start a firefight with that kind of backup?"

"I want the Huey back on the ground," I said. "I don't care how we do it, Clete."

We were in the middle of the road, the engine idling, the heater clanking, the inside of the truck cold, the fog clinging to the ground like strips of dirty cotton. Clete stared at Ludlow's Buick and the number of vehicles behind it, their headlights crisscrossing. "Why do you think all these guys are here?" he said.

"They're running out of space," I said.

"Something like seedpods?"

"Yeah, I think you could say that."

"You don't sound too good, big mon," he said.

"I've got a bad feeling."

"Like this might be it?" he said.

I didn't answer.

"That's exactly the way I feel," he said. "Like it's the bottom of the ninth. Hey, I gotta say something, here."

"What?"

"I didn't mean to lecture you about the Thompson and the greaseballs. My stomach is flopping, that's all. I've had a good life. Most of the downsides have been my own fault. You call it. We'll go out any way you want."

Chapter Fifty

We got out of the truck and walked up the road to Helen and Valerie and Mr. Hendrix. Valerie had shifted her weight on one foot, and blood had leaked and dried down to her ankle. She bit her lip each time she shifted her foot, but said nothing and kept her face empty. I could see Helen was having a go of it as well, and drinking from a canteen she had laced with lemon juice and olive oil to doctor her gallstones, or some combo like that. I decided if we got through this I would join a nutrition club and drink Montana creek water and eat rabbit food the rest of my life.

Mr. Hendrix was stone-faced, his arms folded on his chest, the M1 carbine hung from his shoulder barrel-down. I had the feeling he had come to a conclusion about his willingness to use violence; I also felt it was not a good one.

"Mr. Hendrix, Clete and I believe that Sidney Ludlow is going to leave us for the gators," I said. "That means my daughter will die with us."

He had an expression like the back of my thumbnail.

"How do you know that, Dave?" Helen said.

"Carlucci is behind us and Ludlow is in front," I replied.

"Jerry Carlucci has shot his wad," Helen said.

"I don't think so," I said. "Jerry will probably kill every one of us as soon as we get close to the saloon, then Ludlow and Jerry will be buds again. Maybe later they'll kill each other. But we won't be there to see it."

Helen looked at Valerie. "What do you say, Val?"

"I say we fuck them up," Valerie said.

"Where'd you learn that language?" Helen said.

"The nuns," she said.

Clete laughed. I think he was the only one of us who had the strength to do so.

"You don't have anything to say, Mr. Hendrix?" Helen asked.

"I would like to talk to Mr. Ludlow," he said.

"Just chat him up?" Helen asked.

"You do not understand Mr. Ludlow," Hendrix said. "He wears dark glasses night and day and stares at the sun and the moon, but has no interest in either. His world is one of darkness. He's trying to escape it now. But only on his terms."

"What is he looking for?" she asked.

"A place that has never existed."

"I think I'm gonna end this conversation," Helen said.

It was getting colder, even though the early light was about to break. My bones ached, and my skin felt like my fingernails had been pulled out, and I could feel two or three nerves pressing against my spine. But I wasn't the only one hurting. I could see Valerie getting weaker and becoming more desperate than courageous. She put her hand on the top of the car on her cruiser, then lowered her head and opened and closed her mouth and eyes, like she wanted to go to sleep. For a moment I thought her knees were about to cave. I put my arm across her shoulders. I could feel the solidity in her back and arms, and smell her skin and her hair, and I wanted to tug her against me, or maybe go away with her for a long time. She looked into my face. "I'm all right," she said.

"I know that, Val," I replied.

"So why are you looking at me like that?" she said.

"I think you're nice and wish I was younger," I replied.

"Hang around and see how things go," she said, then winked.

"Okay!" Helen said. "If we're all in accord, start walking five feet apart, your weapons drawn, chambers loaded. Is that satisfactory with you, Mr. Hendrix?"

"I am not sure," Hendrix said. "But I have decided to carry my carbine at a forty-five-degree angle."

"That's very gracious of you," Helen said. "If we get out of this, I will personally drive you to the state mental asylum. Okay, let's see what these motherfuckers are made of."

We started walking through the fog and the creeks that threaded through saw grass where alligators with chests the size of beer kegs waited in sand ponds for nutrias and sea turtles they snapped in their jaws like bear traps. Two hundred feet away at least two dozen men were standing by their vehicles, holding pistols, AR-15s, and cut-down shotguns. I could see Sidney Ludlow in front of them, dressed in a fedora hat and a pressed suit and his dark glasses, looking at a wedge of sunlight on the southeast horizon, like a broken egg yolk buried in a cloud. His son was next to him, wearing a khaki cap and a fly vest, a garden trowel in his hand, as though we were all on an archeological dig.

I had thought better of his father. I couldn't believe he would expose his son to a firefight. Or was I wrong? Was Ludlow there simply to subsume the land, the way many others had? The French and the Spanish and the British, the American troops that were marched across the bottom of Louisiana into Texas and Mexico in 1846, the Union and Confederate soldiers, the oil industry—all of them thought it was theirs. Now we had the cartels and the dregs of Atlantic City and Las Vegas to deal with.

Helen fell down, then got up with Clete's help. But Valerie was the one who worried me. She tripped and went down hard on her wounded hip, then tried to muffle her pain as she wrapped saw grass around her hands to pull herself up. I picked her up and wiped her hands clean and tried to brush the mud off her clothes, then put her .357 in her holster. "You okay?" I said.

"Sure," she replied.

"Stay behind Clete and me," I said.

"In your dreams," she replied.

I vowed that no matter how things came out, Sidney Ludlow was going to pay a price for coming to *la belle Louisiane*.

We walked up to Ludlow, as though joining a picnic.

"Good morning," I said. "But it's time for you to leave."

"None of yous need to be here, Mr. Robicheaux," Ludlow said. "Go to your homes and jobs, and it'll be over. I'll bring your daughter safely to your house."

"When?" I said.

"Five minutes from now," he replied.

I nodded. "Your word means nothing, Mr. Ludlow," I replied. "You convince uneducated people they have an even chance at your games and machines, and eventually take every dollar they have. Tell you what, if you get my daughter down here within fifteen minutes, I won't have to feed you to the shrimp."

He tilted up his face; his eyes were cups of shadow, his mouth small and gray and dry. "I came out here to make peace. To put money in your pockets. To create a city of lights out of a swamp."

"Your hired scum degraded Clemmy Benoit before she died, didn't they?" I said. "Or did you do it yourself?"

His son began to moan.

"You don't talk to me like that," he said. "You don't talk like that in front of Bedford, either."

"Your son owns his soul, Mr. Ludlow," I replied. "You lost yours somewhere down the track. That's why you wear those glasses. You think you can find your soul inside their darkness. It doesn't work that way."

He raised his finger. It was trembling. His son was moaning louder, opening and closing his hands. Ludlow's mouth was twitching. But he couldn't speak. In the corner of my vision I saw the Huey flying at about three hundred feet, the rotos making the strange chugging sound they're known for, headed in the direction of Jerry Carlucci's saloon.

Then our handyman stepped forward, his M1 carbine at port arms, forcing himself in front of Ludlow. "I don't like you," he said. "You shouldn't have children."

"You're the popsicle man," Ludlow said. "The guy who probably shot my employee with a German machine gun. The arsonist who burned Elton Foot to death inside the jail."

"Why did you take your son here?" Hendrix said.

"Because I'm gonna turn this into a beautiful place. Nutcases will not be allowed—"

He didn't get to finish. Mr. Hendrix reached out and pulled Ludlow's glasses from his face and crunched them in his fist, then dropped them in pieces on top of Ludlow's shoes.

We had no plan. I guess that's the way the most important events in our lives go down. We step off a curb before the light has changed, or give up a seat on a subway just before the car goes off the tracks, or leave the key in the ignition with a child in the backseat or unlock the house door to someone we thought was a friend from church.

It started with a solitary pop. Maybe one of Ludlow's troglodytes was drunk. Members of the Mafia are not known for their intelligence. Once in a while someone like Meyer Lansky comes along, and we hear about it for decades. Regardless, guns were popping everywhere, like Chinese firecrackers, but they were lesser in sound than the Huey that had reached Jerry's saloon; it landed briefly, the blades whipping, then took off again, lifting into the sunlight, the shadows shrinking away from the swamp, the goons from New Jersey never suspecting the denouement they were about to experience. Nor did I know who was in the slick, or whether he was friend or foe. All of this occurred in seconds.

Sidney Ludlow grabbed his son's arm and began running for the parked cars, but not in a gentle way. Bedford was weeping and fighting with his father, who in turn was shaking him and tearing his clothes and shouting in his son's face. I did not want to see it. The degradation of a child is the degradation of an adult. It doesn't wash off.

Valerie and Helen and Clete and Mr. Hendrix crouched down behind our vehicles. I stood behind the pickup with the Thompson, and sprayed it over all the greaseballs' cars. I could hear glass breaking and bullets punching through the hoods and grilles, blowing out radiators and setting one gas tank on fire. The Thompson made my right ear deaf. The gas tank blew up in a huge ball of flame, swallowed by a larger cloud of black smoke.

It's strange how the firefight affected me. I wasn't afraid. Maybe because I didn't have time. Or maybe because I couldn't keep my mind off Alafair, and to a degree the rest of our group. If I could get them home, I would have gladly given my life. In fact, I would have considered it a great victory. Plus, I hated the thought of dying in bed, physically sealed in my own secretions, surrounded with beeping machines and morphine bags and catheters and well-intended personnel who joked constantly but whose eyes would never meet mine.

As I fired the Thompson, the brass shells jetting from the bolt, I was happy in a strange way. I was part of something that was bigger than ourselves. That's right, in some inexplicable way we had been refashioned out of the clay, either by an invisible hand or simply Creation, right there on that spot, in Southwest Louisiana, in a swamp, maybe right out of Genesis. Or call it what you wish. Who cares? In the sogginess of the saw grass and mud and clay quicksand I could smell the odor of fish, but in truth it was not fish. It was semen, and it belonged to the Earth; it just used another name.

I curled on my side under an uprooted cypress trunk and changed magazines. The greaseballs were not doing well. They had not expected the amount of fire they would have to eat or how well we could shoot. I think we had another gift, too, namely, the knowledge that this was our land, just the way Woody Guthrie said it was. Maybe its possession came to us at a terrible cost, but that did not mean we had to emulate our ancestors. We could start over. Why not? Each day we could rise with the sun and the cawing of seagulls and the flight of blue herons and winged fish sailing above the waves. Eden might be a lot closer than we think.

Clete crawled on his stomach until he was next to me. He was painted with mud and dead vegetation. "How you doing on ammo?" he said.

"Two mags gone. How about you?"

The mud on his face looked dried and stiff. He touched his cheek, then looked at his hand. "I'm gonna frag some of these cocksuckers," he said.

"You've got a grenade?" I asked.

"I got a few of them."

"Why didn't you throw them already?"

"I was worried about that autistic kid. You think Ludlow put him in a safe place?"

"You know why Ludlow is a psychopath?" I said.

"No."

"He doesn't think he's normal and other people are like him."

"Yeah, I kind of overrated his paternal side." He peeped over the tree trunk, then brought his head down fast. "I'm gonna shake these guys up. Stay cool."

He got on one knee below the level of the tree trunk and cupped his hands around his mouth. "Hey, you guys, I've got four or five old-time, pineapple presents for y'all! You can boogie now or hang around and get the shit blown out of you! It's your call! Enjoy!"

Clete twisted the pull ring out with his index finger, then released the spoon, igniting the fuse, then lobbed the grenade. As it arched into the automobiles of the greaseballs, I saw Clete silently counting: *One motherfucker, two motherfucker, three motherfucker*—

The grenade probably went through a windshield that was already broken because glass and shrapnel rained down on the cars, as though the explosion came from inside a vehicle. I didn't hear anyone scream, but more importantly I saw Ludlow's people shooting blindly, which meant they were not giving up.

Then I saw the Huey coming, with someone silhouetted in the door, a plexiglass shield on his face, swinging an M60 on a mount, blazing short bursts, ripping incredible amounts of glass and metal from the cars, almost like confetti, a long burst showering water and mud in a straight line in seconds, like aerial rounds streaking across a rice paddy in South Vietnam.

Clete was on his back, looking up at the sky, his hands pressed on his ears, his mouth open wide as the slick roared past us. But I could not make out who the door gunner was. He was obviously passionate, swinging his body, measuring his bursts, having a fine time, literally licking his lips, perhaps having an erotic moment. It happens.

"Did you get a look?" I said.

"No!" Clete said, holding his head. "Oh, fuck, is that cocksucker circling around? Gimme your Thompson! I'm gonna cut him off at the waist!"

"Maybe Alafair is still on board," I said.

"Then what are we gonna do?" he replied.

Clete was right. The slick was turning around. The sunrise was now a yellow band stretched across the bottom of the sky. I stood up with the Thompson and shook it at the door gunner. "Show me your face, you motherfucker!" I yelled. "Show me your face!"

Chapter Fifty-One

The pilot had chosen an angle that blinded the people on the ground and illuminated the faces of anyone looking up at the Huey. Both he and the door gunner went overhead again, ignoring us, and opened up on the parked cars and anyone near them. Cartridge shells actually landed on Helen and Valerie's cruisers, but there was no attempt to hit them. I saw several of Ludlow's men who were obviously terrified, looking over their shoulders, one man clutching what was probably a religious medal. The M60 seemed to make them shudder, then dissolve into a pink mist. Six other men were wading waist-deep in a canal, trying to shade their eyes, when they were strafed and eviscerated by the M60, then attacked by alligators. The alligators roiled the water for several minutes, the underside of their tails a rubbery greenish-white, then the water was calm, just like that.

Helen and Valerie and Mr. Hendrix had crawled into a galvanized drainpipe under a levee, but none of us could be sure of the pilot's and door gunner's intentions. I thought we might be done with them, that perhaps they had left Alafair at the saloon and would now cross the bay into a new day. But I should have known better. The countryside was soaked with blood. Someone had to be accountable. There were no electric lights on in Jerry's saloon, and our radios and phones were still dead. Hermann Göring said that the history of wars is written by the victors. He was right. Except he was a failure, and everything he touched turned to shit.

Who was going to write our story? The door gunner? Ludlow and his goons? I was beginning to feel that our time in Golgotha was not over. Or perhaps it was just beginning.

Valerie and Helen and Hendrix gathered with Clete and me and stared at the southern rim of the parish. The sun was a golden bowl under another cluster of black clouds hanging on the Gulf, as though stormy weather would never leave us. The Huey had swung around, made a wide loop, and was now headed toward the saloon again. I felt raindrops striking my head, each of them as hard as a small ball of lead, and saw the faces of my companions and knew what they were thinking. They wanted to go home. Who would not? I cleared my throat and spat, and started to speak, but I didn't know what to say.

Every war has a story about a brave group that will always live in our hearts, but the realities come at a great cost. I suspect that if poppies amid tombstones and waves swelling over a sunken battleship had their way, they would seek a kinder place to be. The wind is the wind; its coldness can be raw. The dead can sometimes be angry. When you feel their touch, you sometimes grab your comrades and hold them tight and pray they never leave your presence.

"You okay, Dave?" Clete said.

"Sure," I said. "How about y'all?"

They nodded, but they were not good actors, particularly Valerie. She was drained out. Helen knew it, too. She looked at Val, then at me, as though saying, *Call it, big boss man.*

"How about you let Mr. Hendrix drive for a while, Valerie?" I said.

"I signed out my cruiser," she said. "I'll sign it in."

That was the protocol: You made sure your cruiser was clean when you left the department, and you did a search when you checked it in.

"I'd be proud to help out, Detective Benoit," Hendrix said. "You've got to rest a little bit."

Valerie didn't seem to think that was a good idea. She looked at me. "Where are we going?" she asked.

"I'm hoping Alafair is at the saloon," I said. "If I could be sure she was there, I would cut through Ludlow and his greaseballs. I think they're beat-up enough not to want any more of us."

"Meaning the door gunner or Jerry Carlucci or whoever is running that Huey might just kill us all?" Helen said.

"It's a possibility," I said.

"That's it?" she said. "A possibility?"

"Yeah," I said. "If I were y'all, I'd plow through Ludlow and his goons. Call it mopping up."

Helen's eyes were pink with strain and exhaustion, the way you feel when mosquitoes are buzzing in your ears and laying their eggs in your veins. "I can't think," she said.

"I'm going to the saloon," I said. "Come with me if you will."

"Dave, are you sure you don't want to hit Ludlow head-on?" Clete said.

"Yeah, I'm sure," I replied. "I won't get Alafair back by shooting at Ludlow and his guys. I'm betting on the slick and Jerry Carlucci. It's a lousy flip of the coin."

I was putting my daughter ahead of my friends. I guess no one could blame me. But it didn't make me feel well. It's just the way it was. Sometimes your spiritual metabolism gets messed up. I heard Clete take a breath. "Okay, let's do it," he said.

"Copy that, Cletus," I said.

"Detective Robicheaux?" Mr. Hendrix said.

"Yes, Mr. Hendrix," I said. "What can I do for you?"

"I've got a confession to make."

"What might that be, Mr. Hendrix?"

He looked into the distance, then back at me. "I forgot what it was."

"I think your sins are probably forgiven, sir," I said. "No, no, you don't have to say anything. You're welcome. Don't say another word. Stay on the sunny side."

I got into my truck, slammed the door, and put Mr. Hendrix in the rearview mirror as quick as I could.

We parked in front of the saloon. The Huey had landed in a pool of shadow in the back. I could see no one inside it. Through a saloon window I could hear music and see neon lights floating inside a 1950s-style jukebox. The main instrument carrying the song was a flute. Yes, like one going back to the American Revolution or a song resurrected from the 1930s. It was Jerry's favorite, "Going Up the Country."

I thought the inside of the saloon would be wrecked, the way the countryside was. Or maybe some drunks would be passed out on a table. Or maybe an over-the-hill, glassy-eyed, lady-of-the-night would be asking for one more Vodka Collins so she could tell one more story about the way things used to be.

But the interior was immaculate, and the only sound was the voluminous echo of the jukebox. We were inside a mausoleum, a tribute frozen in time, one that could be compared to the House of the Rising Sun, where white slavery was practiced and despair and suicide were the norm. However, the fantasy cathedral we call Las Vegas would replace Jerry's saloon, and in my opinion prove that the dumbing-down of America was working splendidly.

I glanced in a bar mirror and hardly recognized my friends or me. I guess that was why I loved them. They were the kind of people who in extreme situations never give up, and as a consequence consider suffering as part of the ride. As George Orwell wrote, they're the ones who "keep their mouths shut in the torture chamber" and "go down with their guns still firing when their decks are awash." But would the words of Orwell help my little girl? Yes, that's how I thought of her, and it's why I cannot bear the thought of a cruel man placing his hands on a woman. I want to grind him up. I believed Alafair would spit in the faces of her tormentors, and the fact she would do that brought me even greater misery.

But I had a bigger job than to simply save my daughter. Valerie and Helen were both hurting and getting worse, and it was unfair to put them in extra jeopardy because all my attention was on Alafair. I put my hand on Val's back. Her muscles were like rope, probably because they were knotted with pain. "Sit down, Val," I said. "I'm going to find Carlucci, then we're going to find a phone that works."

"Yeah, that sounds good," she said, her voice laced with fatigue.

I eased her down on a chair. Her face was only a few inches from mine. I could feel her breath, like a feather, every three seconds. "You worry too much," she said. "I'll just rest a few minutes."

The shirt on her left side was stiff with dried blood. I moved my hand to her shoulder. "Don't give me a hard time, Val."

She closed her eyes for a few seconds, then opened them again. "How many dead people do you think are out there?" she said.

"I don't know. Most of it was done by the helicopter."

"Does it bother you? I mean, our part in it."

"On my first time out an old-time master sergeant in Vietnam told me something I never forgot: " 'Don't think about it before, and don't think about it when it's over.' "

"You don't have dreams?" she asked.

"If I do, I talk to other people and I don't have to get drunk."

I picked up a sugar-shaker from the bar and flung it into the back of the building. I heard it crash and break in the darkness.

Jerry came from the back of the saloon, dressed in a clean western-cut suit, his black six-star Stetson, a fat gold watch-and-chain stretched across a leather vest. "Glad you saw the light," he said to me.

"Where is she?" I said.

"Where is who?" he asked.

"My daughter. The little girl who used to go fishing off your dock."

"She's safe and sound," he said. "What? You think I would hurt her?"

"I think you're morally insane," I said. "I think you would do anything."

"You got it all wrong, Dave," he said. "I saved Alafair from Sidney Ludlow. You want to talk to her? She'll back me up."

The record on the jukebox stopped and changed to another 45 RPM. The needle swung down on the vinyl, followed by a few seconds of static, then Larry Finnegan began to sing "Dear One." If ever there was a heartbreaking symbol to the end of the 1950s, that was it.

"I'll ask you just one more time, Jerry," I said. "Bring her out here."

"Not until I get some agreements," he replied. "I saved her from the shitheads that kidnapped her, but I've got bodies on my property I'm gonna have to explain. I'm also looking at a member of your personnel right now who is looking at me like I'm the stink on shit. Got me?"

"No, I don't *got* you,'" I said.

He pointed at Valerie. "I'm talking about *her*, the one with leopard spots for a hairstyle. She was in the St. Martinville drama class that your daughter was in," he said. "Except your daughter had talent. I paid for the tutors in that class. Valerie Benoit spread rumors about me and 'Nam, so I got her arrogant ass kicked out. She's a bitch. It has nothing to do with race."

"Hey, Jerry," Clete said. "I don't want to disturb you, but if you use that word again, I'm gonna bash your teeth out on the edge of that bar."

Jerry ignored Clete and opened his coat to show he wasn't carrying. Or I thought he did.

"What do I have to do to prove myself, Dave?" he said. "I always backed your play. I rubbed oil on your gloves when we were at the nationals. It almost blinded that kid from Chicago you took down. You didn't know that, did you?"

"You're lying," I said.

He massaged the back of his neck with his fingers, accidentally opening his slim-cut coat again. "Believe what you want," he said. "I keep my word. How many in my profession can say that?"

A small pistol was tucked in the back of his belt. "You have Alafair's .25 auto," I said.

"What?" he said. Then realized what he had done. "Oh, *this*. I found it on a guy out there. He caught an M60 round in the face. I can't believe I used to shoot people with those."

He jerked when he grinned.

"Do you actually think you can cut a deal here, Jerry?" I asked.

"In a state that allows drive-by-daiquiri windows? I think it's possible."

"What did you do to Alafair?" I said. "Who put her in the Huey?"

"Everything that has gone wrong here is on Sidney Ludlow, Dave. Granted, I got my faults, but I probably saved your daughter's life. Now, you want to see your daughter, or do you want to start throwing fists again, 'cause it doesn't make any difference to me."

I guess one of my great failings in life has been my inability to throw former friends over the gunwales. Of course, a cynic might say that Jerry was never really a friend. He could look like one, certainly, and he even had moments when he seemed a charitable man and made you proud to be in his company, like when we were at the Golden Gloves nationals. However, like his father, he viewed the world as his enemy, and actually distrusted people who were honest because he believed them unpredictable.

"I need a phone that works, Jerry," I said.

"Well, you're out of luck," he replied.

"I see," I said. I had the Thompson propped on my shoulder. I got up from my chair and pushed Jerry with one hand, then flipped aside his coat and took the .25 auto from his belt and threw it in the back tables. "Who's the pilot?"

"A guy for sale," he replied. "Or maybe a couple of guys for sale."

"Clete and I are going outside now," I said. "We'd better not find any surprises."

"I'll come with you," he replied.

"No, you won't," I said. "You'll stay there and do what Valerie and Helen tell you to."

"What about me?" Mr. Hendrix said.

I had almost forgotten the handyman. He had followed us, and still had his carbine. I had no idea what was on his mind.

"Maybe you ought to keep guard here, Mr. Hendrix," I said.

"You don't trust me?" he said.

"No, sir, I hold you in great respect," I said.

"I'll stay, Detective Robicheaux. But you underestimate Carlucci. He'll be your undoing."

Then I heard the rotors on the Huey start to whine, and I forgot all about Mr. Hendrix and even Jerry Carlucci, and ran for the back door into the early morning light, holding on to the Thompson, the downwash already hitting me like a big pillow, Clete right behind me.

I started to raise the Thompson, but it was too late. The button man, Cory Diamond, was standing in the door. Alafair was on the floor of the Huey, her ankles and her wrists bound behind her.

Had I blown it? I didn't know. We could have rushed the Huey and gotten her killed, I guess. Or maybe we could have been blown into spaghetti by the M60.

The Huey tilted away, sliding toward the east into the sun, lighting the Huey from the inside. I swore I heard a scream. I wanted to believe it was my imagination. I wanted to eat my gun.

Chapter Fifty-Two

I ran back into the saloon before Clete could get there. I picked up an empty wine bottle by the neck and smashed it and twisted Jerry's shirt and kicked his shin and threw him on the floor and stuck the jagged edges of the bottle an inch from his face and knelt on his lower abdomen until his mouth dropped open.

"You get the slick back, Jerry!" I said.

"No-can-do, Davie," he said. "Sorry."

I pressed the broken edges of the bottle below Jerry's left eye and watched a small triangular split in his skin fill with blood.

"Do what you're gonna do, motherfucker," he said.

I could feel Clete's shadow bending over me. "Ease up, noble mon," Clete said.

"Get out of my light, Clete," I said.

Then Hendrix knelt next to me. "Don't do this, Detective Robicheaux," he said. "He's not worth it. Your daughter would be the first to tell you that."

I held Hendrix's eyes, then threw the bottle across the dance floor and pulled up Jerry by his coat collar and crashed him into a pile of barstools. "I'm asking you in front of all these people—who kidnapped my daughter?"

"It's simple," he said, getting up, one hand on the bar. "I bought Cory Diamond for a million dollars, and the zip for five hundred thousand."

"The zip?" I said.

"Yeah, as in zipper-head."

"You're paying out millions of dollars for what?" I asked.

"To come on my side," Jerry replied. "As you have probably figured out, I had some product in the cargo container, so I told the zip, who I call Mr. Ling, to quit Ludlow and fry the product with the flamethrower and start working for me, which he has happily done."

"Who strafed Ludlow's greaseballs?" I asked.

"Diamond."

"A button man would go up against a Jersey gangster like Ludlow?"

"The families are falling apart up there," he replied. "They can't wait to rat each other out."

"Why did Diamond and the Asian take Alafair away?" I said.

He scratched his cheek. "Insurance?"

Clete was looking at the back of Jerry's head. "I don't like your language, Carlucci," he said. "I don't like your racism, either."

"Why don't you shut up, Purcel?" Jerry said.

Clete stuck a wood match in his mouth. "You know, I really dig your threads," he said. "They remind me of the clothes corpses wore in coffins in nineteenth-century photographs. You just need a bullet between the eyes to have the whole look. I'm ready to help."

Of course, I knew Clete better than that, and so did Val and Helen and even Mr. Hendrix. We would always be ourselves. But sometimes evil takes advantage of the virtuous and the charitable and leaves them with great regret.

We heard the thropping of the Huey, then the ceiling began to shake and in seconds the Huey was hanging twenty yards behind the saloon and thirty feet in the air, the airframe tilting, vibrating in the swirls of grit, faded red and white shark teeth painted on the fuselage, unvanquished for all to see, the pilot grinning behind the stick, a Mongolian cap with earflaps tied under his chin.

"Motherfucker, somebody brought this from Shitsville," Clete said.

"What's the pilot doing, Jerry?" I said.

His eyes were riveted on mine, as though his next words might be the most important of his life. "Get everybody out," he replied.

"I asked you what the pilot was doing," I said.

"We're going to get out of here," Jerry said. "You and Helen and Hendrix and Valerie and even Purcel."

"Did you know you have a nervous twitch?" I said.

"There're storm clouds building on the water," Jerry said. "It'll be pouring again in fifteen minutes. Time to haul ass. Like the 'Hadacol Boogie': 'Louisiana in the bright sunshine, they do a little boogie-woogie all the time.'"

"You're talking like an idiot," I said.

"I'm saying Ludlow will show you no mercy," Jerry said. "He'll take your eyes out with a spoon. He's going blind himself. He hates people like you. The slick can take us out, Dave. We can land in Lafayette, then split."

"Dave, don't listen to this asshole," Helen said. "Get the helicopter on the ground. Shoot one of the blades if you have to."

What was the best way out? Or was there any? I had no idea. I couldn't think straight. I remembered when Sir Charles got his hands on one of our bloopers and started lobbing shit into the LZ when it was full of wounded. That's how I felt now. That's what apeshit is all about.

"Okay, you guys, we keep it simple," I said. "We're going outside and bringing down the Huey and taking Alafair off it."

Helen stood up, then made a sound like a knife had broken off in her side. She eased back down in the chair. "This is the sickest I've ever been, bwana," she said.

"We gotta get her outside," Jerry said. "Right, Dave? We're all in this together."

"Fuck you," Helen said. "The only person you're in this with is yourself, you rotten bastard."

"I'm just trying to help," Jerry said. "The pilot is not gonna listen to y'all."

"You're not giving orders, Jerry," I said.

He squeezed his hand on his mouth. His face was as gray as cardboard. "We gotta organize," he said.

"What are you up to, Jerry?"

He started toward the back door, then stopped. "Can I talk to you?"

"Go ahead."

"Back in 'Nam I got messed up with drugs and shit, and did some bad things."

"Why are you telling me now?" I said.

He started crying. I wasn't ready for it. He never cried when he was a little boy. His father took a strop to him if he did.

"When I came back home, I decided I would do things my way," he said. "That means money talks and bullshit walks."

"So?" I said.

"It's my credo," I said. "I cut a deal with Ludlow. Then I cut another just hours ago with Diamond and the zip, or as you say, 'the Asian.'"

"What kind of deals?"

"I had to tell Ludlow I wouldn't help you in any way. That means at some juncture you might have to go."

"I would have to go?"

"Yeah."

I nodded. “Go on,” I said.

He cleared his throat. “Maybe others might have to go, too.”

I didn’t reply. No one else spoke, either. Jerry took out his handkerchief and blew his nose. Mr. Hendrix walked away.

“You were going to kill all of us, including Alafair?” I said. “A guy I grew up with?”

He looked like a man on a scaffold waiting for a bag to be put over his head. He folded his arms to keep them from shaking.

“Answer my question,” I said.

“I was stringing Ludlow along,” Jerry said. “I didn’t make the transfer of money to Diamond and the Asian guy. They think I did, but I didn’t.”

“But you wanted us to walk outside and get shot to pieces?” I said.

“No, I was gonna straighten everything out. And if I couldn’t, I was gonna eat my gun or let the dink do it.”

He raised his hand as though taking an oath. Clete’s eyes never blinked. But the wrinkles at the corners were flat, his chest calmly rising and falling.

“Listen, Dave,” Jerry said. “People like you and me are dreamers. I’m gonna shut down my place here and go out to Arizona and open a bar in the desert. Come out there with me.”

I couldn’t keep up with his lies or, more charitably, his fantasies. Was he a psychopath? I didn’t know. Psychopaths take their secrets to the grave, even when they face execution and can reveal the burial places where they have hidden the remains of their victims. Was Jerry that evil? Did the term “malignant narcissism” fit Jerry? Maybe. Maybe not. But I knew one thing for sure. The Huey had made another circle around the building. Our time was running out.

Hendrix walked up behind me. “Detective Robicheaux?”

“Yes, sir,” I said.

“The roof of this building is in shabby repair,” he said. “Like yours was, before I fixed it.”

I could not take any more of our handyman's craziness. "Sir, would you take the mashed potatoes out of your mouth?" I said.

"I've got a ladder and a plan," he said. "But I need you two to help me."

Why is it that anger usually comes to us only when it's unjustified?

The previous owner of the building had built it with an attic over the bandstand for storage space and sometimes a sleeping area for musicians who followed what was called the southern circuit, R&B people like Smiley Lewis and Fats Domino and Jimmy Reed and Little Richard and Jimi Hendrix (believe it or not, the latter was a member of Little Richard's band and performed one Saturday afternoon at the television station in Lafayette).

But Jerry was interested in money, not music. Even his western clothes and mustache and gold watch and uplifted chin were borrowed from a soiled mythology, whereas the southern circuit and the musicians on it had their origins in the Baptist church.

Hendrix took us to the back of the stage and showed us where he had propped a ladder that led into the attic. The termites had been busy. A half-inch of sawdust had sifted from the attic to the floor.

Hendrix was holding the carbine with one hand. "I'll need one of you to hold the ladder, and one to steady a piece of plywood I've got laid across two beams. Those beams are like rotted cork. Are you ready to do this?"

My stomach was flopping again. "I don't see an alternative," I said.

"This is the way I see it, Detective Robicheaux," he said. "We make our choice now and save your daughter, or these men will take her away forever. I speak these words because I could not get to my children before they were murdered. I live with that every morning I wake."

I felt like a thorn had entered my heart, just as though someone had pushed his thumb into it. "We take down the Huey?" I said.

"If we do it that way, many things can go wrong. That includes fire or an explosion."

"What would you do?" I said.

"If you get a clear shot, kill the man named Diamond. The Asian man has no grief against you or Mr. Purcel. But Diamond does."

I hated to see Clete take a verbal beating, but Hendrix was right. Clete had shoved Diamond's face into a plate of grits in Victor's Cafeteria, and later stuck a .357 barrel down his throat.

"Yeah, what I did was dumb," Clete said. "Keep the pilot alive."

That was Clete. He accepted blame, even in the worst situations. I was worried about Hendrix, though. He was unpredictable. I believed he shot Jack Raider with the German machine gun, but he also froze on the gun and left it abandoned, which could be interpreted in all kinds of ways.

"May I borrow your carbine, Mr. Hendrix?" I said.

"You have too much weight, Detective Robicheaux," he said. "You'll punch through the floor."

"You're going to shoot Diamond for me?" I said, having to raise my voice, the slick throbbing in again.

"Let the man do it, big mon," Clete said.

There are lot of things you can do when you're tired and you're shaking and your heart is in your throat, but making a clear choice about whether your child lives or dies is not one of them.

"Damn it, Dave, we've got to get it on," Clete said.

Hendrix was waiting, his eyes dead, like a man whose mind saw no images night and day except those in a graveyard.

"Don't miss," I said.

Hendrix went up the ladder first, with me following him and Clete holding the ladder like the columns of Solomon. The floor in the attic was splintered with boards and protruding with rusty nails and carpeted with the tiny fecal pellets of small animals. In the wall was a window-size vent made of thin wood slats fluttering with cobweb. Hendrix and I crouched on two beams and ripped the slats from the vent. Suddenly the Huey appeared at twelve o'clock high, as though floating on an invisible sea, the downwash disintegrating the shingles on the roof.

Because the Huey was hovering at an angle, I could see the pilot behind the stick and Alafair blindfolded and bound on the floor, Cory Diamond standing over her, wearing aviator glasses to meet the morning sun, a man who looked more like a pianist than a button man. He grinned when he saw me, then reached down and squeezed his package.

Hendrix was on his left knee, aiming through the iron sights on the carbine. His shooting position could not be worse; he looked like a contortionist. I could see the rigidity in his body, the quiver in his buttocks, a horse fly walking on his neck; he had become an aggregate of physical and emotional tension that must have been an agony.

Do it, do it, do it, I could hear myself saying.

He pulled the trigger, but the round in the chamber was a dud, probably water-soaked or corroded. Hendrix had to pull back the bolt and hit the side of the carbine with the heel of his hand and clear the chamber and slide another round in, the dud bouncing down the ladder.

In the meantime the pilot saw us. Hendrix lifted the stock to his shoulder and fired four rounds into the Huey, the carbine close to my head. My face jumped and my left ear felt like it was stopped with water.

Hendrix didn't group the rounds. They were spread all over Diamond. It wasn't Hendrix's fault though. He knew this was probably our last chance and he reacted accordingly. But it was not pleasant to watch. Diamond looked like he was jerking on strings, his arms flopping, his mouth open and blurring. Then the Huey swayed, and Diamond went out the door as though on a bicycle.

"Dave!" Clete shouted up the ladder. "I think somebody just hit the deck! That wasn't Alafair, was it?"

Chapter Fifty-Three

I went down the ladder and out the side door just as the helicopter pilot bugged out for the Gulf of Mexico, the Huey's shadow racing across the pale-green tops of the saw grass, the same image I saw from the door of a Huey after I almost got cut in half by a Bouncing Betty. The medic who saved my life was a sweaty Italian kid from Staten Island. He had a rosary wrapped around the canvas cover on his steel pot, plus an inked peace sign and an ace of spades and rubber spiders and a bottle of mosquito repellent. I was sure I was going to die. Down below the shadow of the Huey was racing across the landscape and a ville that had been burned. A red *M* meaning "morphine" had been written on my forehead.

The kid leaned in my face and shouted, "Say goodbye to Shitsville, Loot. You're going home alive in sixty-five."

I memorized his words.

Why mention all this? I'll tell you why. The most important moments in your life, for good or bad, usually involve people and events you never saw coming and you never tell anybody about.

Right or wrong?

I wanted to be that Italian kid from Staten Island, to do for Alafair what he did for me. I wanted to gather her in my arms, or maybe pack her on my back, and carry her to a battalion station, like the one that saved my life. Instead, I was gazing at a hit man, a man who was arguably mad, who looked like he had been pounded into the earth. His lower body was obviously ruined, but he was still alive. He could flop his arms around and keep his head propped on his right shoulder. His bullet wounds were deep and soggy and were probably toppling when they hit him.

He looked up at us and grinned, his head at forty-five degrees, obviously straining to keep his head balanced. “Hope you don’t mind me dropping in.”

“Where were you taking my daughter?” I said.

He squeezed his eyes shut, then opened them. “Sorry, it’s hard to concentrate. What are you saying?”

I asked him again.

“Talk to the chink,” he said. “He’ll be after the five hundred grand he’s supposed to get.”

Clete had stepped quietly next to me. “Do a solid for Alafair, bud. I guarantee we’ll get you to a hospital.”

“Or otherwise I die?”

“You get the hospital either way, Mack,” Clete said.

“You got a cigarette?” Diamond said.

“Yeah,” Clete said. He lit a Lucky with his Zippo and bent over to put it in Diamond’s mouth. Diamond puffed on it without touching it with his hand. I had the feeling he was in deep shock and about to come out of it. It would not be a good moment. Then he coughed and Clete removed the cigarette from his mouth.

I squatted down so I could look straight into his face. His eyes were lustrous, as though they had become feverish. There were no more grins coming.

“Think about it this way, partner,” I said. “You must have family back there in Jersey. Help us and I’ll contact them and tell them you did a good deed for somebody. I give you my word. Clete and I are both on the square.”

“I’m dying, huh? No chance, huh?”

“Who knows?” I lied.

He looked at me a long time. "I played the piano," he said.

"In New Jersey?" I said.

"In a whorehouse."

"Help me with my daughter, Diamond. Do the right thing."

I waited for his reply.

"Hello?" I said.

His lips began moving, his eyes on mine.

"The wind is blowing," I said. "I can't hear you."

He tried again, the angle of his head causing his eyes to see sideways.

"Hang on," I said.

I got down on one knee and put my ear to his mouth. It was an awkward way to listen to a deathbed statement. His skin was deeply tanned and filled with tiny lines, as most Miami Beach wiseguys are. His black hair had threads of silver in it and a touch of tonic, and his breath smelled like copper pennies, which meant he was bleeding inside and probably eating a lot of pain.

"Tell me what it is, podna," I said.

But he couldn't get it right. He was gargling on his blood and his sphincter had failed him. Clearly he was embarrassed, and I honestly felt pity for him. Then his eyes snapped wide and his mouth opened.

"Come on Diamond," I said. "It's never too late."

Then he tangled his fingers in my shirt and twisted the cloth with far more power than I thought he was capable of, pulling me into his face, his forehead hitting mine, his saliva spraying on my skin.

I wanted to shove him to the ground, but didn't.

"Tell me again," he said.

I felt his hand release me. When I pulled myself away from him, his face was as stiff as a painting, his eyes locked on a cloud. My knees and back hurt when I stood up. My hands were shaking.

"He's dead?" Clete said.

"Yeah," I said, and wiped off my face with my handkerchief.

"What'd he say?"

"'The black girl told Ludlow he looked like a frog. Tell the bear I'm sorry. Don't let Ludlow get his hands on your daughter.'"

"That's it?"

"For that guy, that's probably an encyclopedia," I said.

While I watched, Clete found a tarp in a shed and threw it over Diamond's body. It was hard to process Diamond's last words. Was he leaving them to do more injury, like rubbing a stain in the lives of people he could no longer touch? Or having a run at redemption?

Clete read my mind. "Don't believe anything that guy said, Dave."

"I'm not," I replied.

"We're gonna get Alafair back."

"How? It's almost morning and there's still no rescue, no planes overhead, no boats out on the bay or even in the Gulf."

"I dig you, noble mon. But we're still the Bobbsey Twins from Homicide."

He was right. How many cops ever had a title like that, for good or bad? I couldn't help but smile. Clete knew what I was thinking, too. "Fuckin' A, big mon," he said.

We went back into the saloon. Jerry was cooking on a butane stove at the rear of the bar. The others had watched Clete and me through the window. Valerie was the first one to speak. "Alafair is gone with the helicopter?"

"Yeah," I said. "Diamond warned me about Ludlow. He as much said Ludlow killed Clemmy."

"What's that about Diamond?" Jerry asked.

I didn't answer.

"Did you hear me, Dave?" he said. "I've got a first aid kit in my office."

"Nobody is talking to you, Carlucci," Valerie said.

"*Excuse* me, Miss Valerie," Jerry said. "I thought this was my property. Tell me, is it true you exercise by sticking your head up your hole?"

She was sitting at a table, most of her strength gone, obviously in pain. "Before this is over, I'm gonna shoot that asshole," she said.

"He's not worth it," I said.

"So I'll dig the bullets out," she said. "Maybe I can get a rebate."

Hendrix was standing by the jukebox, motioning to me, his body marbled with the neon colors floating inside the jukebox's plastic encasement. I didn't know what he wanted, but I welcomed it. I knew that in a few minutes Clete and I would have to make a move if I wanted to save Alafair's life, and Hendrix would have to take care of Helen and Valerie, and also keep Jerry inside the building. I suspected it would be a harrowing experience, and not one that he would welcome.

"Would you walk outside with me, Detective Robicheaux?"

"Yes, sir, I would be glad to," I said.

But once outside I began to get a little uncomfortable.

"You smell the air?" he said.

"What about it?"

"It's different, isn't it?"

Oh yes, it was. But I did not need Mr. Hendrix to tell me about it. It was a dank, cool smell, like wood barrels of wine in a cellar, or the French Quarter in the early morning when the bougainvillea and bugle vine are wet and dripping from the balconies, and in the brick courtyards the humidity clicks as thick as beads of mercury on the banana fronds and elephant ears. But if you are still my reader, please do not assume too much about the beautiful quality of the gardens I describe. The Quarter is a cautionary environment, and sometimes it generates the same odor as the cemeteries on St. Louis Street, crypts that are split open and vandalized and contain the remains of splendid characters such as Marie Laveau and Dominique Youx, the latter a cannoneer for Napoleon and the brother of the pirate Jean Lafitte.

"So what about the smell in the air, Mr. Hendrix?" I said.

"Don't play the role of the naïf, sir. You well know that your beloved Louisiana is a haunted place and will never give you rest. Why is that? It's because the enslaved have no tombstones, most not even coffins. Their mouths and eyes are caked with dirt. You think they're going to let us go?"

"Speak for yourself, Mr. Hendrix," I said. "I do the best I can for both the quick and the dead."

He looked like I had struck him in the face.

"I didn't mean to offend you," I said.

"I care not," he replied. "We may never leave this island, Detective Robicheaux. You know that, don't you?"

"This isn't an island."

"I think it is. Regardless I want to go with you and Mr. Purcel to find your daughter."

In the south the rain clouds were as purple as plums, but beneath them was a golden bowl that seemed to spill on the bay and streak across the marsh and the saw grass and darkness of the swamp, like a ball of lightning. Then it exploded with amazing energy, illuminating the entirety of the swamp, like a lantern held in the hand of a magician in a medieval forest.

"I need you to stay here and take care of Helen and Valerie," I said. "And also to keep Jerry Carlucci in the saloon."

His face was gray, his mouth dry. "You don't trust me to go with you?"

"That's not true," I said, trying to keep in mind St. Augustine's admonition not to use the truth to cause injury.

"I'll have nothing to do with Carlucci," he said.

"You have to guard him, sir."

"I will not breathe the air he has fouled," he said.

"I think you have more pilgrim in you than you'll admit, Mr. Hendrix," I said, and went inside.

It was not a polite thing to do. But the edges of the civilized world are just that—raw and feral, a bit like being downwind from a charnel house. The starvation of the Indians, religious burnings at the stake, the torture of political prisoners, the napalm bombings of Third World people in grass huts, the millions who walked into the gas chambers and crematoriums with their children, lunatics who are allowed murderous weapons they carry into schools and movie theaters and discount stores—it's a bloody business no matter how you cut it, and the motivation is money and power, no matter what the craven tell us while we count our dead.

My wife Annie Ballard was murdered with shotguns while I tried to run home through a pasture and a pecan orchard to stop her death, the sky as warm and red as velvet, the raindrops clicking on the tops of pecan trees. But I was too late. I heard the twelve-gauge pumps firing and saw the barrels flashing on the walls of our bedroom. Annie had been asleep, with only a sheet on her body. The shells were double-ought bucks. Alafair was in a separate room. She was five years old. One of the men who slaughtered my wife was a Haitian, a former Tonton Macoute. Was he a by-product of neocolonialism? Probably. The world can be unkind. But that doesn't mean we have to accept it.

Clete and I told our group we were driving down a wisp of a dirt road to the Gulf in search of the Huey, and would return when we could. There was sadness in both Helen's and Valerie's faces, or perhaps sickness. Mr. Hendrix was disappointed, but I knew he was a good man and would do the right thing if called upon. If anyone was an emotional question mark about our activities, it was Jerry.

"You won't eat my steak and eggs?" he said. "I spit in them? I don't wash my hands? What?"

"We'll be back," I said. "In the meantime why don't you help Val and Helen? Where's your medical kit?"

"I wouldn't touch this guy's medical kit if I had the Black Plague," Val said.

"You'd better shut your face, woman," Jerry said.

Valerie tried to get up from her chair but was too weak to get up.

"Jerry, you'd better get out of my sight," Helen said.

But she wasn't doing much better. Jerry was turning off the flames on his butane stove. "I want to talk to you, Dave," he said.

"We're done talking, Jerry," I said.

"Come on, Dave," he said. "We've gotta put a plan together."

I touched Clete on the arm and nodded toward the door.

"Gladly," Clete said.

"Is this what I get for a lifetime of being your friend?" he said.

Both Clete and I turned our backs on him and went out the door and into the morning. The sky was a purplish red, like felt, as though you could put your hand on it, like the evening Annie died.

"It's like the world is upside down, isn't it?" Clete said. "Dawn and evening tide are mixed up. Sometimes I think that's why the tree frogs start croaking. It's like death and life can't separate themselves from each other."

"Yeah, I think you got it, Cletus," I said.

I started to say something else, but didn't get the chance. Behind us Jerry banged on the metal door. "I just want a few words, that's all," he said. "And you stay out of it, Purcel."

"Go back inside, Jerry," I said.

"I never told you this," he said. "I was in two crashes and one shoot-down. I could have grounded myself but I got some intravenous skull-fuck in Bangkok and my own boom-boom, and kept my engine running, because I was never a quitter, you got that?"

"You told me this before," I said.

"Not everything. I had blackouts in Bangkok. I think maybe I killed a CID."

"A Criminal Investigative guy?" I asked.

"Yeah," he said. "Then I went nuts. You know, 'get-some, get-some, get-some.' I mean that's what I think I might have done."

"Let's talk about it later, Jerry," I said. "I've got to get my daughter back."

"That means creep your own house and stay away from us," Clete said.

Jerry gave him an ugly look, the kind that says *I'll get you down the road, bub.* Then he looked back at me. "Okay, Dave," he said. "Good luck on Alafair. *C'est la vie*, and all that trash."

Then he walked back into the saloon.

My pulse was beating on the underside of my wrists.

"Forget that guy," Clete said. "Time to dee-dee."

"I've got a confession to make, Clete. I think we're all players on a board. I think we're about to run out of time, too. Look out there on the bay. It looks like a bronze shield."

He was standing by the passenger door on the truck and looked at the bay, his face pink in the rising sun, his green eyes lidless, unperturbed.

"What are you thinking?" I said.

"It's been a gas."

We got in the truck, and I started the engine and headed toward the Gulf. We had probably gone eight hundred yards when the earth jolted sideways, like tectonic plates or steel and rubble grinding each other miles underground, the ponds around us trembling.

"What the hell was that?" Clete said.

"Maybe what we were talking about," I said. "It looks like it woke up Ludlow's greaseballs. There're some cars coming through the fog by the swamp."

"Where?"

"Ludlow is standing in front of them," I said.

"How do you want to play it, noble mon?"

"Ludlow is evil. He'll be consumed by a black flame within him. Let him do it of his own accord."

"How about feeding him to an alligator?"

"That's not fair to the gator."

Clete laughed out loud. It sounded wonderful.

I stopped in the road and was ready to get out.

Suddenly my phone buzzed and lit up floorboards. "I can't believe it," I said.

"Believe it," Clete said, looking at the external mirror. "The power is on in Carlucci's saloon and whorehouse. Want to turn around?"

"Hang on," I said. I picked up my phone. It felt cold and had a hardness that didn't seem consistent with its light weight. Like everything in our environment, it seemed at odds with itself.

"Robicheaux," I said into the phone.

"Dave, get your ass back here!" Valerie said. "That motherfucker shot Helen. I let him go to the men's room, and he came back with a revolver and shot her in the back. I think she's gonna die. Oh, God, what have I done?"

"You're talking about Jerry?" I said. "He shot Helen?"

I felt the horizon tilt and saw a flock of cranes rise from the bay and fly into the sun.

Chapter Fifty-Four

My heart was beating, my breath rancid, bouncing off the phone. "You have electricity?"

"Yes, it just came on," Val replied.

"Did you call 911?"

"I was about to," she said. "Carlucci went out the door. That's why I called you first. He's still got the pistol. Maybe he's gonna shoot you or Clete."

"Why would Jerry want to shoot Helen?" I said.

"She was bent over with pain from her bladder stones. Carlucci mistook me for her. All Carlucci saw was Helen's silhouette."

"It's not your fault," I said. "I think he picked up the .25 auto I threw in the back of the saloon. It's a gun I gave Alafair."

"Are you coming?" she asked. "I need help and I feel awful."

I didn't want to answer. I could do little or nothing to help Helen that Valerie couldn't do. Also, Valerie's training in the army was more recent and probably better than mine. "Get the guilt out of your head. There's one villain in this—Jerry Carlucci."

Just as I said those words, I looked through the back window of my truck and saw him bouncing in his Jeep and banging in the ruts and potholes in the road, either coming toward us or Ludlow and his men or the road that led to the Sabine River and Texas. Once in Texas he could disappear in a metropolitan city and his knowledge of Alafair's whereabouts could be lost forever. My stomach felt like I stepped into an elevator shaft.

Clete was staring at me. "Call it, Streak," he said.

I stared back at him, as though he had the answer. But an answer to a question like that is not one others can give you. I felt the sudden presence of mortality, the kind that's like an anvil that has settled in your chest. I bit my lip and pinched my mouth and wiped my hand on my sleeve, then blew out my breath and looked into Clete's green eyes and at the wrinkles in the corners and the passivity he seemed to acquire when we were up against a wall.

"Hey, Dave, Helen knows the score," he said. "She'd want you to do what your conscience tells you."

Maybe, but what was the right thing? I had no guarantee I would find Alafair that day or any day. In the meantime Helen might bleed to death. The truth was I had no power over any of it. So I squeezed my religious medal in my palm and stopped thinking about mortality and decided that wealth and power and martial victories have no sway in the Big Parade, and neither do the dice when we roll them out of a leather cup, nor does the flagellation we lay on our backs. When you have done your best, you've done your best.

I returned my phone to my ear. "Stay with Helen, Val," I said. "I can't be with you all. Make all the emergency calls you can. For some reason I don't think the weather is done with us. Do you copy?"

"Receiving poorly," she said.

"Bring everybody here you can. Civilians, helicopters, firetrucks, whatever."

"Roger that," she said.

I clicked off my phone and looked at Clete. "It's not supposed to work this way," I said.

"Tell it to the chaplain," he replied.

Clete was bent forward, looking in the mirror at the Jeep closing the distance between Jerry and us. I thought he might make a break for Cameron Parish, but he didn't. The only other places to go were down by the bay or the swamp, but I saw no boats on the bay, and Ludlow and his men had occupied the swamp. Also, it was an unpleasant place now. I had seen three bodies bobbing in the water at first sunlight.

"What's Carlucci got in his head?" Clete said. "He's shot a cop. He's the stink on shit."

"Jerry was always a dreamer," I said. "Hang on, I'm going to cut him off."

"Want to blow out his tires?" Clete said.

"Wait until we see which way he turns."

"If you say so," he replied. He leaned toward the windshield so he could see the swamp. The fog was almost gone, like strips of cloth that are gray and rotten, the stuff of graveyards, the stuff of night feeders. "You're gonna brace Ludlow?"

"He and his people walk out or they surrender," I replied.

"What if they tell us to eat shit instead?"

"Ignore them," I said.

"Just like that?"

"Yeah, I'm surprised they haven't tried to leave already," I said.

"You think maybe we're already dead?"

"I've thought about that."

"There's something that bothers me, Dave. Ludlow's kid, Bedford. In the dark I threw a couple of grenades."

"Diamond and the Huey were laying down most of the fire," I said. "If we hurt Bedford, I think we would know about it," I said.

"Yeah, I know, but it always gets to me when it's over." He huffed air out of his nose. Then he rubbed his face. "Remember what you once told me?"

"Told you what?"

"About dealing with the world and all the shit we've gotten into. You said, 'Let the world break its fists on your face, then gather your blood in your mouth and spit in their faces.'"

"I said that?"

"Yeah."

"Remind me not to hand out advice for a while, would you?" I said. "Plus, that has nothing to do with the mess we're in now."

He hung a Lucky Strike in his mouth but didn't light it. "Did you hear something?" he said.

"No."

"I think my malaria is back. I'd like to stick a hose in one ear and blow everything out the other. You know, get all the mosquito eggs out."

Then he rolled down his window just as the Huey roared over us, both of us clamping our hands on our ears, instinctively ducking, then raising our heads as the pilot lifted away, our heads splitting.

"What did you see?" I asked, trying to get my voice back.

"Alafair," Clete said. His voice was somber, his eyes unreadable, like a roll of green Life Savers.

"What else did you see?"

"Just her and the guy on the stick."

"Tell me the truth."

"She was looking straight ahead. She didn't look at us."

"Come on, Clete. Say it."

"She didn't look down at us because she was scared of the cocksuckers next to her." His chest was rising and dropping, his nostrils flaring.

"But that's not all of it."

"She looked like she had a hunting jacket on. One with a lot of loops or pockets."

"They're setting down by the bay," I said. "The pilot wants the sunlight in our eyes. What did you see in the jacket, Clete?"

"I'd be guessing."

"Right," I said.

"I might have seen something else, too. Did you see a Gatling on the Huey?"

"No, I didn't."

"I'm probably losing it," he replied. "I don't trust anything I've seen for the last twenty-four hours. Forget I said anything."

The sky was changing, the way it does during summer in South Louisiana, when the waterspouts in the Gulf siphon the darkness on the horizon and translate it from a purple wave into spun glass and watch it carry itself to a sandbar before it disappears. When it does disappear you smell the odor of iodine and seaweed and the brass on a ship that is nowhere in sight. It's a magical place, all the more worth fighting for.

"We'll get through this," I said.

Clete bit off a piece of thumbnail and spit it off his lip. "Yeah," he said.

"Yeah, what?" I said.

"I don't know," he said. "I really don't. That's a crazy way to be, isn't it?"

The Huey set down on the edge of the bay, between the sandbars and the swamp, the latter on its way to the Gulf Stream once the saline had eaten its way through the roots that hold the coastline in place.

"Carlucci is headed for the slick," Clete said.

"I see him," I said, turning the steering wheel, leaving the mud road and rumbling down the incline toward the helicopter, everything in the truck rattling, the helicopter blades already winding down, the tide sliding over the helicopter's skids.

"He's gonna get the jump on us," Clete said.

"You think he's going to try to pop us?"

"Maybe," Clete replied. "Maybe just wants a deal. He still thinks he's Wyatt Earp. Somebody should tell him Wyatt and Doc wouldn't let him clean their spittoons."

Clete was getting hyper. But so was I. It's funny about death. When you're around it your heart pounds like a drum, so loud you can't hear your own voice; you get sick on your own stink and your anxiety is like someone ripping off your skin with pliers. At least that has been my experience. And you beg God that if He will just cut you loose this one time, you'll make up for every mistake you ever committed.

The closer we got to the bay, the calmer Clete became. But Clete's calm was deceptive. He was ready to rock. All in the worst way. At least in our situation. He made me think of electric wires sparking in a pool of water after a storm.

"You're not going to 'act out,' are you?" I said.

"When did you start using baby talk? What am I gonna do with you, noble mon?"

He yawned, his spine as straight as a broomstick. His .38 snub lay flat on his thigh, his hand lying on the cylinder and the grips. He turned toward me and wet his mouth. Under his soft breath was a bilious tinge, and in his clothes a sweaty loop under each armpit. "This one is for all the marbles, isn't it?" he said.

"Keep talking," I said.

"Carlucci wants inside the Huey before us so he can take over again," he said. "Then he'll have total control over everybody and everything in his dirty little dominion."

"Let me go out first and keep them split up," I said. "Alafair didn't look at us because Bed Check Charlie has got her terrorized. I'm just not sure about Carlucci. The guy's got a half dozen personalities."

"Dave, you're not listening to me," he said. "You keep thinking Carlucci is a human being. He's not. He's not even a piece of shit. He wants his money, he wants his dope, his saloon, Alafair if he can get his hands on her. Yeah, that's right, he's also a sex addict. That's why he runs a whorehouse."

I didn't want to know how Clete knew about Jerry's sex life. Also I wasn't sold on Clete's objectivity about Jerry. "What's the name of the Asian guy, the name Jerry gave him?" I asked.

"Fuck if I remember."

"Mr. Ling?" I said.

"You keep calling Carlucci 'Jerry.' First names are for friends, Dave, not for assholes. You're scaring me."

We were both worn out. We could not have gone to sleep if we had the opportunity. If I had closed my eyes, I would have seen a molten sun sliding off the earth's rim, into an abyss, never to return, a nightmare I had for years as a child, and sometimes still see today.

Jerry beat us to the Huey and got out of his Jeep, his hands in the air, as though he were pushing us away, taking charge, the man of all seasons.

"What a jerk," Clete said.

I drove across the grass and onto a series of half-flooded yellow sandbars, the tires splashing on the undercarriage, the saltwater probably ruining the bottom of my truck. I could see Alafair sitting in the nose of the Huey, next to Mr. Ling. We rolled down the windows but didn't get out.

"Hey, Dave!" Jerry said, grinning. "I think I got a deal that's gonna be good for everybody."

Clete pushed his snub-nose behind his belt and dropped his shirt over it, then put his Lucky Strike back in his mouth. He looked at me, his face blank. "When we finish this doodah, the Bobbsey Twins from Homicide and all our gang are going back to New Orleans. That's a fact."

"Why are you talking about New Orleans now?" I said.

"Because nobody dies there. You get on the St. Charles Streetcar with a spearmint sno'cone and ride into the Garden District and keep the window open in the shade, with the live oaks flying over your head. I bet you Tennessee Williams is still alive. I bet Louis Prima is still alive. I bet William Burroughs and William Faulkner are."

He was nodding through his entire statement, as though he had found the fountain of youth.

"Are you serious?" I said.

He looked into space. "Yeah," he said.

Ironically the big player in our situation was Mr. Ling, a man we had no knowledge of. His head resembled a baked apple, his mouth a slit. Perhaps he was a mercenary or a degenerate. He made me think of a high school janitor, the kind of guy who worked late hours and threw bags of trash around and had a face like a dirty glove. Yeah, the kind of bad guy nobody notices but should.

He had opened two folding chairs facing out the side door, and now was seating Alafair in one of them, one hand cupping her elbow, her wrists bound in front of her with plastic ligatures. She wore a nylon jacket with at least ten explosives snugged in cylindrical pouches, all of them wired one to the other. There was no tape on her mouth. A bandana was wrapped around her forehead to keep her hair out of her eyes. The fact that he was treating her delicately while simultaneously turning her into a bomb made me want to rip him apart.

She looked at me sleepily, then at Clete, as though she was not sure who we were.

"What have you done to my daughter?" I said to the man named Ling.

He didn't answer.

"Did you hear me?" I said.

Clete was looking at his shoes, rocking them, holding his energies inside his feet. "Cool it down, big mon," he said under his breath.

Clete and Jerry and I were formed in a half circle. There was perspiration on Alafair's upper lip. Jerry had said nothing to Clete or me or Alafair. His face looked out of joint, like a pinball machine about to tilt.

"*Ni hao ma?*" I said to the man named Ling.

"I am Cambodian, not Chinese," he said.

"Did you put narcotics in my daughter's system?" I said.

"I would not do that," he replied.

"Then who did?" My voice was beginning to tremble.

"I'm a very old soldier," he said. "I do not talk of those things."

"I'm not interested in your age, sir," I said. "You've kidnapped my daughter."

Clete looked at the ground, puffing one cheek, then the other. I could smell him. It was a gray odor, like damp towels and shoulder pads and jockstraps thrown on a dressing room floor. "Slow it down, Streak," he said out of the side of his mouth. "We're almost home."

Clete knew better. But he also knew the only argument you win is the one you enter into.

"French Legionnaires captured me when I was sixteen," Mr. Ling said, smiling. "See my hand? The Legionnaires took two of my fingers. They were Nazis and cruel to a young boy who had done them no harm."

On his forearm was a blue tattoo of a nude woman. "They made me their servant," he said. "I thought they had changed their thoughts about me. Would you like to know what else they did?"

"No, sir," I replied. "Please give me my daughter back, Mr. Ling. I'm an honest man."

"Mr. Carlucci owes me a great amount of money," Mr. Ling replied. "My family has had a hard life. The revolution in Cambodia cost the lives of a million people."

"I'm sorry. But I had nothing to do with that. Did you or Jerry Carlucci inject my daughter?"

"Hold on there," Jerry said.

"If you have the money Mr. Carlucci promised me, I will free your daughter."

"I don't know how to say this, sir," I said. "I am sorry for the things evil men have done to you in your young life. But my daughter is not negotiable. It's very important you understand that last sentence."

He smiled. "I understand what you say, but that attitude will not help you or me or your grandchildren or your daughter," he said.

"Why have you not allowed my daughter to speak?"

"Because it is not in her interest," he said.

"Hey, partner, we've got a problem. Don't you dare talk like that about my daughter. If you want to blow us up, do it. Someone will send your parts back to your family."

I guess I lost it. What you could call an existential moment. All sound and movement stopped. Alafair raised her eyes to me, as though saying goodbye. Clete stared at the horizon and a column of sunlight on the water. Mr. Ling cocked his head as though he misunderstood my statement.

How did Jerry react? He beamed. He had already changed clothes at the saloon, and now had the chiseled good-looks and stature of the Earps and Doc Holliday walking to the O.K. Corral, dressed in black, carrying a shotgun and Peacemakers. I never saw him so happy. All he needed was a cut-down double-barreled twelve-gauge loaded with double-ought bucks.

That's when I heard the amplified voice of Boone Hendrix through a bullhorn on Helen Soileau's cruiser. It was not simply loud; it was ear-bursting:

"DETECTIVE ROBICHEAUX! I NEED TO SPEAK TO YOU! NO EXCEPTIONS WILL BE ALLOWED! WAVE YOUR HAND IF YOU UNDERSTAND! I DON'T MEAN TO BE IMPOLITE! NOR AM I A PURITAN!"

Chapter Fifty-Five

Hendrix was driving, and Helen and Valerie were in the backseat. Hendrix got out of the driver's seat and eased the door firmly in the jamb so as not to frighten his passengers. He looked at me. "We need to go," he said. "That includes your daughter and Mr. Purcel. Ludlow is making a move. I saw him through the sheriff's binoculars."

"You didn't get any 911 response?" I asked.

He shook his head. "Detective Robicheaux, don't believe the rest of the events you see here. If you do, you'll be treated as a fool. The same applies to your daughter and Mr. Purcel."

"Who are you?" I asked.

"Why do you ask me such a strange question, Detective Robicheaux?"

"Don't try to duck it, Mr. Hendrix. You know things about the supernatural world. It's nothing to be ashamed about."

The wind was from the south, which meant it would be hotter, the smell of shellfish stronger, a raindrop or two as hard as a BB in the face, sand crowning in the waves, maybe things coming apart once again.

"I'll tell you one day, Detective Robicheaux," Hendrix said. "Maybe there are some things you shouldn't know. Like the future."

His last three words sent a drop from my armpit down my ribs.

I looked at Mr. Ling. I wondered if my question to Mr. Hendrix would be as valid to Mr. Ling. How much can one human being absorb without taking on an aura, one whose iridescence glowed like a rainbow or one that was malignant, oozing with purulence?

I thought of the images modern times have wrought for us: Napalm cascading through a village of grass huts, children and women in a ditch begging for their lives, human bones in a line of gas ovens, civilians tied on wood stakes for bayonet practice, a brilliant flash, then the atomization of two cities within a few days.

I want to be a child again, to be with my parents, to speak Cajun French, to swing my father's nets on his deck, way out on the Gulf, the shrimp skittering, even though oil from a torpedoed tanker was lapping against our bow.

"Who are you, Mr. Ling?" I said. "Tell me what the Foreign Legionnaires did to you. Is it so cruel that you're permitted to pass it on to others? Does your arrogance have no limitation, no charity, no decency? You drape my daughter's body with bombs and tell me what you will and will not do with her. I want to kill you right now, sir. Yes, you. Don't you look away from me."

His eyes were small, as were his other features, and as shiny as acorns. He fiddled with the gray and black stubble on his chin. It was the first time I noticed his teeth were filed to the gums, yellow and black, the gums infected, too. "You do not believe I will explode everyone who is standing here?" he said.

"Maybe."

"What is wrong with the women in the car?"

"One is sick. The other was shot by Jerry Carlucci. They are both policewomen."

"He shot a police officer?"

"Not any police officer," I said. "He shot the sheriff of Iberia Parish. You still haven't told me who you are."

"What if I execute them?" he said.

"I won't let you."

A cloud passed across the sun, and a shadow fell on us and I felt the temperature drop and rain clicking on my head and face. I could see Ludlow and his men and all their cars coming toward us.

"You are a strange man, more like me than these others," Mr. Ling said.

"You're wrong about that, bud," I replied.

He showed no reaction. Instead he stared at Ludlow's people coming toward us.

I know something is about to happen. It's because I can see my mother and father now, Mae Guillory and Big Aldous. When I see them they are always by a road or standing in water, raising their hands, asking me to stay a while. However, if I do, I will stay much longer than just a visit. Right now they are standing on a sandbar twenty yards directly south of the bay. My mother is wearing a simple chalk-like white dress with a purple rose stuck through a buttonhole. Big Aldous has his huge arm around her back, and his other hand holds an umbrella made out of tissue paper and bamboo with flowers painted on it. The sun's reflection is blazing around them. But their skin looks cool and impermeable, and the wind seems to have no effect on them.

I can hear Harry Choates singing "La Jolie Blon," *recorded in 1946, the one he sold for one hundred dollars and a bottle of booze and then was beaten to death in a Texas jail. But I still love that song, as my parents did, no matter how much tragedy lives inside it.*

"Are you looking at Mr. Ludlow?" Ling asked.

"I'm not interested in him," I said.

"I made him my enemy, as I made an enemy of Mr. Carlucci. Now I am left with men I scorn. You, I do not."

"What does that mean for my daughter?"

"To take her, sir," he said. "I will not trouble you anymore."

I felt Clete's eyes on the side of my face.

"Check Ludlow and his goons, Streak," he said. "There's something out of whack."

There were a number of vehicles coming through the saw grass and cattails, the stems and saw grass blades bending under the bumpers and undercarriages and tires, their headlights on, even though they were unnecessary. In the midst of the vehicles four men—greaseballs, rather—wearing suits streaked with mud, were carrying a stretcher, the antique kind, with wood poles that rolled out with the canvas.

At least five greaseballs were carrying funeral candles that guttered and flickered in the wind, the melted wax sliding down the candlestick onto the gripping hands of the bearers.

Sidney Ludlow walked by the side of the stretcher, holding the hand of his son, the body sagging in the middle of the canvas, like water that had collected under a leaky roof. The eyes were sealed, the features partially squeezed because his head was slanted upward and a clean beige blanket with a solitary palm tree stamped on it was folded underneath. Consequently he looked troubled, as though he were having a bad dream. I felt sorry for him. He wore his fly vest and a khaki cap and held an archeological trowel that somebody had placed in his hand. I wanted Ludlow to let his son go in peace, and I felt the men around him felt the same way. But Sidney Ludlow had the mark of all psychopaths. The issue is always about them.

I got one glimpse behind his dark glasses and the expression they held. There was none. But that did not mean he was not enraged. Holding his son's palm, he pointed his finger at Clete. "You killed my boy," he said.

"What?" Clete said.

"With your grenades!" Ludlow said. "With your stupidity! With your whores and fat and the stink on your body you substitute for a culture! I'm gonna have you boiled. Yeah, the real thing."

Clete's face turned gray. "You think I killed him?" he said.

"I heard you yell out 'Enjoy,'" Ludlow said. "That was not you?"

The rims of Clete's nostrils were white and dilated. I could see his pulse racing in his throat, like an injured butterfly. Clete's enemy was guilt, and many times his enemies brought him down with it, but not this viciously.

I stepped between Ludlow and Clete. "Everybody here is sorry for your loss, Mr. Ludlow, but Clete didn't kill your son," I said. "Those wounds are at an angle from the shoulder to the opposite hip. Those wounds are not from a pineapple grenade, either. Bedford was probably hit by an automatic weapon. Probably an M16. If anyone murdered Bedford, it was his father. Yes, you, you son of a bitch."

Ludlow cupped his hand on his mouth to keep his teeth from shaking. Yes, either his anger or his hatred was so great he had no way to speak. He fumbled off his dark glasses and tried to put them into a leather slipcase, but dropped them, then tried to bend over and pick them up, then stepped on them and crunched them into pieces.

"Whadda-you-wanna-do, Mr. Sidney?" one of the greaseballs said.

Ludlow wiped his sleeve across his nose. "Not here," he said.

Then Clete stepped closer to Ludlow and the stretcher bearers and the two goons supporting Ludlow by his arms. "Here's your message for the day, all of y'all," he said. "Do the Hadacol Boogie. If I see y'all again, I'm gonna light you up with that flamethrower in the Huey. Yeah, the flamethrower Mad Man Muntz cooked Ludlow's and Carlucci's dope with."

"Who's Mad Man Muntz?" one of the goons asked.

"The guy who's flying the Huey and about to hose you off the planet with an M60," Clete said.

I can feel the barometer dropping, and the smell of rain, and the promise of a different day. I can still see my parents, the tide not high enough to cover the sandbars, the waves and mist blowing off an old pier, maybe one my mother danced on at a fais dodo, the salt spray shining on their faces, my mother laughing and spinning her three-dollar umbrella on her shoulder, like a Victorian girl rather than a Cajun who could not read or write and thought a three-dollar paper umbrella was a glorious possession, her head slung back, laughing and dancing and singing "La Jolie Blon" *with Big Aldous.*

"I pity you, sir, not so much for your loss but because you immediately tried to blame his death on my friend Clete," I said. "Your son had a conscience and suffered for the pain you imposed on Clemmy Benoit, a poor girl who you thought was going to bring archeologists on land you wanted for your casinos. The only possession you ever had was your son, and now he is gone. Try to respect him and not use him, and maybe others will respect you in turn. But don't come back here. You will not be welcomed."

I did not plan these words, nor did I take pleasure in saying them. For a moment I thought I might try to retract them. But I didn't. Ludlow was evil, a tarantula, the kind that wraps its legs around the heart of its victim. Instead of thinking more about Sidney Ludlow, I hoped Clemmy Benoit heard my words in the ether, among the stars, in a place where the lion and the lamb lie down together.

"Wake up," Clete said, pushing my shoulder with the heel of his hand.

"What's wrong?"

"You look crazy."

"Really?" I said.

I took my Swiss Army knife from my pocket and opened the main blade. I kept it sharp with a whetstone in the kitchen sink at least once a week. "Clete?" I said.

"What?"

"Drop anybody who tries to stop me."

Mr. Ling watched as I cut the straps or loops or buttons of the suicide jacket that he had put on Alafair's body. I could smell him. His clothes, his body, his breath. I also smelled him on the jacket.

"How about getting out of my light, please?" I said.

Mr. Ling was bent over, his arms propped stiffly on his kneecaps. "You sound unhappy."

I cut another loop. Then slipped a canister out of it. I put it in his hand. "Here's a souvenir."

"What is it you have against me?" he said.

"Please don't stand behind me, sir."

"Dave, these things aren't Mr. Ling's fault," Alafair said. Her face was a few inches from mine, her eyes as soft as sleep.

"That's fine, Alfie. Let's not talk about it."

Did she ever hear of Stockholm syndrome? Probably not. But I suspected she was deep in it.

"Mr. Ling told me a story about you," she said.

"Really?" I said, lifting a wire from another canister. I had already removed the batteries inside the jacket, but I didn't want to take any chances. Also I didn't trust Mr. Ling. Nor was I convinced he was made simply of flesh and blood.

"He knew your outfit, Dave," she said. "He said you mistook a peasant boy for a sapper. He said you shouldn't blame yourself. The boy was carrying a potato-masher. What is a potato-masher?"

I looked up into Ling's face. "Did you feed this crap to her?" I said.

"What is crap? I don't know what that is. I think it is probably a profane word. I do not use those kinds of words."

I had already cut the ligatures on Alafair's wrists. Now I slipped the knife through the fabric between her shoulder blades and removed the two halves of the jacket and remaining wire and canisters. Then I put my hands under her forearms and stood up with her.

"I will say this once, but never again, Mr. Ling," I said. "Leave us alone."

"You do not believe I saw the can of food you thought was a weapon?"

"I believe that is a common experience," I said. "I've had similar experiences as a policeman. Everybody screws up. Everybody has a story. Everybody can replicate one."

"Goodbye, Mr. Robicheaux. I hope I have lightened your burden."

"The same to you. But I hope I never see you again," I replied.

I stepped down from the Huey and was on solid ground again, then I placed my hands on Alafair's hips and lifted her into the air and eased her onto a sandbar, our shadows becoming one.

"One question," I said. "There's something under a piece of canvas on the other side of your Huey. Is that a Gatling gun?"

"It's a winch and cable and steel hook. Why do you ask?"

I shook my head and put my arm around Alafair and walked to my truck, with Clete behind us. Then Mr. Ling grinned and yelled out a day and month in the year 1965. But I was not sure of the date or his pronunciation of it. Was he trying to take me back to Shitsville and all its guilt and fear and depression and anger and feelings of betrayal that destroyed many of the best boys in the world, the kind that lives decades, that sleeps under the soil, the kind that drags you down by the ankles and makes you wonder if you're with the damned?

No, I don't think Mr. Ling was trying to do me emotional injury. Instead, I think he wanted to prove he was not a fraud and in truth I was forgiven for the death of the boy tangled in the concertina wire and in some way or another the peasant boy knows how I feel about him and how sorry I am and how admiring of his valor I am.

Now that Alafair was with me again, Clete was too big for the pickup and rode in the cruisers, driving slow, Helen and Valerie shivering every time the cruiser hit a pothole. I would like to say that humanity and environmental normality had reestablished itself at Carlucci's Landing, but that was not the case. A lost look had come into Alafair's eyes, and I knew what it meant. She was revisiting every violent moment in her life, and that's the way it works. You don't just pay your dues. Sometimes you have to pay the interest that goes with it.

In fact, I've come to believe that normality might be an illusion. I think Jerry came to that conclusion. Otherwise, why would he have chosen the *denouement* of a lunatic?

Not sure what I mean? My narration about my parents has probably been a distraction. Sidney Ludlow and his greaseballs had withdrawn from the entire landscape, and in their absence my parents had walked out on the sandbars where the tide was now capping, full of froth and sand and gulls spinning and dipping, my mother's dress floating over her knees. Big Al had his arm around her so she would not slip and go under, because both their deaths were in some way connected with water.

My mother had dropped her umbrella, and watched it float away, and now both she and Big Aldous carried candles, just like Ludlow's people, cupping their hands to keep the flames from guttering out.

Mr. Ling fired up the slick and took off due south, and immediately Jerry began running after it. No, not in his Jeep. Ludlow's goons had slashed his tires. He ran after the Huey. Until this day, I'm not sure why. Jerry was crazy, but his lunacy had always been self-serving and never self-destructive, and was never what we called a yellowbelly. Jerry was Jerry, the son of a Sicilian, a father who took you to baseball games, a father who knew how to smack a homerun over a centerfield fence. I don't know how many times Jerry and I punched each other training for the Gloves, knocking over the spit bucket and slinging sweat and blood and sometimes the mouthpiece through the ropes. But like the froth on the sandbars, and the deaths of my parents, whether by criminality or industry, madness was madness.

I was tempted to run after him, but this time I let Jerry go forever. By that I mean he ran along the edge of the bay, splashing in his pointy cowboy boots, his slim-tailored black coat split down the back, sometimes looking over his shoulder, the kind of malignant behavior that Doc Holliday made acceptable. I thought then, and I think now, he hoped I would join up with him, to forgive him, to take him back to Helen and ask for her forgiveness.

But I'll never know. Mr. Ling circled him several times, unwinding the spool of cable that in my foolishness I thought was a Gatling gun, until Jerry had run into a marsh of waist-high saw grass as sharp as knives and chocolate-colored water and mud that sucked him down like freshly poured cement, all of it bleeding into the endlessness of the Gulf of Mexico, a place where the hull of a Nazi submarine was rasping along the bottom.

Mr. Ling lowered the Huey over Jerry, the blades whirling, flattening the grass, the hook swinging and dropping simultaneously, while Jerry grabbed at it and finally caught it, probably breaking his fingers or tearing the skin from his hands. At first he held on to the steel hook, then pulled himself hand over hand on the cable while Mr. Ling steadied the Huey, until Jerry could force one foot inside the hook and stand erect, holding on with one hand, skimming across the water.

Clete came to my window. "Did you see this bastard?" he said.

"Yeah, I want to find out where he goes," I replied. "Try to keep everybody going."

"Nothing has changed. No electricity, no radios. I think this is more than just a cluster fuck."

"How are Val and Helen?"

"They're both tough," he said. "Dave, you think this is it?"

"What do you mean by 'it'?"

"The End of Days."

"If so, we're with the right people."

He was leaning on the windowsill, his eyes lifted. Then he looked out at the end of the marsh and the beginning of the Gulf. "I can't believe it. The guy's coming back."

The Huey was probably a hundred feet above the water and the saw grass, and Jerry was holding the cable with one hand and waving with the other, like a passenger conductor on the Southern Pacific. My parents certainly saw him. They had put away their candles and were pointing at him, then they looked at me, as though he had found a special place, one like theirs. The inevitable rain clouds of Louisiana were back, and the sun had turned them into golden whales with purple stomachs. Tell me if there is another place on the globe more beautiful than the home of the Great Whore of Babylon.

Then I heard Jerry say something inside me. *Hey, Davie, I lied about rubbing oil on that kid's gloves when we were in the finals. I did it later to a kid in Vegas myself. What a bum. I'm talking about myself, here. Even my old man would be ashamed.*

Tell Mr. Ling to set you down, I said.

I kind of like it up here. It's swell racing over the land and the water and hammerhead sharks in the waves. Why the fuck did I ever want to build casinos on a piece of earth like this?

Because you hang around with people like Sidney Ludlow.

Well, I'm through with that, you can plainly see. You want to know what my gig is now?

No clue, I replied.

You got all that ancient history in your head. You're smart. Give it a try.

Why did you want to shoot Valerie Benoit?

Because she's beautiful and intelligent, and she treated me like I got my brains from the bottom of a pay-toilet.

Did you have anything to do with murdering Clemmy Benoit?

Give me a break. That hurts. You still think I'm that kind of guy?

In a word? Yeah.

Let me tell you about the gig I got. Think of the Knights Templar. And even way back from that time. I'm talking serious history, here.

I'm signing off, I said.

After that Bouncing Betty whacked you, you got hit with the electroshock and a little shake-and-bake and lots of days and nights in the Garden of Gethsemane and strung out with clinical depression and bipolar shit and sweating blood, before you drank yourself through the sidewalk on East Fifth Street in Los Angeles. Right or wrong, Dave? You're one of us.

Adios, Jerry.

Hey, you're looking at Dismas here. I got style. Drop by sometime and throw me a couple of coins. Fuckin' A.

Then I looked through the binoculars again. Jerry was looking straight at me, smiling, giving me the peace symbol, the only time I ever saw him do that. The winch was retrieving the cable, but the altitude of the Huey remained the same, which to me didn't make sense. Why didn't Mr. Ling simply lower Jerry on dry ground?

I was about to ask Clete that question when the slick exploded. The ball of flame was huge, the concussion blowing out the windows and doors, the smoke like the fuzzy legs on a giant spider. The airframe collapsed on itself, burning with the brilliance of a furnace, parts flying everywhere, steam rising from the water, Jerry going down with all of it.

"Jesus Christ," Clete said.

"Yeah," I said.

Clete swallowed. "You want to go out there?"

I got out of the truck. So did Alafair. My limbs and back seemed a century old.

"Did you hear me?" Clete said.

"My radio woke up," I said.

"Mine, too," he said. "Come on, big mon. Let's boogie."

"I gave him an explosive as a souvenir."

"Say again?"

"You were there. The Huey had a flamethrower in it. It was a flying bomb. I made sure of it."

"You risked your life to save them as much as yourself and Alafair," he said.

"I saw my parents. I wanted to stay with them. I want to take Alafair with me. Now."

Alafair put her arm in mine. "It's okay, Dave."

"You think so?" I said.

"Sure, if that's what you want," she said.

"The sun is orange," I said. "I think we'd better leave it for my mother and Big Aldous."

She held my hand and pressed the side of her face against my upper arm. "I think that would be fine, too, big guy. It's surely a nice morning. I can hear wind chimes, but I don't know where they're from."

And we left it at that. A fine morning is a fine morning.

Epilogue

We went to our various homes and spoke little about our experience on Carlucci's Landing, not even amongst ourselves. Oddly enough, I don't think any of us dreamed about it either, the way soldiers come home and sometimes are uncomfortable with the setting of the sun or memories about a friend who didn't make it home; you know that feeling, don't you? Sure you do. You end up in a quiet neighborhood bar and never share the Great Shade that can eat an entire battlefield in a blink. Wow, some fun, huh, boss?

In other words, I was done with all that. In the middle of the night I dropped my badge in Helen's mailbox at her house and became a recluse. It was easy. Clete and Alafair were probably the only people who noticed. Or maybe I had been a pest to too many people and they were glad to get rid of me. I really didn't care. I simply accepted the world, and I'll tell you how. It was the rain.

It began in its early summer tradition when the buttercups were in bloom on the levees and the rain fell almost every afternoon at three o'clock, then the afternoon showers became squalls and began raising the bayous in all the southern parishes and swamps and sometimes graveyards and in New Iberia filled the sky with electricity and mist that dimmed the park across from my house, although I could hear a softball game progressing and the clinking of a ball against a metal bat, you know, the way kids somehow prevail in a situation like that.

In the late hours I embraced the rain and walked under the tunnel of live oaks from my house to the Shadows, then returned from the drawbridge at Burke Street back to my house, the bayou as yellow as paint, the tidewater in some people's backyards, certainly mine, my wooden lawn furniture already floated away. And into my house I went and lay down on the living room floor, my arms and feet spread on cypress planks and throw rugs, the latter masking the hardness of the wood that was underwater hundreds of years, hard enough on which to be crucified while I listened to Merle Haggard singing "T.B. Blues."

I never thought anyone could sing it as well as Jimmie Rodgers, but Mr. Haggard, now gone, with his band might even sing it better than the Mississippi Yodeler. Tell me what you think. That particular recording is the only one I ever believed captured death in a tangible way and made me feel that death could be beautiful and should not be feared.

Hey, don't let Mr. Death put the slide on you. Mr. Death can be a pain in the ass. That's why I like Mr. Chaucer and his collection of obnoxious characters known as *The Canterbury Tales*. They reek of halitosis, facial syphilis, body odor, and every sin imaginable, and yet we find nobility in their weakness and kindness in their hearts. In effect, you wish to join them, people who lived in the fourteenth century. What does this say about the nature of Death? It means to tell Mr. Death to go fuck himself. Chaucer and his creations are still here today, bigger than life.

Regardless, I made friends with the rain, and in all of its manifestations. Louisiana is a baptismal font. That's not a metaphor. It's real. After many midnights, in my slicker and fedora and with my umbrella, I walked through the crypts of Old New Orleans and spoke to Marie Laveau and General John Bell Hood in Metairie and the boys in butternut in Abbeville. I liked them all. While I stood among their crypts, the rain ticking on my umbrella, the electricity flickering in the clouds, they asked me to think well of them, to forgive them for the mistakes they made for a cause they never really understood, to play the song "The Night They Drove Old Dixie Down." Some of them walked with me to my truck, and asked me to come again and to put my hand on their crypts because it will light their hearts and set mine at ease.

However, I do not know how successful I have been. I swore I would never return to Carlucci's Landing, but I broke my vow. Why? I don't know. The gangsters were gone, both the living and the dead. Few pieces of the Huey remained, as though the marsh subsumed the airframe and the shark's teeth painted on the bow, as though the earth wanted to erase its own mistakes, and certainly there was nothing of Jerry's body. I know this because I looked for Jerry's flesh, burned though it might be, yes, me, a ghoul, a solitary figure walking knee-deep in a saline tide, while lightning struck the sandbars where my mother and father danced to "*La Jolie Blon.*"

That's when a game warden in an airboat found me exactly where the Huey and Jerry and the pilot named Ling went down. You could tell he considered me a little strange when he cut his engine, letting his airboat float in its wake, holding a flashlight on his face, forcing a grin on it. He was a young fellow, and I did not know if he was to be trusted.

"Are you Mr. Robicheaux?"

"That is correct," I answered.

"Your daughter Miss Alafair is afraid you got lost out here."

"How could I be lost if she told you where to find me?"

"That is well spoken," he said. "Will you be so kind as to climb on my airboat so I don't have to chase any more crazy people at two o'clock in the morning?"

"Gladly," I said. "Do you have any coffee?"

"Yes, I do."

"May I have some?"

"Yes, you certainly can. But more importantly, if I were you I would get myself on my boat because an hour ago I saw a twelve-foot gator feeding just about where you are."

"Thank you, sir, I will take that under consideration," I said.

Of course, he looked at me as he would a lunatic. I was tempted to ask him if he was on duty when the world turned itself upside down at Carlucci's Landing. But I had learned my lesson when it came to reality. People make up what they need to. The events I saw on Carlucci's Landing were nothing compared to the hurricanes on the Gulf Coast that have curled thirty-foot waves over a city and crushed it like a dollhouse. In 1957 I pulled dead people out of trees in Cameron Parish for a week. The crew I was with wore rubber gloves. They never spoke when they took down the bodies.

"Before we head back, can I ask you something?" the game warden said.

I hesitated. As I said, people my age may want to pass on our wisdom, that is if we have any, but it doesn't work that way. "Sure," I said.

"There's wisps of gas out there," he replied. "Mighty raw, actually. It's not oil or a pipeline. More like a grave."

I nodded but said nothing.

"I was in Desert Storm," he said. "Get my drift?"

"No, sir, I don't," I said.

The clouds were black, cracking with electricity, full of gold pitchforks on the horizon. I did not like his subject of conversation.

"You couldn't take a wild guess?" he said. "Even though you've lived here most of your life?"

"All right, if you wish to talk about mortality, I'll do so. When I was ordered into my first combat, I was very afraid. Then my sergeant told me something I'll never forget: 'Don't think about it before it happens, and don't think about it after it's over.' So I took his advice and have continued to do so. You read me on that, partner?"

"Yes, sir, I do," he said.

"Is there anything else I can tell you?"

"No, sir," he said. "Hop up, Mr. Robicheaux. It's a pleasure to meet you."

I mounted his airboat and buckled myself into a steel-braced passenger seat, then watched him push a button with his thumb and start the propeller inside the wire cage that supposedly kept all passengers as well as the pilot safe. Of course, the cage and the propeller are safe until you lose your leg to one. We roared across the marsh, cutting a channel through all the carpeted vegetation that had been knitted together only minutes earlier, the surface of the water roiling as black as oil. I had not thought about the wound I was about to help impose upon the earth, as slight as it might seem. Life can sure be a slider, can't it?

I had thought that Boone Hendrix had disappeared, but the day after I was picked up at Carlucci's Landing by the game warden, Mr. Hendrix was at my front door. It was Juneteenth, before it was formally adopted as Emancipation Day, which people of color in Texas and Louisiana had celebrated since 1865. The rain was droning on my tin roof, the temperature over ninety, the window air-conditioner dripping. He was dressed in freshly pressed denims, a shaving nick in the dimple inside his chin. He was holding a hand-carved model of a pirogue, complete with a small paddle.

"I thought you might pass this on to a colored boy," he said. "Or a little girl."

"Why would you bring it to me?"

"Carlucci used to make them. So I do it for the children now. But I don't want to have any link with Carlucci. It's like washing your hands."

I started to answer, then decided not to ever enter the brain of Mr. Hendrix again. "I know a child who would certainly like this."

"I've got four more. I might just make a big one, too."

"That's fine," I said, easing the toy boat out of his hand.

He had folded his umbrella and the mist was blowing in his face. "Can I come in, Detective Robicheaux?"

I knew he would do it. "I'm pretty tied up."

"Long hours at your department?"

"Not exactly."

His eyes slipped off mine. "Well, I guess I'll be going along."

"What did you want to tell me, sir?"

"It's that dry rot. There's a mess of it under that wind vane. One flash of lightning and I think your bedroom will be blown into the bayou."

"That's all that's on your mind?"

"I'd like to build an aviary on the back of your property. It would be a fine one, Detective Robicheaux. They'd all be injured creatures."

"What kind of birds?"

"Screech owls and such."

"Screech owls?"

"Yes," he said, his eyes vacant.

He seemed like a man who had come from a lost world, one he never believed would be taken from him. "Come in, sir," I said, stepping backward.

I closed the door, then turned around. He stared at me, his mouth parted.

"This isn't about owls, is it?" I said.

He paused, thinking. "My girls are gone."

"Your daughters? You don't have to explain, Mr. Hendrix."

"No, they're not just dead. They're gone. Why would they go away, Detective Robicheaux?"

He waited for my answer, the rain stringing down his slicker.

"Let's take a ride," I said.

By the time we had arrived at Valerie Benoit's house in St. Martinville, a windstorm had dropped several oak limbs in her yard and water from the bayou was seeping under her house. The limbs were large and thick and heavy and looked like they were not going anywhere. The branches and twigs were riffling in the current on the yard, already wilting, perhaps even dead. Most of her block was dark, but her kitchen was lit by a gasoline generator behind the house.

I could see her through the kitchen screen. The glass window was up, her cat crouched in it. Valerie was cooking a cake. Her hair looked soft and blow-dried and browner and more gold than black. Or was it the other way around? I couldn't remember. She was wearing lipstick and a white dress with pink lilies printed on it. She saw us coming up her walk and beat us to the door and seemed unusually happy. "Hi!" she said, pulling the door wide. "My kitty has been my only companion. What are y'all doing in this rain?"

I used her bathroom and let Hendrix tell his story to Valerie. Maybe to the reader I seemed to have pushed Mr. Hendrix's troubles on her, but I don't think that was the case. I had given my all in my struggles with Hendrix. I think he was probably the saddest man I ever knew. If my loss was as big as his, I would go mad. You ask what the answer is for a poor fellow like that? A well-meaning clod would probably say "prayer." Does that seem disrespectable or irreligious? It is not. It's the recommendation for someone who hasn't paid his bloody, fucking dues. Because when you're in the Shit, you need to talk to people who have been here themselves, such as Jesus and his mother and St. Perpetua and St. Felicity and the millions who died in Hitler's ovens. You don't go easy into that good night. It's a son of a bitch.

When I came back from the restroom, Valerie was slicing a pineapple cake on the stove, and Mr. Hendrix was sitting at the breakfast table. Her back was to him. Neither one of them seemed to have cognizance of the other. I hadn't expected her to wave a wand over Hendrix, but I thought she would try.

"Did y'all talk?" I said.

"About going downtown, we did," she said. "Juneteenth has probably gotten rained out."

"That's it?" I said.

"I don't have the experience you do, Streak," she replied. "I would never try to tell anyone I did." She stood up straight and turned around. "Tell him what you know."

I did not want to do this, and I do not want to do this to you, the reader, either, but the stories I am now telling you are the only ones I can relate to you because they are the only ones I have ever had. If you have the same, this is what will occur: A smiling figure with a rainbow-colored glow, a jewel-like brilliance, will appear. I saw him; I don't care what anyone says. The others I've seen? Or heard? They'll whisper in your ear and tell you you're okay, not to worry about the score, the score takes care of itself, just keep bearing down on the batter. And sometimes they'll speak to you just before you fall asleep, and resurrect the children from your youth, yeah, those kids, the ones who were the best people you ever knew.

So that's what I told Hendrix. There was a long pause. He was sitting on a divan, his hands propped on his knees, his face blank. "My girls don't come back anymore," he said.

"It's because they're safe," I said. "You have to let them go. But eventually they'll return. The biggest pain you suffer is the fact it didn't have to happen. Like the addiction of a drug addict or a drunk like me, there was another way, a simple call for help, a hallelujah mission, if you will. But someone profited off the deal. It's that simple. It's money. And every time you think about it, you want to splatter brain matter on the walls. And that eats a hole in your chest. That's about it, Mr. Hendrix. We let these bastards take us down."

His eyes shifted on mine, the flats of his hands still planted on his knees. "So what should I do?"

"Be the good man you are," I said. "Build your aviary. Get the dry rot out of my roof."

I could not get him to smile.

Valerie's eyes were wet. "Are y'all ready for some cake?" she said.

"I could use some of that," I said.

"How about you, Mr. Hendrix?" she said.

"Not right now. But I appreciate it."

"I have some ice cream, too," she said. "Help me with it, Detective Robicheaux."

"Could I use your bathroom?" Mr. Hendrix said.

"Yes, you surely can," she said.

He went down the hall and closed the bathroom door and turned the deadlock. Valerie opened the freezer in her refrigerator. The frozen air swelled out and covered her face. I got up and walked behind her. She turned and looked at me.

"What's wrong?" I said.

"I've never felt like this."

"Like what?"

"Like I don't know," she said.

I closed the freezer. She placed her feet on top of my shoes and stood, clenching her arms around my neck and burying her face in my chest. I could feel her heart beating, her breath warm on my skin, the dampness in her eyes, on my shirt. Then I saw Alafair's car pull into the yard, the waves from her car rolling up on the veranda steps.

I felt the weight of Valerie's feet suddenly lift off my shoes. I did not know what to do. I heard Alafair twisting the doorbell.

"Is anybody home?" Alafair called. "There's going to be a ceremony at the drama hall after all! Nobody can stop Juneteenth!"

There was another pause.

"Hello?" she said. "Is anybody in there? Dave? The moon is coming up. I think it's going to be a grand night. Will somebody open up the door, please?"

Acknowledgments

I hope you have enjoyed what some will call "the twenty-sixth story" in the Robicheaux series. That's fine to do so, but I see it differently. Dave is not a storyteller, nor is his friend Clete Purcel. I see them as Everyman, right out of the fourteenth century, one man riding with a lance and sword the armor of the knight-errant, the other man as huge and cumbersome as a wine barrel mounted on a mule.

In other words, the characters are the era they live in. It's the Middle Ages. Fortunately, they are blessed with the medieval belief of free will. Secondly, the Earth is still young, the forests thick with trees and so high the sunlight can barely touch the ground. Thirdly, it's a gay, merry, and musical world, the calendar filled with holy days and fairs and contests and games and, yes, plowed to the eyes, which means bloody-well drunk on their asses.

That's why Dave and Clete both make many allusions to the past. But not exactly. They see it as a shining city. My father was something of a historian, but he did not believe that time was sequential. He believed that the past, the present, and the future all happen simultaneously, like God having a dream. And that's what I believe, and so do our friends Dave and Clete. Maybe the Milky Way is much closer than we think. Regardless, the big blue marble is a grand playground and the mysteries in It can be a wonder.

At least that's what Dave and Clete think. No, "think" is a bad word. It's an impression, a moment in time, a click of the camera when the laws of causality are thrown over the gunwales. I think those are the only times I ever learned anything. A medieval artist needed a giant ceiling. The time period is not coincidental. Dave and Clete are wanderers, but they do so without leaving town. If they could, I think they would be fine companions for Geoffrey Chaucer. Who knows? I believe *The Hadacol Boogie* would not be unwelcome by the denizens of the Sherwood Forest.

Once again, I want to thank all the people who helped with the creation of *The Hadacol Boogie*: My publisher Grove Atlantic and Morgan Entrekin, Zoe Harris, Deb Seager, Justina Batchelor, Natalie Church, Rachael Richardson, JT Green, Mike Richards, Sal Destro, Jisu Kim, and Miranda Hency for editing, typography and artwork, and marketing and publicity. Thanks also to the Spitzer Agency, which includes Anne-Lise and Mary Spitzer and Lukas Ortiz and Kim Lombardini. I have now been with them forty-eight years. And to Penelope Glass, who has been an invaluable help for many years.

Also, thanks to both Erin Mitchell, my sidekick and all-around fix-it-lady, and Alafair Burke for the edits in a pinch. You could not have two better friends.

And thanks to all of you all around the world. You are the best people on the planet. I know something about people. There are none better.

Thanks for listening again.
Stay on that old-time rock and roll,
Jim